Praise for James Byrne

Deadlock

"As good as *The Gatekeeper* was, this one's even better. Byrne is a writer who knows exactly what he's doing on every page and with each thrill." —*Booklist*

"My fave new series! If Popeye and Jason Bourne ever had a secret love child, it would be Dez Limerick. He is brilliant, funny, and hella deadly. Fans of Jack Reacher, Gray Man, and Orphan X definitely need to check this out." —Lisa Gardner

"An action-packed chess match between grand masters of death, *Deadlock* is one of the most entertaining novels you will read this year. It's intense, cerebral, and quite hilarious." —*Best Thriller Books*

"Dez is the Renaissance man of spies and is always fun to hang with while he's rendering justice on those who have forgotten the meaning of the word." —Dana Stabenow

"A uniquely imagined, larger-than-life action hero who is sure to delight fans of the likes of Jack Reacher, Jason Bourne, and Orphan X." —*Mystery & Suspense*

"Byrne has created an engaging hero that is a true delight and, with the complex thriller [plot] and impossible odds, makes *Deadlock* essential reading for any thriller fan."
—*Criminal Element*

The Gatekeeper

"A taut, explosive tale with high stakes and authenticity that kept me riveted and fanning the pages. Fans of Lee Child and Vince Flynn will love the hero, Dez, and find themselves enthralled in *The Gatekeeper*."
—Mark Greaney

"Dez Limerick is one of the most interesting, enigmatic, and coolest heroes to ever come across the written page. Byrne knows how to weave a complex tapestry and make his characters come alive. Well-written, fast-paced, and immensely entertaining."
—Nelson DeMille

"Gripping and compelling . . . this one is a keeper."
—*Library Journal* (starred review)

BY JAMES BYRNE

The Gatekeeper
Deadlock

DEADLOCK

A Thriller

JAMES BYRNE

St. Martin's Paperbacks

Published in the United States by St. Martin's Paperbacks, an imprint of St. Martin's Publishing Group

DEADLOCK

Copyright © 2023 by James Byrne.
Excerpt from *Chain Reaction* copyright © 2024 by James Byrne.

All rights reserved.

For information, address St. Martin's Publishing Group, 120 Broadway, New York, NY 10271.

www.stmartins.com

Library of Congress Catalog Card Number: 2023009255

ISBN: 978-1-250-34181-5

Our books may be purchased in bulk for promotional, educational, or business use. Please contact your local bookseller or the Macmillan Corporate and Premium Sales Department at 1-800-221-7945, ext. 5442, or by email at MacmillanSpecialMarkets@macmillan.com.

Printed in the United States of America

Minotaur hardcover edition published 2023
St. Martin's Paperbacks edition / June 2024

10 9 8 7 6 5 4 3 2 1

The folks at Minotaur Books could not be more supportive or gracious with their time and talent. I want to thank Keith Kahla, Grace Gay, Kelley Ragland, Hector DeJean, Stephen Erickson, Paul Hochman, and so many others for making this book a reality.

"Thanks" aren't quite enough for Janet Reid, my longtime literary agent, cheerleader, moral support, and unflagging champion.

To Shirley Haynes, my mom and most fervent reader.

And to my wife, Katy King.

I do love nothing in the world so well as you.

—*MUCH ADO ABOUT NOTHING*

PROLOGUE

Desmond Aloysius Limerick has been ordered to fly into Baku, Azerbaijan, under a false name, carrying nothing but a change of clothes and a paperback Michel Bussi mystery in the original French. He's met by a woman he knows to be a British agent, MI6. She's Pakistani and English, lovely, five-five, with amazing eyes and skin tone. If Dez had any time at all, he'd seriously consider flirting with her. But this is a run-and-gun gig. He's got one job to do, then he's out.

Pity.

The woman says very little to him, just leads him to a car park and a Range Rover and, over the next two days, a mostly silent, mostly nighttime, mostly round-about trip through Georgia and into Chechnya, avoiding border guards along the way.

She drives him to an abandoned warehouse outside Kurchaloy, Chechnya.

Five men are waiting for them. One is blond, handsome, authoritative, American, maybe thirty-five (same as Dez) and six-two (way taller than Dez). He starts by showing Dez a palm, halting him. "From this moment on, no names," the American barks. "I know who everyone is. The rest of you need to know jack. This is my op. There's me, then there's God. Are we clear?"

Dez says, "'Course!"

The American gives him the up-and-down eye, clearly unimpressed. "You're one of these so-called gatekeepers? I call bullshit on the entire legend around you guys. You need to know, I was against bringing you in."

"Don't care, mate." Dez beams and offers his meaty hand.

The American ignores it. He points to the lovely woman, then the four men. "I'm Alpha. She's Beta. In this order, they're Gamma, Delta, Epsilon, Zeta. You're Eta. Repeat it back to me."

Dez nods. He points to the other four men in the same order. "Got us Dave Cander and Mason Diggs. Americans, Navy Intel. Julius Chadha and Robert Barnard. SAS. How d'ye do. I'm Dez."

The tall blond grabs him by his shirtfront and bellows: "The fuck did I just say!"

"Indoor voice, Ray, my lad." Dez turns to the Pakistani-British woman. "Arabella Satti. Ye go by Belle, aye? Know you by reputation, an' it's a good one. Won the distance-shooting competition at Pontrilas, three times running! You're the reason I took this job."

Arabella, the woman who hadn't said two words to him over two days, looks like she wants to jump in the middle of this but isn't sure how. The American sailor boys look surprised but not unpleasantly so.

The blond lad, Ray Harker, is CIA. He, too, has a reputation, which of course Dez investigated before flying to Baku. Harker has a high win-loss record as a CIA field officer. He's known for taking chances and gambling. He's considered one of the Agency's best. Dez doesn't know if the Brits or the U.S. Navy fellas know any of this. He doubts they do. Harker is handsome and perfectly proportioned. If he wasn't a spook, he'd make a damn fine fashion model. Dez, by contrast, is built more or less like a tank: five-eight, barrel chest, wide at the shoulders, thick neck, bowlegged, massive hands. He tends to look boyish at best; goofy at worst. When he was younger, he practiced looking stern in mirrors. Usually just looked gassy.

"When I'm told t'come help the likes of you, I salute smartly," he says. "But ye didn't think I'd come all this way without knowing who ye were and what you're about, did ye? Don't be thick, my son. Joint U.S.-UK operation, on foreign soil. Best everyone knows everyone, yeah? Teamwork makes the dream work. Read that somewhere."

He turns to Julius Chadha. "Saw your big brother play for Tottenham, few years back. Scored twice against Arsenal. Madman! Left foot handed down from the gods."

Chadha, who's Sikh, smiles. "I was there, yeah! That was a good match!"

Ray Harker goes berserk.

There, Dez thinks. Broke the ice. Time to move on.

An hour later and Dez has a better understanding of the dynamics of this disparate group. Brits and Americans. Soldiers and sailors and spooks. Plus one gatekeeper. Arabella's the peacemaker. She'd be in charge if this were a joint UK-U.S. op, but it isn't. It's a U.S.-UK op—all the difference in the world. It means the Americans dreamed it up. That, and that alone, put Harker in charge.

The American sailors, Cander and Diggs, seem rock solid. They don't trust the CIA but they go where they're ordered.

If Harker's clothes caught on fire, the two SAS guys, Chadha and Barnard, wouldn't piss on them to douse the flames. But again, they do as they're told.

When everything's calmed down a bit, Harker lays

out the situation. The mission is to get inside a chemical weapons facility, twenty kilometers due south of the Chechen town of Znamenskoye, and to retrieve the notes, the computer, and the samples of a chemist, Dr. Timur Dachiev. They don't need Dachiev himself; the doctor is a fraud, his postgraduate degree purchased online, and the nerve gas he's "developed" is stolen.

At 1300 hours the following day, the Chechen military will be alerted to a possible incursion by a Turkish intelligence unit. When the border troops move to intercept, the soldiers guarding the chemical weapons depot will be repositioned to the south, to back them up. For ninety minutes, the corridors of the facility will be empty of all opposition.

"Your job's to get those damn doors open," Harker says, jabbing a finger into Dez's chest.

He points to a map laid out on an overturned crate. He points to each of his five people. "Once he's done that—if he can do that—we split up. You two . . ." He points to the American sailors. "You're with me. We take the north side. I'm basement, you're first floor, you're second floor. Belle leads the other team, south side, one person for each floor. Searching the entire building should take no more than forty minutes. All right: Questions?"

Dez raises his hand.

"You can get the goddamn door open. Can't you?" Harker steps into Dez's personal space, looms over him. Dez doesn't take a step back, and he doesn't take a step forward. He just smiles up at the taller but slimmer man.

"Can, aye. But that's not the problem."

"What is?"

"Your plan. It's rubbish, love."

Harker's fists clench. "Your job's to open the fucking door! If I want an opinion from you, I'll reach up your ass and yank one out. Are we clear?"

"You don't even know what a gatekeeper is, do you?

Brilliant." He smiles at the others. "Quite the brain trust ye have here."

"Fuck you! I'm—"

"My job's not to open doors. A marmoset on Adderall could do that. My job's to open 'em, keep 'em open as long as needed, an' close 'em proper. And to make sure that everyone who enters also exits, a smile on their face an' a melody in their heart. Aye? Won't open a door for people with a stupid plan. Will, if ye've a plan less likely t'get everyone killed."

Ray Harker cocks back a fist. One of his fellow Americans clears his throat. "What do you recommend, Limerick?"

The leadership dynamic has tilted considerably.

Dez points to the map on the crate. "Think of this as a body o' water. An' what you're doing is scuba diving. Aye? Which means the buddy system. Splittin' up and searchin' each floor? That makes perfect sense. But two of you on each floor, an' ye never leave your mate. One man on point, one ridin' drag, check your corners, keep each other safe, teams meet in the middle of every floor, everyone home by tea."

Ray says, "That'll take twice as long to search."

"An' look who's the math whiz, then. Aye, that's right. We've ninety minutes. Your way, could have searched the building in forty. My way, you search in eighty, but ye come out alive. Still an idiot, mind you. My plan can only accomplish so much."

Harker sneers. "You're staying outside where it's safe. Easy to talk big, asshole."

Dez laughs. "Does this look like the Kentish countryside t'you, mate? We're in bloody Chechnya! The outside's not noticeably less Chechen than the inside."

They argue for a bit but it's clear that Dez has won over the sailors, the SAS blokes, and Arabella Satti. But Harker needs to save face, so he argues for another twenty minutes. Just to remind everyone that he's the boss.

"One last thing," Harker adds. "The door stays open ninety minutes, and not one second longer. We are gone at the ninety-first minute. Think you can memorize that, Mister Math Whiz?"

Dez says, "Believe I can."

That night, Dez learns that Ray Harker and Arabella Satti are sleeping together, which is fairly dumb while working in the field, but it happens. It's happened to Dez in the past. He keeps his own counsel.

He awakes around three in the morning and knows he won't sleep unless he goes over the details of the chemical weapons warehouse, its security and alarms, yet again. He's pored through them five times and now goes for an even six. He focuses on each detail.

He barely hears Arabella step out of the room she and Harker share. She stands over his shoulder, studying the blueprints and alarm details. She says, "Nervous?"

"Just realized. That novel I brought? I've already read the bloody thing. Remember whodunit."

She touches his shoulder. "I've worked with Ray two other times. He's damn good." She randomly picks up Dez's mechanical pencil, rolls it with her fingertips, back and forth. "He comes across as, well . . ."

Dez says, "Exceedingly American?"

She smiles. "Yes. But he's smart, and he's fearless, and I trust him."

"Hard t'believe no one's ever written a folk song about him."

"Chief, I know why you broke up the dynamic when you got here. You were probably right to do it. But trust Ray. He'll give this mission a hundred and ten percent. Guaranteed."

Dez looks up into her eyes. "Jay-sus, but I hope not. A hundred percent is perfection. A hundred an' ten is showboatin'."

"You know what I mean. He'll be fine. Don't worry about him."

"I worry about everyone, love."

She wanders to a window and looks out on the night. "I don't know why I always wake up at this hour."

Dez, his head bent over the blueprints, says, "It's the nicotine."

"I don't smoke."

"Well, not currently ye don't." When she turns to him, he nods to the mechanical pencil she's holding . . . much the way she always held cigarettes.

She walks back and sets the pencil by his side.

"Started smokin' when you became a sniper, didn't you? Calmed your nerves. I seen it a lot in me mates."

"Yes, but it's a filthy habit. Are you a distance shooter, too?"

Dez barks a laugh. "I could stand at the bottom of a lake an' not hit water, love! That's not me gift."

She says, "Ray will be fine. We all will be."

"'Course you will. Your Uncle Desmond's watchin' out for ye."

The Chechen soldiers pull out at 1100 local time to back up their border guard brethren. Right on time.

Dez is kneeling by the big garage-style door at 1107 hours, the covering of the alarm system removed, red and green leads attached to it with miniature plastic alligator clips, all connected to his tablet computer.

The door opens at 1108 hours.

Dez doesn't enter. That's not his job. He stays to guard the door.

The two SAS soldiers return at 1132 hours. They've got the faux chemist's files.

The two Navy intelligence guys emerge at 1145 hours. They have Dr. Dachiev's laptop.

Arabella Satti walks out at 1202 hours. She has the stockpile of chemical weapons, in a wheeled lockbox not unlike a professional mechanic's rolling tool kit.

And she's alone.

"Ray," she says, eyes darting to the others. "He went after Dachiev."

Dez says, "Don't need Dachiev."

"I know but . . ."

Dez eyes his tablet computer, shakes his head. "Bloody hundred and ten percenters."

He opened the door at 1108 hours. They'll have until 1238 hours. A total of ninety minutes to the second.

Diggs and Cander make a quick foray into the basement to seek Ray and the chemist. They're back in ten minutes, empty-handed.

Chadha and Barnard do a quick recce of the ground floor. Nada.

At 1235 hours, the six of them gather at the door of the compound. Dez, down on one knee by the alarm system, checks the satellite-fed clock counting down on his tablet. The U.S. sailors and British soldiers and the English spy make eye contact with one another. Arabella wipes sweat off her palms with the thighs of her fatigues.

At 1237 hours, she draws her sidearm and points it at Dez's head. "I'm sorry about this. But we wait."

"We don't," Dez says, but softly.

One of the SAS soldiers touches her gently on the forearm. "Belle. You know the drill."

"He'll make it."

"Aye, we have to hope, but—"

"He'll make it!" She's still pointing the gun at Dez's head. Dez keeps smiling up at her. "Hundred an' ten percent. Meaningless number. Sorry, love."

"Don't call me love. We wait."

The clock hits 1238 hours.

Dez reaches for the leads connecting his tablet to the door.

Arabella presses the barrel of the gun against his skull.

"Do what you need t'do," Dez says, and disconnects his alligator clips and leads. The door alarms are reactivated. Whoever's still inside is staying inside.

Arabella holsters her weapon. She turns to the others. "Take the gas and the information. Get to Rendezvous Point A in Azerbaijan."

Dez tucks his tools in his backpack. "Coming along, are ye?"

She addresses the other four. "You have your orders. Go."

Dez shakes his head. "Saddens me to counter your orders, ma'am. But your guvnors brought me in to make sure everyone walks out safe. Means my job was never 'bout the chemicals and the chemistry. 'Twas always about you lot."

She draws her weapon again, holding it by her thigh. Her voice is as calm as a brook in a glade. "Chief. I. Am. Not. Leaving. Ray. Here."

They stand, eyeing each other. Dez looks sad. "Please."

"No."

For a muscle-bound guy, Dez is surprisingly fast. Comes from all the soccer he's played, plus the boxing. Arabella isn't even aware he's moved until her gun is on the ground and Dez is behind her, one massive hand holding both her elbows behind her back, his other forearm around her throat, muscles gently, gently blocking her carotid arteries.

She fights like a hellcat. She's studied martial arts. She's been trained to be a nasty street fighter. Against Dez Limerick: naught.

The sailors and the soldiers watch. Nobody interferes.

Arabella loses consciousness.

"That was a tough choice, chief," Julius Chadha says, a hand on Dez's shoulder. "Had to be done. Ta."

"Thanks, man," one of the Yanks says, and takes Arabella in a fireman's carry.

Dez looks like he's about to throw up. He gathers her gun and his kit, and they light out.

THREE WEEKS LATER

It's Paris. Dez meets a distinguished English gentleman outside a quaint and tiny little bar on the Seine, just off Quai François Mitterrand and near the Pont du Carrousel. They sit on a bench facing the river. The English gentleman—they won't be using their names today; not in public—drinks absinthe. Dez has a stout. The English gentleman says, "We still don't know what happened to Ray Harker. No body. No report of his defecting. He simply walked into that weapons facility and never walked out."

Dez nods. It's a sunny day in Paris and he's wearing plenty of sunscreen because he's fair of skin and burns like a peach. He says, "Arabella?"

"Ms. Satti quite hates you, I'm told."

"Fair, that."

"Our side debriefed the SAS soldiers, and the Cousins debriefed the American sailors. You received high marks from them all. You made some very difficult calls in the field. But they were the right ones. As for Ms. Satti . . ."

"She's a pro. She'll be fine."

"Well, either way, you have the gratitude of the DOD and the Cousins. We analyzed the chemist's plans for that weapon. You and Ms. Satti's team likely saved thousands of lives. We are grateful. If there is ever anything we can do for you . . . ?"

Dez wipes his lips with the back of his fist. "Actually, since ye've asked. Thinkin' of retiring."

"Really?"

He shrugs. "Always wondered what the States are like. Might pop in. Look around. See Disneyland. That'd be something."

The English gentleman's voice drips with condescension. "One would think so, yes."

"Hard t'get lost in a crowd in this world of ours. What with everyone knowin' everyone's business."

Dez scratches his chin. "Know what I mean?"

PART 1

CHAPTER 1

It's been a long day in Los Angeles and in Malibu, California.

Dez is in a guest room of an ocean-side cottage, packing his duffel bag. His electric bass guitar already is stowed away in its nicked and smudged old guitar case, the oval fuzz of passport authority stickers evidence of his travels. Neither he nor the woman he can hear—out on her deck above the Pacific, on the phone, salvaging her multinational corporation—have said as much, but it's likely time to call this affair quits. It's been a good run. Dez will be sorry to say goodbye. He suspects she'll be a little sorry as well, and he also suspects she'll say it first.

His mobile vibrates. He checks. He smiles. He sits on the guest bed.

"Brat."

"Old man."

Dez grins. "Wotcher. In Portland, are ye?"

The young woman on the phone is a vocalist and a songwriter, barely more than a girl, barely a year out of her teens. She says, ". . ."

It's not that she says anything. It's that he can hear the catch in her voice when she tries to. He stops grinning. "What?"

"My sister's in danger."

He says, "Laleh. She's a reporter, yeah?"

"Yeah. Dez, she's in the hospital. She's . . ."

Raziah Swann stops talking. Dez waits.

"Can you come? I don't have any right to ask but—"

"Be there tomorrow."

In the silence, he can almost discern the silhouette-sound of her crying. It's more in the absence of noise, in the rustle of her clothes.

"Desmond Aloysius Limerick," Raziah exhales his name, sniffs. "Goddamn, I think I love you."

Dez says his goodbyes to Petra Alexandris, and they sleep together one last, satisfying time. He leaves her in the morning to tend to her stolen company.

He knows how to pack light. With the exception of the guitar case, everything else he owns fits in a military surplus duffel. His belongings include a number of items he cannot carry onto an airplane. Some he designed and built. Some are illegal in the United States. Two are knives, one with a set of lockpicks in the sheath. Dez has little interest in getting crosswise with its legal system. So for the flight to Portland, he checks everything except his tablet computer and a used paperback, the front cover missing, wrapped in a thick red rubber band. His wardrobe for the flight is what he's worn every single day since arriving in the States: black jeans and a black T-shirt and boots. Dez has a fifty-inch chest and a thirty-two-inch waist and he has to buy the T-shirts online because no stores sell them in his size. He has twinkling blue eyes and a boyish smile, which he's quick to deploy.

The tablet computer is unique, bespoke, and was of great importance in Dez's old job.

The used paperback he's already read, years ago, but for now he's forgotten that and will only realize it right around the time his flight leaves the tarmac.

* * *

As he steps off the plane and activates his phone, Raziah's image pops up, along with an address he has not seen before and a suggested route. She's using Clockjack, an app that integrates all her technology and allows her to connect to anyone she wants with lightning speed. Clockjack is the app of choice for the twenty-something set and the techie set, and Dez doesn't have it. It's like TikTok; it's one of those fads that make him feel old and out of touch.

He takes a Lyft to a small blush-pink condo building in a sector of Portland called Goose Hollow. The neighborhood looks like it grew up in the 1920s and decided to stay there. The topography is hilly and green, with views of downtown Portland peeking out at some intersections. The building is shaped like the letter C—two stories tall, with two units in the east wing facing the street lined with cherry trees, and two units in the west wing, and a tiny garden in between them, with more units behind the garden. The garden is simple and well kept, with a single tree, a stone bench, a little trapezoid of grass, and maybe five flowering plants.

Raziah Swann sits on a window seat behind the big bay window of the ground-floor unit to the east—she's there when Dez waves and steps out of the Lyft; she isn't by the time he grabs his bag and guitar case and crosses the street.

As he hits the sidewalk, Raziah is in the garden, heading his way. She's not racing into his arms because Raziah is cool. Always cool. But she's walking faster than usual, almost skipping, and shrugging her petite body into a cardigan about twelve sizes too big for her. Her Afro bobs contrapuntally with her stride, head down, hair partially masking her smile, and then she's in Dez's arms. Dez weighs two-sixty and Raziah weights about one-ten. She squeezes him tight.

He says, "Brat."

She says, "Old man," but doesn't let go of him. "Hero-man."

"Not that. Think ye owe me five quid."

The condo belongs to the conductor of the Oregon Symphony who is on tour in Europe. She mentored Raziah when the girl had been a high school dropout; had been the first to realize she has a four-octave range and is a gifted lyricist. The conductor's place is lovely and clean and well decorated. The artwork on the walls are originals, mostly charcoals and pencil sketches. Raziah wears cutoff denim shorts and a thin tank and Converse All Stars with no laces. The cardigan would fit an NBA power forward and hangs below her knees. Dez spots her acoustic guitar, and a cheap spiral-bound notebook and lots of pencils. She's been writing music.

She says, "I want to take you to my sister."

Dez says, "I want to pee like a racehorse, then meet your sister."

They agree to this modified strategy.

After, Dez catches the girl looking at him as she sometimes does, head canted forward, that mass of hair obscuring her vivid mahogany eyes. Her father was Black and her mother was Iranian, and her skin is a tone that Dez can't quite describe and had never seen before. She smiles.

"What?"

"I called. You came."

"How it normally works, yeah? Not psychic."

She snugs her fingers in the back pockets of her little shorts, elbows pointing straight back from her narrow frame. "That's not how it normally works. Not in my experience."

"Where's your sister?"

"Good Sam. It's a hospital."

"You said she's *in* danger. Not *was* in danger."

"Her apartment was ransacked. The next day she was mugged by a man who almost killed her, except some witnesses happened by and called the police. Laleh went to the cops, told them everything. She's got a concussion. And I think she's still in trouble."

"Then let's go an' meet her."

Raziah grabs a floppy rattan bag worn cross-shoulder, and they call another Lyft.

Good Samaritan Hospital is in the northwest sector of the city, called the Alphabet District. The neighborhood is an untidy hodgepodge of tiny cottages and huge Victorians, boutique shops and four-star restaurants, all sitting cheek by jowl, bisected by mathematically straight, ninety-degree intersections. The land in this neighborhood is as flat as a phonograph.

Outside the hospital, Dez makes an excuse about needing to tie his boots, and he takes a knee as Raziah races into the hospital on coltish legs. He's spotted a man loitering outside the hospital. The man is clocking Raziah as she races into the lobby. Now, could be he's watching her because she's twenty and graceful and lovely, but Dez doesn't think so. While fiddling with his bootlaces, he spots the second watcher, half a block away.

The two men nod to each other.

They're not watching Raziah; they're watching *for* Raziah.

One guy's Black. The other's Latino. Both wear jeans and windbreakers of gray or black; nothing flashy. Both look tough enough and experienced enough to handle themselves. They begin to move toward the lobby door, but both quickly stop and look away when Raziah pops out like a jack-in-the-box and bellows at Dez.

"Get your ass in gear, England!"

Dez stands and crosses the street to her, side-eyeing the men but subtly. "Yes, ma'am."

CHAPTER 2

When Raziah was here the day before, her sister had been in the Emergency Department, where she'd been diagnosed with a concussion. She's since been moved. Raziah has jotted a room number across her palm with a Sharpie.

Before she can dash away, Dez draws her to a bank of vending machines and goes through the charade of hunting for coins. "Your instincts weren't wrong, love. Two fellas outside were waiting for you."

"No fucking way!"

"Language." He studies the array of candy behind the glass. He's already clocked the room number scrawled across her hand. "Go see your sister. I'll tag along behind, keep an eye on our feckin' playmates."

Raziah could have been expected to look frightened but the emotion that flashes across her light brown, gold-flecked eyes is scalding anger. With her mop of lightning-bolt hair, she can bow her head and hide it. "If they—"

"Well, that's why I'm here, innit. Scoot. There's a good girl."

Raziah heads down the corridor. Dez doesn't really want any candy, and he's a cheapskate, so he changes tactic, drags out his bulky mobile phone, and pretends to read a text. His phone is larger than average, as is his tablet computer. Both have been ruggedized. Both have needed to be.

The Latin guy starts down the hall in Raziah's wake. He's got his hands stuffed in his pockets, and he whistles. Aren't I the most innocent thing ever? It's the single crappiest bit of playacting Dez has ever seen.

The other fella, the Black guy, stays well back, keeping an eye on Dez.

Dez pretends to send a text, then heads down another corridor, perpendicular to the one Raziah took. He doesn't look about to see if he's being followed. Dez takes a left and a left and then quickly leans his shoulder blades against a wall, arms like oak trunks crossed over his barrel chest.

The Black guy comes around the corner and bumps into Dez's elbow.

His emotions march naked across his face: *Shit, who is this/Shit, this is the guy I'm following/Shit, he made me/Shit, be cool.*

"'Scuse me," he rumbles.

"Dez," Dez says.

"What?"

"Dez. I'm Dez. Friends call me tha'. Laleh, you know. Raziah's the sister. You're a thug. Think we're caught up."

The Black guy steps back and, doing so, Dez catches the outline of a pistol in a holster clipped to his belt. This isn't a surveillance gig. It's a snatch job. Or worse.

Dez unfolds his arms and steps away from the wall.

The guy goes for the gun.

As he draws, Dez hits him square in the chest, and the gun goes spinning out of the man's grip.

A lot of people fall over when Dez hits them. This man does not, but takes a pugnacious step into Dez's space and throws a haymaker at him.

Dez can dodge the blow. A sea urchin could dodge this blow, it's so well telegraphed. Dez lodges his fist in the man's breadbasket and dances away.

The man still doesn't fall. He's tougher than Dez presumed.

The guy spots his gun and makes a play for it. Dez anticipates as much and drives his knee into the man's gut.

Now, he topples over, eyes bulging, lips making fish-pucker movements. Dez goes to one knee and whisks up the gun. Now it's a calculation: The other man might have a gun as well, and the other man is chasing Raziah. That would argue for keeping this gun. On the other hand, Dez has fired many, many guns in his lifetime, but you can count on one hand the number of times he's fired a gun that he, himself, hasn't cleaned and maintained.

That, plus the fact that he hasn't a jacket or sweater to hide it, helps him make up his mind. He rises, deftly separates the gun to its component parts, and slides them into a nearby waste bin, lowering everything gingerly. As he does, he notices a boy, maybe fifteen, at the end of the hall, mouth agape, watching him.

Dez makes the *shhh* gesture, finger to lips.

The boy draws out his phone and starts shooting video.

The man he clobbered is gasping, trying to get his lungs to work; he'll likely be up in a minute or two. Dez rounds a corner and spots an orderly and says, "Fella back there havin' a heart attack, mate."

That'll slow him down.

Dez heads back toward Raziah. The room numbering isn't intuitive, which seems fairly stupid in a hospital, so Dez stops at an information kiosk at one of the intersections and reorients himself. Everyone working at the kiosk is on phones or chained to their monitors.

Dez spots a pile of WHILE YOU WERE OUT slips being held down by a steel marble the size of a plum. It's like a massive ball bearing. He snags it, en passant, and hustles down the correct corridor.

He finds the right room number—it's a wing of the hospital with single-occupancy rooms. He spots neither a petite singer nor a hulking bruiser and that concerns him. The sums don't add up. He palms the steel marble and knocks on the door with his knuckle.

He steps into the room and knows he's made a miscalculation.

The Latin guy is in here, check. He has a gun, check. But there's also a white guy, and he, too, has a gun.

Raziah is in the room, standing by the single bed. The woman who sits bolt upright in the bed looks like an older version of Raziah but with much shorter hair. Her eyes are open very wide, the whites showing all around the same mahogany irises that her sister has. One eyelid is inflamed, the skin swollen, and she has a butterfly stitch on her lower lip.

The white guy with the gun stands about five-ten with the lean, muscular frame of a man who's labored for a living. He's blond and his hair is in a short ponytail. He says, "Who are you?"

"Desmond Aloysius Limerick."

The white guy blinks. "What is that, a law firm?"

"Law . . . it's me name!"

"You're kidding, right? Never mind. Where the fuck's Frank?"

"An' who's Frank, then?"

"Frank," the Latin guy says. "The other guy. *¿A quién crees que nos referimos?*"

Dez's hands are quite large—much larger than most men's hands—and he palms the plum-sized steel marble, keeping it hidden. For a brief instant he's sorry he ditched the other guy's gun but then he remembers they're in a hospital. There are places fit for a running gunfight, and there are places that are not, and this is the latter. He says, "They're offering free colonoscopies in the lobby. Man his age, it's not a bad idea . . ."

The blond guy says, "Joe, frisk him."

The Latin guy holsters his gun to do so. He turns to the blond guy. *"¿Donde diablos esta Frank?"*

Dez raises his beefy arms up high. He's wearing a T-shirt with no jacket. He says, "Look, ye daft twat. An' where would I hide a gun if I had one?"

He twirls, so they can see his entire torso. And when he comes out of the twirl he cocks back and sidearms the metal marble, hard as he can, toward the blond with the ponytail.

The marble connects with the guy's head and he folds straight down, his gun clattering to the tiles a split second ahead of his skull.

The Latin guy reacts pretty quickly, moving forward, driving a fist into Dez's gut. Honestly, it's a damn fine punch. Dez is feeling this one, and he will for a goodly bit. The guy sends a jab into Dez's chin but Dez rides it backward, bleeding off its energy.

The Latino figures that'll do for his opponent. He backs off and goes to unholster his sidearm.

Dez closes the distance between them, grabs the man's left wrist—a second into the fight, Dez knows this bloke is left-handed, left-footed—and squeezes, pressing his calloused thumb into the nerve cluster on the inside of the wrist. He also swings his right elbow and connects with the man's neck.

The gun stays in its belt-clip holster.

The guy staggers back, free hand going for the injury to his throat, his left hand immobilized by pain.

Dez makes a play of punching the man in the nose and, when he ducks down, Dez goes with a Thai boxing move, driving his knee into the man's solar plexus.

Joe folds in on himself like origami.

He's down now, on his knees and one good hand. Dez has heard the expression you should never hit a man when he's down. Stupid advice, that. There's no better time to hit a man than when he's down.

Dez makes a fist and rockets it into Joe's ear.

Joe checks out.

Dez kneels, unholsters the man's gun, ejects the mag and the one bullet in the pipe, and deftly disassembles the pistol. He frisks the man and finds a switchblade knife but no wallet. He finds a magnetized card of flexible black metal, polished so finely that Dez can see his face reflected on the surface. This card opens doors. Somewhere. There is no writing on the card, so there's precious little way to know which doors it opens.

Unless you've been a gatekeeper.

Dez pockets the card.

He stands and turns to the Swann sisters. Raziah is on her feet, Laleh sits up in bed, and both of them are staring, not at Dez, but down at the white guy.

Dez circles the bed and checks him out, too.

Ah. That explains the ladies.

The ball bearing caught the blond guy in the temple and killed him. His eyes are wide open, glazed, staring at whatever one sees at the very end. Which, Dez thinks, might well be nothing at all.

Dez puts a hand to his gut. He picks up the room phone and hits zero.

"Can ye get the police to Room 1715 . . . ? Aye, please . . . Miss Swann . . . Aye. Need to report an attack. Also, there's a bit of a dead fella in here, wants cleanin' up . . . Ta."

CHAPTER 3

Hospital security finds a new room for Dez and the Swann sisters to wait until police can arrive. Laleh is more than a little wobbly when she's on her feet, and Dez is reminded that she's concussed. She and Raziah also are spooked to have had guns waved in their faces. Well, that and they saw a man die. Dez is reminded that that's unsettling for some. Once they're in the new room, he offers his baseball mitt of a hand and Laleh hesitates, then shakes.

"Desmond Limerick. Dez to me friends."

"Laleh." She sits on the made bed of the new room. "I . . . um, thank you."

"'Twas Raziah here who said you was in the barney. Right place, right time; that's me."

Laleh looks at her sister. Raziah says, "It's okay. I don't understand half of what he says, either, but I trust him."

"You trust your bass player?"

"He's not *my* bass player. He's my friend. And yes." She turns to Dez. "Are you all right?"

He smiles. "All the lad did was hit me, brat. 'Course I'm all right."

Laleh says, "That other man. Is he . . . did you kill him?"

Dez says, "Did. Sorry about that. Seemed the thing to do. How'd you get hurt?"

As they talk Raziah's phone pings in her bag and she draws it out, checks it, begins scrolling.

Laleh gingerly touches her own left eye and flinches a little. Her finger dances over the foreign material of the butterfly suture in her lip. She's got the same skin tone as her sister but the skin around her eyes is a mottled green. She looks a little nauseous.

"Two nights ago. I was walking to my bike. Coming from my yoga class. The guy you punched? He hit me. I was on the ground, all tangled up in my bike. He drew this . . . *huge* knife . . ." She holds up her index fingers, twelve inches apart. "He was leaning over me when this couple on the street saw him, yelled, and called the cops."

Dez thinks: *Then the lad and his mates came back today with friends to finish the job. Lovely.* "An' how are you holdin' up?"

"They were just about to discharge me when . . ." Laleh shudders.

Raziah crosses to him and stands shoulder to shoulder, showing him her phone. "You're famous." Her hand resting on the middle of his back, the widest part of his torso.

Laleh notices.

It's a video on Twitter. It shows Dez ambling away. It shows the Black guy—Frank—rising, one hand on his chest, wincing, huffing, as orderlies and nurses begin to surround him.

Dez remembers the boy in the hall with the phone.

"There's more. Same kid." Raziah closes that video, opens a second one. The Latino, Joe, in the hospital corridor, handcuffed, police on either side of him. Joe looks like he had a disagreement with a coal train.

The hospital room door opens and uniformed police officers enter.

The rest is predictable.

Dez and the Swann sisters are interviewed, notes taken. IDs are exchanged.

More police arrive. The three witnesses are separated and answer the same questions.

Dez's answers are so short, the police have little to do. "Me? Just arrived. Raziah's mate. Said her sister was in trouble. Never met her before."

Rinse and repeat.

Finally, detectives arrive, because there's a dead guy to deal with. That changes things.

Dez and the sisters are taken to the Portland Police Central Precinct. The cops are gentle with Laleh, due to her concussion. Also with her sister. They're even relatively gentle with Dez.

A nice change of pace.

WASHINGTON, DC—U.S. MARSHALS SERVICE

A clerk is on his break, eating a tuna salad, legs up on his desk, thumbing through Twitter.

He takes a slug of Mountain Dew and promptly spit-takes it across his terminal.

He cleans up the mess, then sprints out of his cubby, up the stairs, to the office shared by senior investigators. He shows his cell phone to the highest-ranking deputy marshal he can find.

The phone plays a Twitter video, on a perpetual loop, showing a Black guy rising, holding his chest, pushing away nurses, getting into a dustup, until a uniformed police officer intercedes. The video is all of twenty seconds long, looping over and over again.

The senior-most deputy U.S. marshal on duty says, "Holy hell! That's Demetrious Givens!"

PHOENIX, ARIZONA—FIELD OFFICE, U.S.
DRUG ENFORCEMENT ADMINISTRATION

Two DEA agents are on a stakeout in a stiflingly hot van outfitted to look like a septic tank rooter company. They've been on monitoring duty of a known drug house for three days. They are one of three shifts. They are bored out of their minds. They expected to find nothing during this surveillance. They have not been disappointed.

Both are on Twitter.

Both spot a video coming from Portland, Oregon. It shows a Latin man who's been beaten, badly. He's handcuffed and being perp-walked through a hospital lobby.

The first agent says, "Funny. Dude looks like Cristian Hinestroza."

The second agent snorts a laugh. "Yeah, that'd be fucking hilarious. That'd be . . ."

The video loops. They watch the guy being perp-walked. They watch his face.

The video loops.

Neither agent has glanced at their black-and-white monitors, or the drug house, for some time now.

The video loops.

The first agent mutters, "What the hell . . . ?"

The second agent makes a secure call on the DEA communications server. "DC now. *Now,* goddammit! You are not gonna believe who just surfaced . . . !"

CHAPTER 4

Portland Police Bureau Sergeant Heywood Washington is in his late fifties, a squat bulldog of a man with a fringe of gray hair around his head and an easygoing demeanor. He's Black. He offers Dez coffee before they talk. Dez accepts the coffee.

"Where are you from?" Washington's voice is higher pitched than Dez had expected.

"The UK, originally. Been visiting Los Angeles awhile."

"Doing what?"

"Music. Guitar, piano. Also some car repair."

Washington writes everything down. He seems more like a psychoanalyst than an investigator. He wears half-glass cheaters. "You killed that man back there."

Dez says, "Aye."

Washington studies him. "You want a lawyer?"

"No. Thanks, though. Good coffee."

"Uh-huh. You have the right to remain silent."

"More than a few nuns suggested I do just that growing up." Dez grins.

"Okay, then. You killed a man by throwing a ball bearing at his head."

"Aye."

They look at each other across Washington's desk.

"You threw a marble at him. And you killed him. Do I have that right?"

"Aye."

"Plus you beat two men armed with guns. You disarmed them both."

"Yessir."

Washington studies him.

"You a cop, Mr. Limerick?"

"Me? God, what a thought! No offense, sorry."

"You a soldier?"

"Not a big one for taking orders, me. Tend to chafe."

"You're a trained fighter?"

"I work out a bit. Healthy body, healthy mind."

Washington studies him.

Dez says, "Ask ye a question, then?"

The cop waggles his pen in the air.

"Them lads had no ID. Had good moves. Had tactics. Pros, them. Have you put names to 'em yet?"

Washington says, "You're not a cop and you're not a soldier, but you frisked the men you'd beaten, and disassembled their firearms, and you looked for ID. You know from good tactics."

Dez sips his coffee.

"Don't worry about who they are, Mr. Limerick."

"Well, y'see, Raziah Swann's me friend, yeah? And her sister I just met, but it's clear the lads were sent to put the boot in. Came at her heavy. A knife, two nights ago. Guns, an' three of them no less, today. So whoever is giving the marching orders can't be too happy about the outcome. Which means Laleh is still in trouble, and so's Raziah, if she's staying with her sister, which sort of makes this something for me to worry about. Yeah?"

"You're protecting the sisters?"

"Appears I am, aye."

"What were you doing in Los Angeles?"

Dez digs out his thin, newish wallet. In it is nothing that predates his arrival in the United States. He slips out a business card and slides it across the desk. "Detective Beth Swanson. LAPD. Ring her up. She'll tell you a little about me."

Heywood Washington takes the card, writes down all the information, and slides the card back. "Think I will. As for those guys, don't worry about who they are. We have fingerprints for all three. We'll tag them shortly."

"Pros, them."

Washington nods. "That seems likely, but it's our problem now."

"I'll stick close to the sisters. You figure out who them twats is, and Bob's your uncle."

"I . . . honestly don't know what that means, but . . . you are free to go, Mr. Limerick. We'd ask you not to leave Portland for a while but, since you said you're still protecting the sisters, I guess that's a given. And you're really not going to tell me who you are?"

"That part's easy," Dez says. "Raziah's playin' a club called the Deep Dive tonight. Asked me to sit in. Come by. Everything to know 'bout me, you can find out by listening to me play."

CHAPTER 5

Laleh Swann informs the police that she has no idea why she was attacked. She's a business reporter. She's not working on any stories that are worth her life. She's not working on any stories that are even going to crack the front page.

She and Raziah and Dez are released that afternoon.

Laleh's apartment was ransacked by whoever threatened her, so she's staying at the home of the symphony conductor, along with her little sister. The three of them pile into another Lyft and get taken from the Justice Center in downtown Portland to the Goose Hollow neighborhood—maybe a ten-minute drive. This one's an SUV and there's plenty of room for the three of them in back. Raziah sits in the middle and Laleh sits on the far-right side and says not a word. When the SUV pulls up in front of the C-shaped condo building with the little garden, Laleh breaks her silence. "Thank you again, Mr. Limerick."

Raziah says, "Come in and have a drink, and Laleh will tell you all about it."

"No," Laleh says, softly but with a solid assurance. "I won't."

They do head into the condo anyway, and the sisters head straight into the master bedroom to argue.

Dez checks the perimeter of the building and finds a

small, five-slot parking lot back there that was created when an old garage or outbuilding was torn down. He sees high hedges all around. One could get into a lot of mischief behind this building and none the wiser. He returns to the ground-floor condo and checks the door lock. A joke. The building is not rigged with an alarm system. Dez finds out everything he needs to know in a matter of seconds.

As he returns, Raziah emerges from the bedroom the way a circus acrobat emerges from a cannon. She whisks up her massive raffia bag and blows wild lightning bolts of hair away from her eyes. "I'm going to find something to eat. What do you want?"

"I could eat crickets and carpet tacks, love. Y'know me."

"Stay and talk to her royal eminence." With that, Raziah kisses him on the cheek and just about leaves a Warner Bros.–style, Raziah-shaped hole in the wall on her way out.

When Dez turns, Laleh Swann stands in the doorway of her bedroom. "Would you like a drink?"

There's a little stone bench in the little garden, next to the little tree, and Laleh says she needs fresh air after staying two nights in a hospital. She pours pinot grigio into small jam jars and they take them outside. She brings a towel to wipe dew off the bench.

"I do need to thank you again," she says.

"Ye don't. What did them bastards . . . sorry, them fellas say t'you?"

"Not much. They . . . the guy you . . . the white guy, he said I didn't get the message the first time and they were waiting for Raziah this time, to make sure I understood."

"Understood what?"

"Not to talk."

"About . . . ?"

She gives him a strangled little laugh that's halfway toward hysteria. "I have absolutely no idea."

Dez waits until she's composed herself again.

She looks into her glass. She whispers, "He called me a cunt."

"Shouldn't've." Dez shakes his head. "Bad form."

And Laleh shudders a little. This time, when she laughs, it's with less hysteria. "They threatened me with a knife, then with guns, but you think it's bad form to use the C-word."

"'Course." He shrugs. "Using a knife or a gun to threaten someone—to get 'em to do this, or not to do that—that's a perfectly legitimate criminal enterprise. Time-honored, ye might say. Calling you that word? Well, that's just ungentlemanly."

Now she really does laugh, and instantly winces and touches her skull. But she keeps smiling anyway. She's barefoot. Laleh has painted her toenails a translucent white.

"Why are you here? Really?"

"Raziah called and said you was in need of a hand. She knows a little about me. Knows I can handle meself in a fight. I'd nothing better to do, so I came. Never been to Portland. Been meaning to."

Laleh speaks softly, looking at the almost colorless wine in her glass. "She's only twenty."

"Aye."

"You can understand I'm wary of the men . . . the many, many men she's picked up in her life."

Dez grins. "Not sleeping together, you know."

Laleh says, "Oh, really." She makes no pretense about believing him.

"I like playing music with her. She's a lovely voice. Gifted lyricist, her. She's a force of nature in front of a microphone. We're mates. That's all."

Laleh's doubt hasn't budged an inch. "I know how men are around Raziah. It's been like that since she was fourteen. Look, all I'm saying is, she makes bad decisions about men. I'm grateful for what happened today, but you and I are not going to be friends and I'm not okay with you sleeping with my little sister. And I thought I should be honest about that."

"Fair." Dez holds up the little jam jar and, after a beat, Laleh reluctantly lifts hers and taps it against his.

Dez drinks. "Why d'you think them fuckwits . . . Sorry . . ."

She smiles. "I work in a newsroom. You can swear around me."

"Understood. Why d'you think they're after you?"

She says, "I don't know. Not for sure. But . . ."

Dez waits.

"I'm writing about a local guy. A professional auditor, who was murdered a couple of nights before I was attacked. I mean, I wasn't investigating his death. I'm not a cop-shop reporter. I don't do the crime beat. I was working on a profile."

"But two violent acts that close together? Three, counting the hospital. Sounds like a pattern, that."

"I told the police. I even sent them a link to the story I wrote. It . . . I can't figure out how they could be connected."

"Then let's find out."

They both spot Raziah, on a bicycle, cruising down the middle of the street with earbuds in, head bobbing to something only she can hear, her massive hair bobbing a fraction of a second out of sync with her skull. She curves the bike into the driveway that leads to the small parking area in back.

Laleh stands.

"Don't hurt my sister, Dez."

CHAPTER 6

Raziah is in the middle of the living room, down on her haunches, all her weight balanced on the balls of her feet, digging steaming, lidded boxes out of her shoulder bag. She produces doughnut-shaped fritters called medu vada, with aloo bonda dumplings, little plastic containers of tamarind and mint chutney, flaky pyramidal samosas, a box of tandoori salmon, another of chicken tikka kebabs, and Indian eggplant smothered in a peanut coconut curry. She also stopped at a liquor store for a cheap Canadian blended whisky and a screw-top bottle of soda water. Dez peers into the depths of her raffia bag. "Haven't an anvil, do ye?"

She grins up at him. "They were out."

Laleh distributes small plates and forks and pieces of paper towel ripped artfully into neat little squares, as if she used a ruler. Dez wonders about people who focus that much on something so mundane. Also glasses of water from the tap, telling Dez that Portland is famous for its pure and sweet tap water. Raziah pours whisky and soda for herself and Dez—her big sister has another few eyedroppers of white wine. "He doesn't care about the tap water," Raziah murmurs.

"Lived in deserts, me." Dez sits on the floor, back to the worn but well cared for couch, and piles food on a plate on his lap. "Endless supply of potable water? Sweet Jesus, what a thing."

Raziah hands him his drink. "Where do we start?"

Laleh says, "We? I never asked for help."

"Never," her sister agrees. "As in: not once, ever, in your life. He's here. Let him help."

It takes a while, Laleh's eyes on her plate and her food and her glass of wine. But she nods.

"You wrote about a fella what died?"

"Conor O'Meara. Do you know what a B Corp is?"

"Do not."

"B Corporations are businesses that maintain a civic duty to take care of the planet. To do well *and* to do good. And the biggest B Corp in Oregon is, obviously, Clockjack Solutions."

Dez stuffs food in his mouth, nods. "Make phones," he mutters around the food.

"Well, software and a website, originally, then apps. And yeah, a lot of people now have Clockjack phones. The company started right here. Four professors at Portland State University in 1990. It exploded, went international. They have this massive R-and-D campus east of here, on the edge of Mount Hood National Forest."

"An' your lad O'Meara?"

"Every few years, B Corps have to get reregistered, to prove they're still good citizens of the planet. Clockjack was getting recertified. Conor was doing the audit. He was heading back to his condo, coming back from watching the Thorns play at Providence Park. He was on the MAX—that's our light-rail system. He was on his way home, to the east side of Portland. When he got off the train, someone mugged him and killed him."

Laleh stops to nibble on her food. The headache and the butterfly suture in her lip make that a chore. She says to her sister, "You ordered everything mild."

"He's English."

"Ah." She nods. "Anyway, all Conor's research into Clockjack was missing. Both at his work and on his laptop."

Dez said, "The plot thickens."

"I guess. Anyway, I pitched the idea of a profile to my editor at the *Post*. But it wasn't an investigative piece. I was just writing about Conor. He went to Lincoln High School and Portland Community College, and U of O. He was a local guy. He was a rock climber and he liked Portugal the Man. I mean, he was just a *guy*."

"He was your friend?"

She nods.

"My condolences on your loss, then. So he was mugged an' killed, and a coupla days later, you was mugged an' almost killed."

Dez sips the last of his whisky. Raziah, mouth full, stretches her arm toward him and snaps her fingers, and he hands her his empty glass. Laleh notices this simple, domestic shorthand between the two of them, and her lips harden a little.

"D'you think this is about Clockjack?"

"I don't think so. I can't imagine how. There's no mystery there. Clockjack is the biggest company to ever originate in Oregon. Well, Clockjack and Nike. I'm not sure which is bigger. It's worth billions."

"Aye, but Conor O'Meara was auditing the company, he died, an' his research went missing. You was writin' about O'Meara, you was attacked, an' your apartment was ransacked, your computer taken. Yeah? Gotta be a connection."

"Tell him the story," Raziah says, then casts an aside to Dez. "This is a great story. This is, like, Peak Portland."

Laleh nods. "So, in 1990, four friends at Portland State University—RJ Sharpe, Teddy Meeker, Joel

Menache, and Carl Hickman—invented Clockjack,
software that allows people to fine-tune their federal
taxes. A couple of years later, they had one of the very
first websites in the world."

Dez says, "Fine-tune how?"

"Portland is very liberal," Laleh says. "Most West
Coast cities are, to one degree or another. But Portland's, like, the People's Republic. One of the legisla-
tive districts in Northeast Portland is nicknamed the
Kremlin. Super-lefty, super-green. Anyway, people here
don't mind paying taxes for social services, and for
Medicare and Medicaid, and foreign aid and, whatever,
parks. But they don't want their taxes going to wars, or
to Wall Street or Big Tobacco or Big Pharma. So the
story goes: This unknown professor at PSU had this
epiphany. This was Teddy Meeker. You know how the
stream of a river can be disrupted, a little, by rocks and
boats and bridge footings? The water eventually flows
all the way down the river; all in one direction, for sure,
but on a micro level, some of the water can get diverted
into, whatever, gullies or ponds. Right? Well, Professor
Meeker had this idea that government funding is the
same."

Dez says, "Is it?"

She shrugs. "A little. Maybe. As I understand it: You
pay your taxes with one check. But the money flowing
into government coffers can be affected at the day, the
hour, and the minute by changes in the bond market, and
procurement schedules, and when budgets are written or approved, and when congressional committees
hold hearings, et cetera. Teddy Meeker thought, if you
could write a program to map out these . . . I don't
know what you'd call them. Revenue currents? If you
could map them out, could you divert your tax money,
say, away from the Department of Defense and into
the Department of the Interior? Or Housing and Urban

Development? If you could, then you could literally pick and choose, cafeteria-style, which government agencies get most of your tax dollars."

Raziah glances up, a V of concentration on her forehead. "That's always seemed far-fetched to me."

"Well, I have the app. I do it." Laleh sips her wine. "Does it work? I don't know. I like to think so."

Raziah says, "I don't make enough to pay taxes."

"Yes," her sister says. "You do. You just don't pay your taxes."

"Whatever. Anyway, it's huge. Everyone here uses Clockjack."

Laleh says, "You're following all this?"

Dez beams. "Not even a little! Terrible with numbers. But keep going, I'll catch up."

"Okay, well, Teddy Meeker wrote the software, which allegedly can track the tiniest changes in the revenue eddies of the federal government. You put your taxes into an escrow account. You're in a coffee shop or the gym or whatever, and your phone pings you: says Defense is only getting ninety-five percent, or ninety percent, of what it normally receives at this hour, on this day, so you dole out some of your tax money right then. And a slightly lower percentage of your own personal taxes goes to buying the next aircraft carrier. You start the escrow account on the first day of the quarter and, by the quarterly tax day, you pay it all out, but riding the micro-eddies. That's the theory."

"An' people bought it?"

"Not at first. Then it exploded. People credit RJ Sharpe. She taught poli-sci at PSU. She became the CEO, the chief cheerleader for Clockjack. The company started making thousands of dollars, then millions, now billions. And she's doing all these TED Talks, on the cover of all these trade mags, traveling the world, proselytizing for the firm. Clockjack now has, I don't know, a hundred and twenty-some-odd apps, all very green and lefty."

"Ye mentioned two other professors, from back in the day."

She nods. "Joel Menache was the original head of software development. His team built the website. Carl Hickman was the company treasurer. But neither of them is around anymore."

"Falling out?"

"No, they both died a couple of years ago. RJ Sharpe is still speeding around the planet, still preaching about how the Clockjack software and apps can lead to a better world."

"An' Teddy Meeker?"

She shrugged. "He was the quiet Beatle. He's still plugging away, writing code. Nobody ever hears much from him. He lives on the R-and-D campus. It's called Gamila. I think it means 'beauty.'"

Dez nods. "In the Egyptian, it does."

The sisters look at him.

He glances up. "Jamila is Arabic for 'beauty.' They give it a hard *guh* sound in Egypt."

Raziah deadpans him. "You speak different dialects of Arabic. How is it you speak—"

Dez blushes, suddenly realizing he's been caught out knowing something that's difficult to explain. "Grew up reading *National Geographic*. Had these amazing snaps of topless women, all over the world. Loved that magazine."

Laleh wrinkles her nose in disgust. Buying it.

The doorbell rings.

Dez says, "Anyone know you're stayin' here?"

Laleh said, "The police do."

Dez unwinds himself from the floor and walks to the door, which is out of sight of the living room.

At the door are two men with badges. One's tall, one's slight. "U.S. Marshals Deputies Garrison and Gliek. Come with us, Mr. Limerick."

Dez shrugs. "Not just this moment, ta. Hungry? We have Indian takeaway."

The taller one—his badge says GARRISON—speaks slower, "Come with us. Now."

"What's this about, then?"

The slighter one—Gliek—says, "Can you tell us about the Black guy you fought at the hospital?"

Garrison glares at his partner.

Dez leans against the doorframe, arms folded. "Oh, sure. So, there I am, in hospital with me mate, yeah? Looking for her sister, and we spot two villains lurkin' about—which was actually three but I'll get to that nutter in a mo—so I sends me mate one way, lure one guy after her, led the other astray, blows were exchanged, blah blah blah, dismantled his gun, went after the other bloke, found him with the third bloke—whom I'd mentioned, ye'll recall—popped Bloke Two in the noodle with me fist, threw a marble at the third guy, called security, who called police. And later noticed signs all over the bleeding hospital, saying workplace violence can't be tolerated, an' hands are not for hurting, an' such, and of course I agree with all that. Wholeheartedly, yeah? But you, know, wrong place, wrong time, an' shite happens. Am I right?"

He smiles big. The two men blink at him.

Gliek says, "Ah . . . wow."

Garrison gnashes his teeth. "Did you talk to the Black guy?"

"Not as such. Not in what ye'd call a conversational manner. His mates called him Frank. He carried a SIG P320. Fifteen stone, five-nine. Right-handed. Looked fit. Weren't no amateur, him."

Gliek says, "Fifteen stone?"

"Two-twenty; sorry. See, a pound in my world's a unit of money, which—"

Garrison cuts in, "Don't need you to get smart with us, asshole."

Dez bats his eyes. "A fella as pretty as me don't need to be smart, does he."

Garrison takes a step toward him and Gliek runs interference. "Did Givens talk to you at all?"

"Who?"

Garrison sneers. "Yeah. You don't know Givens at all, do you? Just got into a fistfight with him in a hospital. What happened? Did you guys come together? Are you part of this?"

Dez has his eyes on Gliek. "Givens is Frank?"

"Yes."

"There's a lot of names start with G here. Getting confused. Mind if I get a pad of paper and we make name tags?"

Garrison says, "Fuck you."

Gliek says, "Did you talk to him? This Frank?"

"Na. Just fought."

"Had you seen him before?"

"I've not seen anyone in Portland before, save Raziah." And Dez goes through the litany again, about his trip up north from California.

"The police told us all that. Unbelievably, I think they're buying your story, Limerick. We are not. Where the—"

Gliek says, "Man, we don't know—"

Dez notes that they haven't asked about the blond guy he killed, nor the Latin guy he beat. Just the Black guy. And they haven't asked if Laleh is okay. "Was there anything else, chums? Selling cookies? Raffles for the village fete?"

The two deputy marshals study him. Garrison pissed

off, Gliek looking confused. Dez smiles, languid. Has all the time in the world.

Garrison says, "You're coming with us."

"I'm protecting the Swann sisters. Should you feel a need to arrest me, please do so. Otherwise, the curry's getting cold."

"All right, you're under—"

Gliek draws a business card. "We're not arresting you, Mr. Limerick. If you think of anything else, let us know. Okay?"

"'Twas a pleasure and an honor," Dez says.

After they leave—Garrison eye-fucking Dez halfway to their SUV—Dez heads back inside. The sisters were near the entry, listening.

Laleh looks a little lost. "All that, and they didn't want to ask me about being attacked, or anything. That's . . . weird."

Dez sits again and fills his plate. Again. "'Tis, that."

CHAPTER 7

After dinner, Dez insists on doing the dishes and taking out the rubbish. He does the first because he's a gentleman, and the second because he's not sure Laleh's out of the woods yet. Someone sent those men after her. Whoever sent them likely isn't a satisfied customer and might want a refund. Or a redo.

So he hauls out the rubbish to the freestanding wheelie bin in the car park behind the condos, then takes the opportunity to walk around the block. It takes him under a minute to spot the first car on surveillance. Then the second one, in the opposite direction.

Bad guys? Cops? Marshals Service? Dez doesn't know. For now, they appear to be benign. If they were violent, they could have moved at any time. He decides to let sleeping dogs lie.

He returns and finds Raziah sitting on the floor, legal pad on her upturned knees, wearing high-end headphones and scribbling lyrics. He recognizes them as Master & Dynamic; expensive 'phones for pro musicians. He knows not to bother her when she's writing. But Raziah spots him as he enters. She pulls down the headphones, still around her neck but the foam bits snug against her clavicle.

He says, "You still playing tonight?"

"You still planning to come help?"

"If you need me."

She says, "It's a cool little club. You'll like it. My guitar guy said he might be able to make it after all. But bring the Ripper. Just in case."

She nods to his guitar case, leaning in a corner near the door.

"Your sister coming?" He has no intention of leaving the sister here unguarded.

Without rising, Raziah bellows, "Laleh!"

Her sister emerges from the bedroom, now wearing makeup and a nice blouse, screwing small diamond studs into her earlobes. The makeup has covered her bruising and split lip, at least a little. "What?"

"Come to the club tonight."

"I'm going out with David. We're meeting up with some other couples." She turns to Dez. "I don't need a babysitter."

Raziah reaches out with one foot and gently kicks Dez on the calf. Dez's calf has the same dimension as Raziah's waist. "Come hear me play. Please? The club's nice."

He looks down at her and grins. "Wouldn't say no."

Americans call it a game face. Dez has seen it in professional athletes and professional soldiers, and he can always spot it in Raziah Swann. It starts as she's about to get to a club to perform her music. Gone is the sloe-eyed flirt with the sexual asides and the sly smile. En route to a club—and Dez played several of them with her in Los Angeles this summer—she grows stone-cold serious. The way her eyes dart, he can tell she's contemplating her reservoir of songs. She's written dozens. She's calculating the strength of her backup band, and its weaknesses. The acoustics of the site, if she's played there before. The differences between a Friday date-night crowd versus a boisterous and drunk

Saturday crowd versus a smaller audience, actual music fans who tend to show up on Tuesdays or Wednesdays. She thinks about the ambient light on the stage. She thinks about the interconnectedness of her lyrics: Perform three of her songs back-to-back and you might catch a soulful, painful subtext of longing hidden in the middle song. But play that song between two others, and the subtext becomes angry and vengeful.

Laleh and her lad leave first. To Dez's surprise, the surveillance cars don't follow Laleh, and they don't stick with Dez and Raziah.

The club is called the Deep Dive. It's in the basement of a four-story, Flatiron-shaped restaurant and boutique hotel on Burnside Street. It's dark inside and much more spacious than Dez had anticipated, making him think the footprint of the basement expands under the adjacent streets. Or maybe that's an illusion. It has a longish bar, a sea of two- and four-top tables, plenty of room to dance, and a slightly elevated stage on the north end with cheap follow spots screwed onto water pipes overhead, adhered with industrial C-clamps.

Dez likes the spot straightaway.

He's introduced to the keyboards and the drums and bass—and indeed, the bass player made it. Dez isn't disappointed; he enjoys listening to Raziah perform. The band is comprised of boy, girl, boy; white, white, Black; all in their twenties. Raziah will be playing lead guitar tonight, though she sometimes doesn't.

Dez asks the bartender, a handsome lad in a topknot and muscle shirt, if he can store his guitar somewhere safe. He catches the eye of the owner. "Her call."

The club owner is chatting up a table but saunters over soon enough. She's tall, with white-blond hair and vaguely Asian facial features, wearing matchstick jeans and cowboy boots with Spanish heels, no shirt but a black leather waistcoat that buckles up the front and is designed to show off her hard-earned shoulders and her long neck. Dez has no idea who designed the waistcoat but he's pretty sure it was made exclusively for her.

"Help you?" Her accent is Eastern European.

"Mate of Raziah's. Can I stash this someplace for a couple of hours?" He drums a little tattoo on the beat-to-hell guitar case.

She eyes him. She's taller than Dez—five-nine, he guesses, without the blocky heels—and likely ten years his senior. She has about the palest skin he's ever seen. She wears her platinum hair in a low pony. She nods toward the case. "What do you play?"

He sets the case down on the bar and pulls out the Gibson Ripper. It's candy-apple red, and the woman's eyes light up. "Ooooh." He hands it to her and, when she strums, Dez spots the telltale calluses on her thumb. "This is a classic, yes? I love the color." She hands it back.

"Ta. Want to play some? Band's not set up yet."

"Perhaps later." She offers her hand. "Any friend of Raziah's . . . I'm Veronika."

She pronounces it the Russian way: *Vero-Nica*.

They shake. "Desmond Aloysius Limerick."

She says, "That cannot possibly be your real name."

"It's a fine name!"

She *tsks*. "Parents do a lot of cruel things to children. Welcome to my corner of hell, Desmond Aloysius. I am normally good with accents." She squints—her eyes are the pale, pale blue of flowering rosemary—and cants her head a few degrees. "Manchester?"

"For a bit, aye. Top marks, you. You're Russian, but not from Moscow. Nor the west. Somewheres out east, I'm thinking."

Her eyes pop wide. "Oh ho! An interesting tongue and a talented ear." Veronika turns to the bartender. "Desmond Aloysius's first round is on me."

CHAPTER 8

The first set starts with a love ballad as soft as a rose petal. The club patrons—maybe fifty people here tonight—hardly notice. So when, without a break between songs, Raziah picks up her electric guitar and hits a power chord, and when she drops her voice into low and growls out the first stanza of a rocker's lament, nearly every head in the place snaps her direction and every conversation withers away. Raziah is five-foot-nil and her weight is barely in the triple digits, and nobody expects this waif to have a four-octave range, but she does. Her lilting butterfly voice had been perfect for the love ballad, but now she torques it down and growls into the mic, the lyrics half protest, half threat.

"You watch my ass/you watch your back.

Don't bring no weapon to a fight/you don't want used on you."

Dez enjoys eyeing the crowd. He loves that moment when the collective *gets* that Raziah isn't your everyday singer. All of the guys and half of the girls have fallen in love with her by her fourth song. Even the gay boys. Especially the gay boys.

Dez has seen this a half dozen times in LA clubs. They're eating out of the palm of her hand. Half fear that palm will slap them down. Half fear it won't.

* * *

Dez sits at the bar and nurses an Irish whiskey, neat, for the first hour. He's impressed by the other musicians. During the band's break, Veronika brings him another drink and one for herself and takes the stool next to him. The vest and trousers reveal an inch of ice-white skin around her midriff and lower back, not to mention the shoulders one can only get by using a professional trainer. She lifts her glass, holding it in midair. "Raziah."

Dez clinks his glass against hers. "Raziah." He sips. "Ta."

"You play with her?"

"In Los Angeles. She's got a voice that'll drop the barometric pressure over the city, that one."

"Yes." Veronika smiles. "But her voice isn't her best asset, my dear Aloysius."

Her tone is mocking but fun. "Dez to me mates. And you're right: Raz could sing campfire songs or Chinese opera, and it'd be grand. But it's her lyrics that make ye weep."

Veronika looks a little surprised. "You get that? Most just see the purring or snarling sex kitten onstage."

"Speak nice. She's me mate."

Veronika sips her drink. "Does *mate* mean fuck buddy in Manchester?"

Dez belts out a laugh. "It does not! Jay-sus, I've socks older than Raziah! You've a mouth on you."

She ups her smile. "Don't I just?"

The second set is better than the first. Raziah wears the slightest sundress and red sneakers onstage, and the dress is limp with sweat when she makes it to the bar, after the set, and kisses Dez on the cheek. She grabs the remains of his drink and downs it in a gulp. Veronika is behind the bar, helping because the crowd has grown, and she's obviously skilled and experienced back there.

Raziah says, "Laleh texted me. She's staying at her boy-friend's tonight. He lives in a high-rise with security and a concierge desk. She's safe enough. And . . ."

She looks a little chagrined. Dez has seen this next bit coming. "And you've made plans for tonight as well, have ye. Let me guess: drums."

She grins up at him from beneath her lightning-bolt hair and suddenly looks like a teenager. "Nah. Key-boards."

Dez studies the boy at the piano, who can't take his eyes off Raziah. Dez looks aghast. "An' since when d'you fancy blonds?"

Raziah laughs. "I'm tolerant like that."

"Fine, then. Some hostess you are. Leave a poor de-fenseless lad alone in the strange city for the night."

She kisses him again. "I do love you, Dez. And I know I said it before, but thank you for coming. Laleh's the only family I've got left."

"Family before everything."

She heads back toward the stage. "I'll meet you at the condo tomorrow morning. I'll bring bagels. Love you."

Frat boys at a table near the back of the club are get-ting frisky, and Dez turns to watch the bouncer have a word with them. From behind the bar, the owner refreshes his drink. "I'm Veronika Tsygan," she says, filling in more of her name. "I overheard part of that. Have you a place to stay in Portland?"

He offers his hand across the bar. "Pleased." He jams a thumb toward the ceiling. "That's a hotel above us, in-nit? Should do."

She smiles and wipes the bar with a clean rag. "You're low maintenance, Desmond Aloysius Limerick of Manchester. I'll give you that."

Dez actually ends up playing two songs with Raziah, but not with his bass. The pianist takes a break and Raziah waves Dez up to the stage. "Do you know 'Killing Me Softly'?"

"Roberta Flack? Not really."

"Right. Doing it in mambo. Try'n keep up." She winks at him, takes up her guitar.

Dez can play by ear. Raziah starts, just her angelic voice and her guitar, and when Dez has her key, he joins in at the piano, filling in where he assumed she'd want, letting her silences hold their own.

The audience loves it.

They do one more, a rockabilly bit, her version of a Jerry Jeff Walker thing, which Dez and Raziah played together a few times in Los Angeles, and it goes swimmingly tonight. After which, he returns to the bar to listen and to enjoy the rest of the night.

Later during the third set, that same table of frat boys gets loud and obnoxious and very drunk. One of them swats a waitress on the butt as she takes their order. Dez glances around and sees that the bouncer has stepped outside. He sets down his mostly untouched drink and slides off the stool.

Veronika is heading toward the frat boys with a scowl that would peel paint. He catches her attention. "Would I be interfering if . . . ?"

She nods her consent.

The frat boys sit in the back, near the door. Dez wanders around to that side. The loudest kid, the one who pawed the waitress, shouts, "Where's that bitch with my drink!"

Dez taps him on the shoulder. The kid turns, gives Dez the up-and-down, then stands, almost chest-bumping him. He's taller than Dez and fifteen years younger, though Dez out-masses him by close to ninety pounds. He slurs, "You got a problem, dumbass?"

Dez grins, all boyish charm. Behind him, Veronika has arrived, along with the club bouncer. Dez said, "Want to see a bar trick? Bet I can guess your sign."

The drunk kid says, "My sign. What're you, queer?"

"Sure, why not." All smiles.

"Go ahead, dude. What's my sign?"

Dez ramps up his smile, steps into the kid's personal space, and says, "'Do Not Resuscitate.'"

The other frat boys aren't quite as drunk. They take in Dez's physique, rise, throw twenties on the table, grab their friend by both arms and haul ass.

Dez is about to walk back to his drink at the bar when Sergeant Heywood Washington, Portland police, touches his forearm, stops him.

"Sergeant! Wotcher, mate. Didn't see you there. Enjoyin' the show?"

Washington nods to the frat boys' now-empty table. "Enjoying both shows. You're pretty good onstage."

"Raziah's good. I just hum along."

Washington says, "I called your friend, Detective Swanson, in Los Angeles."

"How's she doin'?"

"Says the city's quieter since you left."

"She's good people, that one. All wool an' a yard wide. Ask you a question?" Washington nods. "Two cars are running surveillance on the house the Swann sisters are staying at. Or they were, before the show, an' they didn't follow us. Them your lot?"

Washington looks serious. "No. I can have a unit prowl past, see what's what."

"Ta."

"Is it all right if I call you in the morning, Mr. Limerick? I think we should talk."

"'Course."

They shake hands and the sergeant ambles away.

At the bar, Veronika Tsygan smiles at Dez. She says, "That man is a police officer?"

Some people have a keen sense about things like that. "He is."

She eyes him shrewdly. "Tell me, Manchester: What was he drinking tonight?"

Dez says, "Him? Soda water with a wedge of lime. Had two."

Her smile grows warmer. "I watched you tonight. I think very little escapes you."

Dez shrugs.

"Thank you for the help with those idiots. And for getting them out quietly."

"Best fights are the ones never get started."

She leans in close so he can hear her over the music onstage. "Oh, Manchester. I think we can do better than just the hotel upstairs tonight."

CHAPTER 9

Veronika doesn't just own the Deep Dive, she's a co-owner in the ground-floor restaurant and hotel that occupy the same building. She arranges for a room for Dez and they sleep with each other that night and it's pretty magical. Then again, Dez has enjoyed every single sexual encounter he's had since he was sixteen. He's not sure if that makes him a bon vivant or a slut, and he's honestly not given it that much thought.

After, he learns she's Siberian. She's lived in the States for fifteen years and has been naturalized. Votes and everything.

Around three in the morning, Veronika wakes up to find Dez at the little antique desk near the window. He's backlit by the streetlights on Burnside, and the room's peppermint wallpaper lends him a reddish glow. He's working with a tablet computer, applying wires to it.

She wriggles into her panties and his black T-shirt, and crosses to him. "Can't sleep?"

He grins at her. "Lookin' something up." He has a card reader; one of those devices that baristas and bartenders use, attached to a smartphone or a computer, to swipe credit and debit cards.

"Are you a hacker?"

"Amateur," he says. "Picked up a little in me last job. I use it only wisely an' as a force for good."

"Can you spam my ex-husband?"

"Oh, absolutely!" He grins. "That's the fun bit!"

He's wearing only his boxer shorts and Veronika, standing behind him, gets her first good view of the bullet wounds, knife scars, and burns that decorate his solidly constructed body. Making love in the dark, she'd only felt them. He has two tattoos as well: Over his left pectoral is a tattoo of a fleur-de-lis of flames. On the inside of his right forearm is Janus, the Roman god of beginnings and gates, transitions and time, duality and doors, passages and endings.

She looks at an exit wound on his upper back. "*Bozhe moi.* You've been in trouble a lot in your life."

"I've not," he says, attaching a lead to the card reader. "Bit of bad luck, here an' there. Not enough to dwell upon. Mostly I'm the luckiest bastard on God's green."

"You consider this a lucky life?" She traces the exit wound with her fingertip.

"Well, just climbed out of bed with a stunning blond goddess, so . . ."

Veronika Tsygan has a low-timbered, almost masculine laugh. She says, "Keep going. You're on a roll."

He hands her an ID card, a magnetic access card made of a bendable black metal, shined to a mirror surface. Veronika studies both sides of the card and sees no writing, images, or symbols. "What is this?"

"Told you about Raziah's sister, yeah? Being attacked? Took this off one of them bastards."

"Is it important?"

Dez shrugs. Veronika, with her hands on his shoulders, feels the defined muscles of his trapezoid bunch and clench. "Bastard had no ID. This card gets him through a door. Be nice t'know which door."

Because that's how gatekeepers think: *Show me which door a man has permission to walk through, and I'll tell you about the man.*

He swipes the magnetic card through the reader. He waits a few seconds.

Lines of green code on a black background start motoring down the screen of his tablet.

"Can you read any of that?"

"Aye."

They wait. A foreign word scrolls across the screen.

"'Gamila'?" Veronika frowns. "I've seen that word before. I can't think where."

"Supposed to be a high-tech facility on the Columbia River," Dez tells her. He lifts her hand off his shoulder and kisses her knuckles. "Ever hear of an outfit called Clockjack?"

CHAPTER 10

Veronika tells the front desk to book Dez in his room for three nights. She locates a gym for him only a block away that offers day passes. She also points out his window as the sun begins to rise and shows him Powell's City of Books.

His eyes light up. "Heard of that! Ta, love."

Veronika dresses and heads down to her office in the club. Dez walks to the gym, gets a day pass, buys workout togs—gyms are one of the few places he can buy off-the-rack clothes that fit his frame. He gets in an hour on a treadmill and jumping rope, and an hour on a Nautilus machine. He showers. It's just going on eight when Dez checks Google Maps and walks toward a coffee shop. He's halfway there when he spots a toy store. On a whim, he enters. He finds the aisle with marbles and buys three metal ones the size of dates. More ball bearings than marbles, really. Dez liked the efficiency of the one he used on the blond fella at the hospital. And he can't very well walk around Portland with a gun strapped to his hip. This is America, true, but that isn't his style.

Dez heads to the coffee shop and buys a handled cardboard container with a gallon of coffee, plus sugar, creamer, and stir sticks. He's spotted weirdly colorful, motorized scooters all over town. He rents one and whisks his way to the conductor's condo in Goose Hollow, riding one-handed, messenger bag worn cross-body, coffee box in the other hand, grinning like an idiot.

He arrives at the C-shaped building with the cute, minuscule garden. He spots a black Escalade with several short antennas and federal government plates. Raziah and Laleh stand in the condo's bay window. They watch as two men step out of the SUV with badges.

"Mr. Limerick?"

Limerick drops the stand, the scooter remaining upright. "Aye."

They flash tin. "I'm Van Ness. This is Wu. We're with the Drug Enforcement Administration."

Dez slaps his forehead. "*That's* what DEA stands for!"

The men look at each other.

"Sorry. Met a fella in California last week, worked with you lot. Long story. How can I help ye?"

The guy identified as Wu says, "We want to ask you about one of the men you tangled with the other night."

"Line forms on the left. Popular, that one."

Van Ness isn't smiling. "Someone else has asked you about this Joe character?"

That takes Dez by surprise. The U.S. Marshals deputies who visited this condo the day before had asked about Frank, the Black guy. Not Joe, the Latin guy. Dez maintains his poker face. "Police, is all."

Wu says, "How do you know this guy?"

"By punching him. It's a primitive way to meet people, ye, but have you tried them online dating services?" He shudders.

Van Ness says, "You think this is funny?"

"Oddly, kind of, yeah. Not exactly sure why."

"You'd met 'Joe' before."

"Hadn't."

"You don't know anything about him. Just stumbled into him."

"He stumbled into me fist, if we're being technical. Anything else?"

Wu reaches for handcuffs. "You're coming with us. Turn around."

"Arresting me, are you?"

Both men rest their hands on the butts of their guns. "Turn around."

And, as if on cue, a Portland Police Bureau prowl car pulls up behind the Escalade. Sergeant Heywood Washington, in uniform, climbs out, adjusting his utility belt. He joins them and now it's a foursome. He's twenty years older than either of the DEA agents, and he speaks softly, politely. "Good morning. May I see some IDs?"

Van Ness and Wu exchange looks, then hand over their badge folders. Washington takes out a notepad and pen, and writes down the details. He says, "How we doing, Mr. Limerick?"

"Good, Sergeant. Yourself?"

"Fine morning." He hands back the folders. "I heard the DEA petitioned for custody of one of my suspects. The one called 'Joe.'"

"That's right," Wu says.

"Do you have a positive ID on him?"

Van Ness says, "Well, all of what we know is in the custodial petition. You're free to look at that."

Washington tucks away his pad and pen. "I will. Thank you. Do you have probable cause to arrest Mr. Limerick?"

The DEA guys look at each other. There's a pause.

Wu hands Dez a card. "If you think of anything . . ."

"'Course. Glad t'help."

The DEA agents return to the SUV and buckle up, and check their rearview mirrors, hit their turn indicator, and pull slowly away from the curb.

Dez turns to Washington. "Coffee?"

"Please."

"The surveillance on this house, yesterday?"

Washington says, "It wasn't us, and there was nobody here when I asked two uniforms to swing by. I swung by myself, after hearing you play last night. I saw nobody."

Dez says, "I might've failed to mention the two cars on stakeout to the Swann sisters. Since they're gone now, can we keep that 'tween ourselves?"

Washington nods.

CHAPTER 11

Raziah brought bagels and cream cheese. Laleh brought fresh berries from the local farmers market. Dez discovers that Raziah has used the conductor's condo several times—la maestra travels all over the world—and the sisters feel at home here. Heywood Washington accepts a cup and a bagel and turns to Dez. "Detective Swanson in LA vouches for you. She couldn't tell me much about you, except that you had a number of chances to do right by her and hers, and you stepped up. Pretty much all I need to know."

The coffee is utterly fantastic and Dez groans. He's heard this before about Portland. The coffee, and also the microbrew beers. "Makes me feel bad I withheld information from you."

Washington's salt-and-pepper eyebrows rise.

Dez digs out the mirrored black key card and hands it over. "Took this off the fella calling himself Joe."

Washington examines both sides. "It won't tell us much."

"It's a high-access security card to a joint called Gamila."

Both sisters react, Raziah with surprise, Laleh with suspicion. She says, "How could you know that?"

"I'm good with electronics." He leaves it at that. He digs his tablet computer out of his shoulder bag and shows Washington what he found. Washington can't decipher any of the code, but he sees the end result.

"When were you going to tell me this?"

"After Beth Swanson vouched for me."

The cop nods.

Laleh nibbles berries. "Even if that man had been to the Clockjack headquarters, it won't narrow it down too much. There are, I don't know, a thousand employees? Two thousand? Something like that. Plus visitors."

Dez says, "This is a high-access security card. It doesn't open one door at Gamila, love. It opens them all."

She looks skeptical. "You're sure?"

But Dez responds to the police sergeant. "Fella named Conor O'Meara was doing an audit of Clockjack. Conor O'Meara gets mugged an' killed. And his research goes missing. Laleh does a profile of O'Meara for her newspaper. She's mugged. Her apartment's ransacked. By at least one fella what works for Clockjack."

Laleh isn't ready to accept the chain of evidence. "Yes, but my profile had nothing important in it! It's a good story, I think. I talked to Conor's parents, and his two best friends, and his pastor. But so what? I didn't dig up any deep, dark secrets."

Raziah, sitting cross-legged on the floor, says, "That you know of."

"I'd know. I'm a writer. Trust me."

Raziah says, "I'm a writer, too."

And her sister rolls her eyes. "You write *music*."

It's a throwaway line. Not delivered with any heat or speed. Raziah has slowly turned her head to stare at her sister. Laleh hasn't noticed. Dez has.

Laleh already is back on topic. "Conor's investigation wasn't groundbreaking, either. Clockjack needed to be recertified as a B Corp. His audit connects only to public documents."

Dez says, "Drug Enforcement fellas wanted to know about Joe. We also got visited by the U.S. Marshals Service last night."

Washington nods. "Regarding the other guy you beat, right? The marshals petitioned for custody of him. But they won't tell us lowly police officers who he is. Same for 'Joe' and the DEA."

"Two agencies. Seeking information on two ne'er-do-wells. Neither of 'em asks about two of them bastards, or all three. Just the one. And neither agency wants t'talk to Laleh, so it's not about her assault. Assaults. Sorry."

Laleh shrugs. The swelling has gone down on her face and she has better color this morning.

Raziah is quiet, focused on her bagel, head down, that mass of kinky hair obscuring her face.

Dez turns to the cop. "Is your lot investigating Clockjack?"

"I couldn't answer that if I knew, but no, to my knowledge. And thank God."

"Why?"

"Do you want to tell him, ma'am?" He directs this at Laleh. "You're a business writer."

She says, "Clockjack Solutions is one of the largest taxpaying corporations in Oregon. One of the state's biggest exporters, too. It's an economic and political powerhouse."

"Plus, they provide communications technology and computers that we use." Washington reaches into his pocket and produces a Clockjack phone, then tucks it away. "Fire and Rescue, and Parks and Rec, too. The city council would wade in hip-deep if we ever started to think about an investigation of the company. But then again, what's to investigate? We only handle municipal crimes. If there's something big enough to bring in the DEA and the Marshals Service, it'd most likely be out of our jurisdiction."

Raziah stands, long legs unfolding, and takes her dishes to the kitchen.

"And there's this," Laleh says. "You'd expect the Securities and Exchange Commission to lead an investigation of company wrongdoing. Or the State Department, if it was about international trade, or the Federal Communications Commission, if it was about the phones or the website or the apps. DEA is about the narcotics trade, period. Marshals Service is about traditional crimes."

Dez reaches for the coffee. "How many investigative agencies does this country have, anyway?"

"Dozens and dozens." Washington shakes his head. "And before you ask: no. None of them are famous for sharing information with each other. Not a one of them."

Raziah walks into the living room with her massive shoulder bag, headphones around her neck, her guitar on her other shoulder, stuffing a notepad and pens into her bag. "I'm going out," she says.

Dez says, "Fancy some company?"

"Nope."

She's gone.

Dez looks at Laleh. She is unaware that her words— "You write *music*"—stung her sister. She starts cleaning up the remains of the breakfast and notices Dez's look.

"What?"

But Dez turns to Washington. "I'm only in town to help Laleh and Raziah. I've no interest in the rest o' this. Whatever's behind all this is none of my business and I'm glad t'be rid of it."

"So you won't launch some sort of investigation into Clockjack, Mr. Limerick?"

"Friends call me Dez. They stay away from me mates, they've nothing to fear from me."

"Well, I can't investigate Clockjack without getting the explicit permission from the chief of police, and he'd have to get permission from the police commissioner. So if I make even a squeak, this becomes a political hot potato." Washington turns to Laleh. "How about you? You're a reporter. Will you be looking into the Clockjack angle of this thing?"

"I can't. I was attacked. It would be a conflict of interest for me to write about what happened, unless it was, like, an opinion column. Let me sound out my editor. Tell him what Dez learned. I don't think he'll bite. We're a small daily. Places like the *Wall Street Journal* could throw whole teams at this story. We've got exactly one-point-five business reporters." She shrugs. "I'll ask. We'll see."

CHAPTER 12

After Sergeant Washington leaves, Dez turns to Laleh. "Can we get into Conor O'Meara's home?"

"Yes. I talked to Conor's sister. She gave me permission to look around. She's mailing me the keys."

"If we've her permission, we should have a look today, aye?"

"I get that, but without the keys, you can't get in."

"Well . . ." He shrugs. "Never say never."

Conor O'Meara lived off Hawthorne Boulevard on the east side of the city. The lanes are narrow and the sidewalks are packed with pedestrians. Dez counts as many skateboards as he does dogs, and plenty of both. Many restaurants have outdoor seating. The whole area has a shabby-chic vibe, and he likes it. As Laleh's parking, Dez gets the logic of her driving a Smart Car. Parking is at a premium in the inner east side of Portland and the streets are narrow. A normal American sedan could never hope to fit into the space she picks.

She climbs out. "Are you going to break into his place?"

Dez winces. "Harsh term, that."

He rounds the car and she touches his arm. "Stop. Before we do this: Who are you?"

"Raziah's friend."

"I know that. But how do you know how to do the things you do? Beat up guys with guns, hack passkeys, break into homes? Is my sister mixed up with some kind of criminal?"

Dez ponders how best to answer this. He also remembers to whom he was speaking. "Off the record?"

She nods. Her short haircut doesn't bounce and jostle as her younger sister's does when she nods.

"I had an interesting sort o' job, for a time. Developed certain skill sets. All I can tell you is this: I wouldn't use what I know to hurt your sister and that means I wouldn't use it to hurt you, either. You've my word for that."

"Raziah said she's heard you refer to yourself as a gatekeeper."

He starts walking toward Conor O'Meara's place. "Gatekeeper. Comes from the Latin. It means 'friend of Raziah.'"

She sees that she's not getting any more of the story, so she begins walking with him.

O'Meara rented a room in a Queen Anne house in Southeast Portland that had been converted into apartments. It's three stories tall aboveground, with a gabled roof and a veranda and no street-facing garage. It's painted pale blue and daisy yellow, and Dez counts no fewer than five bicycles chained to the railing of the veranda steps. He spots outdoor stairs on the left side of the house that lead to the second floor, and outdoor stairs on the right side that lead to the third floor. He says, "Which one's his?"

Laleh points to the second floor, the south side.

Dez brought his beat-up, faded leather messenger bag. He starts up the stairs and, after a beat, Laleh joins him. At the top landing, he peers through the four rectangular windowpanes in the door. The door opens onto a corridor.

"Everyone on this floor has a key," Laleh whispers.

"Why are you whispering?"

"Aren't we breaking in?"

"It's not the Guggenheim, love."

He rattles the doorknob. Nothing. He reaches into his shoulder bag and retrieves a small folding knife in a green canvas belt-clip sheath. A pocket in the sheath holds a tension bar, a couple of lockpicks, and two rakes. He selects the tools he wants and, four seconds later, steps into the corridor.

She says, "Ex-gatekeeper?"

He says, "Ex–juvenile delinquent."

The nearest door on their left is Conor O'Meara's. Dez has that one open in about the same amount of time, and they step in, closing the door gently behind them.

The room is decorated cheaply but nicely, with second- and thirdhand furniture lovingly restored, a couple of framed black-and-white landscape photos in store-bought frames, and an IKEA bookshelf crammed with novels, essays, historical biographies, and a collection of graphic novels. The apartment has a separate bedroom and bath, but only an attached kitchenette. Laleh shows him Conor's desk under a window that would get good morning light.

"He worked here, when he worked from home. He liked the quiet."

"D'you mind me askin' . . . ?"

"We dated. For a while. And when that didn't work, we remained friends. He's . . . Conor was a good guy."

"His work computer was taken?"

She nods. "I told the police he kept one of those small, knee-high filing cabinets next to his desk. It's missing, too. The entire filing cabinet."

Dez digs out his mobile, with its thick rubber, ruggedized carrier. An alert flashes on it, and he smiles.

"What?"

"Feds are trying to get a locator tap on this phone. Marshals Service, DEA, maybe both."

"So they know we're here?"

Dez looks a little hurt. "'Course not, love! In a way, phones are a gateway to the person owning 'em. Nobody uses my gateways, 'less I says they can."

He swipes away the alert and brings up an app. He taps some keys. "Your mate's story an' notes were erased from the computer at work?"

"Yes."

"Could that be done from afar?"

"Yes. At least I think so. I know he could access his company's database and word-processing stuff from here or from a coffee shop."

She peers over his shoulder; easy to do, they're the same height. Dez is searching for Wi-Fi sources. Seven of them pop up. Laleh points to one called 3Base. "That's him. He was a starting third baseman in high school and college."

The other Wi-Fi sources have names like BigBob's, Tube o' Internets, and EpsteinBarnes01. One of them is labeled 3BaseOld.

Dez taps on the chevron to the right of that one. He taps several commands into his phone.

"What are you doing?"

"Scavenger hunt."

The screen changes to a bull's-eye and an x-axis and a y-axis. A fuzzy glow appears in the southwest quadrant.

Dez has broken into many doors in his career. Some were wooden or iron. Some were virtual. The virtual ones sometimes required finding their nexus in the real world, and this program was designed to do just that. He doesn't explain any of that to Laleh. He also doesn't tell her that he'd written some of the code for this app.

He spins on his heel, slowly, until the fuzzy spot of

light connects to the y-axis. He steps forward and the fuzzy spot slips toward dead center of the bull's-eye.

Dez is facing the room's coat closet.

He tucks his phone away and checks the closet. Coats and jackets hang from the dowel. Below that, he spots Adidas trainers set up on newspaper that is wrinkled and stiff from absorbing rainwater. He clocks hiking boots, and snow cleats that clip onto the soles of one's shoes. He sees a basketball, filled with air and relatively new. Also a baseball glove and a baseball; the ball is inside the glove and the glove is wrapped in a thick, industrial-sized rubber band.

He stands on tiptoe and checks the shelf above the dowel and coat hangers. He takes down one box filled with gloves, scarves, and watch caps. He hands that one to Laleh and takes down the next box: a high school yearbook and a folder with clipped copies of newspaper articles. Sports page stuff of his baseball days. There's a photo of him holding a trophy and grinning like a goofball. When Laleh sees that, she starts to tear up.

Under the last box is an older MacBook. Circa 2010. When Dez tries to pull that down, he realizes it's plugged into a power cord, tucked behind the shelving. He moves the farthest coats on the right-hand side of the dowel and sees the cord, staple-gunned into the wooden rear of the closet, running to the floor and out through a drilled hole.

He unplugs the old laptop and hauls it down. Its black surface is dusty. He beams. "Thing o' beauty this. I had one."

He sets it on the island separating Conor's living room and kitchenette, pries open the lid. He hits the On button. It hums to life.

"What is this?"

"Your lad had two Wi-Fi systems. One 4G, which he used for gaming, TV, music, the internet. What have you. And an older, slower network, that he ran this beauty on."

The screen opens to show a row of folders. There must be forty of them. One is labeled Audits. Dez applies a fingertip to the small, square scrolling pad. He opens the Audits folder.

The most recent one was last modified six days earlier.

It's labeled Clockjack Solutions.

CHAPTER 13

The BBC interviewer drawls, "The consensus is that you tech gurus are just vastly too powerful these days. Gates, Bezos, Elon Musk flying to Mars or whatever. While billions of humans starve. What say you, Ms. Sharpe?"

RJ Sharpe, CEO of Clockjack Solutions, stands in her office on the Gamila campus in the Columbia Gorge. As always, Sharpe is in her uniform, for which she is internationally famous: jeans with no knees, a stretched-out Metallica concert T-shirt, vintage, one shoulder bared, with classic Doc Martens. RJ Sharpe is fifty-five years old and looks far more splendid and relaxed and confident and strong than most people of either gender ever will. Her curly hair hangs to her shoulders with a vivid silver streak running the length of her auburn locks, slightly off-center to the right.

Interviews like this are more or less the only reason she goes to the campus. She's Zoomed the space with sleek steel furniture, no wall hangings, a big horizontal window with curtains back to perfectly frame Mount Hood, TV-newscaster-quality camera and microphones and lighting.

She smiles easily into the camera, on a tripod in front of her wall-mounted computer monitor. "I run a billion-dollar business from little ol' Oregon, Nigel, and

I take an electric bus to work. I don't speak for Bill, or Jeff, or Elon. I don't hardly know them. What I can tell you is that Clockjack does a lot of good, and we could do more, and we will. Wait and see."

She winks into the camera. Her delivery is always like this: quick-footed and positive and vivacious. She always gives interviews standing up, her shoulders swaying a little, as if she can hear music, or as if she can't wait for the interview to end so she can go cure Ebola.

"Your Clockjack phones use tantalum, Ms. Sharpe. Tantalum!" The presenter's eyes narrow. He jabs in the direction of the camera with the blunt end of a fountain pen. "The mining of tantalum has been linked to human rights catastrophes—*catastrophes,* Ms. Sharpe—in Rwanda, the south of Kenya, and even the failed state of Zanj. Places with some of the worst human rights abuses on Earth!"

"True enough. Tantalum is used in capacitors. But we have the documentation to prove that we're using the metal that is mined peacefully, with the profits going to the people doing the mining."

"But *still*!" Nigel scoffs. "That's an awful lot of conflict metal plundered for your profits."

"You got me there." She smiles broadly. "That metal is used in every smartphone and laptop and tablet computer on Earth. And a bit of quick research on Facebook and Twitter and Instagram shows that your own household, with yourself, your wife, your three daughters, and your son, post from no fewer than ten such phones and tablets, Nigel. Ten. From one household. Tsk."

She winks again.

The presenter blushes, his nose going from red to purple.

The interview doesn't last much longer than that.

She rings off with a cheery, "Always a pleasure,

Nigel!" She powers down her monitor, makes sure it's off, and flips it the bird.

She turns to Robert Taylor, head of security for Clockjack Solutions, who leans against a wall, well out of camera range, listening and occasionally chuckling silently, one thumb pad and his eyes scrolling his Clockjack phone nonstop.

"It's going to take a miner's helmet and a lamp to find your boot up his arse." He has a Scots accent.

Sharpe places both hands on her hips, thumb-side up, elbows akimbo, and tries to calm her nerves. She nods. "You didn't have to stay for the whole interview."

Taylor keeps scrolling. "A little moral support. Glad to do it."

She studies him. Taylor is a hard man with a long, sleek, muscled body. More like a swimmer than a wrestler. He wears his blond hair slicked back, sports a goatee and a full set of tattoo sleeves on both arms. He makes no pretense of hiding his shoulder-strap holster or the SIG Sauer.

Sharpe says, "You're pensive."

He smiles up at her, gray eyes squinting. "Do I look pensive?"

"I read people. That's what I do. I read people and I read the times in which they live. You're pensive."

He watches her awhile. He pockets his phone and grabs the fitted charcoal jacket he'd thrown over the back of a chair. "There was a problem. With that auditor and the reporter."

RJ Sharpe presses the pads of both forefingers into her temples as if willing a headache to recede. "Define *problem.*"

"Or perhaps I should define *was.*" He shrugs into the jacket, adjusts the collar and the sleeves. He's a handsome, fit man, and he knows it. "It's taken care of."

"You're sure?"

"It's solved, but there's a new player we didn't count on. The reporter got herself some muscle. He's not with the newspaper . . . we don't think. We don't know who he is. I can tell you he dropped Frank and Joe like they were bantamweights, and neither of them is. He killed Kevin."

She blanches. "Oh my God."

He shrugs. "And according to the police reports, this newcomer killed Kevin by throwing a marble at his head."

She blinks. "A marble."

Robert Taylor smiles. "Isn't that something, then?"

"Are you going to tell me who Kevin and Frank and Joe are? Or were?"

"So you can work up a performance evaluation?" he chides her. "No. Thanks, though."

"Frank and Joe . . . ?"

"Don't worry about them. They'll be fine. We're going to need to make a few hires, though."

Her left eye twitches. "More hires."

He smiles and shrugs. "Business is booming."

RJ Sharpe says, "What business is that? Exactly?"

He smiles and reaches for her door. "None of yours."

CHAPTER 14

Laleh Swann transfers all of Conor O'Meara's notes to her Dropbox account. They find nothing else of interest on the old computer so Dez plugs it back into its power source and returns everything to the closet. They head out.

As they reach her car, Laleh leans one hand on the hood, steadies herself. She's gone pale and she's sweating.

"Jay-zus, girl! You're still concussed! I can't believe I made you drive. Here, let me."

She hands him the keys with gratitude.

Dez ratchets back the driver's seat and begins threading his way back to Southwest Portland.

That's when he spots the tail.

The sides in this whole thing are getting confusing, and Dez can't tell the players without a scorecard. He also dislikes being tailed. Time to shake things up.

He drops Laleh off at the conductor's house. "Mind if I borrow your car a bit?"

She doesn't, and he sits behind the wheel, pulls his tablet out of his messenger bag, plus his phone.

There it is. Federal agencies trying to track his mobile devices. Dez roots around inside the anti-surveillance app, grinning like a little kid. When he's ready, he adjusts the surveillance blocker on his phone and calls an answering machine of his, which he keeps active at a server farm in Estonia.

"Yeah. Me. Need to talk t'you about Frank. There's a petrol station, three blocks from the Swann sisters. Meet you there."

He hangs up. Readjusts the surveillance blocker, calls his own answering machine again.

"Yeah. Me. Need to talk t'you about Joe. There's a petrol station, three blocks from the Swann sisters. Meet you there."

He hangs up and drives three blocks to the out-of-business gas station, thinking: *This should be fun.*

Dez leans against the Smart Car, checking football websites on his phone, as two SUVs squeal up from opposite directions, damn near hitting each other, roof lights rotating.

Dez keeps looking at stories on his phone as Garrison and Gliek of the U.S. Marshals Service clamber out of one SUV; Van Ness and Wu of the Drug Enforcement Administration jump out of the other. Four guns are drawn.

It's a babel of "freeze" and "don't move" and "hands" and "on the ground," and Dez reads that a midfielder for Tottenham shredded his ACL and likely is out for a month. Tottenham had been on a good run, too.

The foursome are drawing nearer, guns out. They'd been shouting at Dez but now they're shouting at each other, too. "Jurisdiction" and "priority" and "warrant" and such. Tottenham face Newcastle on Sunday. They've brought on a young midfielder, on loan from Portugal. Will he make his debut at their newish stadium?

When the Sturm und Drang and the toxic masculinity has died down a little, Dez looks up and beams. "Ladies! Thank you for coming."

All four turn to him. Their guns, too.

Dez waggles the phone. "I've an anti-surveillance suite that's just the very thing. I dropped it long enough to call this conference. Appreciate your time. Thank you."

He can see it in their eyes. The Marshals guys and the DEA guys had wondered why they couldn't get anything from Dez's phone, and then they struck the motherload with a brief talk of "Joe" and "Frank."

Gliek says, "Can we see some IDs, guys?"

Wu says, "Back at you."

With deliberate slowness and care, four badge folders are displayed.

The DEA's Van Ness says, "We want to speak to Mr. Limerick about one of the men he beat at the hospital. What do you guys want?"

Deputy Marshal Garrison says, "Same thing. This is our jurisdiction. DEA has no standing here. Back off. This asshole's ours."

Wu says, "No standing? Are you shitting me?"

Dez leans against Laleh's car, loving the show.

Gliek says, "No standing. That's what the man said. What do you guys know that we don't?"

Van Ness counters, "What do you guys know that we don't?"

Dez's hand shoots straight up. "Oh! I know that one! Me! Pick me!"

Gliek says, "Stay out of this, Limerick."

Wu is like, "Let the man speak."

The hostile glares continue unabated. Van Ness and Wu and Garrison and Gliek stand in the middle of the parking lot, the red-and-blue magnetic lights swirling uselessly on the roofs of their SUVs. Everyone's equidistant from everyone else. Dez is fearful they'll bow and start up a Victorian Regency dance.

Dez says, "I'll explain this slow-like and with small words. I boxed the ears of a lad going by the name o' Frank, and another going by the name of Joe. Aye?"

The feds wait.

Dez points to the marshals. "You lot came to ask about Frank." He points to the drug cops. "An' you lot came to ask about Joe. An' you're all so parsimonious with the details, ye haven't even told each other as much!"

The feds start side-eyeing one another.

Gliek says, "Is this true?"

The DEA guys nod.

The standoff lasts another ten seconds or so.

Van Ness rubs the back of his neck. "Well, suck me."

Dez jerks his thumb toward him. "A poet, that one."

Deputy Gliek says, "Wait a minute. Who the hell is Joe?"

Wu counters, "Who the hell is Frank?"

"An' why, one wonders, are you four fuckwits so uptight? Something's happened, yeah? Something new? Since last we saw one another?"

The silence stretches.

"Holy fuck!" Dez's jaw drops open. "Ye've lost 'em! Haven't you!"

After nearly a minute, the deputy marshals holster their guns and turn toward their car.

A beat, and the DEA guys do the same.

Leaving Dez, a funny-looking little car, and a whole lot of new questions.

CHAPTER 15

Dez drives back to the condo. He draws his phone and texts Raziah. Brat—where at?

He heads into the condo. He finds the older sister lying on her back, on the conductor's couch, shoes off, a cold facecloth over her forehead. Her eyes flutter open as Dez's shadow crosses over her.

She says, "Is everything all right?"

"'Course. Can I call your boyfriend? Have him come get you? I've errands to run."

"I already did. He'll be here soon. Dez?" She raises one arm and Dez takes her hand. "Thank you. For coming. For caring about my sister."

"Gladly." The phone in his pocket vibrates.

"May I ask you a question?"

He nods.

"Did you pick the lock to get in here, just now?"

"Better than ringing the bell with your head throbbing. Yeah?"

She smiles.

Outside, a car pulls up.

"Ford Fusion, blue?"

"That's David." She sits up, folds the cold compress. She looks decidedly better than she did a bit earlier.

"Good, then. Off with yez."

The boyfriend waits by his car. Laleh puts her shoes back on, gathers her things.

Dez says, "My turn: Ask you a question?"

"Sure."

"Have ye heard Raziah perform her music?"

She laughs, then winces when it makes her head throb. "Oh God. Growing up? A hundred thousand times."

"No, I mean now. Today's Raziah."

She glances at him, a little annoyed. "I've heard plenty."

"Should come out to a club some night. Should hear what she's become."

Laleh takes her time; picks her words with care, putting things in her shoulder bag as she contemplates how to answer. "I appreciate your looking after me. Really. I appreciate you finding Conor's notes. And I hear what you say about you and Raziah not sleeping together. It's . . . whatever. Despite everything you've done for us, I'm not ready to trust you with my family. And I don't need advice about my relationship with my sister. No offense."

"None taken."

"There are things you just don't know about Raziah. Okay?" She heads toward the door.

Dez slides his hands, palms inward, into the back pockets of his black jeans. "Know about your step da."

She stops. There's a moment of freeze, neither of them moving. The boyfriend waits patiently outside. After close to five seconds, Laleh turns back. Her eyes are scalding.

Dez waits. This is a calculated risk.

"Raziah told you that."

"No," he answers softly. "Raziah never talks about that. She *writes* about it. It's in her lyrics. It drives her lyrics. Or a lot of 'em."

Laleh stares at him. Tears glisten in her eyes.

"None of my business. I beg forgiveness. But yeah, you ought to come listen to her sometime. You really ought."

Laleh leaves without another word.

Dez drags out his phone and checks the incoming messages. He's got a text from Raziah: Sup.

His thick fingers fly over the tiny keys. Hungry. What's your favorite restaurant in town?

He waits. Outside, a fella he assumes is David kisses Laleh on the cheek and holds the door open for her, then circles his car and drives off. Seems a nice lad. Dez hopes he is.

Ding. He looks at the incoming text. Not "restaurant" Best food=food carts!

He types: Show me.

CHAPTER 16

He meets Raziah at a pod of food carts in the downtown core. Raziah, in a brief summer dress and sneakers, rides her bike in and draws longing smiles in her wake.

The pod is a collective of about twenty-five carts, each with a food theme. The colors are intoxicating; the carts decorated in every imaginable jewel tone. Dez is all grins, and it's infectious; Raziah hasn't said a word, but she's still stinging from her sister's rebuke—"you write *music*," to differentiate that from *real* writing, apparently. But soon she's smiling, too, as they wander. Dez picks a place and orders bandeja paisa, perfectly barbecued chicharron atop red beans, rice, beef, chorizo, plantain, arepa, avocado, and fried egg. Raziah wrinkles her nose at the size of it and goes with a vegan shake.

They find a picnic table and dig in. Dez is aware of how many boys and girls are casting glances at his friend. He's used to it by now.

"So I hear you ended up sleeping with 'Nika last night!"

"Mind yours, ye brat. And did you have a sterling night?"

Raziah actually says, "Bat bat bat," as she cants her head and bats her eyelashes at him.

"'Nuff said." His phone chirps. He glances at it.

"What?"

"Set a Google Alert for some of the Clockjack names Laleh told me about. Which one's Teddy Meeker, then?"

Raziah squints and looks skyward as she racks her memory. "Ah . . . the guy who wrote the code. I think? Yeah. He's the math-head of the original four."

"Aye? Well, our lad is speaking at Portland State University."

"I thought he was some kinda recluse. When is this?"

"Now. Wouldn't mind meetin' the fella. All this has something t'do with Clockjack Solutions, an' that's a fact."

"PSU's really close. Grab your scooter."

They pack up their trash in a bin and head out.

Portland State University is in the heart of downtown and straddles a one-block-wide stretch of park blocks called, helpfully, the Park Blocks. The campus is a hodgepodge of brand-new and architecturally interesting buildings with early-twentieth-first-century brick hulks. There are precious few on-campus dorms, Raziah explains, and most of the students commute from elsewhere in the city. It takes them only about ten minutes to get there, Dez on a scooter and Raziah on her bike.

She locks up her bike. She draws her phone and looks up the event from one of the local newspaper websites. "'Teddy Meeker, former math professor turned internet trailblazer, will speak Tuesday at an alumni donor group of engineering graduates and former faculty in PSU's Willaway Hall. Meeker, a cofounder of the Oregon-grown software giant Clockjack Solutions, taught math in Willaway Hall from 1982 to 1990. . . .'"

She reads silently for a while. "Says this is his first

appearance in Portland in over a year. Says he lives in that R-and-D campus in the gorge."

"Might be a good idea to ask if he knows about Conor O'Meara an' the audit, yeah?"

"What's the plan? Wait outside and see if we can catch him as he walks out? I know Willaway. It's got doors on all four sides."

"No reason to hope for luck, love. We'll catch him in the lecture hall."

"It's a closed-door event."

"Closed doors are sort of me thing."

The one-block-wide grassy park bisects the campus, and it's humming with activity. More food carts and coffee kiosks that draw a steady crowd on a lovely Wednesday. Dez spots the requisite Frisbee game and a black-clad antifa protester denouncing something or other; neither Dez nor the speaker is exactly sure what.

Willaway is a brick monolith, an almost perfect cube, WPA era, decorated on the outside with plenty of bike racks and a thirty-meter-long Black Lives Matter mural. Dez and Raziah stop to study the art for a moment, both impressed. Raziah drags her notebook out of her massive shoulder bag and jots down three or four words. Dez doesn't know which ones. He might hear them in a song someday. Might not. Raziah takes inspiration from a wide array of sources.

Dez uses his tablet computer to conjure up an interior map of Willaway Hall. He studies it a bit, tucks his computer away. "C'mon. Think I see the way in."

They enter, and a man in a space between two of the classroom buildings grinds out his cigarette and draws his cell phone.

"I'm at the thing at PSU. . . . Yeah, listen, a muscle-bound dude with a limey accent just entered with this hot Black chick. . . . Yeah, that's how Frank described the fucker at the hospital. . . . He walked into the same building that Meeker's in. . . . Yeah, I'll head in first and check the room. Get here fast as you can."

CHAPTER 17

Lecture Room 315 in Willaway Hall is set up in atrium style, maybe two hundred and fifty seats in descending arcs. The tech is old-school—literally—with huge chalkboards and an overhead projector circa 1980.

Roughly two dozen people are there, men and women, clustered in the center seats of the first three rows. They look to be retirement age. They aren't here to be lectured to, but are laughing and drinking from lidded coffee cups, and all chatting, sharing anecdotes. Alumni and ex-faculty, Dez guesses.

The man holding court is Teddy Meeker. He's sixty-ish, small-boned, maybe five-five, with a neatly trimmed beard and small, round, wire-framed glasses. He wears khakis and loafers and a dull olive sweater, pilling, the neckline a little ragged. He's sitting on a desk, his butt next to the overhead projector, feet dangling. Out of what Dez assumes is habit, Meeker is holding a length of chalk, even though nothing's written on the vast chalkboards behind him.

He looks up and spots them enter. Dez sits at the end of the top row and waves jauntily at Meeker. The mathematician is likely a bit stumped to see a man in his thirties, built like a much-smaller version of Willaway Hall itself, plus a pretty waif in sneakers and a white sundress with red polka dots. But Dez smiles, and Raziah sits, too, shoes up on the seat-back in front of her, and Meeker goes back to chatting with his old friends.

Dez hauls out his tablet computer, subconsciously kissing the banged-up, ruggedized leather cover. He's bookmarked a *Wired* article about Clockjack and angles it so Raziah can see.

The cover photo shows four people in their early to midthirties. The shot was taken in the Park Blocks of PSU. It's been three decades, and Meeker's hair was both longer and thicker, but his beard is much the same and it looks like he never changed his glasses frames.

"Meeker," Dez whispers, and points to the grinning dude on the left in the photo. His finger drifts to the right. "Joel Menache. He handled the website and administered everything before Clockjack exploded in popularity. I read this article last night."

"Before or after 'Nika rode you like a cowgirl?"

Dez comes from the British Isles, and nobody blushes like his people. His face is the same color as Raziah's polka dots. "Jay-sus! Could ye say that a bit louder? The blue hair at the end mightn't've heard the details!"

Raziah giggles and squirms down farther in her folding seat, her bony knees as high as her forehead. She points to a smiling, dazzling, dark-haired woman in the photo, with one arm around Menache's waist and the other cocked over the shoulder of the fellow at the end. "RJ Sharpe. Damn. Girl had it going on."

"Lovely, aye."

"She still is. I caught a TED Talk on YouTube, all about the power of the internet and social media to create a worldwide environmental movement. I'm not sure I believe her, but can I get a hallelujah: She brings the thunder."

Dez whispers, "Mutant power, that. If I had to speak in public or get a cattle prod to me nethers, I'd need t'think about it a bit."

His finger goes to the last guy in the *Wired* photo, the one on whose shoulder RJ Sharpe is leaning. "Carl Hickman. Taught business studies here. He put together the financing for Clockjack. Article says they made thirty dollars one April and thirty million the next April. Fella had some skills with the green eyeshades and calculator."

Everyone up front laughs at some story Teddy Meeker is telling. A few of the alumni and retirees are standing or reaching for jackets.

Raziah whispers, "Two of these guys are dead?"

Dez nixes the *Wired* article. He's queued up one from the *Portland Tribune*. "Aye. Menache, a year ago July. Car crash. Coming back to Portland from the R-and-D site. His car went into the Columbia. Took 'em the better part of two days t'get both cars out of the drink."

"The other driver?"

"Dead, too." Dez drops the *Tribune* article, pulls up another from the same website.

"Carl Hickman died a month later. Doin' some home repairs. Electrocuted himself. Stopped his heart."

"Wow," Raziah deadpans with laser-like irony. "Shit luck."

"Innit?"

People are trudging up the stairs to the exit doors at house left and house right. Some use canes and walkers. Dez sits and waits for them to pass.

Teddy Meeker stuffs some papers and a couple of hardback textbooks—Dez assumes he wrote them—in a dilapidated canvas backpack. The man's shoes are orthopedic and formless, and there's a coffee stain on the knee of his khakis. If this guy is a dot-com millionaire, he's doing a tremendous job of hiding it.

He could take the left-hand stairs or the right-hand stairs to exit, and he chooses to go left, to exit by Dez and Raziah. Both stand as he draws near.

Meeker throws one backpack strap over his shoulder. The earpieces of his eyeglasses are a bit askew, one lens higher than the other on his face. He's soft-spoken. "Hi. Did you want to talk to me?"

"Desmond Limerick. This is me mate, Raziah Swann."

She offers her hand and he shakes. He says, "Pre-engineering?"

"Pre-Grammys, post-patriarchy, nonbinary, antifascist."

He says, "That's a major?"

She says, "Ought to be."

Dez takes over. "Sir, d'you know about the auditor got hisself killed? Conor O'Meara, by name? Was doing an audit of Clockjack?"

"Sure."

"D'you think we could ask you some questions, then?"

He shrugs and adjusts his lopsided eyeglasses. "Walk me to the streetcar?"

Meeker holds the door for them. There's a proprietary air about him. He hasn't worked as a lecturer at PSU for decades, but he's totally at home in the classroom and the corridors of Willaway Hall.

Dez mutters to Raziah, "Nonbinary?"

She snaps her fingers to a rhythm. "No, but I needed it for the meter."

For the private fundraising function, the entire northwest quadrant of the third floor was closed to students, faculty, and staff, with plastic cones and red velvet ropes in the corridors, plus signage, warning people away. Which is why it's surprising to find men in the third-floor corridor.

Three men. Waiting for them.

CHAPTER 18

There are three guys. All three have the look and heft of soldiers. All look fit. Two of them glare at Dez. The third guy is different. He's blond, his hair slicked back, with a goatee and a full set of tattoos revealed by the rolled-up sleeves of his shirt. The first two are blocking the corridor. The tattooed blond is back a bit, leaning against a wall, smiling softly, fiddling with a pack of gum.

Teddy Meeker looks surprised but not frightened by their appearance. He addresses the blond. "Oh, hey, Taylor. What's up?" He turns to Dez. "Forgive me, this is Robert Taylor, head of security at—"

"Ah, Mr. Limerick doesn't need to know all the details, Professor." Taylor is unfolding a stick of gum as he talks. He sounds Scottish. And he knows Dez's name. That alone tells Dez something useful.

"Pleasure, mate. Taylor, was it?"

Taylor takes those first few bites of his gum, the big ones you use to break up the stick into a chewable wad. He eyes Raziah. "You're not the writer. You're the sister."

"I am *a* sistah." She flashes attitude.

One of the two feisty boys up front eye-fucks Dez. "You're not dealing with street punks this time. This time? You got Rangers."

"Was in the Army, you two? Well then, thank you for your cervix."

Taylor speaks softly, "The lass can go but we'd like a word with you."

Dez beams. "Looking to give Raziah orders, are you? Good luck with that, my son!"

The two Rangers make ready, centering their balance, eyes locked on Dez. Taylor is looking down, still leaning against the wall, fiddling with the silver foil gum wrapper.

Dez says, "Professor, Raziah, stick close, yeah? No wandering about now."

He's gambling that this lot isn't here for mass slaughter. Their mates didn't just traipse into Laleh Swann's hospital room and pop her, right? They're playing a more subtle game than that.

The Ranger nearest to Dez reaches behind his back and draws a collapsible battle baton, its scabbard clipped to his belt. Stowed, it's only about five inches long. But snap it into its deployed format, and it's twelve and a half inches long, made of steel. It's a crowd-control weapon that can break bones and cause concussions when used by someone who knows how.

The man rears back to clobber Dez.

Dez steps into the blow, not away from it. He grabs the guy's wrist, immobilizes his arm, spins him around, braces the man's torso with his other hand, and—*pop*—dislocates his shoulder.

The ex-soldier gasps and falls.

The baton bounces free.

The other ex-soldier swings his own baton at Dez's head. Dez blocks it, forearm to forearm, and drives his fist into the man's gut. The blow is aimed upward and the man's shoes leave the floor by an inch, before he lands again, folds and falls in the fetal position.

The ex-soldiers' plan—if such as they can be said to have had a plan—is shot to hell.

Robert Taylor leans against the wall, eyes down, smiling, nimbly turning the foil gum wrapper into a crane.

Teddy Meeker steps toward Dez. "I don't know who you are and I don't know what this is about, but I'm leaving with these men, and I suggest you get out of here. Now."

"This is about a dead man, sir. A man this mob likely killed."

Meeker shakes his head and adjusts his off-kilter glasses. "You're delusional. These men are a professional security team for a Fortune 500 company. A team you just assaulted. I'm going with them. Leave me alone."

Dez says, "You're a math teacher, aye? Do your sums, Professor."

"You don't know what you're talking about."

"Usually don't," Dez concedes. "But in a bit less than a year, your mate Joel Menache died, an' Carl Hickman died, an' the fella auditing Clockjack died, an' a reporter covering his death was assaulted twice, and should be dead."

"Conspiracy theories? I'm sorry, Mr. Limerick. Seek professional help."

Meeker moves closer to Taylor and his men. The injured guys are helping each other to stand, and both look close to passing out.

Taylor gingerly sets the origami crane atop a water fountain. He smiles back at Dez.

And Dez realizes the quiet blond came with the ex-Rangers for the sole purpose of seeing Dez in a fight.

The Scotsman says, "Be seeing you."

CHAPTER 19

One of the distinguishing characteristics of downtown Portland is that the blocks are short—about half as long as those of most cities. The reason: greed. In the nineteenth century, every merchant knew you did your best business if you had a corner lot, so Portland, never one to shy away from profit, halved the streets and doubled the number of corner lots in the downtown core.

Dez and Raziah take the scooter and bicycle to the boutique hotel, restaurant, and club that Veronika Tsygan co-owns. Dez is uncharacteristically quiet on the way over and Raziah's head is still on the abrupt altercation; Dez hesitates to call that a fight, in that nobody laid a glove on him. She's doing a sort of play-by-play out loud. ". . . and then the dude swings that stick at you and you step *toward* it, like, no way! Like who does that? Then . . ."

They head straight to the Deep Dive. Veronika is there, in leather trousers, boots with Spanish heels, and a man's white tuxedo shirt. She pours Dez an Oregon stout, as dark as a fruit of a date palm. Raziah surprises them both by ordering a Negroni. Veronika approves, and also directs them to a booth that, at this early hour, provides plenty of privacy.

Dez props his bespoke tablet computer against the

uneven brick wall, in landscape format, and they initiate a video call with Laleh.

"God, I haven't done one of these since the pandemic," she laughs. She looks as if her headache is all but gone. She also doesn't appear to be angry that Dez mentioned their stepfather.

"Feelin' better?"

Laleh is speaking on her phone, and looks past it to shoot her boyfriend a warm smile. "David is pampering me."

"Any chance your lad could pamper you out of town?"

She looks startled. "Why?"

"Took your sister to meet Teddy Meeker. Was speakin' at the university here. 'Fraid I made a pig's breakfast of it."

Raziah laughs. They're sitting close enough, and on the same side of the booth, that Laleh can see them both. "What are you talking about? This guy attacked Dez with a nightstick. Dez disarmed him, then *disarmed* him! Dislocated the bitch's shoulder! It was so hot!"

Dez blushes. "Amateur hour, me. Never got t'ask Meeker any questions. Alienated him. Worse, I put us on the radar of the fella behind the attacks. I couldn'ta fecked this up worse if I'd been on their side."

Raziah sips her drink. "Which guy?"

"Blond. Full sleeves of ink."

She wrinkles her nose. "That guy? He hardly said a word. I thought maybe he was, I don't know, an intern or something."

Dez shakes his head. "That bastard was the shot caller."

Laleh cuts in. "How bad is it?"

"Them gobshites attacked you just on the notion that ye might've dug up something on 'em. Now they know

I was askin' questions of one of the foundin' fathers of Clockjack, so they've motivation to try again."

Laleh said, "Oh God."

"Aye, exactly. I went waltzin' in there, dumb an' happy, and convinced them that you, me, and Raziah really do know something. Or are tryin' to learn something. Either way, I made sure they stay focused on you both. Could kick meself."

Laleh is silent, her eyes away from the phone, pondering. She nods and says, "Dez?"

"Aye?"

"Not your fault. I ask people tough questions for a living. I've just scratched the surface of Conor's audit notes. If I find anything incriminating, we'd have ended up on their radar anyway."

"Appreciate you sayin' that. Can you do your research from elsewhere?"

"David's parents own a cabin on Whidbey Island, in the Puget Sound."

"An' where's that, then?"

"In northwest Washington. The cabin's huge. There's plenty of room for David and the three of us. David's here now; he's nodding."

Raziah rattles her ice. "Me? I'm no threat to those a-holes. I don't know anything."

"Neither did your sister, an' they attacked her twice," Dez reasons. "Ye should both be in the wind."

"And not you?" Raziah balks.

Dez laughs. "I can take care of meself, brat. Might just draw them bastards out a bit. See what's what."

Laleh says, "No. Dez? This isn't your fight. You came to Portland to protect me, and you did. You could head back to California, or back to England, or whatever, and be out of this mess. You should."

He starts to protest and she rides over him. "Look, I'll pore through Conor's notes. I've told my editor what

I'm doing . . . although I said we got the research from an anonymous source."

"Thankful for that, then. Ta."

"Anyway, I'll call Sergeant Washington, let him know where I am. Whatever I find out goes in print, and it goes to the police, and after that, we're no longer a potential threat to anyone."

"Not a bad idea, that. I just might head back home. Been ages," Dez lies.

"Good. Raziah, you pack. David and I will meet you at the condo in an hour. Don't worry," Laleh Swann says. "We got this."

Dez and Raziah return to the condo of the symphony conductor. They wait for Laleh and her boyfriend to drive up. Raziah hugs Dez so tight his ribs might bend. She buries her face in his neck. "Thank you. I've never known a man like you."

"Well, few have."

She smacks him in the arm. "Call me when you get to wherever, old man."

He watches them drive away. He pulls out his phone and dials a twenty-five-digit telephone number from memory. He hears anti-bugging technology chirp to life.

He gets a voice mail with no voice, just a tone. E sharp.

"Ye know who this is. An' like as not, ye've been tracing me phone 'round the States, so ye know where I'm at. Here's the thing: Last time we met, you threatened to shoot me if ye ever saw me again. Now's your chance. But before ye do, I've a favor t'ask."

Dez explains the weirdness going on in Portland. Then hangs up.

He makes it as far as the e-scooter when four unmarked SUVs hit the neighborhood, tires screeching, light bars rotating. A helicopter hovers into view. Men jump out of the vehicles; men with guns. Dez has never seen any of them before. The men get him on the ground, and get him handcuffed, and get him in the back of one of the SUVs, which goes screaming out of the neighborhood, the other cars running in harness, the helo pacing them in the sky.

Nobody reads him his rights or asks him a damn question.

CHAPTER 20

Dez is taken into a building via an underground parking structure; he has no idea which building it is. He isn't uncuffed until he's taken to a holding cell. It's a single-occupancy cell, not a drunk tank, with walls instead of bars, a cot, a metal toilet and sink, and harsh fluorescent lights. They take away Dez's messenger bag, wallet, and watch.

They ask him nothing.

The cot looks comfortable enough and the pillow, though thin, is functional, so Dez lies down on his back, arms folded over his chest, and drifts to sleep.

A couple of hours in, a guard brings a food tray and a plastic bottle of water. There is no clock in the room, nor are there exterior windows, so Dez isn't sure how long he's been here. The food is a prewrapped sandwich on white bread and a bag of crisps and a bag of apple slices. Dez's eyes light up.

"Ah! Excellent! Ta, mate."

Dez's enthusiasm for the meal seems to take the jailer by surprise. Dez notes that the man's uniform shirt includes a patch for the FEDERAL PROTECTIVE SERVICE. Definitely a federal building, then.

The sandwich is ham and cheese and surprisingly good. Then again, Dez can't remember ever having a meal he didn't enjoy. The crisps are, well, crisp, and the apple isn't woody. Dez has been in far worse lockups than this one. When the guard comes back for the plastic tray, Dez thanks him and asks if he can get reading material.

The guard leaves without responding.

Fair enough, Dez thinks. It's not a Club Med, this. He lies on his back and crosses his arms and thinks about some of the places on Earth he's been fortunate enough to visit. He thinks about his all-time-favorite starting lineup of the Liverpool Reds. There's a guitar riff in the old Prince song, "Gett Off," that Dez has never mastered, and he plays air guitar, lying on his back, simulating it. After a time, he drifts back to sleep.

He sleeps for what seems to be a solid five or six hours.

In the morning—Dez assumes it's morning—a different guard brings him a lidded coffee and an enormous, mass-produced blueberry muffin, and another bag of apple slices. Dez asks if he's permitted a shower and the guard leaves without responding. Dez digs into his breakfast. The muffin isn't really his thing but he doesn't want to appear ungrateful so he wolfs it down.

He wonders if it's possible to give a Yelp review for a holding cell.

He's guessing it's an hour later when a Black man in a dour black suit and black tie enters, cuffs him, and takes him to an interrogation room with a metal table, two chairs, and a mirrored window. Dez's left wrist is cuffed to an iron ring in the tabletop.

He's there for only about five minutes before a tall, robust man in his late sixties or early seventies enters. The man wears a good suit and lizard-skin cowboy boots and a Stetson. He's got to be six-four, with a full head of silver hair, clipped short. He sets the cowboy hat brim up on the table and pulls out the room's other chair and sits. He produces neither paper nor a recording device.

He says, "Desmond Aloysius Limerick." He speaks the name as if tasting it.

"Morning." Dez smiles broadly.

The man has a deep Southern accent. A deep baritone. Deep brown eyes. "I have spoken to a captain in the Los Angeles Police Department, as well as a sergeant with the Portland police. The former vouches for you and the latter says you've done nothing to make him suspicious of you."

"That's nice t'hear, governor. Ta."

They sit. The man crosses his legs at the knee and adjusts the crease in his trousers.

"We have been unable to find any records regarding your past, Mr. Limerick. No criminal record, here or abroad. You appear to have served in no military units. Nor are you in any law enforcement databases."

Dez looks chastened. "Burdened with a lack of ambition, me. Shameful."

The man's skin is tanned and clings tightly to a lantern jaw and high cheekbones. He does not react.

They sit for a spell.

"Tell me about the fight at Good Samaritan Hospital."

Dez tells it, sparsely and accurately.

"You have never seen these men, prior to that day?"

"No, sir."

"You don't know their real names."

"Sorry."

"You have no connection to them."

"Naught."

"You don't know for whom they work."

Dez says, "Oh, aye, yeah. Sorry. Know that one." He beams like a called-upon schoolboy who's done his homework.

The tall man hides his emotions well but his eyes

glide toward the mirrored window and back. "And how is that?"

"Took a magnetic key card off the one callin' himself Joe. The card granted that bastard—excuse my language—access to Gamila, the research-an'-development campus o' Clockjack Solutions."

The tall man studies Dez with piercing eyes. Dez takes it.

"Where is this key card, Mr. Limerick?"

"Me friends call me Dez. Gave it to Sergeant Washington."

"He . . . did not mention this to the deputies."

Deputies. So this fella is with the U.S. Marshals Service. A couple of rungs higher than those clods, Garrison and Gliek, he thinks. "The good sergeant hasn't been feelin' an overabundance of proactive communication from the various federal agencies generally tripping over each other's dicks this past couple of days. Apologize for me language."

The tall man seems to mull over that.

"You believe these men work for Clockjack Solutions."

"I believe one of 'em had a key card that would open any door at a secure Clockjack facility, aye. Likely inference is that our man works there."

They are silent for a while. The tall man does not fidget. His boot does not bounce in midair. After a bit, he says, "Security personnel at this facility said you have not asked for a lawyer."

"That's right, aye."

"May I ask why not?"

"Don't know any."

"You have not asked the guards why you were detained."

"Never served in law enforcement meself. Feel unqualified to second-guess your reasoning."

The tall man studies him.

"You have not asked who I am."

"Didn't want to presume."

The tall man finally adjusts his body, uncrossing his legs, rearranging them the other way; right leg over left, rather than left over right.

"Mr. Limerick, my name is Chief Deputy Marshal Conroy Sims."

"An' it's a pleasure, sure." Dez offers his right hand across the table. He retracts it when it's clear that Chief Sims will not shake. Dez is not insulted.

Sims says, "I am not inclined to believe your story, Mr. Limerick."

"Well, we've only just met. I grow on people."

"We can tell where you've been and what you've done for almost every day since you arrived in the United States, six months ago. Before that, we can find nothing. The lack of background we can find about you suggests that your history has been professionally scrubbed, Mr. Limerick. Obfuscated."

"Have ye tried alternative spellings of me name?"

Sims sits and ponders. After a bit, he says, "Who are you?"

"Amateur musician. A visitor to this fair country of yours. Friend of the Swann sisters. Told 'em I'd have their backs. Intend to."

Chief Deputy Marshal Conroy Sims says, "No matter who, or which agency, gets in your way?"

"Aye." Dez smiles, then adds, "Sir."

Sims sits.

Dez waits patiently.

"The boyfriend of Laleh Swann used a credit card to purchase gas in Ridgefield, Washington, yesterday. He and the sisters drove to Seattle. They boarded a ferry to Whidbey Island. They have not returned. The sisters are safe."

Dez says, "Only a fool mistakes *hiding* an' *safe*. Ye don't seem like a fool."

So Sims sits a bit longer, his face carved of marble.

After a while, he stands, adjusts the crease in his trousers, buttons the middle button of his very fine suit coat, and picks up the Stetson. He places it squarely on his head; not cocked to the left or right, not too far back or too far forward. So evenly placed that Dez wonders how he did it without a carpenter's level.

"Thank you for your time, Mr. Limerick."

"Quite welcome."

Just before Sims leaves, he pauses.

"Deputy Garrison and Deputy Gliek have been relieved of their duty, pending an internal investigation."

"Well, they're quite dumb, them two. Fair play t'you, sir."

Sims does not disagree. He just leaves.

Five minutes later, a guard uncuffs Dez and escorts him to a room where he finds his wallet and watch and messenger bag. He's asked to sign a form and he does so without reading it.

He's released and, on the street, figures out he's still in downtown Portland.

And that he's regretting that muffin. He starts walking toward the gym that offers day passes.

Three stories up, Chief Deputy Marshal Conroy Sims squeezes honey into a cup of tea in a room full of U.S. Marshals Service investigators. He stirs the drink. "Are we tracking that man's phone and personal computer?"

A techie sits at a desk with a brace of high-end monitors, two ergonomic keyboards, and a stack of communication equipment that is proprietary of a U.S. intelligence agency. He blanches. "Ah. Yessir. It's just . . ."

Sims blows air horizontally over the surface of his tea. "Just . . . ?"

The techie gestures to his high-tech gizmos, all as useful as dandruff. "According to this, Limerick's in Buenos Aires."

A couple of men in the room groan. A couple of them curse.

Chief Deputy Marshal Conroy Sims sips his tea, stone-faced. He stands at a window and watches Dez stroll away with that bowlegged, rolling gait of his.

Sims drawls, "I am fairly certain that he is not."

CHAPTER 21

Dez works out and showers and heads back to the boutique hotel on Burnside Street, where he inquires about extending his stay for a week. There's room, so he pays and heads upstairs and changes into clean—if identical—clothes.

He heads down to the Deep Dive and orders a stout, and a potato and leek soup, and boots up his tablet computer. Veronika is elsewhere.

The U.S. Marshals Service is split up between ninety-four federal judicial districts throughout the United States. In each district, there is a political appointee at the top of the food chain, a United States marshal. The highest-ranking career law enforcement officer in each district is the chief deputy marshal.

Conroy Sims is a chief deputy marshal.

Not for the district that includes Portland. For the district that includes Virginia. Adjacent to Washington, DC. In the political world of federal law enforcement, that would make Sims a big deal, Dez suspects.

And here he is in Oregon, a continent away from his beat, asking about a brace of miscreant muggers.

Veronika Tsygan arrives at some point and takes care of inventory, as workers cart in boxes of booze and food. She has an office adjacent to the bar. Before she heads in, she smiles at Dez and points to the upright piano next to the little stage. "Well? Make yourself useful, yes?" She heads into her office.

Dez thinks *Why not?* He sits at the piano and gets the feel for it. It's a midday crowd, only a handful of tables occupied. When he has a guitar in hand, Dez leans toward rock and blues. At a piano, he tends to congregate with Cole Porter and Johnny Mercer and George Gershwin. Sometimes he'll stray as far left as Leonard Cohen or as far right as Kurt Weill. He's not an excellent pianist but he's good enough. Ten minutes in, a woman asks if he knows "Small World" from *Gypsy*.

"Don't, but give us a key and start in, an' I'll find me way there."

She starts singing. He recognizes the song once she's into it. It's a little raggedy at first but they gel by the second verse. After that, it's "All I Need Is the Girl" and then "Mama's Turn," and Dez knows them even if he didn't think he knew them, and he and the vocalist get a nice round of applause from the small crowd.

After, Veronika brings two whiskeys and sits on the piano bench with him. Dez has pinkish skin and sandy hair—fair Albion and all—but Veronika's skin is damn near translucent. She's wearing her ivory-white hair in a French braid today. She says, "Raziah and her sister are safe, yes?"

"Safe enough for a bit, but it won't hold. You look lovely."

She smiles and sips.

"I'm thinkin' up a more permanent fix for their predicament."

"Do you have a plan?"

"Beginning to, aye."

"Want to tell me?"

"'Course."

"Want to tell me while horizontal and unclothed?"

Dez slams the lid over the keys. "Oh, aye, yeah! That'd be grand!"

She says, "You do know that most men attempt to be cooler about sex than this, yes?"

"Tried being cool when I was a kid. Looked a right prat. No point in it."

"Then by all means, lead on."

Later, Dez lies on his back and Veronika lies on her side, her chin resting on his convex chest, their sweat cooling. Dez tells her what he's thinking.

Veronika asks good, logical questions. She pokes holes in his ideas, or tries to. Later, sitting up against the headboard and using Dez's tablet, they prowl around a map of Portland and figure out a venue for his plan.

His tablet pings a couple of times and Dez smiles softly, checking an app. "What is that?" she asks.

He shows her. "See this? An' this?" He points a finger at the screen. "Someone's tryin' to track me phone. This one here is a federal government site. An' this one isn't."

"A lot of people want to find you."

"Unalloyed popularity has ever been me cross t'bear."

"They can't track you?"

"They can if I let 'em," he says.

"I have two little brothers who are in a very, very Russian sort of business," she says, running her fingertips over the swirls and ridges of bullet and knife wounds on his abdomen.

"The kind with few taxes and fewer questions asked?"

Her eyes are glacier-melt and they twinkle when she laughs. "Exactly, yes. They are in Detroit. They could be here in twenty-four hours, if I asked. They have some experience with brawling."

"Appreciate it, an' if plan A is for naught, I might take you up on 'em."

"Who's this?" Her fingers glide to the tattoo on his right forearm.

"Janus. Roman god o' doors. Among other things. Been known to help me out now and then."

"Hmm." She blinks sleepily. "I have a gun, too, if you need it. The gun is, ah, how you say, unadorned."

As in, unregistered and with serial numbers filed off, Dez assumes.

"Care to see it?"

Dez puts away his tablet. "Thanks, no. Not a fan of the things, if I'm being honest. And I'm not in a tearing hurry t'leave."

Veronika says, "I am open to alternative plans," and rises up to straddle him.

CHAPTER 22

Several blocks down from Veronika's hotel is a brick behemoth, circa 1900. Like Powell's City of Books, it started as a warehouse and morphed into something else; three stories of phonograph records and record players, reel-to-reel tape players, cassette tapes, and used musical instruments. According to Veronika Tsygan, it went under less than a year ago.

It's well after 10 P.M. when Dez picks the lock in the alley-side door and sneaks into the old building.

Some of the merchandise is still there. On the ground floor, he spots an ancient turntable standing on four lacquered legs. The box itself is all wood and red velvet. This graced some bachelor's pad in the mid-1960s, Dez assumes, and it's a beaut. Bring some bird back, loosen your tie, pour a champagne cocktail, and put a little Sinatra on this? You're home free, and here's to ye.

He draws his mobile, adjusts the search blockers. The U.S. Marshals Service still can't track him, but whoever the private party is (and Dez is sure it's the Clockjack mob) now can pinpoint him within a meter. He returns the mobile to his pocket and goes prowling.

The phonograph records are all gone now, but he spots posters that make him nearly weep. The Coasters and the Drifters from the 1950s, Led Zeppelin and the Kinks from the 1960s. Even a vintage Creedence Clearwater Revival. Lovely stuff.

The opposition shows up twenty minutes later.

The villains of the piece have three dark floors to search; each floor the width of the block, one-third its length. A lot of space to cover. Dez shakes his head in sorrow as it takes one of the lads a good three minutes to pick the lock on the rear door to the ground floor. And likely, that lad's the best picklock of the bunch, which is just sad, really. Nobody teaches the classic skills anymore. Cursive writing. How to mix the perfect Rob Roy. Picking a basic padlock. Dez mourns for the world.

Once inside, the men make very little noise. Five men, mixed races, all in their twenties or thirties. Each has a handgun. One man has a mobile, holding it out in front of him, screen up, and likely that's the mechanism they're using to track Dez's phone, which currently resides above them, on the third of three floors. The leader appears to be an Asian man with hair dyed platinum white and with a dragon tattoo on his neck. They quickly scan the ground floor and see nothing alarming. Then again, there's so much space, and so many aisles, and various rooms. It could take them ages to search this floor, but they know Dez's phone is above them, so why bother? The blond Asian leaves one man to guard the rear door, while he leads the other three up the stairs.

Before they arrived, Dez had scrounged up a coatrack from what likely had been the music store manager's office, and set it up right next to the rear door. He'd also scrounged some old coats, left by whoever. If you're looking for a man lurking in a vast space, it's human nature to think he'd be well hidden. Dez hid right by the door as they entered; the last place they would think to look for him.

While everyone else is off searching, Dez steps out from behind the coatrack and pops the man guarding the door once in the nose with a fist almost the size of the guy's skull. He guides the unconscious lad slowly and silently to the floor. He searches him, hides his gun, backup gun, and a knife in the workings of an ancient Victrola.

Just because a gatekeeper allows you to walk through a door does not imply he intends for you to walk out.

Four guys are slinking around upstairs. Dez is in no hurry. He stays down on the ground floor, eyes on a poster of Stevie Ray Vaughan. God, what a shame. Died in a helicopter crash at age thirty-five. Brilliant guitarist, him.

Dez's dance partners didn't think to bring radios. Someone from the second floor sneaks down the stairs. "Psst. Lukens. Hey, Lukens. You spot anything down here?"

Psst? Do people actually say *Psst,* in hopes that it will be heard only by whomever you wish?

Dez carries the three metal marbles he'd purchased from a toy store earlier.

The man coming down the stairs, *psst*ing like a busted water main, is Dez's old friend Frank, from the hospital. Now isn't that interesting? Dez lets fly a ball bearing and Frank's eyes roll up into his skull, his knees give out, and he crumples.

Dez catches him and lays him crosswise atop Lukens. Frank's gun goes into the same Victrola.

Dez hit a guy earlier this week with a marble and killed him. This time, Frank's merely bleeding from a head wound, injured but alive.

Dez heads back to his coatrack.

Two more of the five thugs come traipsing down the central stairs. One says, "Nothing. Shit, I don't—"

Before they'd arrived, Dez spotted an aged aluminum baseball bat. Same place he found the old coats. Dez doesn't quite understand baseball, but he understands blunt objects well enough.

Now he steps out from behind the coatrack and drives the handle of the borrowed baseball bat into the first guy's back, just above his belt. The pain paralyzing him. He reverses thrust and swings the bat, clobbering the second guy, right behind the ear. That guy's out before he hits the floor, but Dez takes a moment to choke out the first guy.

Who, wonder of wonder, turns out to be Joe from the hospital. The Latin lad.

Dez is getting the band back together.

Five hooligans entered; four down.

It's less than a minute later when the dyed blond Asian lad comes racing down the stairs, Dez's phone in hand. He'd tracked it to the cabinet Dez had hid it in. "I've got it. He was here. He . . ." The blond with the dragon ink on his neck spots the four bodies lying on the floor and says, "Oh shit," before Dez clocks him with another marble.

Dez's mobile is ruggedized. No fear of the lad dropping it.

Dez separates the three men he hasn't met yet and uses their belts to bind their wrists behind their backs, and to one another. He hides them in the manager's office. When they come to—nobody dead, that hadn't been Dez's goal—it'll take them some time to get free.

All five of these guys carry the shiny black key cards, like the one Dez gave to the police; the one that opens every door at Gamila, the Clockjack R & D campus.

Back in the main room, Dez arranges Frank and Joe, lying on their backs, side by side. Frank, the Black guy from the hospital, is the first to come to. What had the marshals deputy called him? Givens?

Dez sits on a footstool he's spotted and taps the baseball bat on Frank's knee. Softly. The metal marble tore open part of Frank's scalp. Blood is seeping from the wound and his right ear glistening with it.

"Wotcher, mate."

A sheen of hatred and pain radiate from the man's eyes. He looks at Dez, looks at the baseball bat, looks back again. "Shi-it." Frank rises up on one hip and up on one elbow, the palm of his other hand tacky with blood from gingerly touching his skull.

"Now, here's the part where I get lost," Dez says. "After we tussled at hospital, you ended up in the custody of the local plod. Aye? After that, you was with the U.S. Marshals Service. So how'd you end up here?"

Frank leans forward and spits onto the cement floor.

"Your mate, Joe, here? There's a better'n even chance I ruptured his kidney. He'll be in need of medical attention, that one. I can have help here tout de suite. Can ye tell me how it is our lad Joe is no longer in the custody of the Drug Enforcement Administration?"

Frank glares at him.

Dez brings the bat down hard on Frank's right knee.

"Fuuuuuuck!" the big man howls, rolling onto his back, both hands going to his cracked knee.

"Answerin' me questions is the best way to get the medical attention ye deserve. I know what you're thinkin'—I sound like a fan of socialized medicine, an' truth be told, I am. Better than what you lot have here, I reckon. Aye? What d'you say, love? Gettin' chatty?"

Frank lies on his back, hands wrapped around one knee. "Go . . . fuck . . . yourself. . . ."

"Feeling an overabundance o' knees, are we?" Dez taps the man's left knee with the bat, ever so gently. Then again, less gently.

"Fuck you, bitch! I tell you fucking nothing!" Spittle flies as Frank growls his answer.

"Fair, that. Nothin' but respect."

Joe's eyes blink open. Tears trickle down toward his ears. He tries to rise but the pain in his back is paralyzing.

Dez says, "Joe. Did you know this city has an unlimited supply of fresh drinking water? Unlimited. That's a thing, ennit? Wondrous."

Joe is in exquisite pain. He slow-rolls into the fetal position, both hands cradling his back and his flank. He's drenched in sweat. He lets loose with a wide array of Spanish insults, many of which involve Dez's mother.

Dez sighs. "You beat me fair. I'll not get a word from either of you. I'm banjaxed, me."

It's going on 11 P.M. He stands, draws his phone, and dials. It rings six times. A slow-drawling voices says, "This is Sims."

"Chief Deputy Marshal. Wake you?"

The men at Dez's feet groan.

"How did you get this number, Mr. Limerick?"

"Website portals are just doors, sir. Passwords are just locks. I'm good with doors and locks."

"What do you want?"

"I'm standin' here looking at your ol' mate Frank. The one your lads took off the hands of Portland police. He's out on his own, getting into no end of mischief, him. And next to him is his mate Joe. Now, here's the part you may or may not know, sir. You lost Frank, aye? DEA took Joe, an' they lost him, too."

He waits.

Sims's voice carries no hint of confusion or anger or suspicion. He could have been asking a server about the daily special. "Where are they?"

Dez gives him an address. "Three others here, too. None armed. Well, not currently."

Sims says, "May I hazard a guess, Mr. Limerick? You lured them there."

"Aye, well, waiting was never me forte. Chief Deputy? You've problems aplenty, but I'm not amongst 'em. Someone at Clockjack's making you their bitch. You seek answers, my son? Seek 'em there."

He hangs up.

CHAPTER 23

Dez returns to the hotel around eleven thirty that evening. He can hear music from downstairs in the Deep Dive. They sound half decent and he's tempted to head down and get a drink. But he doesn't want to impose while Veronika's working. He jogs up to the third floor. The hotel doesn't have room service but there is a ground-floor restaurant. Dez thinks he'll wash up, eat, check in with the Swann sisters, and call it a night.

He steps into his room and the roundhouse kick to the back of his head sends him sprawling.

He takes a long, slow five-count on his back, arms and legs spread, caught in mid-carpet angel. Eventually he rises up onto his elbows.

"Arabella."

"Chef."

Arabella Satti, called Belle, from MI6, now sits in the room's one chair. She's wearing a calf-length, paper-thin rain duster, plus a Royal Navy sweater and jeans and boots. She lights up a cigarette with a disposable lighter, sucks down half of it in a go, then rises, opens the room's window, and throws both the half cigarette and the lighter out onto the sidewalk below. The sounds of traffic rise and fall with the opening and closing of the window.

"Yer smoking again."

She says, "I've been saving that last one for the day I got to kick your arse."

"Was a good kick, that," he says. "Nice follow-through."

"Thank you."

Dez sits up, elbows on his knees. "Got me message."

"We did."

"Came to help?"

"I've come to tell you there's a fair betting pool on when and how you get yourself killed, wandering America, getting involved in that which you should not."

"I don't go looking for trouble, Belle. You know that."

She glares down at him. She's lovely, Dez's age, five-five, and his equal in fighting skill, but much faster. Also, a dead brilliant marksman. She says, "No. But you are a magnet for those in trouble. And you've a Galahad complex. What is it this time? Damsel in distress?"

"A friend, protectin' her sister."

The woman sits at the room's desk and studies him. He stays on the floor. "Nameless ne'er-do-wells who seem able to slip free the bonds of gaol, both local an' federal, at will. Know anything about 'em?"

Arabella says, "They sound like gatekeepers."

"They are not."

"I know."

Dez says, "Aha," because it seems like an occasion to say that.

But if he expects his guest to be forthcoming with what she knows, he's disappointed. "How long do you plan to be in exile, *chef*? Are you carrying a lantern, looking for one honest man? Or seeking a salve for your guilty conscience?"

"Enjoying the States. Becoming a better musician. Learning to sleep in."

She waves away his story the way one waves away mosquitoes.

"An' why're you here, love?"

Her voice drops a perfect half octave. "Call me *love* again. Please. I dare you."

"Sorry."

They're quiet for a while.

Arabella says, "Two years ago, I was in charge of a joint British-American operation for nearly a full minute, before someone countermanded my orders, choked me out, and carried me to safety like I was a heroine of a gothic horror story. Can you guess how many missions I've been selected to run since then? Hmm?"

Dez doesn't know, but he's willing to bet it's zero. And it's sexism, nothing less. MI6 should have Arabella Satti running her own show. But thanks to his call in Chechnya, she's hit a glass ceiling.

"Sincere apologies for that."

She ignores his apology. "A few years back, the U.S. Marshals Service arrested a man named Demetrious Givens. He was an enforcer for a Baltimore organized-crime family. He had an impressive number of homicides in his ledger. The *capo dei capi* and the various underbosses decided that Demetrious Givens would be better off dead than speaking to prosecutors. The marshals whisked him into the Federal Witness Protection Program. They relocated him, whilst convincing him to turn state's evidence."

Dez listens.

"Almost five months ago, Demetrious Givens evaporated."

"From Witness Protection?" Dez cuts in. "Not easy, I'd wager."

"You'd win. Givens, his false identity, his paper and records . . ." Arabella makes a magical incantation gesture with her long fingers. "'Hath melted like snow in the glance of the Lord.'"

"Byron."

"Quite. And he—Givens, not Lord Byron—remained amongst the missing until someone punched him in the chest, in hospital, in Portland, Oregon. Of all places."

Dez smiles. "Givens being me mate Frank. Couple of pot roasts with badges let that name drop, few days back."

Arabella picks up a new thread of the story. "Three years ago, the CIA kidnapped a notorious Colombian cartel enforcer, Cristian Hinestroza, from the bed of a whore in Havana. Hinestroza was turned over to the U.S. Drug Enforcement Administration. Where investigators convinced him of the wisdom of becoming an informant."

Dez says, "My Joe."

"Indeed."

"An' he winds up in hospital, in Portland, an' that, children, is how the zebra got its stripes."

Dez leans back on his elbow again. He straightens his legs, crossed at the ankles. He ponders. "Baltimore and Bogotá. Quite a fair distance, them two stomping grounds."

Arabella nods.

"Did Givens and Hinestroza know each other before all this?"

"They appear not to have, no."

He ponders. She's quiet.

"Are the Yanks missing any others from the Witness Protection Program?"

Arabella smiles.

"Aha."

"You said that already."

"Calls for it, doesn't it. How many?"

"That, we do not know. The Cousins are keeping mum. We do know that they have absolutely no idea how this is happening. There is gnashing of teeth at the highest levels of the Justice Department and U.S. Intelligence."

"Enough to draw a fella name of Conroy Sims, chief deputy U.S. marshal for Virginia."

"Quite right."

"Someone's compromised Witness Protection."

She says, "Yes. And after it happened the first time, the Marshals Service revamped their security protocols. They upgraded their computers. They ran sweeping, internal investigations into personnel who had the wherewithal to make all this happen. They took every precaution one could dream up."

"An' yet, with Frank-not-Frank in the Marshals' clutches, and Joe-not-Joe in the DEA's clutches, they once again get Houdini'd away."

"Just so."

"Bloody hell."

Arabella agrees.

"Fella I killed?"

"Whom you marbled to death? Yes, he was in the Witness Protection Program as well. Another missing criminal. From Chicago, this time. And apparently he knew neither Givens nor Hinestroza."

"Does your lot know who's doing this?"

Arabella says, "We do not, though I'd gladly lie about that just for the chance to fuck you over."

"Appreciate the honesty. Them arseholes had IDs for a research-and-development campus owned by Clockjack Solutions."

Arabella's studied nonchalance fades. "You're sure?"

"Aye. Whacking great technology firm that made a name for itself with software that predicts when federal agencies get their funding allocations. You thinking what I'm thinking?"

Arabella stares out the small window onto Burnside for a bit. Dez stays on the floor.

"Well," she muses. "That's intriguing."

"Innit?"

She turns back to him. "Could one of the world's rising tech giants be a clear and present danger to the American government?"

"Dunno. Worth finding out."

They study each other for a while.

"I will not help you, Desmond."

"I know. Like as not, the Cousins don't even know you're on American soil. Aye?"

She neither confirms nor denies.

"Tall blond fella, our age. Scottish. Full-sleeve tattoos on both arms. Goes by the name o' Robert Taylor hereabouts. Head of security at Clockjack. He's part of this. Sure of it."

Arabella takes a while before responding. "It would not constitute our interference in American affairs if we were to seek to identify this individual."

"Would certainly help."

"Helping the Americans is an acceptable outcome. Helping you is not."

"Might have to do one to accomplish t'other."

She mock-shudders.

Dez retains his position of comfort on the floor because it puts her above him. It makes her feel less threatened. He's done this intentionally. (Well, that, and she rang his bell pretty good with that kick.)

She stands and crosses the room, stepping over his legs. She opens the room's door. She says, "You know that betting pool about how and when you die on this mad crusade of yours?"

"Aye?"

"A lot of the money is on the how-and-when being me-and-now."

She closes the door behind her.

CHAPTER 24

Dez grabs a steak sandwich and a beer at the ground-floor restaurant and, while he eats, he does a Google Images search, key words "criminal," "Scottish," "blond," "man," "full-sleeves," "tattoos."

He finds a wide array of rap stars. Also porn.

He heads to the Deep Dive around midnight and catches the last set of a hip-hop trio working a cappella. They're good. Veronika is up to her neck in customers at the bar, so Dez gets a whiskey, enjoys the band a bit, chats up the bouncer who, it turns out, is a Manchester City fan. After, Dez uses his phone to search for the same images, but this time adding Baltimore, Chicago, and Colombia. Nothing. He finishes his drink and heads to bed.

He answers a text from Raziah. She, Laleh, and the boyfriend are safe, and there's a sun porch in the island cabin where Raziah can put on her headphones and bury herself in the search for lyrics and tunes.

Dez answers a text from Petra Alexandris in Malibu, California, letting him know she's working twenty-hour days and that her plan to save her company seems to be working. So far. She thanks him, again, for helping save her company and her life.

Are you being safe up there? she asks.

Course. Always.

He's pretty sure he's never met a more brilliant person than she.

Arabella Satti may be a close second. It's a shame she hates him with such vigor. But of course, he's earned that hatred. Someone, someday likely will kill Dez. He hopes it won't be Arabella. But it might be.

He lies in bed and searches through Google Images, adding *police log* and *arrest.* More rappers, more porn.

He tries a search for *bubble and squeak,* just as an experiment.

Recipes and porn. Just as he suspected.

He lies on his back, one arm under his head, and thinks about his situation in Portland. He'd imagined that he understood it all well enough: thugs threatening the sister of a friend. What could be simpler?

Turns out he'd grasped only the slimmest shade of this thing.

Someone has compromised the Federal Witness Protection Program. Someone can make people in the program disappear, along with the paperwork connecting them to their former lives and to the arresting agencies.

It happened months ago, and again this week.

Dez is a fair, if amateur, hacker. He thinks of website portals as doors, and there are few doors on Earth he can't open, keep open, and control who enters and exits. That's his gift. He knows just enough to know that the math and coding and programming necessary to carry off this accomplishment is way, way out of his arena.

By now, he suspects his old dance partners, Frank and Joe, plus their buddies, are either in the hospital or back in the custody of the U.S. Marshals Service. But if it's the latter, can the deputies hold on to them this time? Dez has seen nothing to suggest they can.

Demetrious Givens, a gang enforcer from Baltimore, and Cristian Hinestroza, a cartel gunman from Colombia, who likely never met prior to Portland.

Who is pulling the strings? Clockjack Solutions? A Green New Deal, ultra-leftie tech company that has cornered the market on people empowerment? Moving master criminals around like chess pieces? It makes no sense. He's been reading everything he can about Clockjack, and the company is, without a doubt, the worst conceivable candidate to play the role of Lex Luthor.

Bonkers.

Dez drifts to sleep, not one inch closer to understanding any of this.

His phone vibrates him awake at four in the morning.

He wakes instantly; instantly aware of where he is and why. A soldier's gift. He reaches for his phone.

A text from Arabella Satti.

Looking in the wrong places.

He goes to the closet-like bathroom and splashes water in his face, then pads barefoot to the little window overlooking Burnside. He has the hands of a boxer but the fingers of a pianist, and he types quickly: How so?

Occidental Ventures.

Dez knows of them. Mercenary bunch, ex-SAS, Green Beret, KSK, Spetsnaz types. In parts of Africa and the Middle East, Occidental Ventures is known to some as Occasional Vultures.

It's not that they have a bad rep.

It's that they've got a fabulously good rep at doing bad things.

Dez switches to Google and modifies his image search.

It takes nearly fifteen minutes before he finds a photo culled from *Housaper,* an Armenian language newspaper published in Egypt. He doesn't read Armenian, but he finds a duplicate of the story distributed by the Sahara Press Service, in Arabic, which he does read.

The photo shows three men, sand-camo uniforms of the British Special Air Service, walking through a bombed-out mosque in Aleppo. Two have their backs to the camera. The third is a white guy with blond hair and an easy smile. It's Robert Taylor, head of security at Clockjack. The photo is a few years old. Taylor carries a Heckler & Koch G3KA4 assault rifle. Chambered for 7.62×51mm NATO ammunition, with the full 20-round magazines, the collapsible stocks, and autofire configuration.

Good weapon, that.

Dez does a screen capture of Taylor's head, shoulders, and torso, and cleans them up in Photoshop. He then runs the image through a Finnish facial recognition site that works for free. It takes the site less than thirty seconds to make a match.

Robert Taylor is actually British Special Air Service Staff Sergeant Gareth MacDonald.

Dez does a Google search for that name.

He's a Scotsman, all right. And he had a distinguished career in the SAS. Fought in every hot spot the Brits had heard of for a good ten years.

After that, an honorable discharge, and MacDonald spent six years with the private military contractor Occidental Ventures LLC. What he did for them was anyone's guess. It isn't hard to imagine what sorts of roles MacDonald found himself in with them.

A bit better than one year ago—as Dez himself began contemplating retirement and the States—Gareth

MacDonald was arrested in Boston, Massachusetts, and charged with assassinating a defense contractor. According to what Dez digs up, MacDonald is currently doing time in Leavenworth as the Yanks and the Brits debate who gets to keep him for the rest of his life.

But of course Staff Sergeant Gareth MacDonald is, in fact, not in Leavenworth. Nor in anyone's custody. He's living the life of Riley with Clockjack Solutions.

CHAPTER 25

For Dez, the next day is all about the research.

He's heard of Powell's City of Books, of course. Possibly the largest and finest bookstore in the English-speaking world. It fills an entire city block, with room after massive room of new and used books, from the popular to the obscure. He spends an hour just roaming the surprisingly non-dusty aisles. He could spend the rest of his day—or the rest of his days—there. But miles to go, as the poet said.

He gets a cup of coffee at the shop that dominated one corner of the ground floor and sits, surrounded by people of every age group, most with teetering towers of books before them. He sets up his tablet computer, sips his coffee, rolls his eyes in ecstasy, then digs into the work.

Dez can hack his way into the websites and servers of many companies, but Clockjack Solutions hires software geniuses by the dump truck full, and it doesn't take him but about three tries to realize he's out of his depth here.

That just means he has to get creative.

He calls the Swann sisters and asks if Laleh has made any progress with the audit paperwork they'd taken. "A little," she admits sheepishly. "I've written dozens of stories about audits. But to see the raw research . . . It's just so much!"

"Keep at it," he says. "An' stay where ye are. Them violent types are still lurkin' about."

"I will. I take it you didn't leave Portland?"

"I'm at Powell's Books! Bloody amazing, this!"

She laughs. "Yes. It is. I'd get Raziah for you but she's . . . I don't know. Zoned out."

"Writin'," Dez says. "She gets like that when she's bein' creative. Best not to interrupt her."

He listens to the pause. The coffee he's sipping might be the best he's ever had.

"You two really aren't lovers," Laleh says.

"Told ye."

"I think maybe you know my sister better than I do."

"No, I just play music with her. Can't know much about Raziah if you don't know her music."

Laleh thanks him again and they hang up.

On his tablet, Dez starts making notes about Clock-jack Solutions. When the company started, and through its first two decades of operation, the leadership remained constant: four former Portland State University faculty members.

RJ Sharpe, the vivacious CEO who dresses like a rock band groupie and who owns the TED Talk circuit.

Teddy Meeker, the recluse code writer who started it all.

Joel Menache, who managed the website and the merchandise.

Carl Hickman, the financial officer.

After nigh on twenty years of their steady leadership, Clockjack Solutions grew into a tech giant. It put Portland on the tech map the way Boeing put Seattle on the aviation map.

But Menache died in a car crash last year and was replaced by Willard Dukane.

And Hickman died a month later and was replaced by Matthew Salerno.

Dez starts by looking up everything he can find on Willard Dukane: his hometown, his university, the other companies he's worked for. The list is hefty, and ninety minutes later, Dez sees nothing surprising about the man.

Except this: He can find no good photo of Dukane. Not a one.

He does the same deep dive into Matthew Salerno.

Ninety minutes later—same results. A solid background but no good photos. He gets a fuzzy, out-of-focus group shot at a fundraiser from last Christmas and only then realizes Salerno's Black. Dez had been expecting an Italian. Well, not mutually exclusive, he thinks.

His work is thorough. He's found all that he can. But something nags. Dez suspects these backgrounds are intricately designed forgeries.

Brilliantly executed, of course. But as fake as an employee satisfaction survey conducted by a pimp.

Dez takes a break and goes wandering the aisles. By sheer chance, he finds a used copy of *The Andromeda Strain,* which he loves but hasn't read since he was twenty.

He grabs a new coffee and finds his old seat in the coffee shop has been taken, so he moves to a different pew. He stretches his back, hears his neck pop, then begins anew.

The current leadership of Clockjack Solutions is RJ Sharpe, Teddy Meeker, and the new folks, Willard Dukane and Matthew Salerno. The latter two, Dez suspects, are not who they appear to be. And Dez hamhandedly managed to alienate Meeker at PSU.

That leaves the charismatic CEO, RJ Sharpe.

Dez can't very well call the public information office at Clockjack and ask to speak to the top boss. He'd end up awash in middle-management types, each wanting to know his business.

He's crafted a fake ID a time or two, and could do so again. But he blew his first contact with Meeker so badly, and he's not going to get a lot of do-overs here. Approaching RJ Sharpe under a false flag seems risky.

He has an idea. Something he's wanted to try for some time now.

After a third cup of excellent coffee and three hours of hacking and code-writing, Dez grins as he leans back and hits Enter.

CHAPTER 26

RJ Sharpe has a spacious tenth-floor office at Gamila, the R & D campus on the Columbia River, but she travels all over the world with speaking engagements, on average, every ten days, year-round. For proximity to Portland International Airport, she purchased a gorgeous home perched on the caldera of an extinct volcano, Mount Tabor, in Southeast Portland. It's a lovely old gothic pile on two floors, with a view of downtown Portland to the west. With five bedrooms, it's way more space than a single woman needs but she loves it beyond words. It's her sanctuary, away from Clockjack.

Equally important, and even on bad traffic days, she's rarely more than a fifteen-minute ride to the airport.

She's in town this week and, as always, she throws on her spandex and helmet, and hits the Rocky Butte and Mount Tabor bikeways. She listens to a *New York Times* podcast as she pedals one way, and to a *Wall Street Journal* podcast as she pedals back. At fifty-five, RJ is in better shape than she was at twenty-five, and she's proud of her workout routines. Not an easy thing to do when you virtually live at airports and hotels around the globe.

She gets back to her home and locks her road bike up in the attached garage. She kicks off her bike shoes and enters the kitchen via the garage, deactivating her home security. She slowly drains an entire tumbler of water laced with vitamins and antioxidants. She strips, throws her sweat-drenched togs in the hamper, and checks her reflection in the bathroom's full-length mirror. Tall, strong shoulders, no Botox, and the age lines on her face are proudly owned. The silver wave runs the entire length of her otherwise auburn hair, curly and to the middle of her back. Her hair hasn't naturally turned silver; the skunk stripe is an artifact of her hairdresser. RJ loves it. She loves that she owns her age. She's happy with where she is.

She plugs in her Fitbit-style exercise tracker and showers. In soft terry sweat bottoms and a tank top, she boots up her computer, knowing that the anti-hacking technology, proprietary of Clockjack, will take a full two minutes to run. They're within ten weeks of selling the technology to Disney. It could be one of their biggest moneymakers yet.

She's standing before the open fridge, digging out the makings of an omelet and salad, when she hears something chirp. Repeatedly.

She pads into her office and checks the monitor. It's her exercise tracker making that racket. It's never done that before. She's expecting to see miles walked and biked, elevation gained, calories burned. Instead, she sees the words Message—Download?

She clicks Yes before wondering what the big brains in IT would have recommended.

Her computer screen begins filling with words.

My name is Desmond Limerick and I want to help. Menache, Hickman, and the B Corp auditor, Conor O'Meara, were killed. A reporter, Laleh Swann, working on the story was almost killed twice. Their stories are online. Look them up. Experienced criminals

are working under Clockjack protection. And
Robert Taylor, alias Sgt. Gareth MacDonald,
was convicted in the USA of murder. You can
look him up, too. My name is Limerick, and I
swear, I only want to help.

The message is followed by two boxes marked De-
lete and Reply.

RJ Sharpe's hand hovers over her computer mouse
for nearly sixty seconds.

CHAPTER 27

The next morning, Dez checks the weather before renting a car and driving to Astoria, Oregon. Then he heads straight to an Army surplus store and buys a waterproof field jacket and a baseball cap with no writing on it.

Before leaving the hotel on Burnside, Dez opens his room safe and takes out a case with two knives. One is a 290-mm fixed-blade knife, made by Coltellerie Maserin, black-coated steel in an olive drab nylon sheath. It lies in a cutout of black foam. Next to that is a folding Raptor blade, with its steel cutting surface that glides into the anodized aluminum handle. Both can clip onto his belt. The smaller knife sheath includes a pocket for lockpicks, rakes, and tension bars.

He rents a Jeep. He jogs across the street to Powell's and buys a spiral-bound map of Oregon, and takes a few moments to memorize the route. Yes, the Maps function on his smartphone will get him there, too, but Dez never trusts technology a hundred percent.

The drive is easy and beautiful. Portland and its suburbs, Dez discovers, are surrounded by an urban growth boundary. The cities cannot spread outward like amoeba, as so many American cities do. When you drive out of the metro area, you *hit* a hard boundary and then you're in farm country. It's a sharp transition.

A half hour after the relatively flat agricultural area, and Dez's rental is climbing into the Cascade Range, a shockingly lovely swath of old-growth forest that leads all the way to within a few miles of the coast.

The message he'd received from RJ Sharpe, by way of her fitness tracker, laid out a time and a place for the Saturday meet. Astoria is about 160 kilometers west of Portland, and as far as Dez can tell, Clockjack Solutions owns no property on the Oregon Coast. There is nothing, he believes, linking the Clockjack CEO to this town. Which leads Dez to think he's not traipsing merrily into the trap.

But then again, that's why he brought the knives. He's been wrong about stuff like this before.

RJ Sharpe said to meet her at 9 P.M. Saturday. That gives Dez plenty of time—he arrives by noon—to do a thorough reconnaissance.

Astoria has layers of history, one atop the other. He can see the prosperous fishing village of the late nineteenth and early twentieth centuries, with elegant, Victorian houses perched on the hills overlooking the vast mouth of the Columbia River. Dez passes several dozen former piers; now just rotting forests of wooden stumps, testament to the many salmon canneries that once gave this area its international fame, but almost all of which vanished along with the salmon. There's a sense of poverty and decay, all too prevalent in fishing villages the world over. But overlaid on that is a historic renewal; a spiffing up of the downtown, its microbreweries and trinket shops, its coffeehouses and bookstores, its antiques shops and wine bars.

The town's economy has suffered, decade after decade, but Dez can see that city leaders fought back. Are fighting back. He likes the place.

The most obvious landmark is the bridge across the Columbia to the state of Washington. It stands tall at the southern end, for oceangoing freighters to pass beneath, aided by river-piloted boats. Halfway across, the bridge drops down to just a few yards above the water. To Dez, it looks like a grazing brontosaurus. It's undoubtedly beautiful. The river beneath it is busy with fishing boats, sailboats, touristy jet boats, the pilot boats, and the enormous, international cluster of freighters, bringing goods to and from the Americas. Including, Dez learns, cars. Many of the Japanese and Korean cars driven in the United States sail under this bridge, en route to vast Port of Portland parking lots, where they'll be loaded on trains and distributed throughout the continent.

He's going to be overnight so he rents a room in a hotel that, in its nineteenth-century brick-painted advertising, offers WONDERFUL BEDS.

It's raining hard. Which would be an annoyance all by itself, but in Astoria—on the ocean, at the nearly eight-kilometer-wide mouth of the Columbia, a town made up of almost nothing but hills—the rain tends to fall hard and at a forty-five-degree angle.

Dez parks and begins his reconnaissance.

His watch tells him the sun has set as he stands on the pier, Army jacket buttoned tight so the wind can't take it, ball cap tight over his eyes and under the hood, fists jammed into his jacket pockets, boots shoulder-length apart for stability against the stinging fléchette raindrops. He's standing on one of the few remaining cannery piers. The stable wooden island atop a few hundred wooden pylons has been turned into a touristy hotel, a four-star restaurant, and a dark, quiet pub that Dez has visited already, earlier in the day, to acquaint himself with the meeting place. The cannery pier is accessible from the city's main drag by a short wooden bridge. The massive bridge to Washington looms overhead in the dark, barely visible in the downpour.

At 9 P.M. on the dot, a Lexus pulls into the parking lot on the elevated pier and parks. A woman climbs out. She wears a boot-length rain duster with an enormous hood, and Dez instantly recalls Meryl Streep in *The French Lieutenant's Woman*. She spots him and walks his way, stepping close.

It's RJ Sharpe.

When they're face-to-face—she's taller than he, especially with heeled boots—she says, "Desmond Limerick?" She speaks loud over the thunderous pounding of the rain on the thick boards beneath their boots.

"Aye. Appreciate you seein' me!"

"There's a pub! It's got good privacy! Do you . . . ?"

He spits rainwater out of his mouth. "With pleasure!"

CHAPTER 28

The pub is dark, expansive, and masculine in décor. Pre–World War II fishing boats hang from the rafters by guy wires. The walls are covered in black-and-white or sepia photos of the heyday of the fishing industry. He spots paintings and photos of sail-powered fishing boats on rough waters; the famed Butterfly Fleet of Astoria.

Dez has spoken to the barkeep already, earlier in the day. He nods to the man and directs RJ to a booth. "What're you havin'?"

"Anything red."

Dez is used to ordering at the bar, United Kingdom style, so he does, a porter for himself and an Oregon pinot noir for RJ. He brings them to the high-back booth, the wood dark-stained, well away from other patrons. Nobody sits at her back and nobody sits at his, and Dez has passed the barkeep a hundred dollars to make sure it stays that way.

They hang their very wet coats on hooks at the end of their respective benches. Both coats form considerable puddles beneath them.

He squeezes into his side of the booth. "Lovely town."

"Well, it can be." RJ sounds defensive. "My mom and dad used to bring us here when I was a girl. It's pretty, when it isn't raining like this."

"Ah. Cheers." He lifts his glass. She does, too, but declines to tap hers against his. RJ takes a delicate sip, nods approval. Dez drinks and makes a face.

"Gah. Insalubrious, that."

She surprises herself with a quick laugh. "I've never heard beer described like that. You sound like you're from England. I would have thought you'd be right at home in the rain."

"England, Ireland, Wales. Lived all over, me. An' I am, aye. It's just . . ."

He winces.

"Are you in pain?"

"Denim. Tends t'shrink when it's wet. Tends t'shrink in places ye'd rather it not."

She smiles. "I've lived in blue jeans most of my working life. I understand."

Dez sips the beer again, makes the same face. Waste not, want not. "Seen your talks on YouTube. You've the gift. Dunno how you do that."

She studies him. "What do you want, Mr. Limerick?"

"Dez to me friends. The reporter who was attacked? Sister's a mate of mine. She asked me t'help."

"And that's why you're here? Really? To protect the sister of a friend?"

"Aye."

She sips wine, studying him. She says, "Are you in law enforcement?"

"I am, on occasion, in the custody o' law enforcement. I hold no grudges. Me own fault, more often than not."

"Do you work for the government? For *a* government?"

"I do not."

"Are you the person who beat up two of Robert Taylor's men and killed one?"

"Technically, I've now beaten up six of Robert

Taylor's men and killed one. And technically, there is no Robert Taylor. But elsewise, aye, that's me."

They are quiet for a while and Dez lets the moment play out. She wears her hair in a ponytail, because of the weather and the hood, and she absently plays with it in one hand. She says, "I don't think I believe you."

"I'm surprised how often I get that."

She sits back from the nicked and scarred tabletop, clearly nervous. She's wanting desperately to talk and wanting desperately not to, Dez thinks.

She buys time. "You should see Astoria when it's not raining. I love it here. Did you know they shot that film *The Goonies* here? It's an old movie. Steven Spielberg produced it."

"Know the film, aye."

More silence.

"I looked up those names you told me about. The auditor. The reporter. They really were attacked."

Dez nods.

"I looked up the name Sergeant Gareth MacDonald."

"Piece o' work, that one."

"You don't know he's Robert Taylor. I contacted HR after you reached out to me. I looked up Robert's résumé. I called one of his references. He gave him a glowing review."

"He's MacDonald," Dez says. "Has a fella on staff name of Frank, used to be a gang enforcer in Baltimore. Has another lad, Joe, was a triggerman for a Bogotá drug cartel. Has more. The dream team of the dregs. Dunno why."

"That's far-fetched."

Dez shrugs. "Lots of things are far-fetched. Spielberg produced a film of evil developers wantin' to turn Astoria into a golf course. Town's nothin' but hills. It'd be a par eleven thousand."

She finishes her drink. "Yes, well, that *was* a hole in the plot."

Dez waits some more. He's awfully good at waiting.

"If all of this is true . . . why?"

"Was hopin' you knew."

"It's impossible. And ludicrous. We're a tech company. Why would we hire violent criminals?"

"Dunno. Want another of them?" He gestures toward her glass. She slides it aside and shakes her head no.

"How many men does MacDonald have? Not the rent-a-cop security fellas. I mean the hard lads, like Frank an' Joe?"

She ponders it, makes fleeting eye contact. "Seven or eight. I think. I've seen the men you mean. They don't . . . fit in at our company. They're with Robert so I never questioned it."

Seven or eight. Good. If that's true, Dez has injured most of MacDonald's entire starting squad. That eases the danger to Laleh Swann, a bit at least.

"Are they workin' on any special project? Something on the fringes?"

"No. They're security. They keep the staff safe and the work sites secure. That's all."

"Who does MacDonald answer to?"

She leans forward, getting frustrated. "He's Robert Taylor. And he answers to me."

"Not to Willard Dukane?"

She sits back, eyes narrowing. "Why?"

"Dunno much about corporate America, me. Have a friend who's CEO of Triton Expediters."

Her eyes widen. "I know who they are, obviously."

"Aye. Well, me friend there would be a few rungs up the ladder from the head o' security. Dukane's your chief operating officer, yeah? Figured security would answer t'him."

She fiddles with her ponytail. "Yes, technically, you're right. But everyone at Clockjack works for me. I'm the boss."

"Fair play to ye."

"Why did you ask about Willard?"

"'Cause him an' Matthew Salerno came on last year. Chief operatin' officer an' chief financial officer, yeah? After your mates Menache and Hickman died. Sudden-like. Then MacDonald shows up. Then the thugs. An' I'm wondering if it's all connected."

"Willard and Matthew have stellar credentials! Teddy and I hired them both. They've been total assets to the company."

"Salerno's good with the money, is he?" Dez digs his phone out of his jeans pocket. "S'ppose he'd have to be."

"What's that mean?"

"Matthew Salerno's a Black fella. I'd figured him for Italian, name like that."

RJ says, "What's his race have to do with . . . with anything?" She's nearing the end of her rope with this conversation.

Dez thumbs his phone to life. "Thinkin' out loud is all. I had time t'ponder, waiting for you t'get here."

"Ponder what?"

"St. Matthew. The apostle? His bones are in a reliquary in a cathedral in Salerno, Italy. Did y'know that? Been there once. Lovely city. Had a grilled artichoke. *Carciofo di paestum.* God, but that was good." He shakes his head in awe.

RJ's hands stop fiddling with her ponytail. She does not respond.

"So I got t'thinking, with all me free time: What if your financial officer's workin' under a pseudonym, too? Like MacDonald. He picked Matthew an' Salerno 'cause he's brought up a good Catholic, aye?"

"Wait . . . what are you talking about?"

"Not a lot of predominately Black, Catholic countries. Ye've got your Angola, of course. Antigua. The Bahamas. Barbados. I'm doing 'em alphabetically, y'understand. Burkina Faso, an' such. Anyway, t'me point, I had some time, so I googled the Black, Catholic countries, plus words like finance, financial, exchequer, criminal, conviction, an' such. Got nothin', nothin', nothin' . . ."

He sets his phone on the table, taps it, spins it one hundred and eighty degrees. Shows her a picture of a smiling Black man, in a fine suit, speaking at a lectern. ". . . till I got this."

She studies the photo. And Dez knows: This is no surprise to her.

"Winston Noel. Jamaican. Handled most of the Gulf o' Mexico cocaine trade for the Sinaloa Cartel. Indicted. Extradited to the States. Was doin' time in a U.S. federal prison."

RJ tries to hide her anger and feign surprise.

Dez grins. "You're a fair poker player, an' that's a fact." He claps slowly, three times. "Had me fooled. Don't mind admittin' it. Not half bad at all."

RJ opens her mouth to say something. But nothing comes out.

Dez sighs. "Ask ye a favor? Can ye at least let me know how many men MacDonald brought here with him?"

RJ Sharpe studies him, her hands clenched into fists. A muscle in her jaw twitches. She says, "You have no idea what's going on here."

"That's damn near always the case with me."

"You . . . for God's sake, you think *we're* the bad guys!"

He nods. "Do, sort of, aye."

She drops her voice to a harsh whisper, leans across the table. "Clockjack is making a better nation! A better world! We are doing so . . . much . . . good!"

She leans back, uses one hand to pry up fingers of the others and ticks off points. "On the environment! On malnutrition! Girls' rights in third-world countries! Childhood obesity! Literacy! Communal agriculture! Land mines! We. Our company. *My* company! We're a force for good!"

Dez raises both palms. "Honestly, I'm beggin' you here: If you use any metaphor that includes omelets an' eggs, I'll hurl. Hand t'God."

Tears glitter in her eyes and her fist-knuckles are alabaster. "Goddammit!" she hisses in a whisper, leaning nearly a third of the way across the table. "You have no idea! None! The things I've had to do to stave off . . . You can't . . ."

"That vein in your forehead's pulsin'. Ye need to relax. Have ye considered yoga? Meditation? Heroin?"

RJ Sharpe slides out of the booth. Reaching for her coat, she bumps the wineglass. It falls, shatters on the pub floor, drawing surprised looks from the barkeep, the waitress, the patrons.

"I'm sorry!" she blurts to everyone. She slams her arms into her coat, rainwater splattering everywhere. Dez sips his very, very bad beer.

"Ye hired thugs an' killers, an' you sent 'em against some pencil-neck auditor never hurt a fly," he says, looking up. "Y'sent 'em against a reporter doesn't even know what it is she knows that's a threat to you an' yours. Y'sent armed hoods to shoot me . . . although, yeah, that one, I mean, who hasn't, right? But killin' Conor O'Meara and beatin' up Laleh Swann? Come on, RJ, me love! You're organized crime, an' you know it. That other stuff? Girls' rights? Agriculture? Literacy? Them's the marketing department of Clockjack. Them are the brochures an' tax write-offs. The rest o' the company . . . ?"

She stares down at him.

He laughs. "You're Murder Incorporated, love. An' well you know it."

RJ Sharpe spins around and stomps across the tavern and out into the storm.

Dez rises and reaches for his coat.

She came to suss out how much Dez has put together. And she brought a welcoming party with her, in case he's learned too much.

Which, clearly, he has.

CHAPTER 29

The hotel, restaurant, and pub were built on a massive old cannery pier, the wooden platform perched atop hundreds of creosote-soaked timbers, sunk into the riverbed. The pier stands about fifteen meters above the Columbia, and Dez had to drive across a short wooden bridge from the city's river-walk to get here. That bridge also sits atop old timbers.

Meaning there's one way onto the cannery pier and one way off. Staff Sergeant Gareth MacDonald and his boys will have that exit cut off.

But that's two-dimensional thinking. Dez had seen the problem with being on the dead-end pier when he'd done his recce earlier in the day.

The hundred he gave the barkeep was partly to provide privacy, but also for the promise of another way out.

No self-respecting gatekeeper ever relies on just one door.

As RJ Sharpe storms out of the tavern, Dez moves to the bar. "Criminal types comin'. Don't mind meeting 'em but don't want to in your establishment."

The bartender says, "That makes two of us."

He takes Dez into the kitchen, past the fry cook, and leads him to a door that faces out toward the Columbia basin. Once upon a time, the fishing fleet would sail up to the pier and the restaurant staff would buy the day's ration of salmon, tuna, or rockfish, and would haul them up to the kitchen with a rope, pulley, and bucket.

Earlier in the day, Dez bought thick yellow leather gloves. It took him a while to find gloves that would fit his massive hands, but now he's glad he has them. He'd spotted an old, flat-bottomed boat tied up under the restaurant. It looks older than Dez, but it floats.

The salt sea air rushes in when the door opens. Dez can smell fish and seaweed. He thanks the bartender and climbs the rickety wooden ladder down to the old boat. The river here is only hip deep and the bottom is thick with lazily undulating seaweed. He draws a small flashlight from his jacket pocket, checks left, right, forward, and gets his bearings. Dez doesn't need to paddle. He unties the boat he's about to steal, reaches for the nearest pylon, and drags it a bit to the west. He reaches for the next pylon and does it again. The old boat glides to the west, bobbing under his boots. He pulls the boat westward, slowly, the downpour obscuring his vision.

A wall of faint light glows behind him. The wall is moving. Dez peers through the rain. One of the ocean-going freighters has just passed under the interstate bridge, heading into the Pacific. The light is dim but helps illuminate Dez's situation a little.

He gets past the edge of the pier and turns the boat to port, toward the land. The rain has soaked his trousers and boots. He keeps using the pier's footings, shoving the boat toward the shore until he's beneath the short wooden bridge connecting the pier to the city's river-walk. There's a ladder here he's already tried and knows will hold his weight. He ties off his new favorite boat of all time and begins to climb.

Near the top, he notes the headlights of a car and the purr of an engine. He peeks over the edge of the bridge and sees a man in fatigues and a Kevlar vest, speaking to the driver of a Subaru. The man has an AR-15 strapped to his ballistic vest, plus a holster with a .45 on his hip. He wears lace-up boots and camo fatigues.

". . . some of those antifa anarchists coming here to vandalize the town," the armed man says.

From the car, Dez can barely hear the driver. "Oh, hell no! Send those assholes back to Portland!"

"Will do, sir. Can you back it up, please? We got this."

The driver backs up.

The sentry's back is to Dez. The parking lot glows under sodium lights, and Dez sees most of the same cars he counted before RJ Sharpe arrived. Her Lexus is missing. He spots three newcomers: all dark SUVs, parked side by side by side.

Three SUVs. That's a lot of men, if these cars are MacDonald's ride. And Dez assumes they are.

The sentry guarding the bridge paces.

Dez is shivering from the cold. Rainwater pours off his trousers and boots, but he maintains his position on the ladder, peeking over the edge of the short bridge.

The sentry walks the width of the bridge. He gets to within one stride of the edge, turns and saunters back the other way. He rests his hands on the butt of his assault rifle, which faces downward, clipped to his ballistic vest. He wears a Vietnam War–era brimmed hat of waxed leather, and water drools off the front and the back.

He gets to one edge of the bridge, turns lackadaisically, and strolls back the other way. He holds himself like a man others should fear. *You don't want none of this,* his body language bellows.

He gets to the far edge of the bridge and 260 pounds of very wet Brit slams into his back.

The sentry goes sailing off into the night. He doesn't even have time to scream.

Dez draws the long, black-coated Coltellerie Maserin knife from the sheath clipped to his belt, near his kidney. It's eleven inches long, powerfully designed, damn near unbreakable. Dez is a little embarrassed to admit he loves this knife, but he does.

The rain is easing a bit. It's still a hard downpour, but the wind has died, the rain falling straight down. What one of the nuns who raised Dez would have called a wee Scots mist. Dez duckwalks to the nearest SUV and, quick-like, peeks in through a side window. No driver. He kneels and slides the Italian-made knife into the right rear tire, twists it just a bit, and pulls it out. If these SUVs are ferrying the choir of the nearest Lutheran church, Dez is going to feel guilty as hell.

He takes out tires on the other two SUVs.

The old pier features the tavern, from which Dez has escaped, along with a restaurant and a small hotel. In front of the restaurant, two more fellas with long guns are talking to patrons and a waiter. Both wear rain hats and camo ponchos. There's some arguing going on. The soldier-types want the patrons to stay inside until someone dangerous can be apprehended. Dez hears the waiter say, ". . . calling cops . . ."

Time is not on Gareth MacDonald's side.

Dez lurks for a while, hiding among the patrons' cars, and soon he's spotted at least five of MacDonald's boys. Two outside the tavern, the two by the restaurant, one stationed outside the hotel. The downpour has kept most people at bay.

The door of the tavern bursts open. Gareth MacDonald and another man emerge. That's a total of eight, if you count the sentry Dez sent into the drink. Seven, now. The other man with MacDonald wears the same paramilitary gear as the others. MacDonald wears black fatigues and lace-up boots, with a squall-line jacket, but without the long gun or the camo. Dez lurks beneath the chassis of a pickup, close enough to hear these two.

MacDonald toggles a small walkie-talkie. "Limerick scarpered. Spread out. Check the car park. Collins and Phillips: Make sure he didn't duck into that restaurant. Grady: Same with the hotel. Over."

Dez grins. Seven men, but three of them are heading indoors. They'll not rush it. Why should they? They've been shivering in the rain for donkey's years.

Dez can't see much, lying under a pickup, but since the Scotsman doesn't repeat his orders, Dez assumes the men have obeyed.

MacDonald burrs to the man on his left, "I want that bastard."

His man goes to his left. MacDonald goes to his right. When they're separated sufficiently, Dez rolls out from under the pickup and, with one swipe, slices through the boot, the sock, and the Achilles tendon of MacDonald's man.

As he falls, Dez drives an elbow into his neck. The man hits the old timber, already unconscious. He was a mercenary when he passed out and he'll wake up a cripple. Dez has no intention of feeling guilt over that.

Dez leaves the AR-15 but takes the man's Colt. It's an M1911. A workhorse. Dez kneels between tightly parked cars and checks the mag, checks the thumb-safety, then tucks the gun into his jacket pocket.

He retrieves one of two steel ball bearings from another pocket.

Three men inside, getting warm. Three outside.

Dez keeps moving, keeps low. His baseball cap and his hood mask his light skin tone. He ditched the gloves once he was topside. He spots one of MacDonald's goons, close by, but then spots another and ducks back down. The timing's wrong.

Dez and the hounds continue their dance for a minute and a half.

When Dez spots one of the guys in close proximity, the others nowhere nearby, he rises and throws the ball bearing, hard as he can.

The gunman grunts and falls.

It's Dez's first spot of bad luck so far: The falling man had not safely indexed his finger. Convulsing in pain, he pulls the trigger of his assault weapon. Dez sees the cloth of the man's camo pants flare, sees the spurt of blood as the man shoots himself in the shin.

It's very noisy. Dez drops, rolls under a Toyota, keeps rolling, gets under a Ford Fiesta and out the other side, rises to his feet.

A bullet pangs off the Fiesta's quarter panel, a foot from Dez's nose.

Dez drops to one knee, draws the Colt, and fires three times, straight up and a little to his right. The bullets will sail out over the Columbia and sink harmlessly. At night, low visibility, in a civilian-rich environ, Dez has no intention of aiming at anything down here on the pier. His only hope is that the sound of the shots will scare MacDonald's men and will draw a quick police response.

He's on his feet, tucked low, moving quickly. He'd spotted a blue dumpster earlier in the evening, to the right of the tavern, and he moves for that spot. Over there, he'll be well clear of the parking lot's powerful sodium lights. He can hole up, see how the men react. See how long it takes for law enforcement to show up.

He sees rotating blue-and-red lights coming from Astoria's downtown core. Maybe ten blocks away.

Gareth MacDonald appears from behind a RAV4, with a collapsible baton, and slams it into Dez's back, right over his kidney.

Dez goes sprawling. The stolen gun skitters away.

MacDonald surges forward, drawing a sidearm. A SIG P226, from the looks of it. Dez is winded from the blow and his back feels like he caught a lightning strike, but he thrusts out with his right leg, his boot sole catching MacDonald on his brace leg, and the Scot tumbles.

Dez rises to one knee and drives his elbow into MacDonald's chest as the man falls. He thinks he feels a rib crack.

A bullet whizzes over his head and pangs into the dumpster. Dez is on his feet, his back killing him, sprinting, bent in two. The police lights are much closer now and he can hear a siren—no, sirens—over the rain.

One of MacDonald's men is racing toward him, firing his AR-15. Almost no one can run and fire a long gun at the same time. Not with any hope of accuracy. The man fires three times. He's got a better chance of hitting the state of Washington than he does Dez.

Dez gets behind the dumpster—it's near empty—and leans his shoulder against it. His back protests madly as he braces one leg against the wall of the tavern, waits, times it, then shoves for all he's worth.

The wheeled dumpster only travels about four meters, but that's enough to collide with MacDonald's man, with a satisfying crunch of bone-on-iron. The man lands on his ass, badly.

Another down, but more coming out soon. Plus the police. Plus—

Gareth MacDonald, on one knee, sights up and shoots.

Dez ducks out of sight.

He backs away from the fight, from the parking lot, from the overhead lights. He's near the edge of the pier now, knowing there's a walkway behind the restaurant. Good reconnaissance; an absolute must. He can get behind these guys, outflank them. Dez can see the map in his head as his boot hits the wooden walkway and MacDonald's second bullet hits him in the back.

Dez is thrown forward, over the railing, into the river below.

It's a fifteen-foot drop. He lands in seaweed and a foot of brackish water.

He swallows water and loses consciousness.

PART 2

CHAPTER 30

Paulson Reese, chief of staff for the president of the United States of America, leaves the weekly meeting of OMB economists and checks in with his longtime secretary. Who says, "You're running an hour and twenty minutes behind."

"Yes, but I'm usually two hours behind at this time of the day, so grading on the curve . . ."

"Uh-huh." She's been with him since his first statehouse seat in Albany and she's having none of it. "Your three o'clock is in your office."

"Remind me . . . ?"

"RJ Sharpe of Clockjack Solutions. She's with her COO. They contributed pretty solidly to the Senate caucus this last year."

Paulson Reese says, "How long do I have to give her?"

"Ten minutes."

Not thirty: Clockjack hasn't contributed *that* much.

Reese greets RJ Sharpe as he does every influential donor: two-handed shake, big smile. The titan of Clockjack is famous for wearing jeans with no knees and rock concert T-shirts when she's onstage or being interviewed, but she's in heels and a Prada power suit today. She bears little of the vivacious energy or humor for which she's famous.

She says, "Thank you for seeing us. This is Willard Dukane, our chief operating officer."

The men shake. Dukane is fiftyish and fit, handsome and confident, in a suit the White House chief of staff recognizes for its cost and style. "How's it going?"

"As crazy as every day around here. Please, sit. I'm glad to get the chance to talk to you both," he lies.

RJ picks up her purse. "Actually, I just wanted to make the introduction. I'll step out. Gentlemen."

She sounds eager to leave.

That is definitely odd, Reese muses. But on the other hand, he's already burned off thirty seconds of the ten minutes he has to give Clockjack, and he isn't worried about making small talk.

"Clockjack is eating Apple's lunch with the teens and early-twenty-year-olds," Reese says, gesturing to one of two matching chairs bracing a low French coffee table. Both men unbutton their suit coats and both sit. Dukane's tie is brown and very skinny with a shiny satin stripe, circa maybe 1965, Reese thinks. Dukane has a certain Rat Pack 1960s style. "You're in the running for the contract with FEMA. The new field communication tech. I can't tell you much about the process but—"

"That's fine." Dukane rolls over him with an easy smile and a dismissive wave. "That's someone else's worry. I came to deliver some good news."

"We're heading into the midterms. I'll take any good news I can get."

Dukane settles easily into his chair, legs crossed, smiling broadly, absolutely relaxed. "The president has to be pretty worried about the rise of Ōscar Maruno in Honduras."

Reese freezes, his smile locked in place, trying to catch up to the shift in topic. "Ah. Not sure I know—"

"Maruno is showing surprising strength in the south. 'Specially in La Paz, Morazán, and El Paraíso. He's resonating with the workers. He's raising money as far away as the Gracias a Dios region. I know you guys are getting nervous. Nobody expected a goddamn land-use attorney to be polling so well. Am I right?"

Reese shifts in his seat, trying to figure out how this tech nerd from the Pacific Northwest knows any of this.

"Here's the good news." Dukane shoots his cuffs. "You'll remember I said there was good news? Well, this is it. Ōscar Maruno's plane crashed on takeoff today, at an airport outside San Pedro Sula. Five people on board and I'm afraid all five died. Tragic as hell. It's a huge loss for the people of Honduras."

"He . . . what?"

Willard Dukane checks his 1942 Rolex Chronograph. "Oh my gosh. Look at the time." He pops up out of his chair as if it's spring-loaded and buttons his jacket.

Reese feels like he's experiencing a 4-g vertical takeoff, like back in his Navy days. He snaps out of it and rises, too. "I don't . . . I'm not sure what you've heard but—"

Dukane offers his hand. "The correspondence that Maruno kept, from back when the president worked for Chase Manhattan? I'm afraid that went up in flames, too. I'm not sure if you guys wanted any of that for the eventual president library. Probably not."

Dukane gives him a wink and a smile. "Hey, I should let you get back to it. Paulson—can I call you Paulson? Paulson, it has been a genuine pleasure. The president's doing a heck of a job. Really first rate. I'll see myself out."

At the door, Dukane makes a show of snapping his fingers. "Oh, I forgot. Clockjack is being besmirched in certain circles. Some nonsense about a low-level criminal matter in Portland, Oregon. You won't have

heard anything about this. Tempest in a teapot. DEA,
Marshals Service. Really making a hash of things out
there. It would be super-helpful if they am-scrayed.
Anyway, a joy to meet you. Here . . ."

He draws a Clockjack phone, turns, holds it at arm's
length, and smiles for a selfie with the White House
chief of staff.

"Thanks again. My regards to your wife. Tell her
happy birthday. Anyway, thanks again. Bye now."

And with that, he's gone.

The man going by the name of Willard Dukane had told
RJ Sharpe to take the limo back to Dulles without him.
When he steps through the visitor's gate at the White
House, a black SUV pulls up and he climbs aboard. The
driver—one of Gareth MacDonald's men—hands him
a satellite phone with the latest Clockjack encryption
suite.

He calls MacDonald in Honduras. "It's me. All
good?"

"All good," the Scotsman replies.

"Excellent. And Gareth?"

"Sir?"

"Still no word on that guy on the Oregon Coast?"

He listens to the intergalactic hiss of the call bouncing off a satellite over the Pacific. "Not yet, sir."

"That's . . . I'm not shitting you here. That's less than
ideal."

"Yessir."

"You shot him."

"Yessir."

"Then where the flying fuck is he?"

"We don't know, sir. As soon as we learn anything—"

"Uh-huh. Heard that before."

He disconnects.

* * *

White House Chief of Staff Paulson Reese sends a secure text to his covert contact at the Central Intelligence Agency and asks about the fate of the liberal Honduran lawyer turned politico, Ōscar Maruno. His contact texts him back within two minutes: No news. O.M. still running strong. Why? What have you heard?

Confused and more than a little fearful, Reese has no time to ponder it. He's off to his next meeting of the day, then the one after that, and the one after that.

It isn't until four hours later, while he's on his way home to Georgetown, in the back of a Secret Service–driven Cadillac, that his CIA friend texts him again.

Call me. Secure line. ASAP.

Reese calls him.

"I don't know what shit you're into over there, but Ōscar Maruno died when his plane crashed during takeoff in some pissant little town in Honduras."

Reese loosens his tie. "So I'd heard. Tragic. Can you have an asset look into it for—"

"Paulson," his friend cuts in, voice raw and agitated. "The crash happened fifteen minutes ago."

CHAPTER 31

Dez wakes up in a bed, in a bedroom. Nothing unusual about that.

Except he remembers exactly where he was and what happened when last his eyes were open. Some people coming out of a trauma have gaps in their memory. Not Dez. Comes from being shot more often than your average fella.

The room is pleasant, clean, dull, with the kind of carpet real estate agents call timeless mushroom and everyone else calls off-white. There's a chest of drawers, the top of which is piled high but neatly with medical supplies. There's a bedside table. There's a window with curtains, and the sun is out and the day looks pleasant.

Dez hurts like a son of a bitch.

He smiles, thinking, *Well, survived another one, my son.*

He drifts to sleep.

He wakes up.

A man sits perched on the edge of the bed, wearing a tracksuit and one spotless white sneaker; a broken-ankle cast on the other leg. His left eye is reddish and a little swollen, and Dez spots a shiny new scar on his upper lip. Crutches lean against the side table.

Dez whispers, "Be damned."

Alonzo Diaz offers him water from a lidded cup with a flexible straw. He sips.

Alonzo says, "Now who looks like two hundred pounds of bad hamburger?"

Alonzo became Dez's friend in Los Angeles. He's the house staff for Petra Alexandris, the CEO of Triton Expediters. He's also stood up to exceedingly violent men who wanted to do her harm. He paid for it with the blows to his face and to the broken ankle.

Dez croaks, "How long?"

"Three days, honey. And not for nothing, *cabrón,* but I was the one who washed you, and you weigh a ton."

"Aye, but I'm light on me feet."

Alonzo laughs, seated sideways on the bed, unconsciously rubbing at the ache in his right leg.

"What're ye doin' here?"

"Roy Rogers rode into town on Trigger and asked Petra all about you. He told us what happened. She has to be in DC to, you know, take care of that thing. She sent me."

Roy Rogers. Dez thinks back on the cowboy boots and the Stetson worn by Chief Deputy U.S. Marshal Conroy Sims, and he nods.

"Roy Rogers wants to ask you a bunch of questions. Are you up for it?"

Dez smiles sleepily. "Could ye stop him if you wanted to?"

Alonzo brushes stray hair from Dez's forehead. "Watch me."

Conroy Sims enters the bedroom after Alonzo steps out. He wears a conservatively cut suit and snakeskin boots but no hat. His face looks carved from marble. He brings with him a dining room chair, which he sets down, exactly perpendicular with the bed. He sits and adjusts the crease in his trousers.

"Mr. Limerick."

"Wotcher. Your deputies rescue me?"

"An Astoria PD boat responded to shots fired," the older man drawls, his accent as thick as molasses barbecue sauce. "They saw you fall and fished you out of the river. You were taken to a local hospital. When you were stabilized, I had you transferred here."

Dez thinks about all that for a while. Alonzo had helped him to sit up, his wide back supported by three pillows. Sheets and a blanket covering him from the waist down. He sees the stretch bandage around his torso, plus two square, medicinal-smelling bandages over his right-front and right-rear flank, just above belt height, about ten inches apart.

"Was shot on a Saturday. This would be . . . ?"

"Tuesday."

"Where's here?"

"A house I'm renting in the Portland suburbs."

"People behind this have cracked the Witness—"

Sims says, "A house *I'm* renting, Mr. Limerick. You are not in the Program."

Dez ponders that. Sims waits. Dez thinks that Sims has mastered the art of waiting quietly. Dez has known snipers who can do that.

"The Swann sisters are in Washington. You need to—"

"The Swann sisters are in Virginia. At my house, with my wife."

That, Dez did not see coming.

"When we met, you reminded me that *hiding* is not the same thing as *safe*. I had the sisters relocated. Off the books. Nobody knows but the men I trust the most. We moved the sisters just in time, too, because we've received reports from Whidbey Island of strangers in SUVs asking about them."

"Laleh's boyfriend?"

"With his family in Canada. I imagine you have a lot more questions?"

"The men I fought?"

"One dead, broken neck," Sims drawls with a lack of emotion. "One with a severed Achilles tendon. One shot in the leg, possibly self-induced. One with a broken arm from running into a dumpster. You'd taken out their three vehicles, and whoever was leading them didn't want a firefight with the Astoria police and Clatsop County Sheriff's Office, so the rest gave up."

"An' then evaporated from custody."

"That they did."

Of course.

"How bad am I hurt?"

"The bullet entered through your back, grazed your abdominal muscles, and exited via your side. Your intestines, your stomach, were not compromised. The fall and drinking half the river did you more damage than the bullet." Sims's brown eyes go to Dez's tightly packaged torso, to his constellation of scars. "You've been shot before, sir. I would say this likely was the least of them."

"Always was the lucky one. Petra Alexandris didn't send me lad up here, and we both know it. Alonzo took a beating 'bout a week ago. He's in worse shape than I am."

Sims smiles and frowns at the same time; different quadrants of his face expressing amusement and confusion. "That's right. He insisted on coming. He says you saved his life, and that of his boyfriend, and that of his employer."

"Dramatic, that one. Wasn't half as exciting as all that."

Dez reaches for the lidded cup of water and winces in pain. If asked, on a scale of one to ten, that bolt would have been a seventy-three. But he keeps reaching, and Sims makes no show of helping him.

Dez isn't the only one in this room who's ever recovered from battle wounds, he suspects.

"Where's the investigation into Clockjack?"

Sims says, "There is no investigation into Clockjack. None whatsoever."

"That's daft. They're behind this shite."

"May well be," Sims says with an icy void of emotion. "But the orders from the Justice Department are that my agency is not to go anywhere near Clockjack. The company is off-limits."

"Why?"

Sims sits awhile, pondering that question for his own edification. "I do not know."

"DEA?"

"Same orders from on high. Do not touch."

They're both quiet for a while.

"Am I on painkillers?"

"Yes you are. Very powerful ones."

"Aye, well, that explains it, then," Dez says, realizing that, for the last minute, he's been looking at two Conroy Simses.

He slides back into sleep.

CHAPTER 32

He awakes Wednesday morning.

It's early, the sun only beginning to rise, based on the salmon glow from the window. Dez throws off the covers and tries to sit up.

He succeeds, and also succeeds in not throwing up, but narrowly.

He studies the stretch bandage around his torso and the bandages over the entry and exit wounds, both just over his hip. Through and through.

He studies the medical supplies stacked neatly on the chest of drawers and guesses them to be worth more than a thousand dollars. He wonders if Chief Deputy Sims purchased them, or had them purchased, to avoid a U.S. Marshals paper trail.

He spots both of his beloved knives amid the medical supplies. He blushes; it says something wrong about your lifestyle if you have *beloved knives*. Worth some introspection, that, but not today.

Dez gets to his feet and shuffles like an old man to the bathroom. In the mirror, he looks a fright. He is ghostly pale, with purple bags under his eyes, his hair sticking up randomly. Massive bruises decorate his back and shoulder and chest from the fall. He uses the facilities and washes his face and torso and arms with a facecloth. Any other man would have been bearded by now, but Dez has never, ever been able to grow a proper one. Five days, and peach fuzz is all he has to show for it. Pathetic.

He spots his own Dopp kit, the one he'd left at Veronika's boutique hotel. He shaves and brushes his teeth.

His back aches and his gut aches and his legs feel weak and the world spins a little when he moves. Getting shot sucks.

Wearing only boxers, Dez uses one hand on the wall to brace himself and goes exploring.

The home has three bedrooms. He discovers that, for the past several days, Alonzo Diaz has been sleeping in one and deputy marshals have rotated off shift in the second. Dez recognizes the dour young Black deputy who uncuffed him, the night he'd been held in federal custody. The deputy shakes his hand and then uses a store-bought, preloaded flip phone. "Chief Deputy? It's Vega. Limerick's up."

Dez smells coffee. He finds Alonzo in the kitchen. Alonzo is chopping onions and cilantro, wearing an apron over his tracksuit. The track pants zip at the ankle to make room for his ankle cast and, somehow, the debonair Latino makes it look dashing. He washes his hands. "Well, well. Sleeping Ugly."

Dez gingerly circles the peninsula cabinet separating the kitchen from the living room. He draws Alonzo into a hug, their foreheads touching, Dez's hand on the back of Alonzo's skull, and holds the moment.

"Who do I have t'kill for a cup of that?"

Alonzo pours him coffee. Dez sits at the counter. He inhales the aroma of the coffee, his body protesting as he fills his lungs. "Finally found something you're good at."

Alonzo says, "You know that A above middle C that the Phantom hits in 'Music of the Night'? I once held that motherfucker for forty seconds. Who's your papi now?"

Dez laughs and his wound protests.

They chat as Alonzo makes huevos rancheros, but done up as a breakfast sandwich inside an English muffin, which Dez thinks is sacrilege until he realizes the bread absorbs the yolk and the creamy sauce, and now he can't imagine having it any other way. He devours his. Alonzo makes sure his cup is never more than one-quarter empty. Conroy Sims and another deputy arrive as he finishes the breakfast.

"Sir," Dez says, not getting up.

The man carefully doffs his Stetson and sets it brim-up on the kitchen counter. "Yesterday, you were full of questions, Mr. Limerick. Today's my turn."

CHAPTER 33

Alonzo gets more coffee perking. Chief Deputy Sims eyes him and says, "Sir, we have some sensitive—"

Dez says, "He stays," and limps over to a living room chair, lowering himself gingerly.

Sims stiffens. "This is a law enforcement matter."

"An' it's a bang-up job ye've done so far, enforcin' the law. Alonzo sees patterns I don't. Wouldn't kill ye to get a different perspective now an' then."

Sims stands his ground for a moment, then concedes. He chooses the couch, so he's sitting at ninety degrees relative to Dez. The deputy who identified himself as Vega sets a digital recorder on the glass-and-brass coffee table, equidistant between them. The deputy raps his knuckle twice on the glass and watches the audio level bob, then steps back.

Two deputies, the chief deputy from the district of Virginia, Dez, and Alonzo. Law enforcement in suits, Alonzo looking sleek in his tracksuit, Dez in his boxers. An odd allotment of allies, Dez thinks.

He starts in. "Started last year, near as I can tell. Nothing interesting had happened at Clockjack for twenty-odd years. Then, last year, two o' the four partners who created the company died within a month of each other. Joel Menache, chief operating officer, an'

Carl Hickman, chief financial officer. They were re-placed by Willard Dukane an' Matthew Salerno."

"We know all that," Sims says, but not with impa-tience or annoyance. Just putting it out there.

A thought hits Dez. "Is Laleh Swann still workin' on the audit documents?"

"She is, from my home, but now she has two foren-sic accountants helping." Before Dez can protest, Sims holds up a palm, traffic-cop style. His skin is sun-leathered and wrinkled. "The accountants do not work for the Marshals Service. They work for my wife. They are not officially involved in any way."

"Aye. Good. Want to talk to the sisters."

"And they to you. What's the importance of the deaths of Menache and Hickman?"

"Menache: Dunno yet, but that's the inciting inci-dent, so we'll get back to it. Hickman was replaced by a Jamaican accountant, Winston Noel, who used t'handle the Gulf o' Mexico cocaine trade for the Sinaloa Cartel."

Conroy Sims hardly moves but it's obvious the other deputies hadn't known this. Sims says, "You're sure?"

"Wasn't. RJ Sharpe asked me t'meet her in Astoria. I dropped it on her, t'see if she knew. She did. That's when she sicced MacDonald on me."

Sims nods to one of the agents, who steps away and draws a burner phone. They aren't using U.S. Marshals Service comms. Good, Dez thinks. Smart. The man with the phone sounds agitated and Dez hears him whisper the name Winston Noel.

Sims says, "Who is MacDonald?"

"Gareth MacDonald. Former SAS. Former merc. Goin' by Robert Taylor, these days. Head o' Clockjack security."

Sims says, "Joshua?" Deputy Vega also rises and also draws a flip phone, stepping away to call it in.

Sims inhales, holds it, exhales, says, "My lord."

"Aye." Dez smiles at him. "You've the thick end of this thing now. They wasn't messin' with the Witness Protection Project, playing silly buggers. They're buildin' a criminal empire. Winston Noel, 'cause from what I read, he's dead brilliant at launderin' international money an' all the criminals and ex-soldiers they could ever need, 'cause you lot rounded 'em up for them. They turned the Witness Protection Program into the world's largest supermarket. Can roam the aisles, pick an' choose who they need. Like your lad Demetrious Givens, an' the DEA's Cristian Hinestroza."

Sims picks at lint on his trouser leg. "You figured out who they were. The men you beat senseless in that record store."

"Aye."

"May I ask how?"

"Baseball bat, mostly."

"No, I mean, how did you identify Givens and Hinestroza?"

Dez sips coffee. He's no intention of giving up the assist he got from Arabella Satti and MI6.

Sims ponders quietly.

Alonzo has moved to the counter stool where Dez ate his breakfast, his injured leg elevated on the rung of the next stool over. He interjects, "You said two of the four people who started Clockjack died last year."

Dez nods. "Did."

"So the other two are still on the job?"

"Aye. RJ Sharpe, CEO. Teddy Meeker, head math nerd and code writer."

Sims surprises Dez by half turning on the couch and addressing Alonzo. "What do you make of that, Mr. Diaz?"

"I'd be surprised if RJ Sharpe is an evil mastermind. I've seen her TED Talks. She's flashy and showy. Jazz hands." He demonstrates. "She's the center of attention. She *wants* everyone looking at her."

Alonzo turns to Dez. "You've met the math guy?"

"Have. Unassuming fella. Professor."

Alonzo makes a face. "No offense to Professor Moriarty, but I'm not seeing that dude as your supervillain, either. Who does that leave? The COO? What'd you say his name was?"

Dez grins. He turns to Sims. "Told ye he was smart." He turns back to Alonzo. "Willard Dukane. An' aye, process of elimination. He's my pick for the shot caller, too. I searched online and couldn't find a photo of the man. His biography's an excellent forgery, I think. Also, he was the first new face at Clockjack. The first big change. It all started with Dukane."

Sims studies him.

"All ends with Dukane, too. That'd be my guess, mate."

CHAPTER 34

ROLLA, MISSOURI

The woman going by the name of Lisa Bagley hears the doorbell ring as she places the puffy ball of concentrated detergent in the rickety old washing machine. She stands and cranks the setting to COLORS and gets the machine going.

The doorbell rings again.

"Hold on," she says, dashing to the door. She feels much older than her twenty-four years. She suspects she's going to end up with arthritic knees, like her father.

She won't.

She opens the door to find Gareth MacDonald standing on her WELCOME! mat, his Clockjack phone set on video, and with a .22 Magnum with a sound suppressor.

ATLANTA, GEORGIA

The man called Willard Dukane pours a powerful four fingers of scotch whisky into a heavy-bottomed tumbler. He's standing at the wet bar of a plush suite. Normally, there is an elegant view of Atlanta's downtown core, but today, he has the shades drawn. He opens a mini-fridge and pulls out a small bottle of seltzer for himself.

He carries the tumbler across the expanse of the

penthouse suite. He moves easily and with rhythm and grace, like a man who's studied ballroom dancing, which he has. He holds the almost-full glass just by the pressure of the pads of his thumb and three fingers, from above, like the claw in an arcade's glass box of stuffed animals. His trousers rise a little higher than the style of the day, and his white shirt blouses more, and they look good on him. He pays a tailor for his 1950s wardrobe. The clothes are all new and bespoke; only the ties and belts and watches are vintage.

Reverend Willis Boyle eyes the glass like it's a life preserver tossed into the ocean of turmoil that has become his world. He drains the first quarter of the whisky in a go.

Boyle sits in one of the room's plush leather chairs and Dukane chooses the cream-colored couch opposite him, cracking open the lid of the seltzer. The room around them is clean and minimalist, more metal than wood, light colors and high ceilings. Even with the drapes closed, the room glows.

He says, "You, sir, have had one hell of an unlucky run. But I've got to tell you, all things are possible if you have faith."

Reverend Boyle drinks another quarter of the whisky. "Not words we real Americans expect to hear from you Silicone Valley elites. I hope you don't mind my saying."

"Sili*cone* is a polymer. Sili*con* is an element and . . . you know what? Completely unimportant. Forget I said that. I hear you, Reverend. I do. With the liberals and the Washington swamp and the mainstream media all bearing down on you, it can seem like too much for any man's shoulders."

The third quarter of the scotch is gone.

"Thank you, Willard. I surely appreciate the kind words."

The fourth fourth is gone, and Dukane stands,

takes the tumbler, walks back to the spacious and well-appointed wet bar, refills it but with only one finger this time. He returns it. "The whore who claimed you slept with her, starting when she was fourteen, well, talk about troubles piling on . . ."

Boyle takes the glass back. "I, ah, wouldn't use that word to describe her. A liar, certainly."

"Ex-liar." Dukane returns to the couch.

"Excuse me?"

"Ex-liar. Past tense. Draw your cell phone for me, will you, Reverend? Indulge me."

Confused, the man reaches into the inside pocket of his jacket. As he does, his phone springs to life.

An incoming video awaits him.

Boyle glances at the smooth-talking executive opposite him, who sits with both elbows thrown back over the top of the couch, an expansive gesture, comfortable in his skin and in any given room. He smiles, nods to the phone.

It's a Clockjack phone.

Reverend Boyle brings it to life and thumbs the awaiting video to action. It's a six-second clip from Gareth MacDonald's phone.

The thick crystal glass doesn't break when Boyle drops it on the carpet, the thin layer of whisky flying, spraying the chair and his trousers.

He falls to his knees and barely avoids throwing up all that good booze.

He kneels like a penitent, face green, eyes bulging and glassy.

The man called Dukane sips his seltzer. He purrs. "*Ex*-liar."

Boyle doesn't look up. "I didn't want . . . her dead. . . ."

"Of course you didn't. You're a man of God. You didn't kill her. You're a thousand miles away from her. Heck, you didn't even order it done. Yet, done it is. She has departed this Earth. She now faces the stern judgment of our lord God. And not"—Dukane sips—"the grand jury that the Atlanta DA was about to impanel."

Boyle kneels in a puddle of whisky, hyperventilating.

"You have done so much good, Reverend. Your association has been a political kingmaker in the South for three decades. And with one of Satan's minions dispatched, you can continue to help steer the moral ship of this great nation."

"I . . . that bitch lied about me," he tells the whisky-stained rug.

"Hallelujah."

"I detest violence . . ." the reverend says, eyes down.

Dukane waits.

". . . but . . ."

That's all Dukane needs to hear. He caps his bottle and rises. He crosses to the wet bar, gets a clean rag, runs water over it, wrings it out, walks back, and hands it to the reverend. Boyle stares at it, then takes it and washes his face briskly. He uses the rag to daub at the stains on his trousers.

"Hands. Don't forget to wash the blood off your hands."

Boyle looks up sharply, fear in his eyes.

"Whisky. I meant whisky."

Twenty minutes later, a fresh drink tucked into him, Reverend Willis Boyle looks more like his normal self. His breathing is better, his color better. For the first time in months, he can sense a light at the end of his personal tunnel.

At the door to the suite, Willard Dukane slaps him on the back. "You're a powerful influence for good with the House and Senate, sir, not to mention state legislatures. Praise God, that will continue until you retire in a few years. And do not worry. There is nothing connecting you to the death of that poor deluded girl."

He snaps his fingers dramatically. "Well, except the video, sent to a phone registered in your name."

Boyle staggers.

"Fear not. Even if the DA should ever catch wind of such a video, Clockjack would *never* cave in and produce that link. Never! We've faced down subpoenas by the feds before, and we'll do it again."

He grasps both of the man's shoulders and looks deeply into his eyes.

"In the meantime, three Republicans on the Senate Foreign Relations Committee voted two years ago to continue a trade embargo with the African country of Zanj."

Boyle says, "Zanj?"

"It's near Kenya and Tanzania, and it's just a big, sandy clump of nothing on the Indian Ocean. The embargo is coming up for another vote next week. And I'm afraid, we at Clockjack need those three honored lawmakers to vote against continuing the embargo. Think you can influence them, Reverend?"

Boyle studies him for nearly a minute. Then nods. "It's done."

"Marvelous!" Dukane claps him on the shoulder. "This is why I love working with God-fearing men."

CHAPTER 35

Dez is quick to heal. His body is in terrific shape, he eats well and he's resilient.

It still takes a week in the suburban house before he's feeling up to snuff.

Alonzo knows firsthand all about physical therapy and how to keep flexible while recovering from an injury. He dotes on Dez, commandeering the kitchen and defending it against all invaders. He also knows more than Dez does about stretching and yoga, and he teaches him how to work out without reopening his wound.

Chief Deputy U.S. Marshal Conroy Sims is told he needs to return to Virginia. His Justice Department overseers are getting a lot of pressure from on high to leave Clockjack alone. The pressure on his bosses is coming from Justice, and the pressure on Justice is coming from the White House. And that pressure, Sims learns, is considerable.

Dez has been stuck in the suburban home for eight days, and he's going a little stir crazy. Sims tells him that he's scouted out a park, not three blocks away, near a creek. He, Dez, and Alonzo stroll that way a half an hour before nightfall. The park is small and quiet, and the creek meanders lazily through it. There's a walking

path and benches. They sit and Sims produces a silver
flask with his initials, containing good Kentucky bourbon.

Dez is no longer limping. Alonzo is, but he's using a
dashing black cane that he'd picked up years ago, when
he studied tap dance. The three men sit under a towering
Doug fir and watch the slow-moving creek, and pass the
flask around.

Sims's voice is as slow and meandering as the creek.
"What do you plan to do, Mr. Limerick?"

Dez has long ago given up on getting the chief
deputy to call him by his nickname. "Go after them
bastards."

"How?"

"Dunno yet. Got a few notions."

"Oh, Miss Swann, the elder, wants you to call tonight. She and the forensic accountants have discov-
ered something."

Dez nods.

"I wish the Marshal Service could do more. The political pressure we're under is . . . unlike anything I've
experienced before. I'm sad to say that the Drug Enforcement Administration backed down right after you
were shot. They've already moved on to other things,
rather than risk the wrath of the Justice Department."

"Clockjack can call in powerful favors," Dez says.

"I do not relish fighting a rearguard action against my
own government, so I'll do as I'm told, Mr. Limerick."

"Wise, that."

Alonzo sees a dog-walker with a Scottie dog and—
being nuts about Scotties—limps over to make a friend.
Thirty feet away, he kneels and rubs the dog's ears. The
dog-walker, an elderly lady, giggles and takes a photo
of the two new best buddies. Alonzo hams it up for her.

Dez and Sims sit on the bench and watch the funny
scene. Sims's voice is smoky and slow, his eyes on the

dog and those cooing over it. "Mr. Limerick," he drawls. "I suspect you are going to have to kill a few men."

Dez sips bourbon and hands the flask back. "Aye."

After a beat, Sims nods and takes his own sip.

Back at the rental house, Sims makes his goodbyes and clears out. His men, too.

Dez video calls the Swann sisters, using anti-eavesdropping technology built into his phone.

Alonzo heads into the connected kitchen to clean up.

Laleh, in Virginia, sits on a flowery couch. She's been crying.

"Are ye all right?"

She daubs at the corners of her eyes with a Kleenex. "I am. Ignore me."

"Raziah?"

"She's writing music. She's spending, like, fourteen hours a day at it. She's filled a bunch of notebooks."

"Gets like that, her. What'd you find?"

Laleh pulls herself together, looking more professional. "From what I've been able to tell by the audit, one of the members of the Clockjack leadership began negotiations to sell the company."

"To who? Sorry. Whom."

"A Chinese firm. One of those big telecoms that, bottom line, is actually the Chinese military."

Dez sits back. Ponders that. "Was it Menache or Hickman wantin' to sell?"

"No, it was Teddy Meeker, the math guy."

"Hmm. Okay. An' the other three original founders?"

"Opposed, I guess. But the leadership is a foursome and each of them controlled twenty percent of the stock. Twenty percent is in public hands. Menache and Hickman were dead set against the sale."

"If it'd happened, the Clockjack that herself, RJ

Sharpe, raves about in all them speeches, it would've become a thing of the past."

She says, "Sure. On the other hand, I think Sharpe and Meeker and Menache and Hickman would have been worth something like four billion dollars each."

"The newcomers? Dukane and Salerno?"

"It looks like they're on board with the sale to China."

Dez lets that simmer.

Laleh says, "I'm not through with the audit reports. Not by a long shot. I'll keep sorting through this stuff. What are you going to do?"

"Have a bit of a confab with someone."

"Who?"

"Still working that bit out. Are you all right, then?"

"Frightened," she says. "Homesick. Perpetually angry."

"A lot o' that going around, love."

They're both quiet for a spell. Laleh says, "Dez?"

"Hmm?"

"I've . . . listened to her music. Raziah." She's tearing up again. "You were right. The abuse she . . . we endured. It's all right there."

"It is if you've ears to hear it. Most don't."

She whispers, "You did."

Dez hasn't much to say to that.

"Raziah was hypersexualized. Early. She acted out by flirting and . . . more."

"Aye."

"You didn't fall under her spell."

"'Course not. Mates, us."

Laleh holds the wadded Kleenex under her eyes, then leans out of the camera frame and whisks up more tissue, leaning back in.

"I don't sense the same . . . wildness in her this year. The old Raziah would have conquered both of the auditors and the deputies guarding us by now. She'd have mowed them down. They wouldn't have known what hit them. Instead, she's pouring her heart, and her confusion and her pissed-offedness into her music."

"Aye."

"You saw it first."

"Always been lucky with me mates."

From the kitchen, Alonzo smiles.

"Silver lining in this bloody mess: Raziah's a good soul, an' so are you, an' if this draws you both closer . . ."

Laleh says, "Thank you."

"Signin' off, love. I've cogitating to do."

She wishes him good luck and disconnects.

Alonzo, up to his elbows in sudsy water, shakes his head. "You do get past people's defense shields, Red Coat. You got past Petra's and I didn't think anyone could do that."

Dez laughs. "You did."

"Well, sure. But you're mortal. I'm Cuban."

CHAPTER 36

Dez comes up with a cunning master plan.

Step one: Break something at Clockjack's Columbia Gorge facility.

Step two: Get invited in to fix it.

Dez's master plans tend to look like he pulled them out of his arse if he thinks about them too long. So he usually doesn't.

The thing to break ends up being Clockjack's fleet of electric maintenance carts. The company has ten of them at Gamila. Some are used by grounds maintenance personnel. Some are used by campus security. Two each are used by custodial services and the IT department's roving band of help desk personnel. The four-wheel scooters get plugged in every evening to power up. When plugged in, they also download diagnostic information to the South Korean company that manufactures them.

Dez learns all of this by hacking around, in between bouts of Alonzo's physical fitness regimen. It's been nine days since Dez was shot and he's in as good a shape as he's going to get.

Step two is Clatskanie Repairs, a small suburban company that has the contract to fix the South Korean carts. The company is on retainer. The owner of the four-person company, Pyotr Wiznowski, had been thrilled, seven years earlier, to win the contract. But it hadn't ended up being a gold mine for him. For the simple reason that the Koreans make one hell of a good electric cart, and the damned things almost never need repairs. In seven years, Pyotr Wiznowski has netted $183 off that retainer contract.

On the tenth day after Dez was shot, he sees Alonzo Diaz off at Portland International Airport, hugging and slapping him on the back. "You're a good man, you."

"Learn to duck that big stupid head of yours."

"I will. Give me love to Petra. An' your lad, Michael. Tell him to keep writing."

He watches Alonzo with his fine black cane, limping through security.

Dez moves out of the house in the suburbs and into a small, sterile chain motel near downtown Portland. He has access to a handful of identities linked to banks in Europe, so for now he's flying under Clockjack's radar. He hopes. He changes into another pair of black jeans and another black T-shirt. He sits on the room's bed and sends some quickly written code to the South Korean company's mainframe. Then he gets a Lyft out to the suburbs, to the business of Pyotr Wiznowski, where he introduces himself and says he's looking for work.

And tells the owner that he's an absolute genius at repairing little electric scooters made in South Korea.

Pyotr Wiznowski's massive, steel-wool eyebrows rise, corrugating his forehead. "You're kidding!"

"Why? D'ye have some work along them lines?"

CHAPTER 37

Turns out, Dez quite enjoys his time commuting to Gamila with Pyotr Wiznowski. The congenial and obese man checked Dez's (very fake) credentials and his years of work repairing Korean carts. He signed Dez on the spot as a contractor for this gig. And if this job works out, there could be a month-to-month freelance contract in it for him. The heavyset Pole, with his massive mustache and eyebrows, is a font of hilarious stories. He's a natural-born raconteur, and Dez finds himself laughing and sharing his own (edited) stories as they tool out on Interstate 84, beyond Portland and its suburbs of Troutdale, then Corbett. The view is stunning, the Columbia River as impressive as Dez has always heard. Not as wide here as at Astoria, but still amazing. The gorge rising steeply on the Oregon side, thickly forested, with the occasional glimpse of some of the most beautiful waterfalls he's ever seen.

It takes them forty-five minutes to reach the R & D site for Clockjack Solutions. They take an exit just past the Multnomah Falls Lodge, rolling south and steeply uphill, away from the iconic river. Dez catches sight of a small dam—huge, really, but not on the Hoover or Grand Coulee scale—before Pyotr's Ford F-150 is swallowed up by the fir forest of the gorge and the outskirts of Mount Hood National Forest.

His first sight of the campus isn't what he's expecting: no imposing perimeter fence with guard towers and razor wire. There is a fence, all right, but made of the same wood they've been passing through, vertical posts, a little haphazardly thrust into the ground, seeming more rustic than security-minded.

The road leads to a gate and the gate is rolled open, inviting. The sign for the facility is on the inside of the fence, not outside, and Dez can't read it until they've crossed the threshold.

GAMILA.

BUILD FOR ALL PEOPLE

THINK OF THE EARTH

INSPIRE, CONSPIRE, PERSPIRE—WE'RE IN THIS TO-GETHER.

SCREW UP AND START OVER. AND OVER.

WELCOME.

"It would've taken 'em less time to carve 'Trespassers'll be shot.'"

Pyotr laughs. "They're a little hippy-dippy, but they seem nice."

It's the same forest inside as outside; very little of the vegetation has been cleared on the campus. The well-groomed road is gravel, not asphalt—permeable, so the famous Northwest rains will reach every root they're supposed to. The air is sweet and oxygenated the way it never is in the city. Just inside the gate, Dez spots a small cabin made of horizontal logs. Maybe two or three rooms, tops, all on one floor. Pyotr Wiznowski parks out front and a wholesome young man in a Captain America T-shirt, cargo pants, and sturdy boots ambles out of the cabin.

He's packing a laser-reader gun, like a shelving clerk at a grocery store. He looks to be in his early twenties.

Pyotr kills the engine. "I'll take care of—"

But Dez has hopped out of the passenger side. He thrusts his hands into the back pockets of his jeans and inhales deeply. "God, but the amount of oxygen out here'll make ye drunk."

The kid laughs. "High on life, dude. I'm Dylan. You guys got work orders?" He gestures to the business decal on the Ford's door.

Pyotr has been here before and knows the drill. He produces his phone. Dylan holds his laser scanner up to it and they hear a pleasant chime.

The young man draws his own phone from his cargo trousers.

"Cool. Pyotr Wiznowski? And, ah, Karel Kaye?" The kid struggles with the pronunciation of both names. He snaps a phone-photo of Pyotr. Then he takes one of Dez.

Click.

Dez feels the bespoke phone in his hip pocket vibrate. He pulls it out, checks it. The readout scrolling across his screen is in Cantonese, which Dez can't read, but that's okay. He knows what it's doing.

The kid says, "Pyotr and Karel. What're those, Russian?"

Pyotr says, "Polish."

Dez says, "Czech."

"Cool. You guys are cleared. Here." The kid taps at his phone, and Pyotr's phone chirps. His GPS maps program blinks to life. Dez peers over the man's shoulder and sees a map of the campus and one road lit up like a magical ley line.

Dez clears the Cantonese scrolling on his screen and steps up to the kid, handing him the phone. "We've several scooters to fix. Might have to separate. Give me the map, will ye?"

"Cool." He does.

This close, Dez can see that the kid is in his mid-to-late twenties, but the clothes and the haircut make him look younger. He's also physically put together. Dez notes calluses on the kid's thumb and the web between his thumb and first finger. The best way to get those calluses is to spend hours on the shooting range. Dez has those calluses.

"Never seen a phone like this," the guy says, hefting it. Dez's phone is thicker and heavier than most smartphones.

"All the rage in Prague, them."

"Cool. Okay, don't separate until you get to the X," Dylan says, and hands back the phone. "When you get to the X, a girl named Jenny will meet you and help you figure out where these carts are."

"That's a big ten-four." Pyotr climbs back behind the wheel of his truck. Even climbing into his truck leaves him a little winded.

Dez climbs into the passenger seat. "Cheers, mate."

Dylan flashes him the peace symbol. "Cool."

CHAPTER 38

Pyotr puts the balky transmission into gear and heads deeper into the campus. The GPS map on their phones shows them they're going the right way, although they see several gravel paths diverging here and there, all with old-fashioned wooden signposts listing buildings. Dez draws his tablet computer with its ruggedized leather folder and transfers the Gamila map to his tablet. As his new friend and erstwhile employer drives slowly forward, Dez uses the pads of his thumb and forefinger to expand and contract the map, showing him the perimeter of the campus and two dozen buildings. Gamila sits on 312 acres of wooded land between the Columbia River and Mount Hood National Forest. Dez checks the map index: eighty-one buildings. The footprint of the campus is amoeba-like with no sharp angles anywhere, and the southern sector is dominated by an eight-acre lake. Some of the largest buildings are around the lake, and most feature fanciful and foreign names designed to rob the place of any austerity: The administration building is Patronne, the feminine French word for "boss." Software development buildings—there are more than a dozen—include names such as Elektricheskiye (Russian for "electrical") and Ikerketa (Basque for "research"). Which goes to explain why the campus is named after the Egyptian dialect's word for "beauty," Dez supposes.

Pyotr and Dez are starting to see a lot more people now; close to two thousand people work on the campus, they've learned. Most walk or ride bicycles between buildings. A few ride stand-up electric scooters, like the one Dez and Raziah Swann rented in Portland. Pyotr's Ford has the only combustion engine they've seen so far.

The digital maps bring them to a modernistic, three-story structure with outdoor tables and parasols, and several people drinking coffee or eating salads and sandwiches. The company canteen, Dez assumes. The lawn outside the canteen is dotted with several food trucks, offering an international array of street food.

A young blond woman with a high ponytail, wearing cuffed khaki shorts and a khaki shirt, and clunky hiking boots, waves them down. Like Dylan at the entrance, she appears to be in her early twenties but possibly older. She moves like someone who's athletic and limber. Dez would put down good money she's been through at least basic training in the military. Clockjack Solutions has gone to great lengths to camouflage its security personnel.

Dez takes a moment to study the people on their lunch or coffee breaks, or who are strolling or biking around the campus. The immediate hit he gets off the staff is counterculture: men with beards and ponytails, women with tattoos, a lot of rainbow flags on backpacks, most everyone wearing T-shirts or sweatshirts, jeans or leggings, stocking caps or baseball caps, and sneakers or hiking boots.

The security doesn't look like security so as not to spook the engineers and tech-types in this kicked-back, Northwest culture, Dez assumes. Smart.

The blond girl, Jenny, scans them with her phone. "You're here about the carts?" She has a Southern accent. "Every damn one of them froze up. They're charged up and everything, but . . ." She shrugs.

Dez turns to his new friend. "Best if we split up, yeah? Try an' diagnose more than one of them at a time."

Pyotr says, "Why not?"

Jenny hesitates. Security, maintenance, grounds crew, and IT are all inconvenienced when the go-carts don't go. It will be marginally harder to monitor Pyotr and Dez if they separate, but not impossible.

"All right. There are some parked behind this building here, at the charging station," Jenny says, and points. "Two more are over there, in El Garaje."

She points north and Dez sees an unadorned building ("garage" in Spanish) that clearly houses the Clockjack fleet of vehicles. The cutesy names of the buildings is another attempt to distract the bohemian workforce from the fact that they work for a powerful multinational.

Dez points to the fleet housing. "I see 'em. I'll take that lot, shall I, mate?"

Pyotr slaps him on the shoulder. "Go nuts, my man."

He unlocks the pickup canopy and hauls out a tool kit. Dez has his messenger bag over one shoulder. He ambles off with that rolling, bowlegged gait of his, whistling, toward the company motor pool.

He spots two of the Korean-made carts, still plugged into an e-station, both fully charged. Down on his haunches, Dez pops the hood on the cart farthest from the door and the majority of the passersby. He draws his tablet computer and activates a subroutine, which is in Cantonese.

A little better than a year earlier, Dez had done a favor for a hacker out of Hong Kong. The girl was all of nineteen and had one of the keenest analytical minds Dez had ever encountered. She had an ex-boyfriend make a bid to rekindle their relationship, whether she wanted to or not. Dez met up with the ex and made a powerful counterargument, which involved the sweeteners of moving on to better things, not looking back, bygones being bygones, the better part of valor, and the abundance of fish in the sea, and also the opportunity to retain the use of his knees for the foreseeable future. The ex had been persuaded by Dez's debate skills. As a result, the hacker from Hong Kong had bequeathed unto Dez an anti-snooping app for his tablet. It is a thing of pure and transcendent beauty.

Dez activates that app now. His tablet is its own Wi-Fi hotspot, so he doesn't need to log on to Clockjack's internet system.

When Dylan of the gatehouse sent Dez's photo to the campus security, it included a virus filled with lovely Cantonese chicanery. Somewhere in the bowels of Gamila, security has the photo of "Karel Kaye." And now that the virus has had time to spread, Dez has access to the campus security system.

Online, he tools around the security site until he gets to the campus CC security camera feeds. He pulls up live camera footage of Pyotr, sitting in a cart, his own laptop plugged into the diagnostics. Dez toggles to another camera and spots himself, crouching next to another cart.

Dez begins recording the image.

He works around and in the cart for five minutes—mostly checking football scores and not actually working. At the five-minute mark, Dez bops into the campus security system and supplants the CC camera feed at the motor pool building with the five minutes of looping tape, showing him doing jack shit but looking industrious as hell.

He stands, glances around to see if Jenny or any other security personnel are nearby, then ambles away.

Dez sends a code to the South Korean carts and a countdown begins. One of the carts—one that Pyotr is running a diagnostic on—will spring to life in twenty-five minutes. That'll start a cascade, and all of the carts will be working within three hours.

There. Done.

Easy to fix things when you're the one who broke them intentionally.

CHAPTER 39

Dez heads over to the company canteen and gets a coffee he doesn't really want. He eavesdrops on staff conversations: Some are highly technical, but a lot of them are about sports and politics and television shows. There's a heated discussion about the merits of Xbox versus PlayStation. Two women talk about caring for their aging parents. He overhears nerds discussing comics and anime. Others are bitching about their bosses or their workstations. Gamila appears to be exactly what it looks like: a largish workplace with more engineering degrees and physics degrees than the population at large. The staff is more diverse than Dez believes the Pacific Northwest to be in general.

He's wondering how all these people got out here when an electric bus pulls up to the front of the canteen. A couple dozen people alight; a couple dozen board. Change of shift. The bus pulls out, heading back to Portland.

Dez has been out and about for seven minutes now and nobody's realized he's missing, thanks to the looped video he's feeding the security folks. He owns the security department's computer, so he'd know if they did.

He checks the security system and discovers that three of the four principals are on campus today. Their magnetic key cards even tell him where they are. Teddy

Meeker, the former math professor who wrote the original Clockjack code, is in his office in the admin building. The chief financial officer is in his office, too, in the same building. The security system has him listed as Matthew Salerno, but Dez knows he's Winston Noel, former drug lord from Jamaica.

Willard Dukane, head of special projects, is in a conference room on the far side of the campus. Security indicates sixteen other people are with him, hearing some sort of presentation, like as not.

A Google search shows that RJ Sharpe, the charismatic CEO who set him up to die in Astoria, is speaking in Brussels. Good. Dez wants to get reacquainted with her, but not just yet.

The security computers don't show the whereabouts of the head of security, also known as former SAS staff sergeant Gareth MacDonald. That's interesting, all by itself. Security can't tell you where the head of security is?

Both Meeker and Noel are in the admin building. Dez heads that direction. He really wants to meet Dukane, but the man's way over on the far side of the campus.

He notes that the admin building features a maintenance access and maintenance stairs. The access is on the underside of the ground floor, in part of the building that's out over the lake. He doesn't need this alternative entrance today, but he could in the future. He tucks that thought away for later.

The administration building is the tallest building on campus but also sits the lowest. It's within a ravine that runs from near the Columbia River dam to the on-campus lake. It's ten stories tall, mostly glass, asymmetrical, modernistic and gleaming, and sits on the shore of the lake. In fact, about a quarter of the building is on stilts and hovers over the lake. It's a pristine setting and, as Dez draws nearer, with no trees in the way, he gets his first glimpse of the snow-capped Mount Hood, towering over the site to the south. The mountain is snowcapped all year long, Dez has been told. It's stunning. He sees swans and nutria enjoying the lake.

He spots a small research building on his way to the admin building and ducks in there first. Dez is carrying the black-mirrored key cards he stole from the lads he brutalized in that record store. With a card in one hand, and his tablet computer in the other, Dez steps up to the door of the research building and taps the card against the magnetic lock embedded in the wall.

The door clacks open.

On the tablet, no sirens blare and no red lights blink. In fact, it's monitoring this specific building on his screen and there's no evidence that a lock just disengaged.

When Dez smote those lads in the record store, he figured someone at Gamila would deactivate their key cards. But when he realized that the head of security, MacDonald, wasn't even logged in to the system at all, he thought the same might be true for MacDonald's thugs. And it is. The job of updating or deactivating cards probably falls to some junior technician. A technician who was never made aware of MacDonald's thugs or their key cards to begin with.

Dez has the keys to the kingdom.

CHAPTER 40

As Dez reaches the admin building, his phone buzzes. It's Pyotr, telling him that one of the electric carts just started up.

Dez types back: Genius! Nothing here yet.

He taps his mirrored magnetic card on the card reader at the admin building and the pneumatic door hisses open. Dez saunters in, big as life.

There's a receptionist behind a desk, who glares at him and reaches for a phone as Dez heads for the elevators.

Uh-oh.

Well, he was never going to have unlimited time on the campus. That was a given.

He heads up to the top floor, following a diagram on his tablet, and comes to the office of Teddy Meeker, head math nerd of this whole pack; the guy who did his sums and launched a multinational corporation. Dez unlocks the door with his card, then politely raps with a knuckle the size of a warship rivet and enters unbidden.

He isn't prepared for how cluttered and dismal the office is. It likely has a stunning view of the forest, but the vertical slat curtains are pulled. The room's desk isn't impressive; it looks like particleboard crap to Dez's untrained eye. He spots five . . . no, six . . . no, *seven* bookshelves, all crammed with countless books and documents and reams of paper held together with rubber bands, brass brads, or binder clips.

Teddy Meeker sits behind the desk, facing an ultra-new, Clockjack-brand desktop monitor, clacking at the wireless keyboard. He wears a shabby cardigan over a plaid shirt. He wears black plastic reading glasses low on the end of his nose. He could use a haircut and a beard trim. He doesn't look up, but says, curtly, "What?"

Dez closes the door behind him. The room smells of paper mold and dust. "Wotcher, mate."

Meeker looks his way. "What do you . . . ?"

And then recognizes him.

Dez slips his tablet into his messenger bag and raises both hands, palms out. "Calmly now, friend. We've no need of drama."

Meeker looks at him. After a moment, he pivots back to his keyboard and monitor, and resumes typing.

Dez can see him finish a paragraph in a document, then hit Save. He turns back, removes his glasses, and begins cleaning them with his cardigan. "Hello, again. They called from downstairs, said one of Taylor's goons was coming up."

That explains the scowling receptionist and his phone call. He wasn't alerting security, he was warning Meeker. The receptionist must have recognized the mirrored magnetic card. Or maybe the guy thought Dez looks like a goon. That thought hurts, if he's honest.

"Can we talk?"

Teddy Meeker studies him for a while, cleaning his glasses. He reaches up and uses one fingernail to tap a shallow ceramic bowl on his desk, shoving it an inch Dez's direction. The bowl holds assorted Life Savers. Dez has worked in many parts of the world where the exchange of food or tea is a prerequisite to serious conversation. He recognizes the gesture for what it is, and steps forward. "Ta."

He takes a spearmint, shucks its wrapper, pops it in his mouth. There's a cheap folding chair in the corner and Dez gestures toward it.

"Please."

Dez deploys it and sits. "You're a busy fella. Appreciate your time."

"What do you want?"

"Clockjack's been infected by a criminal element, an' they tried to kill a friend of mine. Your bursar lad, Matthew Salerno? He's a Jamaican drug lord who is supposed to be in jail right now. Robert Taylor's name isn't Robert Taylor, it's Gareth MacDonald. He's an ex–British soldier and a mercenary t'boot. An' my guess is: You know all this, sir."

Meeker studies him for a while. "How did you get on campus?"

"With very little difficulty, thank you very much. I've a talent with doors an' gates."

Meeker nods. "When you dropped by PSU, and when I saw how interested MacDonald was in you, I tried to dig up your record. I couldn't. It's been professionally redacted."

Dez smiles and nods, leans back in the metal folding chair. "That'd be nigh impossible for most people to figure out. But you're the one who used the Clockjack government-monitoring programs to crack the code on the Witness Protection Program. You're the reason Demetrious Givens and Cristian Hinestroza and the other hoodlums are here in Oregon."

Meeker reaches for the candy dish and preens a little. "That's right." He pops a candy in his mouth.

"You're the reason the sister of me china was almost killed."

Meeker blanks. "Ah . . . China?"

"Aye. China. China plate. Mate." Dez waits for

comprehension to dawn and it doesn't. "Swear t'God, this continent has got to start speakin' English."

"Wait. So in this context, 'China' is code for—"

"What say we move past it, sir. Given that you're the cause of all this sorrow, option one would be for me to beat the ever-loving shite out o' you."

"I see that."

"On the other hand, always was a better listener than a fighter."

Meeker says, "Whew. Okay, so you figured out that Willard Dukane isn't really Willard Dukane?"

"Aye. He was the first big change here. When Joel Menache died in an auto accident, Dukane came on the scene. His background's a fake. A good one, mind ye."

Meeker nods. "Do they know you're on campus?"

"Will soonish."

"They'll kill you."

"Won't be the first to try."

"What do you need to hear from me?"

"How it all started. An' the abbreviated version'll do."

Meeker thinks about it awhile. He uses the pads of his thumb and forefinger to rub his eyes. He looks tired. "Tell me what you've figured out and I'll fill in the rest."

"Fair, that. You was hoping to sell Clockjack to the Chinese. Would've made ye mad rich. Menache and Hickman weren't having any of it. You called in Dukane to stop Menache, and to get the sale to China."

"Oh. Wow. You actually know more of it than I assumed. That's all accurate."

Dez frowns. "Any particular reason you're being so forthcoming to a perfect stranger such as meself?"

Meeker says, "When we met at PSU, you just looked like a dumb guy who pumps iron. Now I know more about you. And I can't see any way this whole thing here doesn't end with the people behind it killing me, the way they did Menache and Hickman." Meeker smiles a little. "You seem the safer bet."

"Understood. So why were you in favor of the sale, an' the others not?"

Meeker looks at Dez as if Dez is dim. Dez is used to that. "The *money,* Mr. Limerick. I mean, we're all making millions here. The four of us. The Chinese were offering billions with a B."

"But RJ Sharpe and the others didn't want their B Corp baby owned by the Chinese military?"

"Yes. Exactly. RJ was the worst. It was all about our reputation. Reputation is good. Reputation is great. Have you tried buying a steak dinner with reputation?"

The man's a math nerd, Dez reminds himself. End of the day, the dollar figures were on one side of a greater-than-or-equal-to symbol, opposite *doing good.*

"Joel was dead set against the Chinese. Carl Hickman, I could have brought around. If I could get three of us: game over. If I could get two of us, plus persuade the stockholders who own the twenty percent out in the public, game over."

"So: Dukane."

Meeker nods. "His name is John Kite. Do you know who that is?"

"Don't."

"Look him up. He's . . . sort of infamous. Kite came from this old money, New England business family. Fourth-generation fortune. His family owned . . . I don't know, a couple dozen companies. He was chairman of the board for most of them. He was totally corrupt. He'd subcontracted to organized crime to keep unions out of his factories. He had business opponents intimidated or killed. He bribed elected officials and law enforcement. He sold prohibited technology to North Korea and Iran. He even had a defense contractor assassinated. He was a force unto himself. Then an interstate, federal task force caught up with him. Indictments were handed down. For murder, murder for hire, conspiracy. Even treason."

Dez thinks back to the curriculum vitae of Staff Sergeant Gareth MacDonald. The man got caught in the States assassinating a defense contractor. He and Kite had been in business together before this thing in Oregon began.

"I'll guess Kite turned state's evidence, rolled over on his mates?"

Meeker smiles. "That's right. He was in the Witness Protection Program."

"Which you'd cracked."

"Oh yes." Meeker preens. "The first big breakthrough for Clockjack was the taxpaying software, which lets users ride the tides of federal tax cycles to direct where their tax dollars go. At least a little. When I was working on that, I figured out how to get into several very secure government sites. One of which was the U.S. Marshals' Witness Protection Program. I never did anything with this information. But sometimes, when I had insomnia, or was just bored, I'd scour around inside it, looking at some of the people our government has been hiding."

He smiles and fiddles with his reading glasses. "You'd be amazed who our government is hiding away. Did you know that—"

"Elvis? Aye. Owes me ten quid. So anyway, when you needed to stop Menache and Hickman from nixing your China deal, you turned to . . . ?"

Meeker looks a little chagrined about being put back on subject. "I went looking for a ruthless man. A man who understood the importance of maximizing the value of a company. A man who could do the things others couldn't."

Dez says, "Like kill your mates."

Meeker looks directly at him and pauses. "Killing Joel and Carl was *not* the solution I had in mind. I'd hoped there would be a better way."

"How'd this Kite fella proceed?"

"I reached out to him through his false ID in the protection program. I offered to get him out, set him up with a new identity, and to pay him handsomely. He agreed and—*poof*—I made him disappear from the federal databases. When he got to Portland, I laid out the problem to him. He asked me if I could duplicate the trick; get another person out of WITSEC. I told him I could."

"Winston Noel, the moneyman?"

Meeker shakes his head. "No, he came later. Gareth MacDonald, Kite's chief enforcer. He had me bring MacDonald out first. And that's when Joel Menache died in a car accident."

Dez leans forward, elbows on his knees. "Aye. That makes sense, then. John Kite is a business genius but not a killer. He's the kind what hires killers. Chances are, he'd hired MacDonald t'kill the defense contractor you mentioned, back in the day. He brought in MacDonald and did your mate for ye. Made it look like an accident, yeah? But now the sale to the Chinese is back on the table. Ye might've been able to bring Carl Hickman around, you said. So why kill him?"

Meeker settles a bit in his chair, eyes averted, straightening notepads on his desk.

Dez waits.

"Kite told me he could handle Joel—handle him, not kill him—but only if I gave him Joel's job. Made him head of special projects. I turned him down. I told him I'd set him up with a brand-new identity and a couple million dollars, and we'd never see each other again. He agreed. Then he said he needed a right-hand man; that he'd already selected a guy. He said the guy was going to do some dirty work, and if I never knew who this guy was, I'd have deniability, should anything go wrong. I told Kite I'd bring in his man. That was Gareth Mac-Donald."

Dez nods.

"Then Joel Menache dies in a car accident. Kite came to me, with his pit bull, and again told me he intended to take Joel's position, head of special projects. Again, I said no way."

"An' then?"

Meeker reaches out and adjusts some of the messy piles on his desk. He buys time.

"I'm sort of a recluse, Mr. Limerick. Nobody really notices if they don't see me for a week or two, or more."

"So I've heard."

"The one thing I can do . . . the one thing that I do better than anything else? It's math. My brain reverberates with it. I work on mathematical formulas while I'm in the shower. When I'm out walking. When I eat. It's part of my soul."

The man looks pained.

"I have an apartment on the ninth floor. MacDonald came to see me. He, ah, gave me a drug. The effect of the drug was to muddy my brain. Made it impossible to focus on anything."

"Including your sums."

"Yes." A rueful smile. "That's John Kite's genius. He sees the strengths and weaknesses of others. He robbed me of math for two solid weeks, then asked again if he could, pretty please, with a cherry on top, have Joel Menache's job."

He shrugged a little under the shapeless, pilled cardigan. "And I said yes."

Dez leans back, folds his arms over his chest.

"Not long after that, Carl Hickman died; electrocuted working on his home in Lake Oswego." Meeker barks a mirthless laugh. "Working on his home. Carl Hickman couldn't screw in a light bulb. But this guy MacDonald is damn good at his job. The police investigated and called it an accident. Kite ordered me to bring in Winston Noel as the new financial director."

"An' RJ Sharpe?"

Meeker's face flushes. He looks indignant. "I don't know. Honestly. John Kite's willing to sell to the Chinese. Fact is, he seems disinterested in it. It could go either way, and he wouldn't mind."

"Interesting, all by itself."

"I thought so, too. Noel is just a moneyman. He does Kite's bidding. So when we outvoted RJ, I thought she'd go ballistic. And . . . she didn't. Nothing had changed."

Dez ponders this. He'd been assuming Kite was doing all this for profit. Selling to the Chinese military might net him upward of four billion dollars. And he's, allegedly, disinterested in that? Dez does not yet see all the parts of this game.

He asks, "How much does RJ Sharpe know about the deaths of your mates?"

Shrug. "She's the company cheerleader. The carnival barker. That's always been her role, to play us up on the international stage as the model of a progressive, green, socially responsible company. She did that before Kite took over the company. She's doing it still. Does she know that Kite and his goon had Menache and Hickman murdered? Yes, I think she must. She's damn smart. But . . . 'reputation.'" He makes air quotes and sounds as if he disdains the very word.

Dez ponders all of this. "So Kite's taken over your whole company? Soup to nuts?"

"No, not really. The things that Clockjack makes, we still make. You saw all those hardware and software developers out there. They're still making our apps and tech. The marketing teams, the lawyers, the sales teams. None of that has changed. But Kite has a second business. He's running it through Clockjack Solutions. I don't know what he's doing, but they're raking in money, and Noel is using Clockjack money to finance whatever the hell it is Kite's people are doing. I don't know what it is they're doing, but it's expensive."

Dez ponders that. "And it requires the services of Gareth MacDonald and his thugs. Right villains like Demetrious Givens an' Cristian Hinestroza."

Meeker looks puzzled.

"They're two gobshites going by Frank an' Joe. Plus, I've had the distinct pleasure of meetin' . . . dunno, really. A dozen of MacDonald's villains, total."

Meeker blinks at him. "A dozen?"

Dez counts in his head. "More or less, yeah. Dunno how many he has."

"Well," Meeker ponders, "he has more than a dozen."

"D'you have a guess as to how many?"

"Roughly?" Teddy Meeker reaches for the Life Savers. "Three hundred."

CHAPTER 41

Dez blinks. "Three hundred?"

Teddy Meeker smiles indulgently. "Come on. I want to show you something."

He stands and shrugs out of the cardigan, throwing it over the back of his chair, missing, not noticing it puddle to the floor. Dez says, "Three hundred men?"

"I'll explain."

Meeker leads Dez out of his office and to a door marked STAIRS. They don't pass anyone else on this C-suite floor. A door at the opposite end of Meeker's office bears a gold plaque and the words MATTHEW SALERNO—CHIEF FINANCIAL OFFICER. Another corner office door is marked RJ SHARPE—ROCK GODDESS.

"Where's John Kite's office, then?"

"He picked the fifth floor. All of it," Meeker says. "Actually, my key card no longer works on that floor. Who knows what he's up to down there?"

Meeker sees where Dez's eyes have strayed. "That's RJ's office but she's rarely here. She works from home on Mount Tabor, because of its proximity to the airport."

Meeker uses his own magnetic card—his is metallic gold—to open doors. They're on the top floor and Meeker surprises Dez by turning to his left, toward the upstairs. There's only one flight, with a right-angle turn landing in the middle, to get them to the roof.

Meeker's card opens the door.

The roof is a garden. A big one, well kept, and Japanese influenced. Dez sees all the traditional elements: water, stone designs, gently arching bridges, the *yukimi-gata* or snow lanterns. He spots the white blooms of serviceberry. Meeker notices. "These are native of Oregon. Actually, the design, the horticulture, is Japanese, but there are no invasive species here."

"This is what ye wanted to show me?"

"This?" Meeker says. "No."

"Good. 'Cause if ye had an idea of me snow-lanterning the shite out o' MacDonald's men . . ."

Meeker smiles and walks to the eastern edge of the roof, his hand kneading one shoulder while he gently twists his spine. Dez imagines the man has been sitting and typing in that gloomy, ill-lit, poorly ventilated office all morning.

At the edge of the roof, Meeker points to a building, maybe a kilometer away. "When that's finished, it will house Kite's new special project. Project 404. It's essentially dorms."

"For three hundred men?"

"No. Sleeping quarters for, I'd say, fifty guys, maximum? Something like that. Plus a huge gym, and a medical facility, and a cafeteria. MacDonald has been bringing guys in, twenty, thirty at a time, training them, then moving them elsewhere. Outside the USA, I think."

They're ten stories up, and even though the footings of the administration building are in a gully leading to the lake, Dez gets a better perspective of Gamila. He can see more buildings up here; more of the gravel pathways that make up the streetscape of the campus. He also sees—for the first time—that Gamila is laid out on a hilly tract of land made possible by the upriver dam he'd spotted when they'd arrived. He's much closer to the dam than he realized. It likely defines the eastern edge of the campus.

Meeker watches Dez's eyes and sees what he's staring at. "Lower Hood Dam. We bought it from the Bonneville Power Administration. Raised the river level on the other side and let three indigenous tribes renew their sacred fishing. We paid for the restoration. We and the tribes get the hydro energy for free and the tribes even sell some energy on the open market for profit. The footprint of Gamila is such that we share a border, or a suspected border, with the tribes. For every widget we sell, worldwide, the tribes get some of the profit. Since the campus opened, the tribes have seen increases in home ownership, high school graduation, college acceptance, median family income, and health outcomes. Including mental health and behavioral health."

"Ye really did start out trying to do good."

He chuckles. "That was RJ Sharpe. All the way. That thing—to be good stewards of the Earth—that was her mantra from day one. She and I are both Jewish. There's this concept, *tik*—"

Dez says, "*Tikkun olam.* Healin' the world. Aye."

"Well, that was RJ from go. Joel and Carl agreed, right at the start, that we'd be a different kind of company."

Dez's phone and tablet both vibrate. He checks the tablet. "Security just figured out I'm missin'." He takes a moment to end the video loop of himself in the motor pool.

"Then you haven't much time."

"True."

"You also don't know what Gareth MacDonald's really up to."

"Draining the Witness Protection Program of hoodlums like Givens and Hinestroza. To enforce John Kite's will."

Meeker says, "That's only the operational part of it. Here in Oregon. You said you'd met maybe a dozen of those street-level hoods, and you're right. You've met almost all of them. That's not the three-hundred-plus guys MacDonald's had imported. And they didn't come out of WITSEC."

And here Dez was feeling proud to have wrapped his brain around this thing. "What, then?"

"Have you ever heard of a government program called the Wolf Pack Count?"

Dez's mind reels. "Jay-sus. Yeah, that I've heard of. Only in the abstract, though."

"Okay, well, after nine-eleven, the spies and the cops at the federal level decided that it would be a good idea to keep tabs of every person on Earth who gets special forces training, and who then quits, or gets dishonorably discharged, or gets tried for any kind of crimes. The thinking was: We should know the cream of the crop of the world's mercenary class—even future mercenaries. It was a master list of every highly trained, disgruntled, and morally unencumbered killer on Earth. And the staff and mainframes needed to keep such a list of mercenaries were housed—'"

"Within the Witness Protection Program," Dez says, and sighs.

"That's right. A registry of the world's most highly trained bad apples."

"Now in the hands of John Kite, former Fortune 500 arsehole, an' Staff Sergeant Gareth MacDonald, the very model of the modern major terrorist."

"Bingo."

"This isn't just about releasing ne'er-do-wells to do Kite's dirty work here in Oregon. He's building an international army. Nations would pay any price for that kind of trained military unit. Anyone needs to win a war, they just swipe right."

"Swipe . . . ?"

"Nobody ever gets me jokes." He's looking at the size of this clusterfuck for the first time. He's bowled over by it.

Meeker says, "Shouldn't you get going?"

Dez says, "Aye," but doesn't move. "Irony, this. You, bein' done in because ye invited a viper into your company, but the fella ended up being more than simply criminal. Him being a sociopath an' all."

Meeker freezes up a little. He rubs his sore shoulder again. "Ironic, how?"

"Well, you bein' a sociopath yourself, an' all."

Dez studies the dam, and the campus, and the forest, and the glistening top of Mount Hood. After a moment, Teddy Meeker says, "Sure. No question. Petards. Am I right?"

"When you brought in Kite, you were well sure that he'd end up doin' your mate Joel Menache. You say you didn't, but that's shite, that. 'Course you did. Was countin' on it."

"But not necessarily Carl Hickman," Meeker responds quietly.

Dez laughs. "The *necessarily* there's the dead giveaway, my son. Ye'd known them fellas since the 1980s. And killin' 'em fell well within the window o' outcomes you could live with."

They stand awhile.

Meeker says, "I think sociopathy is a spectrum. Like Asperger's? I present on the spectrum. Not as far down as John Kite."

Dez doesn't call horseshit on that, even though he's thinking it.

Meeker looks at his watch. He says, "You should go."

"Aye. You're right. And the good news is: I've decided to help you."

Meeker turns to him. "You have?"

"I have. John Kite, Winston Noel, Sergeant MacDonald. Mad as hatters, the lot of 'em. An' now they've their hands on the list of every ex–special forces fuckwit with a grudge an' a hard-on. That's an army, that is. Can't walk away from this."

Meeker rubs his aching shoulder. "Well. Good. Thank you."

"I'll need a way to contact you without them bastards knowin'."

Meeker recites a telephone number. Dez says, "No head for numbers. Write it down for me."

Meeker scrounges through his pockets and finds a pen, writes on the back of a coffee shop coupon from his wallet. "They don't know about this number. They're not monitoring it."

"Good. Ta. So here's the good news. I'm here t'help."

"Thank God. And the bad news?"

Dez hits him.

Teddy Meeker lies on the immaculately mowed grass of the faux-Japanese landscape, on the roof of a futuristic building tucked between a dam, the mighty Columbia, and the splendor of a national forest, legs akimbo, arms akimbo, fully unconscious.

Dez is too honest with himself not to admit that that felt good.

He takes Meeker's gold-mirrored key card and strolls back toward the stairs.

On the tenth floor, Dez uses Meeker's card to let himself into the office of RJ Sharpe, CEO. Well, also Rock Goddess, according to her doorplate. Dez appreciates anyone who doesn't take themselves too seriously. It's an odd office: no desk, no filing cabinets, no laptop or desktop computers. Dez spots a high-end video camera on a heavy tripod, and boom mics—wearing what looks like wooly jumpers; he can't think of a better way to describe them—standing on tall, counterbalanced poles. Track lighting that can be controlled by a remote control. Sound baffles on the ceiling and east and west walls. A third wall is dominated by a window facing south and the opposite is a massive computer screen.

This isn't an office, it's a studio set of an office.

He slips out, crosses the tenth floor, nods amiably to a passing clerk of some sort, and steps into the office of the chief financial officer, the former Winston Noel.

Noel is a Black man, Jamaican, in his sixties, overweight, with stylish tortoiseshell glasses and balding hair the color of aluminum. His office is immaculate, his suit coat hangs properly over a coat hanger, the sleeves of his crisp white shirt turned up exactly once, each forearm. He looks up from the documents on his desk and says, "Yes?"

Dez strides into the room swinging the door closed in his wake. His smile is infectious and Winston Noel smiles back. Dez doesn't break stride, just barrels into the room and raises one foot, sole on the edge of Noel's antique desk, and shoves, hard as he can.

The desk slams into Noel, slams him back into his ergonomic chair, and slams the chair and the man into the wall. His computer crashes to the floor. Books and documents go flying.

Dez circles the desk and tosses the coffee shop coupon with Meeker's phone number on the blotter. He uses one hand on Noel's forehead, pinning him back into his chair. Dez's hands are large and strong and precise. He presses the pad of his thumb and the pad of his index finger against the major arteries of Winston Noel's neck.

"Name's Desmond Aloysius Limerick. See that card? Your lad Teddy Meeker gave me it. That's his private number. Teddy brought me in to finish you an' Kite. Remember this when you awaken, Winston my son. Ye can't trust Meeker. Best kill him an' be done with it."

The blood has been cut off to Noel's brain and Dez can tell when the man's unconscious. He checks the door. No one seems to be aware of the disturbance. He returns to the side of the unconscious man. Dez picks up Noel's right arm in both of his massive hands; one near Noel's elbow, the other over his wrist. He twists, the way one does when cracking a crab shell.

Under the shearing stress, the unconscious man's scaphoid, lunate, and triquetrum bones crack, the wrist separating from his radius and ulna.

It even sounds like cracking a crab shell.

Dez sets his arm down and carefully breaks the moneyman's left wrist as well.

Noel's agony fights against the imposed unconsciousness and twice Dez has to stop what he's doing, apply pressure to Noel's blood flow, and send him deeper.

In between, Dez retrieves Noel's gold-mirrored magnetic key card. From his messenger bag, he digs out his tablet computer and his card reader, and slides Noel's card into the slot. He watches as fast-cascading rows of green numbers on a black background flash across his screen. When the program is completed, Dez returns the man's key card to his pocket.

He has taken Teddy Meeker's key card, too, but didn't bother replicating it.

Dez turns and saunters out.

Behind the campus canteen, four security personnel have surrounded Pyotr Wiznowski and are demanding to know where his employee, Karel Kaye, is. Now it's five security personnel. Now six. Wiznowski is stammering denials as Dez rounds the corner, driving one of the "miraculously" working carts and towing another, inert one behind.

The blond ex-soldier who'd identified herself as Jenny spins on him. "Where the hell have you been?"

Dez stands straight, hands kneading his lower back, as the carts slow-roll to a stop. "Bolshoi called. Lead dancer broke her leg an' couldn't go on. Thank God I know the number."

Security personnel use two-way radios to check with the security office, where the monitors show Dez, standing there and snarking at Jenny and her mates. There is some yelling. Confusion reigns.

"Two more of the carts are working now," Pyotr, bless him, changes the subject.

And as he speaks another cart blinks to life.

Five minutes later, Dez and Pyotr climb into the old Ford pickup. The blond ex-soldier listens to her two-way and motions to two of her guys. "Trouble at the admin building. Probably got the *toner low* symbol and are freaking out. Again. Head over there anyway." She turns to the men in the pickup. "Mr. Wiznowski, Mr. Kaye: Drive straight to the gatehouse and check in with Dylan before you leave. Don't stray off the path."

"Will do." Dez gives her the thumbs-up and grins as Pyotr guns it.

CHAPTER 42

It's all hands on deck.

John Kite recalls Sergeant Gareth MacDonald to Portland, even though the Scotsman is overseeing, not one, but two military incursions. One in Kenya and one in Tanzania. MacDonald leaves both missions to trusted seconds and flies straight back.

Kite also tells RJ Sharpe to get back fast. She doesn't argue, she books the next flight home from Brussels.

Two nights have passed since campus security was breached. They meet on the private fifth floor of the Gamila headquarters building; the floor that Kite has turned into the headquarters of his covert business within a business.

Using an ultra-secure Clockjack conferencing system—the company had been making business meetings carbon neutral long before the COVID-19 pandemic—Winston Noel attends the meeting from a hospital bed in Portland.

Kite and Teddy Meeker wait for Sharpe and Mac-Donald to arrive for the briefing. Kite looks as retro and uber-trendy as always, with his vintage eyeglasses and baggy suit and satin tie, an inch and a half wide. But he's missing a bit of his Rat Pack cool. He's holding a leaded glass of rye, neat. Meeker has a microbrew beer and it isn't even nine in the morning yet. He also sports a swollen cheek, one eye blackened.

Sharpe enters, dragging her carry-on luggage in her wake, and nods to Kite's drink. "Am I going to need one of those?"

Kite sips. "Oh, I'm pretty sure, yes."

MacDonald arrives with her, his Scots brogue deep and buttery. "We had a break-in?"

"We did."

Sharpe eyes Teddy Meeker's shiner. "My God. What happened?"

Kite turns to the massive, flat wall monitor connecting to the hospital. "Winston?"

Noel is on some serious painkillers, based on the dilation of his eyes. He sits up in a bed, supported by many pillows. Both arms are raised, on foam platforms to his left and right. Both arms are encased in metal rods and springs, some of the rods penetrating the skin of his hands and wrists and arms. RJ Sharpe couldn't see the screen before, from her angle, but now she can.

She gasps.

"He calls himself . . . Limerick." The Jamaican's voice is slow and raggedy from the drugs and the pain. "He bust into my office. He said he'd come to finish . . . John and me. He knew our names. He . . . broke my wrists."

Sharpe throws a hand over her mouth, eyes wide.

MacDonald shakes his head in wonderment. "He told you his name."

Kite sips his rye. "Tell them what else Limerick said?"

Noel looks like he was within a second of drifting to sleep, but stirs himself. His left eye droops from the drugs. "He said . . . Teddy sent him."

Meeker freezes, beer bottle two inches from his lips. With no real emotions, he says, "Oops."

Kite reaches into his trouser pocket and withdraws
a coffee shop coupon with a phone number written on
it. He sets it by Meeker's chair. "Here. You dropped
this."

Meeker inhales a little, exhales a little. He finishes
taking his sip of beer.

RJ Sharpe has her eyes glued to him, and her eyes
are obscured by tears that haven't fallen yet.

"Oh, Teddy."

Meeker shrugs a little and holds the cold glass
bottle against his swollen cheek.

Sergeant MacDonald—ever the soldier—says, "Orders, sir?"

Kite gulps his drink. "Well, I want this Limerick guy
dead, for starters."

MacDonald doesn't snap to. He just deadpans Kite.
"What?"

MacDonald says, "I've met the man. Limerick. He's
trained. He's smart. Disciplined. He came here, did Mr.
Noel like that." MacDonald nods to the monitor, where
Noel has drifted to sleep. "Grassed on Meeker. Left a
calling card. Not figuratively. Left an actual, fucking,
honest-to-God calling card."

Sharpe is staring at Meeker, whom she's known for
more than four decades. She uses the heel of one hand
to wipe tears off her cheeks.

Kite says, "This Limerick sounds like he's one stupid bastard."

"Not him," MacDonald says. "Limerick didn't do all
that to Mr. Noel's arms 'cause he doesn't like the man
personally. He took out your moneyman. We've operations in the field that need materiel. Warlords whose
palms need greasing."

MacDonald turns to Meeker. "Limerick didn't keep
his relationship with Meeker a secret. He grassed on
him 'cause he wants us fractured. Limerick *wants* us

going after him. He's invited us to. We do, and he has us reacting to his plan. Not ours."

Kite crosses to the wet bar and splashes more liquor in his glass, quick-draining it, then repeats. "What do you recommend we do?"

MacDonald nods to Meeker. "How'd you contact Limerick?"

Meeker scratches his thin beard, studiously ignoring the question.

Kite looks from his top mercenary, to Meeker, and back. MacDonald gives him a slight shrug.

"Teddy boy? Answer the nice Scotsman's question, please."

Meeker does not.

"Remember what happened the last time you tried to rise up on your hind legs?"

Meeker directs his answer to RJ Sharpe, rather than to Kite. "Last time, they kept me drugged. Just enough that I couldn't run my numbers. It was hell. That's how they got me to bring in that fat bastard on the screen there."

Sharpe stands, waits, her long muscles fairly vibrating.

"It wasn't a barrel of monkeys, was it?" Kite says.

Meeker leans back in his chair, the bottle again against his cheek. He looks to John Kite, who stands by the wet bar. "So to start," Meeker says, reverting to his inner professor, "you need to understand the difference between risk and uncertainty. From an economist's point of view, I mean."

"You're talking yourself into hell, friend."

Teddy Meeker rolls on, ignoring him. "When an economist talks about risk, it's a given that all consequences are known. A stock will rise, it'll fall, it'll hold pat. That's the risk. It's all completely predictable and quantifiable. But future human events are unknowable. That's uncertainty. We can chart the likely rise or fall of a company's stock, but not whether the CEO is embezzling and will get caught, or if a night guard will drop a cigarette that burns down the warehouse."

Kite is still angry, but now he's curious as well. He makes a rounded waving gesture with his glass. *Go on . . .*

"The first time you drugged me, the risk was that I wouldn't be able to do math, which for a mind like mine, that's like being castrated. The uncertainty was: You're a lunatic but a lunatic with a goal. Would you keep your promise? Would you keep drugging me because you found it funny? Would you kill me? I couldn't tell. Not knowing, I calculated the risks versus the uncertainty and opted to help you free Winston Noel, and then all of MacDonald's goon squad."

"That was a smart play, friend."

"Yes, but now it's a matter of risk and complete certainty, which, for an economist, is a whole new ball game. When I tell you what you want to know, will you keep your promise? No, of course not. That's a given. Will you keep drugging me because you find it funny?" Meeker shrugged, his puffy cheek riding up and down on the cold glass against which it was pressed. "Maybe. Will you kill me? Definitely. Eventually. For absolute sure."

He turns his tired eyes on RJ Sharpe. "You, too, by the way."

He turns back to Kite. "Last time, the calculus of risk versus uncertainty led me to the conclusion that helping you was the smart investment. This time, the calculus of risk and zero uncertainty tells me to tell you to go fuck yourself."

John Kite studies the mathematician for a while. Sergeant MacDonald stands at parade rest. RJ Sharpe stands and vibrates.

Teddy Meeker turns to her. "This would be a good moment to get that drink."

CHAPTER 43

After sneaking onto the Gamila campus two days ago, Dez hacks into the computers of the South Korean cart maker and sends a glowing report about Pyotr Wiznowski's work, recommending a hefty bonus for keeping the people of Clockjack Solutions happy.

He checks in with the Swann sisters. Raziah is writing music like a madwoman; thick notepads of new lyrics.

Laleh has been slogging through the B Corp accounting of Clockjack. She peers at Dez through the pinhole camera of her phone. "I found something really, really weird."

Dez says, "Tons an' tons of Clockjack money pouring overseas?"

She gasps. "Yes! How did—"

"Lucky guess, love. Where's the money going?"

"It's not just a lot of money, Dez, it's Clockjack's entire R-and-D budget. It's millions. It's been going to organizations in . . ." She pauses, dons reading glasses, checks a legal pad. "Kenya and Tanzania."

"What kind of organizations?"

"Not Red Cross, I can tell you that. Political organizations. Maybe even military ones. I can't be sure, because this isn't my area, but I think Clockjack is disrupting the governments of Kenya and Tanzania."

Dez ponders that. "All of them countries, or portions of 'em?"

"Good point. Portions. Like, fomenting rebellion in Kenya's southern region, and Tanzania's northeastern region."

Dez has worked in Africa, but not that far south. He brings up an image of the continent in his head. "There's a tiny little country, right smack in the middle of that region."

Laleh checks her notes. "Yes. I looked it up. Um . . . Zanj. It's what the International Crisis Group calls a failed state. It was financed by piracy for a while, until an international crackdown on the Indian Ocean. Since then: cocaine and heroin."

"Okay, love. I'm beginnin' to see the edges of this thing now, and there's not a chance in hell I would've without that brain of yours."

Laleh smiles, blushes.

"You're a wonder. Your sister and you both. Tell the brat I'm working on gettin' the two of you out from under this thing. My love to Marshal Sims an' his wife."

"Thank you, Dez. Seriously. Thank you."

Dez rings off. Next, he dials a twenty-five-digit telephone number from memory. It's the same number he called when he reached out to Arabella Satti of MI6.

"This mess has gone international, Belle. Need your help. Don't care what you think of me. We need to end this."

He hangs up.

He gets a text forty minutes later.

Deschutes Brewery Portland Public House.
Two hours.

Which means Belle never left Portland. *Interesting,* Dez thinks.

The brewery is a massive restaurant, not far from Powell's. Easy for two people to get themselves lost in so big a place, and to chat with some privacy. He takes one of those electric scooters and gets there early. He gets a table and asks for a pint and a chip butty.

The waiter, all tattoos and lumberjack beard, says, "What's that?"

"Chip butty? Serious-like?"

The guy shrugs.

"Bonkers. Ye've never had that? It's brilliant. Take chips—French fries, to the likes of you—between buttered white bread, yeah? Add brown sauce, ketchup, a little mayonnaise—"

The waiter says, "Dude, at this point, I'd pay you to stop describing it."

"Philistine. Fish-an'-chips, kindly."

Arabella Satti shows up exactly on time. She glides elegantly into the booth on Dez's side, so they'll be shoulder to shoulder and can speak sotto voce. She apparently has been here long enough to order herself a vodka martini with two olives. Dez makes a mental note of her drink of choice. Several eyes in the room follow her.

Arabella smiles sweetly. "Have you suffered from festering boils on your testicles?"

"I have not."

"God answers all prayers; sometimes the answer is no."

"Ye look a sight."

She does, in a fawn-colored leather bomber with fur collar, ivory shirt, leather trousers, and suede ankle boots. Spies learn how not to get noticed, but the side effect of that is learning the opposite.

She says, simply, "How bad is it?"

Dez leans his shoulder into hers, keeping his voice low. "A group of very well-financed criminals have rooted themselves within Clockjack Solutions. The leader's an indicted Fortune 500 CEO, name of John Kite. The money's being laundered by a Jamaican drug lord, Winston Noel. Our lad Gareth MacDonald, former SAS? He's serving as field commander. Here." He takes a slip of paper out of his satchel and slides it across the table. "I wrote all the names down, seein' as how you went to private school."

The insult gets a laugh out of her and she's more surprised by the laugh than Dez is. "Cheeky bastard."

"I thought them fuckers was gathering criminals to pull off heists here in Portland. Was thinkin' way too small, me. They're importing a few criminals to run interference for 'em in Portland, aye, but more importantly, they're also importing special forces blokes to build an army. As big as three hundred soldiers. So far. Calling themselves Project 404."

Arabella's smile fades. Dez studies her eyes, the color of maple syrup.

"I'd meant to ask ye if Six had heard any hint o' this. Now I'm thinkin' I don't have to ask."

Arabella sips her drink. "No, you don't. Yes, we have. They're in East Africa. Stirring up anti-government forces in—"

"Kenya and Tanzania."

"Exactly. Threat analysis has been pinging for months, but nobody knows where they're coming from. They're fast and efficient. Some warlord needs a few dozen men. They show up, mow down the opposition, then disappear like thistles on the breeze."

"This is them, aye. Project 404."

"Four oh four," she says. "File not found. Clever. And you're sure about this?"

"Am. Got inside their operation long enough to prove it. Also kicked 'em in the acorns, just for laughs."

Arabella says, "You risked your life simply to annoy them?"

Dez grins.

"Wonders just ceased. Why are they doing this?"

"I've a theory, and it's only that. Bloke name of Meeker got the ball of shite rolling downhill by hacking the Witness Protection Program. That got all of the primaries in this scheme together. Next, started gathering mercs by hackin' into the Wolf Pack Count."

"Oh, fuck me," she exhales.

"My reaction exactly. The big brains behind all this is John Kite. My guess is: He knows the hack into Witness Protection can't last forever. The hack into the directory of the world's likely best-trained mercenaries can't last forever. Hidin' inside Clockjack, and in Oregon, can't last forever."

"So he's building himself a theme park," Arabella says. Her tactical mind is a wonder. It took Dez ages to figure this out and she just leaped to the same conclusions between sips of her martini. "Some place with no extradition. Like Zanj. Vast stacks of money to buy warlords there, and mercs to stir up anti-government rebels in Kenya to the north and Tanzania to the south. This John Kite will build himself a Xanadu where U.S. law enforcement can't touch him, with enough money and enough soldiers to make his own little city-state."

"Maybe even more'n that," Dez says. "Kite's thinking about the future. Did a bit of research into that part of the world. Zanj has maybe the world's largest untapped resource of a chemical element called tantalum."

Arabella picks up her own mobile and waggles it in the air. "Which is used in every mobile and personal computer on Earth. Not to mention nuclear reactors, and aircraft parts, and missile parts. If Zanj wasn't run by Indian Ocean pirates and cocaine cowboys—if it had a stable government and it ever got around to mining its tantalum—it could become a new UAE."

"Aye. Tiny city-state, all the money they'd ever need. I think that's Kite's endgame."

"So warn the Yanks," she says.

"I would. Problem is, a fella name of Teddy Meeker dreamt up software that lets him hack the ever-loving fuck out of the federal agencies. Plus, I talked to a right ledge at the U.S. Marshals Service. He's under heavy political pressure to stay well clear of Clockjack. The pressure's comin' down on law enforcement and intelligence agencies alike."

"And would this John Kite have the balls to carry something like that off?"

"Would, aye. Man's brilliant. Lobster-shit crazy, mind you, but brilliant. Now he's got an army, and vast sums of Clockjack money, and his eyes on an exit strategy, to become the next high-tech power broker of East Africa. And t'ride out his years in comfort."

Arabella thinks about this awhile, her eyes unfocused, calculating. After a moment, her eyes snap-lock onto Dez's. "It appears I need a new drink."

Dez gets her a new martini and himself a new beer. When he's back, Arabella says, "What do you want?"

"I've disrupted 'em. Took out their finance boffin. Got the leadership fightin' amongst themselves. Likely did enough damage to recall MacDonald from whatever he was up to in Africa. Bought a bit of time."

"Where do we come in?"

"Your lot can't operate on U.S. soil. But knowin' what you know now, could the Aunts and Uncles step in, try an' disrupt the hot spots?"

In Western intelligence circles, an informal alliance of high-level intelligence leaders is known as the Aunts and Uncles. When necessary, high-ranking career agents in England's MI6 can reach out to high-ranking career agents in Germany's BND, Spain's CNI, France's DGSE, America's CIA, and others. The back-channel communications allow for actions to happen quickly. It's rarely used, as Dez knows.

Arabella says, "Anything's possible."

"Good. If you an' yours can make sure the mercenary operations go balls-up, I can get into Clockjack and decapitate this thing. I'll just need time."

"Do you need weapons?"

The offer surprises him. "It's America, love. They've guns everywhere. When American homeowners clean out their rain gutters, they find assault weapons. I can find whatever it'll take t'get the job done. What I need is their field operations t'know that you lot know who they are, and where they hail from. Get the word out about Project 404 an' the Clockjack connection. Rob 'em of their anonymity. Get the buyers—the warlords, the drug lords, the strongmen—second-guessing the resource. That'll preoccupy 'em whilst I make a right nuisance of meself."

"Your gift to the world."

"Aye." He takes it as a compliment.

"How can you stop this group?"

"Brisk conversation."

She finishes her drink. She sums up the situation. "A high-tech juggernaut of a company, serving as an exoskeleton for a three-hundred-man mercenary army, well financed and well orchestrated. Versus a retired, guitar-playing lunatic with a hard-on, a righteous mien, and a false sense of adequacy."

"Could be a laugh."

She studies him. "But you could have told me all this over a secure web link. Or by phone. There is something else you need from me."

Dez drinks some of his beer, pondering the situation. He is not one hundred percent sure he should share this next bit with Arabella. After a moment, he turns to her and lays out a contingency plan that he wants up his sleeve.

The kind of contingency plan he prays he'll never need.

Arabella is shocked and lets it show. "You're bloody serious!"

"Am." He speaks softly. "Unfortunately."

"You'd actually do this?"

"Not happily. Not without some soul-searchin'."

He drinks more beer.

"You want me to . . . ?"

"Aye, an' with a video link from your scope."

She ponders, and he gives her the time to do so. The lively restaurant thrums around them. Dez is asking the moon and the stars, and it's not like Arabella Satti is all that fond of him to begin with.

She stirs herself at some length. She studies him.

"When you choked me out and left Ray Harker to die in that factory in Chechnya, I hated you."

"I know."

"MI6 hasn't given me tactical control of a field team since. I doubt they ever will."

"Wasn't my intent, and I apologize."

Her eyes dart from his left eye to his right and back again.

"I do this thing for you, and word ever gets out, my career won't simply be stalled. I'll be waitressing. I'll be out. I can't do it. I can't."

Dez opens his big, calloused hand, palm up, over the table.

After a beat, Arabella places her hand in his.

He squeezes.

"I understand. I do. I need an equalizer, and this

would do, but it's also not a thing you can bring yourself t'do, and I can respect that."

She squeezes his hand back. She stands.

Arabella says, "You and I will never be mates. Too
much between us. But I can respect what you're doing.
And I'd help if I could."

"You've already helped. Grateful."

She heads for the door. She looks over her shoulder.
"Good luck, Limerick. Save the girls."

CHAPTER 44

Gareth MacDonald knocks on the door to John Kite's office.

"Come!"

The entire fifth floor of the admin building on the Gamila campus has been turned over to Kite and MacDonald, and to Project 404. It serves as the command center for Kite's plan to flee the U.S. and set up a tiny sheikdom in Zanj. Safe from extradition, and sitting on a buried and unbelievable fortune of minerals.

Kite isn't sure, but suspects he is really going to enjoy this potentate gig.

His corner of the fifth floor hovers out over the lake, with a view of Mount Hood, and a spacious balcony. It's elegantly appointed with Kite's usual flair for 1960s pop. He's created a kind of space-age, bachelor-pad vibe. Kite has an artificial strip of grass adhered to the floor, complete with a regulation golf hole at one end. MacDonald often finds the man practicing his putting, and today is no exception. Kite putts and misses, to the left, by an inch. He uses the putter head to nudge the ball back up where it started. He stands over the ball, putter straight down, adjusting his weight from leg to leg. He's wearing cream-and-brown saddle shoes, and his suspenders perfectly match the brown of the vamp of the shoes.

"Want to know what I like about this Desmond Limerick guy?" he says. "He's driven to do good, to do the right thing—which is a character flaw, but I'm not judgmental. I get that. But here's the thing I like: He's not above going for the funny while he's doing it."

MacDonald says, "Sir?"

"Breaking into this place was pretty much impossible, right? Getting back out again? Impossible."

"Pretty much," MacDonald concedes.

"Limerick broke in here using the name Karel Kaye. It took me a while to figure it out. Carol Kaye was a legendary Hollywood bass player. That was her, laying down the bass line for the theme song to *Mission: Impossible,* late sixties. I mean, breaking into this place was an impossible mission, but our fella, Limerick? He doesn't just carry it off. He goes for the rim shot."

MacDonald thinks about this awhile. He finds himself smiling, a little impressed. Kite takes another swing; misses by the same one inch, again to the left. He bats the ball back to the other end.

"I've a crazy idea, sir. I think I can reach out to him."

Kite glances up. "Who?"

"Limerick."

"You mean, reach out to him with the business end of a shotgun?"

"No, I mean parley. Sergeant to sergeant."

"And how do you know this dude's a sergeant?"

A quick, self-satisfied smile flicks across MacDonald's handsome features. "'Cause I'm a sergeant, aren't I."

"You *were,* sure."

The Scotsman shrugs. "I've served with all kinds. The laziest, stupidest, most corrupt sergeants you can imagine. And the really good ones. Like to think I was a good one. Oh, corrupt as fuck, of course. Don't deny that. But I know a good sergeant when I see one."

Kite is intrigued now. "And what are the telltale signs of a good sergeant?"

MacDonald says, "Takes care of his people. Gets them out of harm's way. Deals with problems. Rarely asks permission in advance. Breaks rules to get the job done. Never seems hurried or worried."

Kite smiles. "You do seem to be describing yourself."

"And Limerick. I'll bet every coin in my pockets against every coin in yours, sir. Man's been a sergeant."

"And that knowledge is going to help you track this shitbird down?"

"I think we might have some of the same friends, from back in the day, sir. Might be able to send word to him. Get him to meet with me."

Kite looks lost. "And why, in the name of holy Mary, mother of fuck, would you want to do that? You want to recruit him?"

MacDonald shrugs. "Possibly. I'd rather have him inside the tent, pissing out, then outside the tent, pissing in. But even if I couldn't buy him off, I think the man's a realist. If he sees he's got no chance against us, he might back off. I'll offer up the sisters, the Swanns. If I say they're no longer a target, Limerick might walk."

Kite studies him. MacDonald stands, waits.

"You're serious."

"I am, sir."

"You think you can make this all go away with, ah, what's the word I'm looking for . . . ?"

MacDonald says, "Words."

"That's it."

"If Limerick's what I think he is, and if I keep sending these scum-of-the-earth criminals against him, we're just going to keep piling up bodies. From a cost-benefit analysis alone, it's a loser."

"So you'll talk to him. And if he won't play ball?"

"Then we stop sending drug runners and Mafia hit men after him. And we send our fucking army. Sir."

CHAPTER 45

The time had come for some solitude and some research and planning.

Dez finds a house in Portland he can use as a base of operations. He knows very bad men are looking for him, and he has no intention of jumping from hotel to hotel. It's inconvenient.

The house he finds gives him plenty of room to spread out blueprints; some of which he gets by paying a fee, some of which he hacks. The house has high-speed internet access, too, which is vital in the research phase. Also plenty of refrigerator room for beer. The essentials.

He scours the United States Geological Survey, which is a federal agency, as well as the Oregon Department of Geology and Mineral Industries. He learns everything he possibly can about the Gamila campus.

He goes online to buy a high-quality AR-15-style rifle. An ArmaLite knockoff. That fact that one can buy such a gun online is totally bonkers, Dez thinks. But there it is. The site he goes to is overseas but it provides him with exactly what he requires at this time.

He's getting everything ready when his phone and his tablet computer both ping. It's an unusual sound, so he checks the source. It's an email on a server that Dez has used very few times over the past five years.

It's a sort of Bat-Signal, if you will. It is not to be ignored.

The email contains an international telephone number and nothing more.

Dez checks the perimeter of the house he's been using and spots no trouble. He makes the call—not on his phone—but via his tablet computer, routing the call through two servers, one in Kazakhstan and one in Uruguay. Even with the big brains at Clockjack Solutions searching for him, it would take a miracle for anyone to track this call.

He dials.

The voice that answers is familiar. Masculine, with a laugh hiding just behind the words, always. "*Cousin? This is you?*"

Cousin is a high compliment to the Kel Tamasheq. Outsiders call them Tuareg; a nomadic tribe of North Africa.

Dez replies in his halting Tamasheq; he's good, but not fluent. "Mojahad! I am pleased to hear from you, cousin. Is everything all right?"

"Yes, yes. My people are well. Well enough."

Mojahad is a *chef de tribus* to a clan that has known nothing but strife in Chad and Libya for as long as anyone can remember. He and Dez are mates. Dez has saved his life and he has saved Dez's. And equally important, it was Mojahad who gave Dez his first bass guitar.

"I am owing a favor to a man," Mojahad says. "This man wishes to speak to you. *En parley.*"

The Kel Tamasheq don't hold much love for the French. Using the term suggests how important this is.

"The man, cousin?"

"A soldier, like us. A sergeant, like you."

MacDonald.

"I would be foolish to trust such a man," Dez says, picking his words carefully. It's been ages since he's spoken this dialect.

"This man is owed a favor by the *amenokal*. He is making this plea on that debt. I believe him to be good for his word."

An *amenokal* is the leader of several clans in the Kel Tamasheq. A sort of sultan. Gareth MacDonald has called in serious markers to have this call made. Which means he has spent time with the nomadic tribes of North Africa. As he might have, when he was SAS.

"There is a message for me?"

Mojahad relays the message.

"And you believe I should trust this man?"

Mojahad says, "I would trust him this one time, at this one place. But not elsewhere. I believe he will honor parley. Once."

"That's good enough for me, cousin."

The man on the line laughs. He switches to English. "Your dialect is for shit, *chef*."

"Aye. Been living in the States. Not a lot of call for it hereabouts."

"I miss you. I hope you are well."

"I am making friends and allies, cousin. I am trading favors and I benefit from the trades."

For a nomad like Mojahad, this statement is a big deal. "This is good. Stay healthy. Trust this man only once. And do not underestimate him. He's a great soldier. As good as you. Nearly as good as me."

"I'll meet with him. But when the music changes, then the rhythm of the dance must change also."

Mojahad laughs. "I taught you that."

"Aye. You did."

"Stay safe, cousin."

Dez disconnects and thinks about how many strings and favors Sergeant Gareth MacDonald had to pull to get a tribal chief of the Tuareg to play the intermediary. And how much MacDonald has figured out about Dez.

It's an uncomfortable amount.

Dez sends a text to the number his old friend, Mojahad, gave him.

CHAPTER 46

The restaurant is in a shabby sector of downtown Portland called Old Town Chinatown. It appears to have been serving breakfasts from the same location since World War II, judging by the black-and-white photos on the wall. The place has seven tables, rickety and sunfaded, and the shelves hold an obscure array of political tchotchkes from Oregon's past.

The waiter is overweight, jowly, and unsmiling. If the restaurant has been serving food since the 1940s, his apron might have been in use, unwashed, just as long.

Dez scouts the neighborhood yet again—his fifth pass since the sun came up. Hours ago, he broke into a low-income apartment building, accessed the roof, and scouted for snipers. He spotted an alcove across the way, in the entrance of a gone-bust sporting goods store. It's shaded and deep, and the windows around it are grungy enough to obscure the vision of onlookers. If Dez wanted to do a street-level stakeout, that'd be just the thing.

He's taken every precaution he can think of besides the obvious, which is to turn down MacDonald's invitation to parley.

Dez goes with his gut and, at the precise hour, 8 A.M., he enters the dingy restaurant and sits opposite the blond Scotsman.

MacDonald has ordered blueberry pancakes, and by the time Dez sits, he's devoured half. He's got coffee, which came in a white ceramic cup, black piping, that seems like an artifact of the fifties.

"That any good?" Dez asks.

MacDonald rolls his eyes. "Fecking unbelievable. Everything here is. An' cheap. Should be a line 'round the block to get in here. Not them fancy, gentrified places, with their avocado toast an' whatnot."

The waiter comes by. "Coffee," Dez says. "Black. Four eggs, over easy. Hash browns. Bacon."

The waiter doesn't even nod. He just turns the table's second white-and-black cup right side up and pours, spilling a bit, then walks away on tender knees.

MacDonald scarfs his food. "How's your gut? Where I shot you?"

"Healing, thanks. If you knew to reach out to the Tuareg, an' to me cousin, then you know who I am."

MacDonald nods, eyes on his food. He swallows, follows the food with a slurp of coffee, wipes his lips with a brown paper napkin from the tin dispenser.

"When I was SAS, I heard about your old unit, Sergeant . . . it is sergeant?"

Dez says, "*Maréchal des logis-chef,* if ye please."

MacDonald smiles. "Thought so. *Chef,* it is. I heard about you lot. Thought it was an urban myth. Soldiers trained to do one fecking thing brilliantly: to take a door, hold the door, *own* the door." He shakes his head in wonderment. "Gatekeepers."

Dez sips the very hot coffee. It's terrific.

"My mates, SAS? We could get through any door. *Any* door," MacDonald says, using the edge of his fork to cut off another triangle of the three-high stack of pancakes. He chews, eyes rolling. "So good. Anyway, we could get through any door. But stupid twats that we were, we didn't know what to do once we got

inside. We figured, if we lose one man or two, and accomplish the mission, well . . ." He shrugged. "That's
not bad odds. Losing men's what you do when you're a
soldier, aye? It's the price you pay for doing business.
But then I heard about you lot, *chef.* Gatekeepers. Soldiers given the training, and the education, to understand how to keep a door. What've you got? You don't
mind my askin'. Degree in electrical engineering, is it?
Structural engineering?"

The waiter waddles their way with a plate of eggs and
crispy hash browns and perfect bacon, and two slices
of unasked-for sourdough toast, cut into triangles. Dez
lifts his hand, two fingers spread.

MacDonald grins. "Double major. 'Course you are.
Masters or doctoral?"

Before Dez can answer, the morose waiter plops
down the plate in front of him. "You from Scotland,
too?" he mutters.

"Ta," says Dez. "For a bit. Couple a' years growin'
up. Edinburgh."

The waiter fills both coffee cups. "Worst goddamn food on the planet. Hands down. Tribes in South
America eating ants and grubs, telling themselves,
shit, at least we're not in Scotland." The man's unsmiling face never changes. He sounds sad to have to share
this information. "Tell you guys something. This is
free advice, me to you. Cows' stomachs aren't musical
instruments, and they're not entrées. Okay? Just stop
with that shit. There. Free advice. Tip accordingly."

He shakes his head in sadness and waddles away.

Dez takes a forkful of eggs, and then a forkful of
the potatoes, and then snaps off a rasher of bacon. He
looks at MacDonald and says, "Jesus preserve me."

"Told you. I'm running an extra fifty kilometers a
week, just to make up for the carbs I'm getting here, but
I'm fecking addicted."

Dez is near tears as he tries the toast. "Transcendent," he says around a mouthful of food.

Chewing, MacDonald nods, agreeing. He says, "I've family in Edinburgh. A sister in Stirling, two uncles in St. Andrews. That whole area."

Dez chews his food like it's a timed event.

"You need to leave us alone, *chef.*"

Dez nods. He adds Tabasco to his potatoes.

"We'll forget about the Swanns. My word. Sergeant to sergeant. You walk away, they're off the table."

Dez pats grease off his lips with a paper napkin. "Your guv'nor, Kite? He's psychotic. Kite's got a skull full of badgers. Your word's worth shite if you can't control the man ye work for."

MacDonald takes no umbrage at this. "First thing to know is: The man's only interested in his profits, and his creature comforts, and his safety. Yeah? If he thinks you an' the sisters have no impact on his life span, and his creature comforts, then you mean naught to him. He'll forget your name in a week. Second thing to know: He couldn't fire a gun to save his life. Hands have never formed a fist. He wants you dead, he goes to me. If I say I've sworn to leave you an' yours alone, what's he going to do? An' before you ask: Every man jack of that outfit answers to me alone. Not a one of 'ems ever even had a conversation with Mr. Kite. If I swear the sisters are safe, you should get 'em to invest in a retirement home. They'll need it."

MacDonald's plate is empty. The waiter waddles over, takes the plate, tops off the coffee cups. "Caber toss," he says, his jowls quivering when he shakes his head. "Throwing a log, calling it a sport. Seriously. What the fuck, dudes."

Dez wonders if the waiter hates Scotland only, or if he's more egalitarian than that. "Lived in Ireland, too," he says, just to see if the guy will take a swing.

The waiter takes his now-empty plate, stacking it on MacDonald's. He picks them both up, and the utensils. "Drunks," he sighs. "Plus, rugby? That's not a sport, that's a prison riot."

When he's gone, MacDonald reaches for a small jar next to the napkin dispenser that holds toothpicks. "Second day here, I told him me grandfather lived in Australia. He told me kangaroos are the world's biggest, scariest rats."

"Could be that's true. Never been."

MacDonald says, "Marsupials. Do we have a deal? You leave us alone, the sisters live an' never have to look over their shoulders. My people leave you alone."

Dez also reaches for a toothpick. The food was unbelievably good and he's in no hurry to finish the coffee. He says, "So Kite's bugging out?"

MacDonald sits sideways on his side of the booth, the toothpick exploring. Dez mimics him. They've the place to themselves. MacDonald says, "Aye. An' soon. Can't tell you where, but these two things will be the gospel truth: From where he's going, international law enforcement will be able to do fuck all to him. He'll be our lad from Krypton, yeah? Bullets bouncing off the big red S."

The failed African state of Zanj, but Dez doesn't let on that he knows. "An' the second gospel truth?"

"If U.S. law enforcement can't touch the guv'nor, what the fuck will he care about a lounge singer and a reporter from Portland, Bumfuck, Oregon?"

That's all a pretty good argument for standing aside. It actually is. Dez hadn't known how the parley with MacDonald would go, and finds himself impressed.

But he needs to know more.

"First, Kite'll need a place with no extradition," Dez says. "Second, he'll be giving up the money spigot of Clockjack when he leaves, so he'll need an ongoing funding source, once he's there. Third, would have to be a stable place, yeah? I know dark corners in South America, Africa, Far East'll get you one of them three. Maybe two. But all three? 'Less your man's joining Starfleet, I don't see him finding his utopia."

MacDonald grins. "That's the beauty bit. It's already set up, *chef.* Kite's mad as a hatter but he plays the long game. He's measuring the drapes already."

"An' how do I know that's true?"

MacDonald studies Dez and Dez studies his coffee cup. The waiter mopes by and refills.

MacDonald says, "Okay. I'll tell you something coming up, on your word of honor you'll do naught to interfere."

Dez needs the information. He needs to know more. He says, "Word of honor."

MacDonald leans in closer. "Ever hear of an assassin calling himself Thiago?"

"Have. *Washington Post,* was it? Did a piece on him. Decades-long manhunt. Supposed to be God's gift to the godless."

"He's all that. I met with the man, Thursday last. D'you know Malpensa?"

"Do." Dez has been to the airport serving Milan, Italy, many times.

"Right. I met him. We shook hands, and we both watched while Mr. Kite's bank put money in Thiago's bank. That money? Had two commas amid the zeds. Following me?"

Dez is. "You're havin' someone assassinated?"

"Not just someone. Someone big. It'll happen within twenty-four hours, and it'll make headlines. And as soon as that happens, you know I'll be handling the transit for Kite and his mob, from here to that utopia you were worried about, *chef.* We'll be in the wind. You an' the sisters, free of care. You've my word on it."

They sit for a spell. It's a lot to take in. The waiter brings more coffee, and the checks. MacDonald takes both checks, throws down money for both and a hefty tip. It was he who called for parley. Fitting he buys.

Dez said, "You didn't try to bribe me."

"Your skill set?" MacDonald laughs. "Jesus, but you could name your price. Not a private military contractor on Earth wouldn't build a trebuchet to hurl bales of money your way, just to get you on their team. I knew money wasn't going to do it."

"I'll take that as a compliment."

"Was meant as such. And you never ragged me about being corrupt. About takin' a quid from a stark raving madman and killin' for money."

Dez says, "Every professional soldier takes money for killing. Every time the paymaster came 'round, I took me envelope. An' spent it, too. I don't judge."

MacDonald slurps a little more coffee, then edges out of the booth and stands. Dez does, too. He holds the cup and calls across the not-well-cleaned room to the waiter. "Can I get this t'go?"

The waiter never looks up from the sports section of the *Tribune*. "No."

"Okay. Ta."

MacDonald offers his hand. Dez shakes.

"Gimme twenty-four hours?" Dez says. "I need to watch for them headlines Thiago's delivering. And this decision isn't all on me. Got to talk to the Swanns."

"Fair." MacDonald nods and exits first.

Dez waits a full minute, then exits, too.

The parley is complete.

CHAPTER 47

Dez is expecting company, so he does some shopping. He uses a false ID to rent a car. Online, he finds a place that likely will have what he needs for the coming days. He drives to a suburban mall. The store now is called, simply, Bud's, but he can see from the old signage that it used to be a Linens 'n Things. A guy in a Jamaican beanie and tie-dyed shirt says, "Help you, man?"

Dez points to the old signage. "D'you think, when they was starting up that old chain of stores, they just couldn't come up with a second noun?"

The guy nods. "I've pondered that a lot. Linens 'n Bricks, Linens 'n Ramen. Pretty much any second noun would have worked."

"First interview at a bank, to get their seed money, yeah? Like, 'I'm opening a chain o' shops. Plan to sell linens and at least one more physical object, but haven't figured out what, yet. Down to marmosets and sheet-rock, I think. So, about that loan . . . ?'"

The guy laughs and helps Dez find the very items he's needing. Folded cardboard boxes with lids, a couple pounds of nails, bolts, and nuts. He even finds a couple of air cannons; those funky devices used by cheerleaders to shoot T-shirts into the upper decks of stadiums. One end rack has prepaid mobile phones, two to a pack. Finally, small and inconspicuous GoPro cameras.

"This place is a bloody marvel!" Dez says.

"You need it, I got it, brother," Jamaican Beanie says to the flourish of hip-hop moves.

"You're a gem, you. Shoulda sold Linens 'n Things t'you. Would still be thriving, them!"

Dez drives back to the house he's been squatting in.

All this shopping, and buying an AR-15 knockoff from the Philippines, has begun to take a toll on Dez's savings. So he snoops around the house and discovers a Post-it Note of logins and passwords. Dez is amazed how many otherwise-intelligent people do that. With the passwords, it's child's play to break into the home-owner's foreign accounts and to drain them into one of Dez's overseas accounts. There. No further problem of rapidly dwindling funds. Dez had been sure easy money would find its way to him. It always does.

But now he's having second thoughts about his par-ley with Sergeant Gareth MacDonald. Can Dez trust this man? It was a parley, and it was backed by a fairly powerful and influential Kel Tamasheq chieftain. And the simple truth is: Dez doesn't harbor much animosity for MacDonald. The man's a soldier. He follows orders. The same's been said of Dez, years past.

Different time, different place, and they'd have been mates. Dez is sure of it.

But something's nagging.

MacDonald was at the airport serving Milan, a week ago Thursday. To meet with an illustrious assassin. Dez has heard about an app, which he downloads into his tablet. The app works like this: You give it a specific time and a specific place, and it'll search Twitter and Facebook and Instagram and TikTok and lord knows where else, looking for social media photos that correspond.

Dez does the research and inputs the exact latitude and longitude for Malpensa. He sets the parameters and hits Enter.

He takes a long hot shower, dries off. He raids the kitchen for bottled water.

He sits in an easy chair with his tablet on his lap and begins zooming through hundreds and hundreds and hundreds of social media snaps, taken that day, in that airport in western Italy.

It takes him ninety minutes to spot a girl, mugging for the camera with her mates. And behind her, not twenty meters away, is Gareth MacDonald.

He was there that day. So far his story is holding up.

Dez scans more. He finds two more images of MacDonald.

Two hours in, he spots MacDonald shaking hands with another man near one of the many bars in the departures area. The other man is blond, handsome, holds himself with an authoritative air. He's maybe six-two.

The famed international assassin, Thiago.

Dez calls the twenty-five-digit number. The one that summons Arabella Satti of MI6.

She calls him back inside of five minutes. "The Swann sisters?"

"Still safe for now," Dez whispers.

"You sound oddly less idiotic than usual. What's wrong?"

"Sending you a snap."

"All right."

He does. It'll take the photo a minute or more to snake its way through the MI6 antivirus filters.

"Gareth MacDonald," he says. "Taken a week ago Thursday, at Malpensa. He's meeting with an assassin name of Thiago."

Arabella says, "Heard of him! We've never been able to get near him. No Western agency has. Limerick, if you've a photo of Thiago . . . My God! This is huge!"

Dez says, "Aye."

A pause, and she says, darkly, "What? What is it you're not telling me?"

He says, "Wait for it."

"All right. Ah . . . image coming in now. That's Mac-Donald, with the full sleeves of ink, yeah, and . . ."

Her voice fades out.

Dez waits.

Arabella whispers, "My God."

"Aye. Thiago. The famed assassin. Once known as Ray Harker, CIA. Your former lover."

CHAPTER 48

The following day, John Kite calls Gareth MacDonald into his fifth-floor office.

"We had some super-shitty luck today. Our evac is delayed. We'll be here another week."

MacDonald senses something very, very wrong. "That killer. Thiago. He was hitting the Tanzanian president today. Did . . . ?"

Kite is fixing himself a highball. "Nope. The president's alive. It looks like British intelligence got wind of the hit and interfered." He doesn't sound overly worried. "This puts us back a week. No more. I've got contingencies." He sips his drink, sighs.

"Thiago?"

"Apparently he didn't get captured. There was a shoot-out. He got free, I guess. Whatever. I just need you to know that this affects our exit date. So: Plan accordingly."

MacDonald stands for a bit. He has a masterful poker face, and right now it's showing nothing. Nothing at all. He hasn't told his employer that he used the information about Thiago and the hit to convince Limerick that they would all be leaving the States, and soon.

British Intelligence stopped the hit?

Limerick is British.

Kite says, "What?"

MacDonald nods. "Just thinking, sir."

"Okay. Whatever. And this, ah, Limerick guy?"

"Oh, he's still a threat," MacDonald says, and means it. "Wish talking had been enough. Wasn't."

"Well, since we're delayed here in Oregon, I'd say sooner rather than later. Capisce?"

MacDonald nods. "Aye, sir. Think I know where t'start. You used your political muscle to get the feds to back off Clockjack. My sources tell me the last federal cop to leave Portland was a deputy U.S. marshal from Virginia. Virginia's a long way from Oregon. A very, very long way."

Kite said, "I'm from America, bubba. I know it's a long way away."

MacDonald says, "The distance from Portland to Virginia is about the same as the distance from London to Damascus, Syria."

Kite sips his drink, smacks his lips. "Okay, I didn't know that. What's your point?"

"I want to see what this marshal in Virginia—this Conroy Sims—is to Limerick. See if there's a connection."

"So you can track Limerick down?"

MacDonald says, "Not trying to track him down, sir. Looking to track down the sisters he came to Portland to protect. They went missing 'bout the same time that U.S. marshal left Portland. Like I said before: Sergeants take care of their people. The Swann sisters are Limerick's people."

"And you think this marshal might lead you to them."

MacDonald nods. Kite ponders, but only a little. He makes a *chk* noise with his cheek. "It's good. It tracks. Get on it."

Gareth MacDonald returns to his cubicle on the fifth floor of the administration building on the Gamila campus. MacDonald could have asked for an office, with a door and everything, but he prefers to work in a bullpen atmosphere. A trio of his men have been finalizing plans to take a team to Kenya. It will be a small team: just five guys. A justice minister is about to have a fatal auto accident. With the assassination of the Tanzanian president, it would have destabilized the whole area enough for Kite's new army to grab the Zanj region. But even without that killing, taking out the justice minister should create chaos.

MacDonald absolutely does not believe in coincidence. The Thiago hit failed because Desmond Limerick fucked him over. Simple as that.

Outside this one-floor cell of a company within a company, the Clockjack Solutions campus is operating like normal, with a bit fewer than two thousand employees coming and going, two shifts per day via their electric buses from Portland. MacDonald had recommended shutting it all down but John Kite had wanted it to be business as usual around here until this weekend, when Kite and company would disappear forever.

But now they're delayed.

"Listen up," MacDonald says, clapping his hands once, gathering his top guys. "This Limerick arsehole's coming for us. Winston Noel's undergoing surgery in Seattle for his wrists. Nothing I can do about that. But John Kite, RJ Sharpe, and Teddy Meeker are here in this building, and they are confined to the campus. On my orders. How many soldiers we got on hand, an' not en route to Africa?"

One of his guys scans a duty roster. "Ah, looks like twenty-four, Sergeant."

"Good. They don't ship out as planned. They're on garrison duty. This fucking campus just became a fortress. Understand? We—"

"Sergeant?" A Canadian merc enters the room. "Got something on this Limerick."

MacDonald nods.

"He just bought an AR-15 online from a service in the Philippines."

"Jesus bless. You've got a mailing address?"

"Right here." The Canadian hands him a sheet of paper. "It's going to a street address in Portland."

MacDonald studies the address. He does a double take.

"Sergeant?"

"Jesus, Joseph, and Mary!" MacDonald says, then barks a genuine laugh. Dez Limerick is many things, but boring isn't one of them.

"Don't believe it. The fucker's been squatting in Miss Sharpe's house!"

As MacDonald is making this observation, back at RJ Sharpe's house, Dez's phone vibrates.

It's Arabella Satti.

"We blocked the hit. The Tanzanian president is safe." Her voice sounds as if her words could scald the phone out of Dez's hand.

"Harker?"

"Got away."

"Bloody hell."

"Limerick?" she says. "These bastards, Kite and MacDonald, have been working with Ray Harker. Ray Harker! I need them to pay for that. I need them stopped. The favor you asked? For the Swann sisters. I'm in. All in."

He says, "Sure, are you? It's a huge fecking ask, Belle. I wouldn't—"

"Fuck you, Limerick," she snarls. "Do it."

CHAPTER 49

Gareth MacDonald is airborne, busy with other matters, so he sends a soldier named Sandoval to deal with Limerick. Sandoval is good. A former Spanish GEO—pronounced "hey-oh"—or a special forces soldier for king and country. He's a solid leader of men. Spain's Grupo Especial de Operaciones is as good in their way as the SAS is in theirs; responsible for countering terrorist threats. And like most soldiers trained in counterterrorism, Sandoval and his lot are nifty at creating terrorism as well.

The best terrorists MacDonald has ever worked with are disgruntled anti-terrorist soldiers. Hands down.

Sandoval brings eight men to Mount Tabor, the quiet, heavily tree-covered neighborhood on Portland's east side. The homes are perched on the flanks of a small and nonactive volcano. The streets are tree-lined, the properties deep enough for front- and backyards, all neatly fenced off from one another. The streets run at steep inclines. The city of Portland maintains a water reservoir in the caldera at the top of the mountain, surrounded by a lush park.

All of the men have photos of Desmond Aloysius Limerick. The mad bastard was kind enough to get his snap taken when he walked, calm as you please, onto the Clockjack campus.

All of them have been told how good Limerick is; how he damn near took out the entire Astoria unit by his lonesome. No one is taking him for granted.

Sandoval deploys his crew like this:

Three men in a van at the bottom of West Tabor Summit Drive.

Sandoval and two other men are in a second van higher up, above the home owned by the Clockjack CEO, RJ Sharpe.

Three men are on top of Mount Tabor, in the park, carrying golf bags and dressed as civilians. When the coast is clear, those men begin moving slowly downhill, over back fences, avoiding dogs and kids.

Sitting in his van, Sandoval is alerted that the foot team can see the rear side of RJ Sharpe's expansive house. Lights definitely are on inside the home.

Gareth MacDonald is monitoring the team's comms from the inside of a C-130 Hercules, crossing over the Rockies, en route to the East Coast.

John Kite and RJ Sharpe are in Kite's office, fifth floor of the admin building, on the Gamila campus. They, too, are monitoring Sandoval's communications.

Sharpe has just returned from a speaking engagement in Miami. She holds her arms across her midriff, as if from a stomachache, pain behind her eyes.

"The man invaded my house," she says softly. "My house!"

"Balls," Kite says, and clicks his tongue. He's making her a martini. "The size of honeydew."

* * *

On the sylvan streets of the Tabor neighborhood, Sandoval's foot team can see the back of RJ Sharpe's house. Van no. 1, above the house on the hillside street, is ready. Van no. 2, below the house, is ready.

Sandoval says, "Team one: Proceed."

His foot team has approached the back of the house from the park atop the old volcano. Two of the three can climb a robust old oak tree and sneak onto the roof over Sharpe's back porch. The third man stays on the ground and unzips his golf bag, revealing a Sten gun.

Sharpe has informed the team that she keeps the window cracked in her bedroom to let fresh air in when she sleeps. Even telling these soldiers that much feels like an invasion of her privacy. Let alone knowing Limerick is inside her house, even now.

She had wondered why the teams didn't simply use her keys to get in.

"Shock and awe," MacDonald informed her. "Want to catch Limerick fast. Man's too smart to get taken otherwise."

The team up in the tree is being led by a Belgian soldier. Slowly, quietly, they step onto the recently reshingled roof, make it to the master suite's window, silently glide it open.

They climb in, set down their golf bags, reveal their own assault weapons.

They can hear a muted voice coming from the first floor.

The Belgian whispers into his mic, "He's here. We're in place."

Sandoval, in the upper van, says, "Team two: Deploy."

The guys in the lower van climb out and start hiking uphill toward Sharpe's home.

Sandoval and one of his guys—both dressed as

civilians, both with backpacks—climb out of their van and start strolling downhill toward the house.

When both teams are abreast of Sharpe's mailbox, Sandoval speaks into his wrist mic. "Go go go."

Softly.

He and his guy sprint up to the front door. The other three back them up from behind cars parallel parked on the street.

Sandoval's guy doffs his backpack, revealing a tactical battering ram: a short, round piece of hardened steel the shape of a bongo drum, with two steel handles. It's a simple and effective breaching tool. The man grabs both handles, rears back with the ram, and slams it into Sharpe's door. The door splinters, the hinges and the locks disintegrating, the door itself surfing into her living room.

Sandoval enters first, SIG Sauer drawn, clean entry, checking his corners.

The man with the ram steps out of the way as the three on backup surge through the door.

The two guys up above, on the second floor, do a room by room—practiced, clean, and smooth.

The third guy who hiked down from the park—but who didn't climb the tree—leaps onto the back porch and uses the butt of his gun to shatter the lock on the sliding glass door. He steps into the kitchen.

Clockwork.

The team finds no one on the second floor, no one in the kitchen, no one in the living room. Two men check the garage. Nothing.

They gather in the living room. The voice that Sandoval's guys heard comes from a TV, set on a Premier League game. West Ham versus Chelsea.

Sandoval speaks into his wrist mic. "We're clear. The house is empty."

* * *

In the admin building on Gamila, RJ Sharpe sighs with relief. The idea of that man being in her house creeped her out.

Aboard the C-130, Gareth MacDonald says, "Copy that. Is anything out of place? Over."

Sandoval looks around. "Is Miss Sharpe moving? Over."

In his office, Kite turns to Sharpe. She shakes her head, brow knit. Kite leans into the mic set up on his desk. "That's a big negative. Why?"

In the house, Sandoval says, "The cardboard boxes. They're all over her living room. We—"

The transmission is cut off as his men begin to scream.

This is how Dez used the cardboard boxes, the two pounds of bolts, nuts, and screws, and the air cannons he purchased at Bud's. He stuffed the cannons with the small, sharp bits of metal and hid them under the empty cardboard boxes in RJ's living room. He set up a GoPro camera on the mantel of Sharpe's stone fireplace, hidden behind a spray of dried flowers in a Japanese vase. Then he rigged the air cannons to fire remotely, powered by his phone. He arranged the cannons so the muzzles point at every square meter of space within a horizontal plane, twenty-five centimeters off the floor. A perfect enfilade.

Thanks to the GoPro, he watches the arrival of the assault team from the comfort of a Starbucks two blocks away from Mount Tabor. When he determines that all of the combatants have gathered in the living room, he fires the air cannons by remote.

The nails, nuts, and bolts turn the cardboard into confetti.

And also the soldiers' feet and legs.

All eight of the combatants are wounded, but nobody is wounded higher than their knees. Their feet and calves and shins are torn to shreds.

Dez dials 911. He gives them the address. "Eight foreigners. With assault rifles. All down an' injured. Could be Al Qaeda." And he hangs up.

He calls all four television news channels in Portland—he has their numbers in speed dial. He gives each the exact same spiel. Accent on the words "Al Qaeda." "The house," he adds, "belongs to RJ Sharpe. Boss of Clockjack Solutions. Aye. Looks like these terrorists might've been livin' there."

And hangs up.

He uses a bent paper clip to slip the SIM card out of his prepaid mobile he bought at Bud's and drops the card in his untouched venti decaf. He does not know why the large coffee is called a venti and not, say, a "large." Venti is Italian for "twenty," and the coffee is twenty ounces, so that tracks. But the iced venti is twenty-four ounces, and they don't call that one a venti-quattro. Who made up this naming system? It's daft.

Dez has no intention of bothering to pick up the AR-15 he ordered from the Philippines. It's not even here yet and it's already done all the damage he needed it to.

But there is one more message he wants to send. And this one's important.

Across the street from the Starbucks, he steps into a 7-Eleven and gets a bag of popcorn.

Dez walks up West Tabor Summit Drive toward the commotion. He's not the only one. Ambulances are here. Police cars, too. TV news stations have brought SUVs with massive giraffe-necked microwave transceivers, reporters and videographers scrambling amid the neighborhood onlookers to get a shot of the story of the day.

Dez suspects that Gareth MacDonald has a medical facility on standby, and nearby, but Dez doesn't want these men quietly evacced to that site. He wants them on live television. He wants the camera crews camped out at area hospitals. He'd told the TV crews about RJ Sharpe, and he wants camera crews and TV helicopters all over Gamila like flies on elephant dung.

TV crews watch as the wounded men are carted out on wheeled gurneys. Eight men; all eight bleeding from their legs. Some bleeding *out*. They're transported in a cocoon, EMTs in close, a scrum of cops around the EMTs, the media outside the property, catching every image.

Videographers scan the crowd. Of course they do. They always do.

Will John Kite and/or Sergeant Gareth MacDonald be watching the live footage? Of course they will.

They'll see Dez, who's shouldered his way to the front of the lookie-loos.

Grinning like a kid at carnival.

Chomping on a bag of popcorn.

Best show in town.

Aboard the Hercules, 25,000 feet over the Midwest, Gareth MacDonald is using a laptop to watch live coverage from one of the Portland TV stations.

He spots the shit-eating grin first. Then the popcorn.

Message delivered.

Desmond Limerick has declared war.

CHAPTER 50

It comes down to this.

Dez gave his word to Gareth MacDonald not to interfere with an assassination in Tanzania.

But when Dez realized that MacDonald had aligned with that former CIA officer, current freelance assassin and lifelong arsehole Ray Harker, well, that's a whole different kettle of fish, isn't it?

Dez's actions in Chechnya, those years ago, was right, and proper, and garnered the praise of the British and American military types on scene, and the MI6 mandarins in London. But it also did near irreparable harm to Arabella Satti's career. Tough enough for a *girl* to become the shot caller for a foreign op. Worse yet if she's rescued, against her will, by the big, strong men she's supposedly leading. At the time, Dez hated doing that to Belle, and that was before he even considered the sexist shrapnel he'd be casting into her career path. He sees it now and regrets it wholly.

A chance for Belle to bring her boss's attention to the very much alive Ray Harker could get her back on the fast track. Which, Dez believes, is where she should have been all along.

Getting her there just meant lying to MacDonald.

Turns out, Dez is okay with this. Cheap at twice the price.

But here's the other side of the equation: Mac-Donald said the Swann sisters could have been safe from all this, once Kite and company relocated to the East African coast. Could've been true. Could've been a lie. Could be MacDonald spoke true and his barmy-as-birdshit boss, John Kite, is so far gone into his own personal psychosis he'd have the Swanns hunted down anyway out of spite.

Go with MacDonald's offer, and the Swann sisters might be out of dire trouble.

Fuck over MacDonald, and the Swann sisters could most definitely still be in the barney.

That part was a very tough call to make.

Dez spent a portion of his time on this Earth as a sergeant. A master sergeant, if you will. A *maréchal des logis-chef,* thank you very much.

The definition of which is: he who makes the tough calls.

Dez's next task is to reach out to the Hong Kong Collective, the informal association of hackers and crackers who live to piss off the Chinese politburo. It's from one of them that he got the virus that messed with Clockjack's internal security at Gamila. Her name is Peng Shanshan but everyone calls her Spot.

It's ten in the morning in Portland, meaning it's 2 A.M. in Hong Kong, but these are young party animals and, as far as Dez can tell, they never sleep. Spot gets back to him quickly.

D-Dawg. Did u buttfuck Clockjack???
Righteous dude!

Shanshan, alas, learned her English from rap videos and role-playing games.

Dez: How did you know?

Spot: Bitches tried to Trojan Horse my program??? Imma oh no you dinnit!

Dez thought this might happen. MacDonald's crew found Dez's virus in their computers and attempted to modify it, hoping Dez might use it again to sneak onto the campus. Do so, and they'd know he was there. It's a good ploy but they don't count on the twisted mind of Peng Shanshan. The kid's brilliant.

Dez: Figured. Hoping to lure me back in, the twats.

Spot: Lame! LMFAO!

Dez: Thanks, love. Any signs of your X?

Spot: Boy Bye!

Dez signs off. She's a nice kid, that one. A completely amoral criminal, mind you, but who's without faults?

MacDonald found Shanshan's virus at the Clockjack campus. He figures that's Dez's way back in, should Dez need it.

Yes, but . . .

When Dez was in the office of the Jamaican drug lord, Winston Noel, he ran the man's gold-hued key card through the card reader on his tablet, then returned the card to Noel's pocket. He'd also kept the black metallic cards he'd taken from the thugs in the record shop. Using his computer, Dez has transferred all of the properties of Winston Noel's gold card onto one of the black cards.

It's a sad and pitiful gatekeeper who relies on only one lock and only one door.

CHAPTER 51

Chief Deputy U.S. Marshal Conroy Sims sports an impeccable suit and well-cared-for cowboy boots. He gets his hair trimmed every other Tuesday and he works out on a treadmill and with free weights every weekday morning in his garage. At sixty-nine, he wears the same size clothes as the day he enlisted in the Marines at age eighteen.

He read about the raid on RJ Sharpe's house yesterday. That's the work of Desmond Aloysius Limerick; Sims is sure of it.

Before leaving for work, he sits at the cozy kitchen nook, dappled by light filtered through trees in his backyard. Sitting opposite him on the facing bench are the Swann sisters, Laleh and Raziah. His wife, Kelly, is at the stove, hovering over five identical glass baking dishes, each with a slightly different variation of cornbread with jalapeños. Kelly's catering business is about three times as profitable as Conroy Sims's law enforcement career.

The older of the sisters, Laleh, has been poring over the audit reports of Clockjack Solutions, looking for anything to explain the lawlessness they suspect hovers over the international high-tech company. Sims has introduced Laleh to his favorite black tea, Lapsang souchong, and both of them have cups on the built-in table beneath the backyard window. Raziah has a Diet Coke.

"They've been pouring money into insurgency efforts in Kenya and Tanzania," Laleh says. "My friend Conor O'Meara, he was just trying to help Clockjack re-up its status as a B Corp. But he stumbled on this. That's why they killed him."

Sims sips his tea, nods. Out of the corner of his eye, he can tell that Kelly is listening. She has a soft spot in her heart for intelligent young women.

Laleh is enjoying herself. Even her sister, Raziah, isn't snarking. Sims had sensed tension between the sisters when he'd first had them spirited away to Virginia, but they've been talking late into the night, night after night, and seemed to have found some mutual understanding.

Laleh says, "I'm trying to find enough—"

A bullet smashes through the kitchen window and embeds itself in Conroy Sims's jaw. He pitches straight over, to his left, not even toppling his teacup, landing on the black-and-white tile floor, his head bouncing once. Neither Laleh nor Raziah have even screamed as the door between the kitchen and the garage cracks open. The first man through shoots Kelly Sims in the back, severing her spine, using a .22 with a sound suppressor. The second, third, and fourth men through head straight to the living room, Sten guns to shoulders, spreading out, searching the whole house. Behind them, the first man who entered puts two more bullets into Kelly Sims, and now Laleh starts screaming.

Gareth MacDonald enters from the garage, silenced .22 auto in hand. Raziah recognizes him from the confrontation at Portland State University, but she's still in shock. Sitting closer to the window than her sister, she got hit with flying glass from the sniper's bullet. Tiny beads of blood begin blooming on her left cheek and her neck and her exposed left shoulder.

MacDonald puts two bullets into the skull of Conroy Sims, whose body twitches on the floor, a pool of blood spreading.

Laleh is screaming, and Raziah is silent and bleeding and in shock. MacDonald's three guys on reconnaissance report back over the radios that the house is clear.

MacDonald holsters his .22 and draws a dart gun, quickly tranquilizing both sisters.

They're unconscious inside six seconds of the darts' impact.

MacDonald nods to his men. Two guys grab Laleh; two grab Raziah. They carry the deadweight girls out of the kitchen, into the garage, and into the van of the carpet-cleaning company parked in the driveway and canted at an angle so no neighbors can see the sliding side door.

When they kicked in the kitchen door, they set off alarms. That was the plan. MacDonald needs the Marshals Service to know Sims is dead and the sisters have been taken, the sooner the better. The word has to get back to the West Coast, and to Desmond Limerick. Again: the sooner the better.

The alarms don't bother MacDonald's team. From first trigger pull to keys in the ignition, the mission took forty-seven seconds.

CHAPTER 52

Deputy U.S. Marshal Joshua Vega of the Oregon field office reaches out to Dez. He's given the Marshals Service his contacts. They meet in Director Park, which is one of those urban parks without a blade of grass or a single tree, just a wading pool for the kiddies, scattered tables and chairs for downtown office workers to enjoy their lunches, and artfully random sets of stairs that are catnip to the skateboard crowd. They meet by a human-sized chessboard made of pavers. Dez has seen Vega before. First, when Dez had been held overnight by the marshals. This had been the serious guy in the dour suit who'd uncuffed him. Later, at the suburban safehouse after Dez had been shot.

Deputy Vega inhales deeply, then exhales it all. "This is the hardest thing I've ever had to tell anyone."

"Raziah and Laleh."

From Dez, and it isn't even a question. Why else would the deputy ask to see him, and why else would he look close to puking? Dez feels his blood pressure drop a little. He doesn't get overwrought when bad news comes. He's been a soldier. Bad news always comes for soldiers.

He says, "Sims?"

Vega chews the inside of his cheek, eyes murderous. "Dead. His wife, too. In their kitchen. Pro job. Double taps to their heads. No fiber, no prints. In and out inside a minute."

Dez says, "The sisters were taken." Again, it isn't a question. He knows this for sure. Gareth MacDonald would get no benefit from killing the Swanns at this point. He will later. He'll have to. For now, he needs them so he can control Dez.

Deputy Vega gets this. "They're going to contact you. They're going to make demands. We want to put a tap—"

Dez pats him on the shoulder. "Appreciate it, but no."

"I know you're hurting right now. But that wasn't a request."

"'Twas, an' the answer hasn't changed."

"Limerick, these assholes—"

"An' what's your plan, mate? Ignore all the political pressure you're gettin' from Washington? Lure a professional cadre o' soldiers into a trap? You're out-manned, out-trained, out-gunned, out-budgeted, and out-politicked. And let's say your brilliant scheme pays off an' you arrest the lot. You've no more chance of keeping 'em than you did Demetrious Givens an' his merry band of mouth breathers. Ye'd make a pig's breakfast of it, an' you'd get the Swann ladies dead. More importantly, you'd get *me* dead."

Vega tries to interject but can't think of a goddamned thing to say. He's a cop, born and raised. His instinct is to go for a sting, and arrests, and convictions. Their standard playbook. Which won't work here.

"Fuck."

"Joshua, was it? I am truly sorry to hear about Sims an' his wife."

Vega works to control his pain. "He, ah . . . he liked you. Said he trusted you. Gotta say, Limerick, you're taking this damn cool."

Dez shrugs. "They's soldiers. I'm a soldier. This

was always going to come down to combat. I wish you lot could've kept Raziah and Laleh safe, but if wishes was horses, we'd all ride. Kite an' MacDonald have made their play. I'll make mine. An' we'll see how it all works out."

A beat, and Joshua Vega says, "I can't just do nothing."

Dez says, "Want to bet?"

CHAPTER 53

Dez needs to do more shopping, and he won't find the items he needs at Bud's, marvel of modern commerce that it is.

That night, Dez picks a fairly impressive lock on a Portland Parks and Recreation site. By *fairly impressive,* he means he had to go to the lockmaker's website, glide through its defenses, and download the code that would undo any of their locks. All of which takes a full six minutes of his life, which, in terms that a 'keeper would understand, makes this a truly memorable lock.

He steals a goodly amount of fuel oil in big red plastic jugs. Plus largish bags of fertilizer featuring ammonium nitrate. Dez studied chemistry, among other things, to become a 'keeper. He's always been more than a little amazed by ammonium nitrate, because it's hygroscopic as a solid—that is to say, it absorbs water—but it does not form hydrates. Amazing, that. Dez had done a term paper on the properties of ammonium nitrate.

He also steals a shovel. It's a good one, oldish, nicked, tar-stained, the handle's color darkened, he suspects, by decades of the sweat of men's hands. Dez loves shovels. They are second only to duct tape as the world's most valuable tool.

Dez steals a roll of duct tape, too.

He hit a couple of ATMs on his way in and leaves five hundred dollars of RJ Sharpe's money behind.

Dez will steal, when needs must, but he is not inconsiderate.

Dez has kept his mobile untraceable, which means MacDonald can't call or text, but he can drop that protection at any time. It's how he lured the DEA and Marshals Service into a confrontation at a garage. Now it's time to let MacDonald find him.

The next morning, Dez activates his phone but routes its signal through a half dozen servers around the globe. They won't be able to track him, but they should be able to call. And they will.

It's a waiting game now, and Dez doesn't mind waiting so long as he has his guitar. He plays it acoustically, just noodling around, picking bits of songs he's loved or is trying to learn. The guitar's always been a good time killer.

His phone lights up. Dez answers the call, puts it on speaker, his hand returning to the guitar strings. "Aye."

Gareth MacDonald says, "Limerick. I imagine you know the drill."

"Likely, aye."

He strums. No need for threats or swearing or yelling, these two. It would be an insult to their professionalism to fall back on cliché.

Dez says, "Time an' place?"

MacDonald says, "Is that Mark Knopfler, then?" Meaning the tune he's hearing.

"'Tis."

"Brilliant. Underrated."

"Oh, aye."

MacDonald says, "Gamila. One hour. You'll be wanting proof of life, *chef*. Hold on."

Dez stops playing. Laleh Swann says, "Dez?"

"Aye. Holding up, are you?"

She sobs. "God, they killed them. Conroy and Kelly. They shot them."

Kelly would be Mrs. Sims, Dez guesses. "I know, love. I'm coming for yez. Be there sharpish. Put your sister on, yeah?"

He waits.

"Dez." It's Raziah. Her voice is cold, as hard as a whetstone. She rattles off the rest as fast as she can, all one word, one breath: "The Clockjack campus in the gorge the admin building I count five in here but there are more outside they'll kill us when you get here so—"

Dez says, "Raziah?"

"—so *don't fuck around!* Come with the police come with the military bring a fucking A-bomb get these—"

"Raz?"

She stops.

"It's all right, love. MacDonald and me will come to an understanding. Professionals, us. It's going to be fine."

She says, "Kill him."

"Aye. Put him on, please."

A wait, then MacDonald says, "Yeah?"

"Yeah, thanks. Appreciate it."

"One hour?"

"Give me ninety minutes. Need to secure transpo."

MacDonald says, "That's reasonable. All right. But leave your vehicle outside the gate and walk in."

"Will do."

"Wish this had gone different, *chef.*"

Dez says, "I understand," and disconnects.

He picks up the phone and hits speed dial, calls Arabella Satti. "MacDonald and his lot killed a chief deputy U.S. marshal an' his wife, and he's got the Swanns. I'm sorry about this. Ready?"

She says, "Go." And hangs up.

Dez tucks his phone away. He peers through the windshield of his rented Jeep, taking in the towering firs, and the sweep of the Columbia, and the showy, snowy peak of Mount Hood. It won't take him ninety minutes to get to Gamila. He's been there all night.

CHAPTER 54

There was a half-decent possibility that all of this wasn't going to happen at Gamila. But upon arriving the night before, parked in the rental just outside the rustic but subtly electrified fence, Dez had used the ID he'd stolen from Winston Noel, the chief financial officer, and the still active virus from his Hong Kong hacker, to access the Clockjack email system and campus intranet. That's where he learned that RJ Sharpe, CEO, had ordered a complete evacuation of all Clockjack personnel from the Columbia Gorge campus. Even IT and security had been given the boot, at least temporarily. According to the Gamila security computer, the only people on the entire 312-acre campus are Sharpe, John Kite, and Teddy Meeker.

But that's only because all of MacDonald's men, and MacDonald himself, never show up on the security feeds. The criminals Kite had originally imported to do his dirty work, and the three-hundred-plus soldiers of Project 404, MacDonald's gig-work guerrillas, are the ghosts of Gamila.

As are Raziah and Laleh Swann. Dez is sure they're here as well.

Last night, just after dusk, Dez snuck into Mount Hood National Forest. He bypassed the very fancy fence around the Clockjack campus using his stolen shovel and digging under it. Low-tech solutions often are the right ones.

He has the rest of the supplies he bought at Bud's or stole from the Transportation Bureau's stores. It's all the stuff he'll need to even the odds here.

Winston Noel's pass can open any door for him. Clockjack's big brains tried to pry loose the Hong Kong hacker's dormant virus but failed. Dez has access to the campus security feeds. Gamila made a good fortress for Kite and MacDonald, so long as they controlled the egress and the security system.

Now it's Dez who's the ghost of Gamila.

Dez checks the Jeep's dashboard clock and sits, noodling through tunes for an additional twenty minutes, then starts up the engine and drives back through the national forest. He returns to the state highway, more or less where he'd gone off-road the night before. He heads straight for the Clockjack campus.

He arrives about eighty-five minutes after MacDonald called him. As if cutting it close. He parks outside the wooden, asymmetrical fence and climbs out with his tablet computer but without his usual messenger bag.

He walks through the gate, arms akimbo, and spots the welcome sign again.

GAMILA.

BUILD FOR ALL PEOPLE

THINK OF THE EARTH

INSPIRE, CONSPIRE, PERSPIRE—WE'RE IN THIS TO-GETHER.

SCREW UP AND START OVER. AND OVER.

WELCOME.

The last time he'd quipped that it would have taken less time to carve *Trespassers will be shot*. The joke doesn't seem as funny this time. Five soldiers await him, each dressed in forest-camo, each with a Heckler & Koch SP5, the lightweight but durable 9mm automatic pistol. A gun Dez greatly respects.

One of the five is Gareth MacDonald.

"Chef."

"Sergeant."

"Stand where you are, please."

Dez does. He waggles the tablet computer in the air. "For you."

"What is it?"

"Insurance."

MacDonald thinks about that for a moment. He makes a gesture to one of his guys. The guy unclips his HK auto from his Kevlar vest, hands it to another merc, walks over, and frisks Dez. Smart move, not bringing a gun within Dez's reach. Not that a machine pistol would have done him a bit of good, the odds he's facing. But good tactics nonetheless.

Dez carries no weapons. Not even his knives.

Finished, the soldier backs off. MacDonald—dressed as the others—steps up, maybe ten paces from Dez. His eyes dart to the tablet. "Want to give that to me?"

"I do."

"Won't explode on me?"

"That'd be a fine trick, but don't see how it'd help me much. Or the sisters."

MacDonald says, "Don't pretend to be naïve. It ill suits you, *chef.*"

Dez shrugs.

A couple of beats, then MacDonald closes the gap, his hand extended.

Dez opens the cover and presses his thumb on the Home button to activate it. He hands it to MacDonald.

"It's a live feed," Dez says softly. "You'll recognize it when you see it."

MacDonald studies the video. He goes deathly still. He watches it for about fifteen seconds.

He draws his mobile, searches for a contact, and makes a call.

Nobody answers. MacDonald lets it ring twenty times. Twenty-five. Thirty.

Dez says, "Call's being blocked."

MacDonald pockets his phone and drops the tablet in the grass and steps forward and punches Dez in the mouth.

Dez is a good fighter. Well-trained. Experienced and quick with his hands and feet. He could have dodged the blow, or deployed measures to counter it. Or even stepped back out of its range. But he knows Gareth Mac-Donald is going to go through some very strong emotions here, and it's best to let them play out. It'll speed things along. The first emotion is rage.

It's a fearsome punch and Dez lands on his ass.

The four soldiers look surprised. There had been a plan, Dez assumes, and decking their prisoner hadn't been part of it.

MacDonald leans down, grabs Dez by his T-shirt collar, and cocks back. It's another staggering blow, and Dez sees stars. MacDonald hits him two more times, in the face. The last blow, Dez's shirt rips along the seams. MacDonald throws the shredded cloth aside and Dez slumps back down, dazed. Blood drools from his mouth and nose.

MacDonald walks in a tight circle, shaking his open right hand, which must hurt considerably.

Dez wonders if his cheek is broken, or any of his teeth. He's breathing okay, so probably he didn't break his nose.

A soldier says, "Mac?"

MacDonald paces in a circle, ignoring his men.

Groaning, Dez slowly rolls over. He gets his palms

flat on the ground and leverages himself up to his knees. His ears are ringing, his vision blurred.

He stands, shirtless, gasping, bent over, hands on his thighs.

MacDonald steps into him and throws a left-handed haymaker.

Dez counters with his right forearm. "Enough," he gasps, and hawks up a gob of blood, spitting it to the ground.

"Hey, Mac?" someone pipes up.

MacDonald doesn't even turn to address his man. "Shut the fuck up." His eyes are locked on Dez.

Dez stands, breathing heavy, woozy. Blood spatters his black jeans.

MacDonald cradles his right hand against his bulletproof vest, two fingers swelling noticeably. Dez has often heard that he's got a thick skull. Apparently true.

The Scotsman stares at him. Dez waits.

Time passes. The four mercenaries wait, unsure of what's happening. Birds sing and the breeze rustles the giant fir trees all around them.

MacDonald draws a VP9 Tactical auto from his belt holster. It's a left-handed, cross-body draw, and it's clumsy as hell; his right hand swelling mightily. He aims the gun at Dez's chest, center mass, his elbow locked. His finger is on the trigger, not indexed.

Someone tries again. "Mac?"

Dez does not move.

After a longish moment, MacDonald drops his left arm, gun facing the ground.

His eyes never leave Dez. "Landers. You and Hurley head back to base. Speak to no one. Radio silence. Get the hostages. Bring 'em here."

"You sure we—"

MacDonald's eyes stay on Dez but he points his gun at the mercenary. "Yes. Go."

The guys hesitate. But MacDonald has installed good unit discipline. His orders run counter to whatever plan they had for Dez, but two of the guys split off. They have one of the South Korean–made electric carts hidden behind the log cabin visitors building. They drive down the path, deeper into the campus.

MacDonald says, "Wait over there."

The other two soldiers move over to the visitors building. Out of earshot.

The Scotsman's voice is tight. He's very near tears. "I told you I had a sister in Stirling. Didn't think—"

Dez spits another gob of blood into the grass. "Aye, but I already knew. Did the research on you, early. Found out your SAS pay—damn near all of it—went to care for your only sibling. A little sister in Stirling, with autism. Know she means the world t'you."

"You fucking bastard."

Dez says, "Aye," and means it.

MacDonald picks up the tablet computer again and studies the image. It is coming from a night-vision scope. He can see a measure for distance, and another measure for wind velocity. The image vibrates and moves slightly on an irregular basis. This is a live feed. Gareth MacDonald has spent countless nights peering through countless sniperscopes. He knows exactly what he's seeing.

The image in the exact center of the crosshairs is his sister. Sitting in an overstuffed chair, reading a book. MacDonald knows his sister can sit like that for hours and hours.

"I am going to kill you."

Dez says, "I know," and sounds sad. "Couldn't assume Sims would keep the sisters safe. He'd been the last copper to pull out of Portland after Kite put the screws to whoever in Washington, DC. Chances of you making the connection with Sims was too high."

MacDonald glares at him.

Dez says, "You're an excellent soldier, you, an' a smart man. But don't give me your moral outrage. Ye shot Sims's wife. Two to the head, execution style. Would've cost you days, at most, maybe hours to figure out how to get to the Swanns without killin' the chief deputy an' his wife. I'm sorry I'm using your autistic sister. But do not play the offended hero on the moral high ground with me, mate."

MacDonald studies Dez. "Would you?" he asks. "Have her killed?"

"Mission objectives, Sergeant. I'll do what it takes to achieve mission objectives. Same as you."

They wait like that for seven minutes until they hear the buzz of the electric cart returning.

With both returning soldiers, as well as Raziah and Laleh Swann.

CHAPTER 55

The returning soldiers roll to a stop near Dez and Mac-Donald. One drives and one holds a machine pistol on the Swanns. When the cart stops moving, MacDonald nods to his men. He points his auto at the sisters. "Down."

Laleh looks terrible—a nervous wreck, barely hanging on. Raziah hasn't taken her mahogany eyes off Dez since the cart cleared the forest-lined lane. She's never seen him without a shirt; didn't know how many bullet and knife wounds are stitched across his taut, pink flesh. The left side of his face is beginning to swell.

Both sisters step out of the cart, Laleh on shaky legs, Raziah stiff-kneed, her whole body rigid, radiating anger. Dez notes that her left cheek, and the left side of her neck, and her left shoulder, have all been scratched up, as if by flying glass.

Her eyes scrape MacDonald, likely taking a layer of flesh with it. She turns back to Dez. "Are you all right?"

"Am *I* all right!" He wipes blood off his chin with the back of his hand. He points back toward the main gate and the folksy, inspirational greeting sign. "Jeep, through there. It's unlocked. Tuck yourselves in tight, if you will. With you shortly."

The sisters look to Dez, to MacDonald, to Dez, back again. They're having a tough time believing any of this.

MacDonald says, "Tell 'em, hero. They deserve to know who you are."

Dez nods. He's right. "I have a sniper, in Scotland. Right this moment. Ready to kill MacDonald's little sister. But I won't have to make it happen. You survive, she survives."

The sisters stare at him, unsure how to react to that.

Dez claps his hands, once. He has outsized hands; it sounds like a rifle shot in the forest. "Burning daylight, ladies. Off with yez."

Raziah grabs her sister's hand and starts toward the gate. Laleh is slow to react. Shock does that to you. Raziah tugs and Laleh either has to move her feet or topple over, so she moves her feet.

MacDonald walks backward, in an arc, to keep Dez and also the moving women in his sights. He takes a good, penetrating look at the Jeep parked outside.

Dez groans, bends at the knees, and retrieves his tablet. His head is still ringing like a chime.

The women get through the gate, to the Jeep, and climb in. It's a Wrangler, which means it has rear doors and a full back seat, and the sisters look particularly petite back there in the cavernous space.

They're out of earshot. MacDonald says, "If Janey lives, I'll do the sisters proper. Two to the skull. Won't feel a thing. If she's not . . ."

Dez says, "Aye."

"When I kill you, it'll be face-t'-face. I'll want you fully aware when I kill you."

Dez says, "Could be tougher to do than to say."

"It's already happened." MacDonald keeps his eyes on the Jeep. "You just don't know you're dead yet."

As soon as the Jeep pulls out, MacDonald is on his walkie-talkie. "Everyone. Limerick's Jeep has been passing through tall grass. He didn't just get here from

Portland. I want every building, every inch of the property searched! Now! Fucker's left us some surprises; I'm sure of it."

He toggles to another channel. "Mr. Kite. I'm on my way t'you. We've a new development. Out."

CHAPTER 56

John Kite and RJ Sharpe stand in the exact middle of Kite's office and watch as two of MacDonald's soldiers search every inch of the desk, the shelves, the wet bar. One guy even gets down on his knee and peers into the six-inch-deep putting green hole drilled into the floor.

Sharpe glances out the window and sees a line of soldiers, probably twenty guys wide, slow-walking across the campus, their eyes on the ground.

MacDonald enters in fatigues and boots, pistol in a hip holster.

Kite says, "What the hell—"

"Limerick," MacDonald cuts him off. "Briefly: He kidnapped my little sister and has a sniper on her, right now, in Scotland. Sniper's got a Bluetooth transmitter on his scope, so I could see what he saw. I let the Swann girls go to save my sister's life. And I don't need to hear any shite about my decisions, aye?"

Kite tries to interject and says, in this order, "He did . . . You what . . . ? I . . . what?"

MacDonald says, "Limerick came in a truck that has grass and weeds stuck to it halfway up the side panels. He wasn't in Portland when I called. My guess is, he was here, last night, leaving us surprises."

Sharpe nods to the window. "Looking for what? Bombs?"

"Man's got engineering degrees, ma'am. Plus, battlefield experience. Of course we're looking for explosive devices. An' booby traps. An' trip wires. The lot." He turns to Kite. "We're going to keep you two here in the admin building until further notice."

Kite says, "Why?"

"I've two dozen soldiers I've been holding back, keeping here till they get processed for Africa. Got another eleven flying into the States soon. We can't guard the entire campus. It's three-hundred-plus fecking acres. But we can make this building a fortress."

"We have all this high-tech security around the campus. We—"

"If I had to guess, he's cloned Meeker's pass card, or Noel's. And the virus we thought we'd neutered in our security computers? Don't doubt for a minute it's still fucking us over."

He lifts his walkie-talkie off its belt clip and toggles it. "Edwards. Aye, me. Shut down the security computer. Completely. Pull the fuses. We don't own the system, Limerick does. Out."

He holsters the radio as Kite says, "A quick reminder: You work for me. Ease up on the orders, Sergeant."

MacDonald stands at parade rest. "Sir. I take your pay envelope, so I take your orders. You want a third-world warlord neutralized, consider him neutralized. You want to destabilize Kenyan oil pipelines, count 'em as unstable. But when it comes to protecting you, I'll do what I deem necessary. Aye? There are two topics in this world upon which I do not take orders from you. One is protecting you. And the other is killing Limerick. Am I clear, sir?"

Kite blinks several times. "And how."

"Good." He turns to one of the men who's finished checking the office. "Get Meeker, he's coming with us, too. I want a cocoon around these three."

The soldier nods.

RJ Sharpe says, "Limerick has those sisters? Then what's to stop him from putting them, and himself, on an airplane to, whatever, Phuket, or Rio de Janeiro, or Bend, Oregon? He could hide with them, anywhere, and wait for the federal authorities to figure out what's going on here."

"He'll hide the girls, good and proper," MacDonald acknowledges. "But he can't hide them forever and I will find them eventually. And I'll have them killed. But Limerick's not done with us. Not at all."

Kite says, "You sound like you know the man."

"I know his type. First, he wanted to protect the sisters. Then he wanted to solve a mystery. Now his goal is to win a war. Won't stop till he does."

RJ says, "You admire him."

MacDonald nods.

Kite laughs. "Oh great. That's all we need. You going soft on the enemy."

MacDonald cold-eyes him. "In my kit is a bottle of fifteen-year-old, double-casked, single-malt Macallan. The day I kill Limerick, I'll crack the seal and drain that fucker till it's bone dry. He's a damn fine soldier, as smart as they come. I'll mourn him after I've washed his blood off my hands. Sir."

CHAPTER 57

It's one of those funny little chance happenings in life, but RJ Sharpe speculated that Dez could hide the Swanns in Phuket, or Rio de Janeiro, or Bend. It was just an offhand remark but it hit a bull's-eye. Dez doesn't take Interstate 84 west to Portland, he takes it east to Hood River, then catches Highway 35 south, going around the far side of glistening Mount Hood, through the Warm Springs Reservation, and into Bend, a city in Oregon's high desert. He travels on, through the town, and takes them to the nearby resort community called Sunriver.

He texts one-handed as he drives. Brothers?

Ding. Oh, you'll love them.

Dez's duffel bag is in the back of the Jeep and he long ago changed into a fresh black T-shirt. He drives, the Gibson Ripper electric bass guitar in its case riding shotgun. His face feels and looks like hamburger, but his nose has stopped bleeding. The sisters huddle in the back of the Jeep and ask few questions. Both of them sleep, and it's the first time they have since they awakened after being narco-darted in Virginia. That stuff is still in their system, in fact, and only time and sleep will reset their internal clocks.

From the back, Raziah whispers sleepily, "Where are we?"

"Sunriver."

He pulls off the highway and into the community, which includes a world-class golf course. He spots deer by the side of the road, grazing.

"Would you have killed his sister?"

Dez doesn't respond.

Beyond a rustic lodge and a set of hotel rooms, Sunriver features lots of rental condos. Dez checks a note on his phone, and the GPS map, and wends his way through the forested community, to a specific condo. He parks outside.

A very beefy guy in a tight T-shirt under a leather bomber stands outside. The guy has shaved his skull and wears a neat goatee. He has vaguely Asian facial features and is pale. He looks like he could bench-press the Wrangler. He's so muscle-bound his arms hang like parentheses around his body.

Raziah wakes her sister and they step out onto the driveway. Dez nods to the small, detached, two-bedroom house. As they reach the door, another man steps out. He, too, has a too-tight T-shirt and a shaved skull and a neat goatee. He's nearly perfectly identical to the first guy. He gets out of the way as they enter, and both men follow them in.

Veronika Tsygan is in the attached kitchen, behind an island, making cold-cut sandwiches. A pot boils behind her, and Dez can smell tomato soup. Raziah spots her and crosses quickly. The women freeze in a long, perfectly still hug.

Laleh looks confused.

Dez says, "'Nika here owns a bar in Portland where Raziah sometimes plays. These are her brothers. From Detroit. Well, from Siberia by way of Detroit. This is, ah . . ."

The first bald, goateed gym rat says, "Vladimir."

The other bald, goateed gym rat says, "Skip."

Dez lets that settle in. "Aye. Well, anyway, Laleh Swann, these are the Tsygans. Veronika, Vladimir, an', apparently, Skip. Which, truth told, I did not see that one comin'."

Veronika and Raziah are still frozen in the hug. Over the slight girl's shoulder, Veronika takes in Dez's battered face: puffy lower lip, inflamed cheek, swollen left eye.

"I've rented this place, an' the next one over. Should be safe. Plus, there's about six hundred pounds of Tsygans twixt you and trouble, so that's good."

Laleh has hardly moved and hasn't uttered a peep.

Raziah breaks the hug and wipes tears. Dez can see the shallow cuts on her cheek and neck and shoulder. He's sure it happened at Chief Deputy Sims's assassination.

Veronika studies Dez and shakes her head. "Should I see how the other guy looks?"

"Fresh as a daisy, I'm sad to admit. On the upside, I'm pretty sure the fucker broke a finger or two on me skull."

Laleh seems to snap out of her shock a little. She hugs Dez, but lightly and quickly. She shakes the hands of the Tsygan brothers, then crosses to the kitchen island and shakes Veronika's hand.

"Thank you."

Veronika touches her upper arm, gently, and peers into her eyes. "I've soup and sandwiches," she says, "but what I think you need is sleep."

"I . . . thank you. Yes, please."

"My brothers and I are staying in the next condo over. There are two rooms for you here."

Laleh nods. "Thank you. Can I speak to Dez for a second? Raziah and I?"

The trio moves into one of the bedrooms. Veronika has provided Dez with a dish towel wrapped around a half dozen ice cubes. He groans, eases himself down on the floor, back to the wall, presses the cold cloth to his swollen cheek and nose. When making introductions, he noticed that his jaw was clicking. Likely not a good sign. The sisters sit side by side on the king-sized bed. They hold hands, all four hands, a great pile of nervous fingers.

Laleh starts. "You risked your life to come save us. I didn't think that would happen."

"Noble, brave, an' true," Dez says. "Also, had me eye on a couple of them sandwiches, so if we could move this along . . ."

"We saw two very nice people, who'd shown us Christian kindness, slaughtered in front of us."

Dez sobers up. "The marshal an' his wife. Aye, sorry. I shouldn't make light. Ye've both been through hell."

"That man . . . ?"

"Sergeant Gareth MacDonald."

"You had a sniper and threatened to kill his sister."

Dez says, "Aye."

Raziah says, "Did you? Would you?"

Dez says, "I've a friend in British Military Intelligence. Well, not sure 'friend' is the term. Exactly. She actually doesn't like me much an' has threatened to kill me a time or two."

Raziah says, "You define 'friend' differently than other people."

"True, that. Anyway, this friend of sorts agreed to help me because I was fairly certain that MacDonald would track you down. Didn't know he'd kill the deputy an' his wife. But I had to have a contingency plan, should MacDonald take you."

"This friend trained a gun on a little girl?" Laleh asks.

"From a distance, aye. The little girl never knew."

"But the threat was real."

Dez says, "The friend—an' ye don't need to know her name, but I'll tell ye anyway because she's very brave, and she could get fired or prosecuted for this, and she helped save your life. Her name's Arabella. Anyway, she agreed to hide in the dark and point a sniper rifle at the child, and to transmit what her scope saw to my tablet. That's as far as Arabella would have gone. Not one chance in a million she'd actually pull the trigger. I'd bet every dime I stole from RJ Sharpe that Belle didn't even load her weapon. But MacDonald had t'believe me bluff, or it wouldn't've worked, and him and his lads would be diggin' three graves in the national forest right about now."

The sisters take all that in. Raziah says, "I had to ask."

"I understand."

"Are you mad at me for doubting you?"

"Never."

"Are you going to kill MacDonald?"

"Am," Dez says. "Have to. He's never going t'stop coming for you, an' for me. So this ends with bloodshed. No other way."

Laleh says, "I'm a Christian and I majored in world history. An eye for an eye has never worked. Never. This . . . this awful . . . *person* . . . these men, they killed two innocent souls and they wanted to kill my baby sister and they wanted to kill you and me. But violence begets violence. You should go to the FBI. To whoever. The authorities should deal with this."

Softly, Raziah squeezes her sister's hands and says, "Conroy Sims *was* the authorities. Dez tried it that way."

They sit side by side for a while.

Dez says, "Bloke behind all of this is called Kite. He's got the money and the connections t'put political pressure on law enforcement. Sims was riskin' his career hidin' you. We've run out of authorities to turn to. Gonna have to end this the only way left. An' yes. Violence begets violence. Truer words, love." He begins leveraging himself up to his feet and falls over the first time he tries.

"I'm going to attack about half them sandwiches, then I'll kip down for a couple of hours, then I'll head back. You should be safe here. Them two plow horses out there will stay tucked in close, just in case."

Raziah says, "You think those guys could take Mac-Donald's soldiers?"

"I think them lads could *eat* MacDonald's soldiers."

He makes it to the door, trying not to show that the act of standing makes him dizzy. He sure hopes he isn't concussed.

Raziah says, "You could die doing this."

"Needs must when the devil drives." He leaves.

Laleh says, "I have no idea what that means."

Raziah side-hugs her. "I've stopped trying to translate him into English."

CHAPTER 58

Dez eats plenty. Then sleeps for about ten hours. The swelling in his face has gone down when he arises, a bit after midnight, and he's breathing all right through his nose. His fear of a concussion is gone; he's been concussed before and knows what that feels like. It was as worthy a beatdown as Dez has experienced in some time, but it was the best way for Gareth MacDonald to bleed off his righteous anger and that feeling of helplessness. If Dez had done anything to avoid the beating, the man's anger would never have ebbed enough for him to see the logical path out of this imbroglio; one that involved three very-much-alive young women.

It's been sixteen days since Dez was shot in Astoria. It's been an interesting couple of weeks.

He sleeps on the couch, in the same condo with the Swann sisters. In the morning, after he showers and takes his body weight in Tylenol, he finds the Tsygan brothers in the condo, waiting for him. On the kitchen island is a well-used canvas duffel, unzipped to show a lot of blued metal.

"Veronika's idea," one of them rumbles, but since they're identical, he's no idea if it's Vladimir or Skip.

Dez groans as he sits at a barstool and sorts through what Santa brought him. He digs past all of the guns and spots what he'd hope to spot: cleaning rods and jags, cotton patches, a bronze bore cleaning brush, and a small jar of Hoppe's No. 9 solvent. Dez has rarely carried a gun into battle that he hasn't disassembled and cleaned himself.

Next, he pulls out two matching MP-443 Rooks. They're PYa's, or *Pistolet Yarygina,* and Dez has used them before. A fine firearm. Weighs in at about thirty-four ounces, less than eight inches long, takes a 9×19mm Parabellum round. Eighteen-round box mags, fixed iron sights with the dot-and-notch design that Dez fancies, and a front blade. Good for up to about fifty meters, more or less. Dez is not the world's greatest shot but he generally hits what he aims for.

He fieldstrips the Rooks, cleans them, reassembles them. The hulking brothers make coffee with plenty of sugar and milk.

Nobody speaks for the first twenty minutes as he cleans both guns. Eventually, one of the twin golems growls, "Are you sleeping with our sister?"

Dez looks up and beams. "Oh aye! Couple o' times, anyway. Grand! Bloody goddess, that one. Unbelievable. It's women like that, they write songs about!"

He shakes his head in wonderment and keeps cleaning and reassembling the guns.

"That is . . . not the answer we usually get," says the other. He takes a beat, then adds, "She likes men who can cook."

"I can cook!"

Tweedle Huge says, "French food. Also Italian, too."

"French and Italian. Got it."

Tweedle Huger adds, "Also chocolate."

GAMILA

Around midnight, Gareth MacDonald hears his walkie-talkie chirp. He's lying on a cot he has moved into an office on the fifth floor of the admin building, turning it into a bivouac. He's been staring at the ceiling, unable to sleep. The two swollen fingers of his taped-up right hand ache. He's lucky he didn't break them. Lights and shadows crisscross the ceiling of his room as sentries with flashlights cover the campus grounds. He levers himself up on one elbow and reaches with his left hand, cross-body, for the radio on the desk next to his cot. "MacDonald."

It's one of his techies. "We ran a Griess test on that Limerick guy's T-shirt. The one you ripped."

"Aye?"

"Positive for nitrite."

MacDonald sighs. "Okay. Out." And sets the radio back down.

He rises and moves to the office window, barefoot, wearing only his camo trousers. He draws a cigarette, lights it. Besides the full sleeves of tattoos, ink covers about a third of his muscled back. John Kite's office faces south, over the pristine little campus lake, and Mount Hood dominates the view. This office faces east, onto the whole of the campus. MacDonald watches his men methodically patrol the grounds. He's got twenty-four soldiers at Gamila now. Twenty-four well-trained, well-armed men from armies representing seven countries. Well, men kicked out of armies representing seven countries, at any rate. They've searched every building on the campus. MacDonald also had bomb-sniffing dogs brought in from his old private military contractor, Occidental Ventures, or Occasional Vultures. The dogs sniffed up nothing.

He's got twelve of his guys guarding the admin building. Of the others, half are stationed along the southern perimeter of the fence, scanning Mount Hood National Forest with night-vision binoculars. One of those guys found where Limerick had dug his way in, under the fence, likely using the cheapest of soldier's tools; a damn shovel. The good ones cost around fifty dollars. That fence had cost four million dollars to electrify.

He's got two heavily armed guys in a powerboat to the north, out on the Columbia River.

MacDonald stands and watches two soldiers patrol the grounds using the buddy system; nobody's ever out of sight of someone. He spots the wink of the overhead drones his tech division put up; they've got infrared cameras to look for heat signatures. He hears the heavy thrum of armored personnel carriers he's had brought in. Project 404 purchased a half dozen German Dingos, heavily armored, MRAP-style—mine-resistant, ambush-protected—infantry mobility vehicles. Basically a rolling fortress on a Daimler chassis. If Limerick's planted IEDs around the campus, moving one of these trucks here will have paid off big-time.

MacDonald smokes.

He's got John Kite and RJ Sharpe holed up here in the administration building. The math brain behind everything, Teddy Meeker, is here, too.

MacDonald finishes the cigarette and taps another out of the pack.

It's nearly 0030 hours. He has no idea what Limerick's next move will be. But it will come soon.

Dez quietly leaves his electric bass guitar outside Raziah's room and, at 1 A.M., climbs back in the Jeep and reverses course, leaving Sunriver, gassing up at an all-night station in Bend, heading north around the east side of Mount Hood. There is almost no traffic at this hour. Dez keeps to the speed limit and listens to the BBC World Service on the Wrangler's satellite radio system. He's packed the remainder of Veronika Tsygan's sandwiches and bottles of water. He can see the Milky Way.

Veronika's brothers, the goateed bison, stay in

Sunriver. They'll protect their sister and the Swanns. They are amiable hoods engaged in some sort of criminal activity in Detroit. They're not soldiers. They'd be in Dez's way if they came. That, plus they'd want to share the sandwiches.

He reaches Interstate 84, which parallels the Columbia River, at the town of Hood River and starts heading west. Toward Gamila.

CHAPTER 59

Around four in the morning, Gareth MacDonald heads to Kite's office on the fifth floor of the admin building. He's surprised to find John Kite awake. Kite is practicing his putting, yet again. He's wearing a very 1960s sweater-vest and chinos and saddle shoes.

MacDonald says, "Can't sleep, sir?"

Kite says, "Nope," and putts.

"Well, glad you're up. I've ordered a helo for you and Miss Sharpe. It'll be here at dawn."

"I thought we were hiding in the Fortress of Solitude."

"That was before we ran a nitrite test on Limerick's shirt. Man's been buying explosives. Or making 'em. Now I want you out of here."

Kite retrieves the ball, again using the head of his putter to gently nudge it across the break room floor. "Sweet Mother Machree, who is this Terminator?"

MacDonald says, "Gatekeeper. A special sort of soldier. Smart and educated and highly trained. The word on 'em is a gatekeeper can get through any door, hold any door, control egress through any door. I figured them for an urban myth until, well . . ." He shrugs.

"So we vamoose?"

"Aye. Got your private jet landing at Port Elsner,

in Washington. Helo takes you there, jet takes you to a mate of mine running a small paramilitary group outside Lethbridge, Alberta. Good soldiers. Solid as they come. They'll protect the two of you till I get Limerick."

"I still need Teddy Meeker."

"Aye, sir. Him, too."

Kite putts. Misses. He calmly retrieves the ball, bats it back up to the starting point. He finally looks up. "You're supposed to be as good as it gets. Baddest of the badasses. Plus, you know, you've got your own army. This guy's tough, but he can't be that tough."

MacDonald shrugs again. He has little interest in debating the military merits of Desmond Limerick with a man who's never served a day in uniform.

Kite thrusts a hand into the pocket of his pleated trousers and rests the putter across his shoulder. He looks like he should be on the back nine with Bing Crosby and Peter Lawford. "You can get him?"

MacDonald says, "Aye, sir."

"You think he's coming here?"

"He's not hiding from us. He could, but not indefinitely. He's coming."

"Well, let me say this, paisan, and then we'll forget about it: I am not happy that this one guy has caused you so much trouble. The man is shaking my confidence, Gareth. I'd be lying if I said different."

MacDonald says, "Understood."

"You kill this nutsack, then hey, it's all water over the dam. But until you—"

MacDonald pivots and sprints out the door.

Kite blinks. Twice.

"I . . . Hey! I was talking here!"

In the corridor, MacDonald runs and draws his walkie-talkie. "Yamada! Gessler! Check the dam! Check the fucking dam! Limerick's got engineering degrees! Check—"

That's when he feels the floor begin to vibrate under his combat boots.

CHAPTER 60

Before taking his beating and rescuing the Swanns, Dez had dug a tunnel under the fancy fence, separating Gamila from Mount Hood National Forest, as a bit of misdirection. He wants them looking on campus for his traps. Looking anywhere but the Lower Hood Dam.

Dez also used his skills with lockpicks and security systems and websites that night to breach the dam that holds back thousands of tons of water on the mighty Columbia. The security computers inside the dam soon identified Dez as a friendly.

He'd found fifteen spillways built into the convex dam, which consists of nearly three million cubic yards of concrete. The spillways are massive doors for river water. And when has Desmond Aloysius Limerick ever had any trouble with doors? Spillways number two through fourteen hang directly over the river. Hit any of those, and the river levels would rise on this side; fall on the eastern side.

The first of fifteen spillways is on the state of Washington side of the river and hovers over dry land.

The fifteenth of fifteen spillways rises over the easternmost end of the Gamila campus.

Dez reprogrammed the spillway computer that night, giving him access to the fifteenth of the fifteen spillways.

And this morning, at 4 A.M., the hour of the wolf, Dez sits in the driver's seat of his rented Wrangler, kisses the ruggedized leather cover of his tablet computer, thumbs it to life, and fully opens Flood Gate No. 15.

He'd noticed his first day here that a ravine runs through the campus, from the foot of the Lower Hood Dam in the east, diagonally west and south, culminating in the administration building and the lake over which it hovers.

The water Dez has released will want to follow that same route. He thinks MacDonald either garrisoned his troops—and Kite—in the admin building or in the almost-completed barracks building that Teddy Meeker had shown him from the roof of the admin building. Either way, thousands of tons of water now are vectoring along the ravine, straight for both buildings.

That done, Dez switches to the app on his tablet that he had used to screw up—and later to "fix"—the ten South Korean–made electric carts on the Gamila campus. Fix them he did. But that doesn't mean he ever gave up operational controls of them.

The ammonium nitrate and fuel oil he stole from the Parks and Rec site pair well to create an explosive known as ANFO. Been around donkey's years. Dez likes it because, gram for gram, it offers a decent heave energy—that's the bit causes the most physical damage—but with a low emulsion content. He combines his ANFO explosive plus duct tape with the box of GoPro cameras he'd bought at Bud's, thanks to the funds generously donated to the cause by RJ Sharpe. Dez thinks maybe she can write it off as a tax deduction, but possibly not.

The night that he'd waited in the national forest for first light, and his chance to rescue the Swanns, Dez's to-do list included ordering the ten little carts to unplug themselves, evacuate the campus, one at a time, and to await him on a side road a mile from the campus. There, he'd loaded them with his improvised explosive devices and the cameras.

Is MacDonald expecting explosives? Probably. He's damn smart. But mobile explosives?

With the flood coming from the east, Dez uses his tablet to order the ten bomb-laden carts back onto the campus from the west.

After eight of his driverless carts roll through the gate, into the campus, Dez's Jeep Wrangler hits the entrance at sixty miles per hour, races past the pithy wooden greeting sign, and slams into the visitors building. MacDonald had left only a single guard there, not figuring for a second Dez would waltz in through the front. The mercenary had been calling in, hoping to ask if anyone knew why the carts were moving at night, so his back is turned when Dez hits the building, killing the man on impact.

Dez climbs out and grabs a walkie-talkie from the corpse, returns to the Jeep. From his duffel in the passenger seat, he retrieves a roll of what might well be the greatest invention in the history of humankind: duct tape. He depresses the Send key, tapes it down, then jams the walkie-talkie up against the Jeep's radio. He finds an oldies station and cranks it up.

Iron Butterfly, "In-A-Gadda-Da-Vida." Dead brilliant.

Dez shoulders his messenger bag and starts marching into the campus.

CHAPTER 61

MacDonald sprints for the lobby of the admin building and stops at the guard desk. He knows there's a set of binoculars hiding in a cabinet. He whisks them up, feeling the floor vibrate under his boots. He's got men on guard duty down here, and he hears his guys muttering the words "earthquake" and "tanks."

He steps outside the building and peers into the night. Because of all the trees, the campus isn't well lit, even when he needs it well lit. He's had a full crew on alert through the night; once the primaries are in the air, heading to Canada, everyone can get some sleep. He spots soldiers near the barracks hall. A drone zips by overhead. The Dingo armored personnel carrier is parked outside, a soldier on top, manning the turret-mounted, 12.7 mm machine gun. One of the campus's electric carts whizzes into view from the west.

MacDonald raises the binoculars and peers east.

He spots whitecaps.

Limerick has breached the fucking dam.

Through the lenses, he sees smaller trees snap in half as a wall of water, five feet high, barrels through the campus. Headed right for him. He sees men sprinting for cover, and a few climbing trees. One is climbing a tree that snaps like a toothpick when the wave front hits it. The man and the tree are instantly submerged.

This isn't enough water to topple the admin building, or any of the campus buildings. Inundate them, yes. Will it kill some of MacDonald's men? Certainly. But this building should be . . .

MacDonald freezes— Who's running the electric carts at night?

He turns to the west, peers through the binoculars, spots the cart he'd noticed earlier. Two of them are running. No, three.

And nobody is driving them.

The nearest one plows straight into the northwestern corner of the admin building and explodes.

The concussive force drives MacDonald off his feet and onto his ass, three feet back. Glass shards rain down on him. The brilliant flash of light blinds him. The pressure against his eardrums feels like the punch of a heavyweight champ.

The carts! The fucking carts that Limerick used to get onto the campus the first time!

The water is close now as MacDonald scrambles for his feet, eyes dazzle-blinded, his elbow screaming at him after slamming into the ground. He sees a flash, in the distance, and thinks the almost-completed barracks building is taking fire, too. He gets to the entrance of the admin building, dashes inside, and begins sprinting for the stairs.

The building rumbles as another electric cart hits it and detonates. Overhead lights blink out, sputter, and kick back in.

The carts are coming from the west. The river water is coming from the east. It arrives and, halfway up the first flight of stairs, MacDonald turns and sees gushers of water smashing windows, pushing open the doors, and pouring into the lobby. He spots a body, floating facedown, arms and legs akimbo, bouncing hard off the reception desk. One of his men.

A third explosion rocks the building and the lights flicker off. After a beat, yellow emergency lights erupt. MacDonald draws his walkie-talkie. Classic American rock 'n' roll blares on the primary frequency.

Limerick.

Some of MacDonald's men will have the forethought to switch to the secondary, backup frequency. That's SOP. Or it would be if a wall of water wasn't slamming into the campus and if wheeled IEDs, like gaily painted torpedoes, weren't zooming about looking for targets.

He switches freqs and clips his radio back to his belt.

John Kite is still in his fifth-floor office when Mac-Donald gets back up there. Kite's eyes are as wide as saucers, gripping his putter like some kind of weapon. His voice is an octave higher than usual. "What the—"

"Stay where you are!" the Scotsman bellows. "We've lost the campus!"

MacDonald leaves, races up the stairs, and reaches the guest apartments on the ninth floor. He finds RJ Sharpe and Teddy Meeker out of their rooms. Sharpe is wearing sweat bottoms and a T-shirt and is barefoot, her hair messy. It's just past 4 A.M. Meeker is buttoning his blue jeans, wearing a PSU Vikings sweatshirt, his cheek crisscrossed with pillow marks.

"We're evac'ing. Take what ye need, because you'll not be returning!" He points a finger at Meeker's chest. "That means whatever you need to maintain access to the Witness Protection Program and the Wolf Pack Count. Aye?"

Meeker nods.

RJ Sharpe says, "Limerick."

"Aye."

"How?"

"Unimportant. I'm getting the three of you to Canada."

"You're coming with us?"

"Limerick," MacDonald says. "It ends here. Now."

CHAPTER 62

Limerick has no idea how many soldiers are on the campus, but it's not three hundred. Arabella Satti of MI6 was able to confirm that mysterious and extremely successful bands of guerrillas have been popping up in Kenya and Tanzania, and in the failed state of Zanj. That means fewer men here. But so what? Dez is tough and trained but he can't take on two hundred guys, or one hundred, or fifty. He couldn't take on five, if they were the right five. Hell, MacDonald nearly separated Dez's skull from his shoulders all by himself.

So this cannot be a stand-up fight. The odds are breathtakingly against him for that.

Dez knows how to fight, but he knows how to skulk, too. Thankfully, everyone will be distracted by his flood from the east and his bomb carts.

He checks the virus his Hong Kong hacker helped him slide into the Gamila security computers and finds nothing. The idiots finally thought to shut down the damn system. Took them long enough. It's all right. Dez no longer needs that back door.

He stays off the unpaved, tree-lined, and well-marked lanes of the campus, dodging through the branches and over unlevel ground, vectoring east toward the admin building and the new barracks. A few times soldiers pop into view and Dez either hits the ground or ducks behind trunks and artfully scattered boulders. Soon he sees the glow of fires, and knows he's heading in the right direction.

He's still a good quarter mile from either building when he reaches the rush of water. It's going like gangbusters through the ravine that connects the dam and the little lake in the south-central sector of the property, but Dez is a good ways away from that, and out here, the force isn't sufficient to knock over trees or kill soldiers.

Elsewhere, the flood hits the campus generator, and every electric light in every nonessential building blinks out.

Dez wades through thigh-deep and fast-running water, letting trees and boulders serve as anchors here and there. He can see that his ANFO surprise—ammonium nitrate and fuel oil—has started fires in both buildings he pre-targeted. He wasn't one hundred percent sure the carts would follow a programmed track, but he's well pleased with his little darlings.

Men are rushing around, attempting to put out the flames, which is a bit bonkers in the middle of a flood, Dez thinks. The water'll take care of the ground-floor fires without much assistance.

He's in an equilateral triangle with the buildings now, hiding behind a glacial erratic a meter and a half in diameter, with the admin building at his twelve o'clock and the Project 404 barracks at his nine o'clock. Dim yellow emergency lights flicker in both buildings. As Dez watches, every window on the second floor of the barracks shatters, glass arcing into the floodwaters, soldiers on firefighting duty ducking for cover.

For all of the windows to explode simultaneously, either the air pressure inside the buildings has greatly increased—it has not, Dez ventures—or the explosions have damaged the physical integrity of the building. If that's the case, the building could be falling apart.

Behind him, a male voice booms, "Hey! You!"

Dez turns and spots a soldier jogging toward him, rifle at the ready. Dez responds in Spanish, and makes the universal *Come on hurry!* gesture with his hand.

The merc keeps running toward him, slogging hip-deep against the current, but with his gun down now. "What? I don't speak . . . Jesus, I told 'em to hire English speakers. How the fuck are we supposed to fight—"

Dez straightens his right arm, jabbing the guy in the nose. He grunts and falls back, arms straight out at forty-five-degree angles, splashing into the current. Dez didn't want to risk firing a shot from the Russian-made Rooks, thus drawing any unwanted attention. The merc floats in about two feet of water and sinks, slowly, beneath the waves.

Before he floats away, Dez takes the man's radio. Sure enough, MacDonald's men have switched to a backup frequency. Dez doesn't mess with this one. He needs to hear what MacDonald and his lot are chatting about.

Behind Dez and a bit to the east, more windows shatter in the barracks building. A lightning-bolt-shaped crack wiggles its way from the lower left corner of its façade to the upper right.

If MacDonald is hiding his primaries in there, he'll have to evac them. Quick-like.

And if they're not in that building, chances are they'll be in the admin building.

CHAPTER 63

In the yellowish glow of the fifth-floor emergency lighting, MacDonald checks his watch. He has a civilian helicopter inbound from the suburban Hillsboro Airport. It's scheduled to reach the campus right around dawn, which is perhaps thirty minutes away. There's a helipad atop the new barracks building, but thanks to that madman, Limerick, the building's in danger of failing. MacDonald has tried to raise the pilots on the secondary radio frequency but they haven't switched yet, and they won't until they get close enough to pick up the classic rock that Limerick used to screw up the primary frequency.

A helo can't land on the admin building roof because of the Japanese garden up there. Too much stuff, from strings of lights to tiny round pebbles, could get sucked into the intake or the propellers. That means they need a new LZ before the bird arrives. One outside the floodplain. All of the land of Gamila slopes toward the little lake. If MacDonald wants to connect Kite, Sharpe, and Meeker with the helicopter, it'll have to be at the highest point on the property. Which would be near the main gate.

MacDonald tries to raise the soldier manning the gate. No response. Either that man hasn't yet switched to the secondary frequency, or . . .

He turns to the soldier nearest him. Another SAS man he's known and fought with for years. "Burke, working on that head count?"

Burke nods. "Think we've ten left, Sergeant. Those are the ones on the backup frequency, anyway."

Ten. They'd started with twenty-four. "Understood. Head to the main gate. Take Haddad; the new lad, the Moroccan. I think Limerick's on the campus."

"Sir."

MacDonald turns to his last soldier on the fifth floor. "Check stores. We should have a Zodiac here. We were going to deploy it to Zanj, but it should still be here. Get it, bring it back. We're moving out the principals."

The soldier nods and heads for the stairs.

The only people left on the fifth floor with MacDonald are John Kite, RJ Sharpe, and Teddy Meeker.

The sun is rising but still obscured by a heavy tree cover as Burke and the Moroccan soldier, Haddad, slog their way from the admin building toward the main gate. The water was fast-moving and thigh-high near the buildings, but gets slower and shallower as they wade westward. "If I wanted to fight in swamps, I woulda stayed in Cambodia!" Burke grouses.

"Don't like this England man, this Limerick," the Moroccan mutters, keeping his voice low. "He everywhere. He got us chasing tails."

"Yeah? If I get him in my sights, we'll see if he bleeds mysteriously, too."

The sky is brighter out here near the gate, and the helicopter out of Hillsboro is much lower now.

As Burke and Haddad draw near, they hear music coming from the visitors center. It's funk. They circle the little log cabin and find a Jeep smashed into the building. Burke spots a dead soldier. He'd never gotten around to learning this kid's name.

He checks his walkie. The pilot has switched to the secondary frequency—after getting an earful of Parliament-Funkadelic on the primary frequency. Burke starts issuing landing orders.

Haddad lights a red flare and drops it in the grass behind the Jeep, keeping an eye open for leaked gas or oil from the vehicle. He jogs twenty feet and drops another, turns forty-five degrees and drops another, and another. He's created a smoky, glowing red baseball diamond, right inside the gate. MacDonald had been right: This site is above the Columbia River flood-waters.

The flares define a landing zone.

Burke cradles his automatic rifle, scanning the scene. Haddad does the same. "Boss? Bring down the helo or get this England man first? Don't like him being behind me."

Burke nods. "Best guess: He came in through the gate, took out the guard shack, and moved eastward on foot. He's after the primaries. No reason he'd stay out here." He lifts his radio to his mouth. "You have an LZ! Bring it down! Over!"

The pilot gives him the thumbs-up through the bubble canopy.

Over the sound of the rotors, Burke bellows into his radio, "MacDonald! Bird's here! Bird is down! Bring the package! Bri—SHIT!"

The helo's parallel skids are a foot off the turf when one of the electric carts whizzes in from outside the gate.

Dez now has binoculars he stole from a drowned soldier. The sun has risen, still mostly behind large stands of trees, the light penetrating the foliage and casting long shadows everywhere. Dez is backlit, where he's standing. His clothes are water-drenched from the waist down. It's going to be a beautiful day. With the aid of the glasses, Dez can see the main gate of Gamila, and the visitors center, and the hovering helicopter, now quite low. He glances from the glasses to his tablet and sees the exact same tableau, but from the point of view of the GoPro lashed to the explosives, lashed to the cart. He doesn't know either of the two soldiers he spots through the glasses. The white guy to one knee, H & K butt to his shoulder, lines up and fires a steady pattern of slugs at the oncoming cart. He's spotted the bundle Dez had left bungeed to the bonnet; he's aiming at that.

The ANFO bomb explodes under the man's assault.

Dez hopes the cart would hit the helo first. It doesn't, but he lucks out. The steering wheel is catapulted into the air and connects with the chopper's rotors. Sparks flash. The two soldiers hit the dirt, arms over their heads.

Dez watches through the binoculars as one propeller sheers off from the rest and scimitars into the visitors center. It stands, canted at a forty-degree angle, vibrating like a tuning fork.

The helicopter falls only about three feet but that's enough to crush one of the skids. The bird tilts wildly and the surviving propeller blades chew into the grass and dirt entry path, splintering.

The white guy is lying on his stomach in the tall grass; he raises his head from beneath his arms and surveys the scene.

The Black guy appears to be swearing a blue streak, holding a broken arm, blood soaking through his sleeve.

The pilot emerges from the downed helo, pistol in his hand, panting a little, wild-eyed. He's unhurt, but his ride is history.

Right, Dez thinks. Scratch one egress.

Dez watches the pyrotechnics with his cart attack and the helo and all that because he's standing amid the Japanese garden atop the admin building. Where, below him, if he's right, all of his targets are nicely ensconced.

CHAPTER 64

MacDonald has gone from twenty-four soldiers to ten in very little time. He lost the Moroccan to a broken arm but gained the uninjured helicopter pilot, so that's net-zero. But now comes news that a team he'd originally tasked to a conflict in Kenya has been rerouted and just landed at a small airport in Troutdale. Not only does this give him an additional eleven men, but they're equipped for a standing fight in hostile territory. They've got full field kits, automatic weapons, grenades, top-end body armor, helmets, the works. Once they secure ground transportation and hightail it out to Gamila, the odds will turn back in MacDonald's favor.

Limerick seems to be a master of the "cry havoc and let slip" school. But all of that relies on surprise.

MacDonald's surprise has passed.

He's on the fifth floor of the admin building, in Kite's kitschy office with Kite, RJ Sharpe, and Teddy Meeker. Kite has cracked open the sliding glass balcony door to air the place out. Meeker needs a beard trim and a haircut but he appears otherwise spookily unruffled. Instead of her rock goddess attire, Sharpe looks thin and angular in sweats. Kite is losing some of his Rat Pack cool, and MacDonald thinks the man's been hitting the sauce a little hard. Which, given that it's dawn, is problematic.

RJ's Clockjack-brand cell phone vibrates and she pulls it from the side pocket of her sweat bottoms.

Meeker sits on a couch and checks his email on his own phone. "This guy Limerick." He addresses nobody in particular, shakes his head. "He's a pip, this guy."

Kite says, "We wouldn't be in this mess except you ratted us out to Limerick, buddy boy."

"I did." Meeker looks up and adjusts his glasses. "The law of unintended consequences."

Kite studies the math wiz. He sips a scotch and soda. Meeker is really getting on Kite's nerves now. Which is why nobody has noticed that RJ Sharpe has read and reread a text on her phone five times. She's sitting in a chair in the far corner of the office, head down, elbows on her knees. The newly risen sun is shining through the sliding glass door to the balcony. Sharpe stands, tucks the phone back in her pocket, runs one hand through her curly auburn hair.

"I'm going up to the roof. To smoke."

MacDonald says, "Don't think that's wise."

Meeker says, "You don't smoke."

"It seems like a good time to start." Sharpe walks up to MacDonald and holds out her hand, palms up.

The Scotsman studies her awhile. She stares right back.

"We don't agree on much," he says, digging a pack of cigarettes and a lighter from his camo trousers. "But yeah. This'd be a good time to smoke 'em if you got 'em, ma'am."

MacDonald checks his watch as the CEO exits. His guys from the Kenyan job should be here in forty-five minutes.

The elevators are out, thanks to the main power being cut and the damage the building took, so RJ Sharpe heads for the stairs. A lifelong bicyclist, she has the lung capacity of a college athlete. She draws her cell phone again and, in the stairwell's yellowing glow of the emergency vapor lights, reads the text.

> Your office. Alone. You and me have no quarrel. Help me, and you can leave. Limerick.

She stops on the tenth floor, checks behind her to make sure MacDonald hasn't followed her, then steps into the C-suite floor. There are four corner offices up here. One belonged to Joel Menache, who died when his car went— She stops herself. Who died when Teddy used his math skills to draw John Kite and Gareth Mac-Donald into their world to kill him.

One corner office belongs to Winston Noel, who's in Seattle, recovering from surgery to both splintered wrists. Another corner office belongs to Teddy, who could hole up in there for days, even weeks, poring over his math problems.

Sharpe heads for the fourth corner of the executive level. Her office. The door is unlocked. She steps in, eyes scanning. She can see just fine, lights off but with the drapes open, Mount Hood glowing white like the Paramount Studios logo come to life. Her office features no desk, no table. She uses it so rarely, it always feels like someone else's work space.

"Morning." The voice comes from behind her, not from the empty office. She turns. Desmond Limerick had been hiding in one of the other offices, a gun in his hand, waiting to see if she'd come alone, likely. He gestures toward the office door by flicking the barrel of the handgun.

Inside, Dez closes the door and locks it. He's been here already and left his shoulder bag on a chair near the door. He slides the gun into the bag. "Sorry for the melodrama."

Sharpe runs her hand through her hair; her nervous tell. "Did you mean what you wrote?"

"John Kite is conspiring with Sergeant MacDonald t'kill me friends. I've no intention of letting either of them off the hook. Sorry, can't be done. You an' me, though . . ." He shrugs.

"I lied to you about Astoria. I lured you into a trap. You got shot."

Dez laughs. He leans back against the office door. "People been shooting at me me whole life, love! Never hold a grudge against that." He lifts his T-shirt and shows her the most recent exit wound. "See? Healed up nice. No muss, no fuss."

She studies his eyes. "I got an alert that some of my banking accounts saw an unusual transfer. Was that you?"

"Was, and I'm grateful as hell for the loan."

She studies him. "I don't know what to make of you."

"Nor I, you. Teddy my lad told me about how you started the company. The four of yez. How you were the moral North Star. You're Jewish, aye? *Tikkun olam? Healin'* the world."

She nods. "In my faith, it's"—she searches for the right phrase—"aspirational. To act in a way that's beneficial to all. It's important. Clockjack *is* that. I explained it to you in Astoria."

"Clockjack *was* that, love."

"No," she says, and takes a step closer to him. "All the things I told you. The poor. Subsistence farmers. Educating girls. Fair-trade goods. All of that. We're still doing all of that."

"While hiding a terrorist organization, Project 404, which plans to topple a couple of governments in

Africa. Love, ye can't be both. Ye can't harbor that, an' believe you're the hero o' the piece."

She straightens her back, eyes narrowing. It's been an exhausting few days, Dez has no doubt, and she's in no mood to be lectured. This woman has been a chief executive officer and a media darling since Dez was a teenager.

"Oh please. Kite and MacDonald are blowing up parts of the world that would blow up anyway. They prolong a war in Africa? So what? If that war ended, the next would flare up within weeks. They blow up some oil pipeline in Tanzania? Order the hit on a cabinet minister? Forgive me if I don't cry tears for the narco-state petrogarchs who run that black hole of a continent!"

Dez shakes his head in wonderment.

"Here's a mental exercise." Her eyes are bright. She's in her zone now: engaged in one of her speeches, the speeches for which she's world-famous. "You've been helping your friends here. You've been risking your own life for them. Haven't you?"

"I try."

"Okay, well imagine if you had cancer. Imagine the Swann sisters had asked for your help, but your body was busy fighting itself. *Devouring* itself. But it hadn't weakened you yet. Would you have answered their call?"

Dez doesn't hesitate. "Would, aye. I've nowhere near enough friends in this world. Do what I can for 'em."

"Even if you had cancer?"

He nods.

"Project 404 is a cancer inside Clockjack Solutions. That's all. I'm the CEO of Clockjack. Under my leadership, we've addressed childhood hunger and literacy on four continents. We've provided broadband to huge swaths of rural America. We've all but eradicated dengue fever in parts of the Caribbean. And Clockjack? The core of our business? The apps and the phones? They empower the people! Our tech is like . . ."

She appears to be reaching for a metaphor, although Dez is convinced this is a well- and oft-rehearsed speech.

". . . our tech is like antivirals. Keeping people healthy. Making them stronger and more resilient. And we provide all that, while battling a cancer within ourselves. Within Clockjack. John Kite. Sergeant Mac-Donald. The ransacking of the Witness Protection Program. The Wolf Pack Count. We're strong enough to live with that, while serving the rest of the world. By *healing* the world. By living the oath of *tikkun olam*. Do you honestly not get that?"

Dez studies her awhile. She's a remarkably handsome woman, a woman of strength, and great charisma, and purpose. And he can see why tens of millions of people have been ensorcelled by her speeches. He says, "Help me and you're free to go."

She peers into his eyes, decides she's out of options and might as well trust him. "What do you need?"

"How many men does MacDonald have? An' who's in the building now?"

"I lied last time you asked me that."

"When the music changes, then the rhythm of the dance must change also. African friend of mine taught me that."

"All right. I heard him say he's down to ten or so, but he's got eleven more on their way. I don't know who all is on the ground floor, but some of his soldiers are. John, Teddy, and I were on the fifth floor, just now. MacDonald's with them."

"Good. Outside, door between your office an' Teddy Meeker's. It's marked Valve Room. It's unlocked now. There's maintenance stairs leading to the ground floor, an' look for a maintenance hatch in the floor.

Also unlocked. It leads to the lake. Jump in. It's about waist-deep. Wade to the far south side of the lake. When ye get to the fence, turn left. East. Ye go one point five kilometers, ye'll find a hole I dug under the fence. Other side's the national forest. Head west, back the way ye came, an' you'll reach the county road in about three kilometers."

She says, "And you're just letting me go."

"Am. Aye."

She watches him awhile. Dez is running short on time, but it's probably a good idea to let her get there on her own.

"Thank you."

"No purpose served in killin' you," Dez says, amiably. "Off with you, now. Skedaddle."

On the fifth floor, MacDonald checks his watch. He's got his ten men deployed in and around the admin building. His backup crew is en route. Smart move would be to hold tight and wait for them to get here. But . . .

. . . but but but . . .

They'd be safe in the admin building if they weren't facing a gatekeeper. This bastard is trained to open any door and to keep it open.

He draws his walkie-talkie. "Burke? Over."

"Sarge?"

MacDonald toggles the Send switch. "Head back to the storeroom. We've battery-powered motion detectors. I want a two-man team to set them up on every floor of the stairwell. Limerick's coming. Mean to trap him here till the others arrive. Over."

"Roger that, but there's maintenance stairs, too. Northern side. I remember from when I studied the blueprints of this building. Over."

MacDonald could draw his weapon and shoot himself in the temple. It never dawned on him to study the blueprints of this building. "You're a good soldier, Burke. Bring enough sensors for both stairs. Also, make sure the elevators can't be restarted. When the backup team comes, we go floor by floor. An' we catch this rat-fucker once and for all."

CHAPTER 65

Two soldiers—one armed with an automatic weapon, one with a backpack full of battery-powered motion sensors—goes floor to floor, installing them. They test each one and declare them good.

They do the same with the narrow and poorly lit maintenance stairs.

Another team removes the governor from the elevator machine room. Without that, even if Limerick could reroute power to the elevators, they still wouldn't run.

The backup team is ten minutes out.

Dez is on the roof, keeping an eye on the campus. RJ Sharpe said more soldiers are en route but he hasn't seen any enter through the gate yet. He's got the radio he stole from a dead soldier. MacDonald knew his primary and secondary frequencies were compromised, and now both of them have gone dead. He's spreading the word, face-to-face, to switch to a third freq, likely as not. That's okay. Before everything went silent, Dez heard about the motion detectors in the stairs. And it gives him an idea.

He quickly gathers what he needs: the hose that campus maintenance uses to water the lush Japanese garden, and also the extension cord for the strings of festive lights and the Japanese lanterns.

He uses his folding knife to shear off some of the rubber coating of the extension cord and to expose the wires within. He loops the long cord around his shoulder.

The garden hose is quite lengthy, to serve the whole garden. Dez turns the water on high, then drags the hose to the door to the stairs. He enters the stairwell, wedges the nozzle in the doorway so water pours into the interior, then sprints down, splashing as he goes.

MacDonald and two of his men have set up a laptop computer on John Kite's desk. They've loaded the monitoring app for the motion detectors. And one of the detectors, on the tenth floor, lights up.

"Ho. He's in the building. Tenth floor." The soldier, who's from Thailand, grins at his boss.

MacDonald toggles his walkie-talkie. Four of his men are in the lobby. "Burke: Limerick's in the stairwell. Tenth floor. Get ready."

"He's moving down," the Thai soldier narrates, eyes glued to the laptop. "Nine . . . eight . . . seven . . . wait."

"What?"

The man frowns. "Look."

He points to the motion sensor indicators on the screen. The ones marked ten through seven are lit, and as MacDonald watches, number six goes green.

"That's not right."

"What's not right?"

The soldier says, "They're motion detectors. They detect motion."

"So?"

Number five goes green. The soldier points to the row of lights. "So they should blink off about five seconds after he's out of sight. They're detecting motion on all these floors. *Current* motion. Limerick—if it is Limerick—is on every floor."

The light for the fourth floor goes green.

"How's that possible?"

The Thai soldier shrugs. "Maybe he's not as alone as we figured."

MacDonald toggles his walkie. "Hold up. Hold up. Limerick may have allies. Over."

The third floor goes green.

Dez races through the water that's pouring into the stairwell, aware that the mini-deluge is triggering every motion sensor on every level. RJ Sharpe said the Clockjack executives and MacDonald were holed up on five. He gets to six, pistol raised, and throws open the door.

This floor is mostly a cubicle farm, with private offices in the four corners. He spots no one now.

He goes to one knee and plugs in his extension cord. He unloops it, walking backward to the stairwell door, opens the door, and lodges the cord in between the door and the doorjamb. It's about two meters off the floor. The now very wet floor.

He races to the southeast corner office of the sixth floor—an office facing Mount Hood—and fires three shots into a window, shattering the glass.

That should get them running his direction.

Dez uses an office chair, sweeping it back and forth to dislodge any glass in the window. That done, he steps up onto the windowsill and crouches.

Directly over the balcony of John Kite's executive office, one floor below.

He can hear yelling from the stairwell now, but dimly. "I'm on eight! . . . We're at the fifth floor! Over!"

MacDonald has deployed most of his remaining men to box Dez in.

He is on the windowsill, half in and half out of the

building, concentrating on the noise from the stairwell. "On my mark: Go!"

He hears the crack of the sixth-floor stairwell door being kicked open. Followed by a scream. Whoever Dez just electrocuted, when the electrical cord dropped into the water, hadn't safely indexed his finger, and Dez hears the long rattle of automatic fire echoing from the stairwell. Around him, the emergency lights dim and flicker and die. The backup generator shorts out when the wire hits the water.

Dez grabs the windowsill with both hands and lowers himself out the window. When his arms are straight, he releases his grip and drops about five feet onto a table on the fifth-floor balcony.

Only sunlight illuminates John Kite's office, meaning Dez is backlit, which is good for tactical reasons. He spots an Asian soldier sitting at Kite's desk, eyes on a laptop. Dez holds one of his steel marbles. He rears back and lets fly, just as the soldier spots him from the corner of his eye.

The man grunts and crumples to the floor.

John Kite does a perfect Hollywood spit take, a fine fan of whiskey and soda water traveling a good meter and a half.

"Cricket," Dez says. "All-league bowler, three seasons running."

Teddy Meeker is sitting on the couch, in the semidark, thumbing through messages on his phone, facing away from Dez. He sees the soldier collapse; see's Kite's comedic reaction. He doesn't even turn around to see who it is; just returns to his messages.

Kite is choking, coughing up booze from his airway. Dez approaches him. "Waitwaitwait!" The man gasps between coughs, his eyes watering, shoulders hunched in.

Dez takes Kite in his arms, standing behind him. "You're John Kite, then?"

"Please wait! I'm rich! I'm very rich! I—"

"Sent thugs t'beat up a girl who was no threat to you an' yours. Sent gunmen to kill her. You're shite, John."

"Waitnopleasedon't!"

Dez braces Kite's shoulders with one arm, uses his other hand to twist Kite's head, sharply. His spinal column snaps like a celery stalk.

His corpse goes limp. Dez eases it to the floor.

From the couch, Meeker says, "Hi, Limerick."

"Kite woulda kept comin' for the girls. Even if he was safe in Africa, yeah? But you won't. Right?"

Meeker finally looks up. "Why would I? How would that benefit me?"

Dez says, "Now you're doin' your sums, my lad."

MacDonald has fewer men now, for sure. How many? Dez doesn't know. He hears something and walks out onto Kite's balcony.

Three big SUVs have arrived on campus and come to a halt just before the deepest of the floodwaters. Men begin to deploy.

Now is not the time for a stand-up fight.

Dez moves to the desk and shoves the unconscious Thai soldier to the floor. The man's moaning, coming to, so Dez breaks both of his thumbs. He won't be holding a gun in the near future.

Dez opens a Word document on the laptop they'd been using to monitor the stairwell motion detectors.

SGT. MACDONALD—PARLEY. TWENTY-FOUR HOURS. SAME DINER. LIMERICK.

Back out on the balcony now, Dez heaves himself over the edge, grabs decorative brick motifs, and lets himself drop to the balcony on four. Same trick to the third floor, then to the second. He's over the little lake, which is much deeper thanks to the flood, and he jumps in.

He can get to the fence and be gone before Mac-Donald sets up a search pattern for the whole 312-acre campus.

CHAPTER 66

RJ Sharpe's hair is a bedraggled mess and her limp clothes are grimy with caked-on, dried-on mud, from when she'd climbed under the campus fence. Mud streaks her face and neck. She flags down a passing Greyhound bus on Interstate 84 and tells a sob story about being marooned in the national forest. The driver gives her a ride to the downtown Portland station. She estimates that fifteen people are on the bus, but they don't recognize her.

She has no purse, no ID, no money, and her Clockjack phone got fried when she went wading through the lake.

Downtown, she takes the calculated risk of hopping on the MAX Blue Line train to Gresham without a ticket. The chances of running into one of the fare-takers or transit police is minimal. One of the stops is only blocks from her house on Mount Tabor.

She gets there, only to remember, too late, that it's a crime scene, still blocked off with police warning tape. She's too tired to care. One of MacDonald's men shattered the lock of the sliding glass door to her kitchen, so she goes around that side. Police warning tape crisscrosses the door, and she ducks under it. Glass glitters on her shiny floor, along with muddy footprints and dried leaves, further aggravating her.

First things first: She needs a drink. She walks into her living room, pauses, then bends over and throws up into a potted plant. She's had nothing to eat since the night before, so it's mostly just gut-crunching dry heaves.

Her living room is spattered in blood. Bits of cardboard are everywhere, as are bolts and nuts and screws. Many of them blood-soaked. Fingerprint powder cakes every surface. The walls and the furniture she'd spent months meticulously gathering are shredded by flying debris, but only in an area about a foot off the floor. Anything higher than that is undamaged.

But the blood is everywhere.

She keeps dry-heaving, her back arched, tears flowing down her cheeks.

Sharpe eventually rises on shaky legs and stumbles up to her second-story bedroom. She sits on her bed, holding her aching abdominal muscles, and sobs for a time.

She strips and takes the longest shower of her life. In clean clothes, she boots up her desktop, looking for news about the attack on the Clockjack campus.

Her default setting is Twitter. And she's trending.

RJ Sharpe has trended before. It's a point of pride that her TED Talk speeches often make news.

She checks her email: dozens of notes from journalists asking for comments.

She goes back to Twitter and searches for her name. She finds a video.

It was taken in her office. Which she'd had rigged to serve as a network-quality video set. On screen, she's wearing sweats, hair uncombed, talking to someone off camera.

"Oh please. Kite and MacDonald are blowing up parts of the world that would blow up anyway. They prolong a war in Africa? So what? If that war ended,

*the next would flare up within weeks. They blow up
some oil pipeline in Tanzania? Order the hit on a cabinet minister? Forgive me if I don't cry tears for the
narco-state petrogarchs who run that black hole of a
continent!"*

She checks a counter.

The video's been shared well over twenty thousand
times.

She sits like that for a little more than an hour. Realizing why Dez lured her to her office. Why he let her
live.

Dez isn't just trying to destroy Project 404. He's
killed Clockjack Solutions. The company's days are
over.

And the bastard didn't even have the decency to
shoot her and put her out of her misery.

CHAPTER 67

After RJ Sharpe's stunning revelations—which went out on Instagram, Twitter, and Facebook—a joint task force of FBI, the U.S. Marshals Service, and Oregon State Police raid the Clockjack campus in the Columbia Gorge. They do not find Sergeant Gareth MacDonald, nor any living soldiers. The authorities do find a large number of dead mercenaries, some Americans, some from several other countries. Just like the wounded men Portland police had taken out of Sharpe's Mount Tabor home, days earlier.

At Gamila, the authorities find the body of Willard Dukane, head of special projects at Clockjack, and his fingerprints quickly identify him as one of the most wanted white-collar criminals in the Western Hemisphere, John Kite.

His spine has been severed. He likely died instantly. The cause of death is not immediately clear.

They find Teddy Meeker, the genius behind the Clockjack technology, in the same room as Kite's body. He does not seem fazed by the destruction—the dead bodies, the collapsed barracks building, the flooding from a clearly malfunctioning spillway of the Lower Hood Dam. He has nothing to say about any of that. An FBI medic checks him out and determines that Meeker may be suffering from a complete mental breakdown caused by post-traumatic stress.

Once the feds have identified John Kite, their colleagues in Seattle drop by a hospital and check in on the CFO of Clockjack. And of course his fingerprints identify him as Winston Noel, drug lord from Jamaica.

The feds have not told the media or the community that they'd lost all control of the Witness Protection Program. But now they figure out how WITSEC was compromised. Forensic auditors will spend the next ninety days weeding the federal computers of all hints of Meeker's Clockjack programming.

Nobody finds RJ Sharpe, CEO of Clockjack. But her personal bank accounts have been emptied, and rumors persist that she was seen on a flight from Turkey to Northern Cyprus, which does not have an extradition treaty with the United States.

CHAPTER 68

From a motel on Interstate 205, the soldier called Burke steps directly between Gareth MacDonald and the door.

"Sergeant. No."

MacDonald smiles. "Get out of my way, lad. Do it fecking now."

"Every law enforcement agency, and every intelligence agency, in the Western Hemisphere's got a shoot-on-sight order out for us. You know this. This isn't some stupid Western, you and John Wayne, *High Noon,* who draws fastest. Jesus Christ, man. You're a pro. You're not going after Limerick."

MacDonald keeps smiling. "Am. Have to. Him an' me, and that's all there is left in the fecking universe." He checks his diver's watch. "Transport's coming. You and the last two guys. Get 'em over the border to Canada. Me mate's waiting to pick you up in Calgary. You're the last of the crew in the States. I'll kill Limerick and catch you up."

Burke studies his boss's eyes. MacDonald doesn't look manic. Or even angry. And he keeps smiling.

"Fuck it. Coming with you."

"Suit yourself."

Burke steps aside and MacDonald reaches for the door. "Don't think John Wayne was in *High Noon,* though."

*   *   *

MacDonald and Burke wear Carhartt jackets and Portland Timbers baseball caps, pulled low. They carry only their SIG Sauers, clipped to their belts under their jackets. They get to the Old Town Chinatown diner, the one with the fantastic food and the world's rudest waiter.

Burke peels off and crosses the street to stand in an alcove, eyes on foot traffic and cars. The alcove is perfect; serving a now-closed sporting goods store, full view of the street, darkened so nobody this close to dawn will spot Burke unless he wants to be spotted.

The diner is on the right-hand side of the street, and they'd already scanned the left-hand-side roofs on their walk in, looking for rifle barrels and the glint of light off a telescopic lens. Nothing.

MacDonald walks into the place and the world's rudest waiter hands him a cell phone. "Your friend gave me twenty bucks to give you this. He also prepaid for an order of the blueberry pancakes. You want 'em?"

MacDonald takes the phone. "Walk into your kitchen. Stay there."

"This is my place. I'll walk where—"

MacDonald draws his gun and the world's rudest waiter steps into his kitchen.

Only one number has been preprogrammed into this phone. MacDonald hits Speaker and connects.

"The question," says Desmond Limerick, "is this: Are we talkin' as soldiers, or as blokes?"

MacDonald stands at the door of the otherwise empty restaurant and turns the OPEN/CLOSED sign in the window.

Dez says, "If it's soldiers, then we've no worries, aye? You fought me for a paycheck. And because you're a good soldier, a good sergeant, who obeys orders an' gets the job done. But the man givin' the orders is dead.

And the company signin' your checks isn't doing so anymore. As a soldier, ye've no need to keep fighting with me."

MacDonald thinks about that. "But if we're just a couple of hard lads grew up in council estates? What, then?"

"Then you're mad that I had your sister targeted. She's unharmed, but still. I went for your family, and it's personal."

MacDonald stands by the cash register. He speaks softly. "You went for my family."

"Had to. Aye? Couldn't negotiate with Kite. Psychotic, that one. Had to have something that you prized greater than duty. Was me only play."

MacDonald doesn't respond.

Dez asks, "Is it business? Or is it personal?"

"Walk away? Bygones, an' that?" MacDonald shakes his head. "Would be the smart play. An' my sister's fine, sure. You used her for leverage, but just enough leverage to solve your problem, an' not one ounce more. Fair play to you."

Dez says, "But . . . ?"

"But we went toe-to-toe, and you won fair. You outthought me and outfought me. I had the best-trained mercenary army on Earth, and you took it apart brick by brick. Too many people saw that. Know about it. I'm a soldier, an' a sergeant, an' a mercenary. It's who I am, Dez. It's how I define myself."

"Your problem wasn't you, and wasn't your men, Gareth. It was Clockjack. Kite had a skull full of ferrets. RJ Sharpe? She wanted to make speeches and wow the crowd, with absolutely no care in the world how that came about. Noel? Unimportant, a paymaster, but still: a drug lord. Your troops was fine, but you were takin' orders from fuckwits an' lunatics."

For the first time, a spare smile ghosts across Mac-Donald's features. "Aye, but that's the same for every army, the world 'round. Innit?"

"That's true. That's true," Dez says with a small chuckle. "Was up to me, we'd walk away."

"I admire you, Dez. You're a good soldier. But I'm comin' for you. Comin' to kill you."

MacDonald waits through the longish pause.

Dez finally sighs. "Let me return the compliment. You're an excellent soldier an' a damn good sergeant. Come by it naturally. You see every angle. Right people in the right place."

"Thank you."

"Like that alcove across the street. Best surveillance spot on the whole—"

MacDonald is out of the restaurant, banging into the door so hard the glass cracks. He draws his SIG as he dashes out into the street. A Nissan screeches to a halt; MacDonald shows the driver the business end of his pistol and the man ducks down behind his dashboard. MacDonald keeps running, eyes up, head on a swivel, hits the other sidewalk. Gets ten feet down and spots Burke, in the alcove of the gone-bust store. He's on the pavement, on his back, unconscious. A small trickle of blood is visible near his right shoulder.

A metal marble the size of a fig is still rolling around in the alcove, bouncing off a rain gutter.

MacDonald does a 360, gun out, all the traffic stopped, people ducking and some running away. Some getting it on video for their social media feeds.

MacDonald never lost his grip on the phone. He raises it to his ear.

"North," Dez says.

MacDonald spins north. Spots Dez, two blocks away, on the sidewalk. On the phone. To the left of him is a pod of maybe two dozen food carts. To the right is a stubby, three-story municipal building.

Dez points to it, and speaks into the phone.

"An' that is a Portland police substation."

He tosses the phone in a trash bin and wanders into the food cart pods.

CHAPTER 69

During his first surveillance of the neighborhood, during their first parley, Dez spotted the alcove of the former sporting goods store. Around dawn, it would be a dark and inconspicuous place to watch the diner. It had a full view of the street. It was perfect. If MacDonald brings backup, Dez thought at the time, I'll find 'em here. But he won't bring a lot of backup. They're all wanted men. A good sergeant, MacDonald will be getting his guys out of the States, as fast as he can.

Dez recognizes the man in the alcove. He saw him at the scene of the helicopter crash on the Clockjack campus. Dez takes him out with a single sidearm throw of the last of his metal marbles and keeps walking, the phone in his left hand, speaking to MacDonald.

Dez gets two blocks away, standing across the street from a police substation, when he sees MacDonald dash into the street, cross it, and spot his downed mate.

MacDonald is wanted by every law enforcement agency in America. Dez made sure to get the photo of MacDonald, the one Arabella had led him to, to the local media. He's seen the photo on the websites of the *Portland Tribune* and Oregon Public Broadcasting and KOIN 6 News.

MacDonald will come for him here. In the byzantine maze of food carts. But he won't come guns blazing.

This pod of carts is the same one Raziah showed him when he'd first hit town. Must be two dozen carts, ranging from fried chicken to Vietnamese street food, from Iraqi to Mexican, from Cajun to fish-and-chips in greasy cones of newsprint. No breakfast joints, and none of the carts are open yet. It's even too early for the food staff to be prepping. Right now, it's just a former parking lot filled with gaily colored trailers, their wheels removed or chocked.

A dozen police units, mostly SUVs and a couple of older sedans, are parked at ninety degrees across the street. There are other city and county services in that building, too, and even thirty minutes past dawn, the place is bustling.

Dez zigs and zags around trailers. He sees no one. He carries his 290-mm fixed-blade knife, the black-coated steel Coltellerie Maserin. Also his folding blade, clipped to his belt. He's owned these two blades since before coming to the United States. They are the only items, besides his bass guitar and his bespoke tablet computer and phone, that predate his arrival in America.

Dez peeks around one corner and spots four uniformed police officers, each with a notebook, and each with a lidded coffee cup, doing a quick confab at the bumpers of their cars.

"We won't be using guns," MacDonald says.

Dez turns. MacDonald has a fixed-blade knife, too. Of course he does.

"Wish we could've walked away from this," Dez says.

"Aye, an' one of us will, *chef.*"

They circle each other. They can hear the chatter of the cops, if not their actual words, across the street.

"Picked your spot well."

Dez nods his thanks.

They circle each other.

"I bested you in Astoria. Dumped your sorry arse in the sea."

"Did," Dez concedes.

They circle each other.

When Gareth MacDonald makes his move, it's lightning fast. It's a slickly synchronized series of step-ins and slashes and a kick-feint-kick, the latter of which clips Dez right where MacDonald's bullet had exited his torso, so many weeks ago.

Dez stutter-steps back, on his feet but hurt. The kick took its toll. He recognizes MacDonald's knife. A Chaos Bowie. At 266 mm, its hardened handle forms aluminum knuckles. An American-made knife, and a fine one at that.

MacDonald moves forward, knife leading the way, slashing horizontally at Dez's gut, and Dez stutter-steps back, avoids it. There's just no question about it now. MacDonald is faster than Dez. His knife's like an extension of his arm. Dez is one hell of a great fighter, but he hasn't been training like one, not for the past seven months or so. He's a much better musician today than he was when he hit the States, but he's lost a step or two as a fighter.

Plain as day, when seen against the likes of Gareth MacDonald.

MacDonald swings left, then right, the knife's knucks catching Dez above the ear, staggering him. He rides the blow, a bit, so it doesn't take his skull clean off. But he goes to one knee, one hand on the pavement.

He rises and MacDonald sends a swivel kick to his right arm. Dez's knife spirals away, skitters toward a Basque food cart across the way.

MacDonald moves lightly on his feet, dancing a bit, a trained fighter, loose and limber, eyes focused on everything: on Dez, the pavement, the carts. They hear the murmured chatter of the cops across the street.

Dez doesn't go for his small folding knife. He has a notion that involves keeping his hands empty.

Dez sweeps right, fakes left, moves in to throw a haymaker at the man, and MacDonald backs away, the Bowie knife sweeping, steel glinting under the street-lights, and an arc of blood erupts from Dez's right forearm.

Dez backs up.

The men circle each other.

Dez makes a run at MacDonald who slips spritely out of the way.

Dez collapses against one of the food cart walls, gasping. He's holding on to the one-meter-long bit of two-by-four, bolted to the cart's now-locked window, upon which often sit a tip jar and a cup of napkins, and maybe condiments. It's where you stand to order; where you hand over your gelt and get your food.

Dez is wheezing, gasping for air.

MacDonald comes at him from behind. Knife extended, parallel with his ulna and radius. Dez has a nice, wide, powerfully muscled back. What a target.

MacDonald is a half step from contact when Dez spins, his powerful hands ripping the bit of two-by-four from its bolted moorings. He keeps spinning, even after the wood connects with the side of MacDonald's head.

MacDonald's knife spirals away.

The man lands on his side, on the asphalt.

The whole fight, Dez only landed one blow.

But it was the right one.

MacDonald rolls over onto his back. His mandible is separating from his temporal bone, his jaw fully separated on the left side, blood pooling around his neck and shoulders. His left cheek is crushed. His left eye is missing.

The Scotsman is choking on blood, body convulsing.

Dez gathers his own fallen knife and sheaths it. He stands, hands on knees, panting, and waits for Gareth MacDonald to die.

He stands straight, adjusts his jacket, runs a hand through his hair, shoves his fists into his trouser pockets, and walks out of the food cart pod, across the street, weaving between police officers in mid-conversation.

Dez enters the substation and goes to the information desk, tucked behind bulletproof glass, and asks for Police Sergeant Heywood Washington.

Washington doesn't work at this station but they can contact him.

"Tell him it's Dez Limerick, would you? Tell him I've something for him."

"Yessir. Can you wait?"

Dez puts a hand on his own flank. At the spot where MacDonald's bullet exited his body, weeks earlier. The spot where MacDonald's first good kick of today caught him. He pulls his hand back and it's tacky with blood.

"Oh, aye. I can wait," he says, and the world goes dark as his knees buckle.

CHAPTER 70

You'd think, given the trail of bodies Dez has littered about Oregon, that the police would have rounded up a silver platter for his oversized and very thick head, ready to serve the Multnomah County district attorney.

When he wakes up in the intensive care unit at Oregon Health & Science University, he finds out that Deputy U.S. Marshal Joshua Vega has thrown a protective cocoon around him. Sergeant Heywood Washington, Portland Police, backs Vega up. At the right levels, into the right ears, it's being whispered that Dez avenged the murders of Chief Deputy U.S. Marshal Conroy Sims and his wife.

Law enforcement is giving Dez a wide berth.

Dez lost plenty of blood while he was unconscious, but they poured a whole bunch more back into him. Between the gunshot wound in Astoria and reopening it today—not to mention a few slices from Mac-Donald's Bowie knife—it's been a festive couple of weeks for Dez's body.

A young ER doctor on the last hours of another brutal shift peers into his eyes with a penlight. "I'm not your mom or anything, but you should avoid getting into any more fights."

Dez is drugged to the gills. "Always avoid fights," he slurs. "Just not always successfully."

Raziah Swann visits him the second they move him out of the ICU and into a regular hospital bed. Later, Laleh and her boyfriend come, too. Dez decides he likes the lad. David, was it?

Veronika Tsygan drops by. It's a very sweet gesture and he's grateful. Her brothers, Vladimir and Skip, have returned to Detroit, but they send him a case of vodka, plus a medovik, a Slavic layer cake made of honey and condensed milk. It's horrible, but Dez thinks, *well, cake is cake,* and he forces it down. The vodka he donates to the Deep Dive.

The U.S. Justice Department files criminal conspiracy charges against RJ Sharpe, in absentia, and Teddy Meeker and Winston Noel, whom they take into custody. Sharpe has the money to hide anywhere on the planet, but Dez suspects she's going to regret her Instagram and YouTube celebrity status.

Alonzo Diaz calls from Los Angeles. "What did I tell you to do?"

"Learn to duck that big stupid head of mine."

"One job. *Estupido cabro.* One job. . . ."

Dez suspects he's made a friend for life with that one.

Sergeant Washington shakes Dez's hand and wishes him nothing but luck.

Before he leaves OHSU, he gets another handshake and a thanks from the dour deputy U.S. marshal, Joshua Vega. Surprisingly, the deputy does not release his grip on Dez's hand.

"This is from our field office, and the Virginia field office, and from the family of Chief Deputy Sims, and the family of Kelly Sims. And this is from me: You call and I'll answer. Lifetime membership, Mr. Limerick. Be safe now."

"Ta, mate."

Dez emerges from the hospital. He tries to take a deep breath of fresh air, here in Portland's sylvan West Hills, but his side wound reminds him not to do that.

He settles for a shallow inhale, a slow exhale.

He says, "You're well, love?"

Arabella Satti emerges from a darkened recess behind Dez, out of his line of sight. She thinks to ask how he knew she was there, but doesn't. He turns to face her.

"There's an international manhunt for the assassin Thiago. Now known to MI6 and the CIA and the world as Ray Harker. The director of operations made me field team leader. The director of intelligence is routing every lead to me. The hounds get Ray's scent, it'll be my team, following my lead, first through the door."

Dez says, "Good. As it should be."

"You should be there, too."

"Me? I'm a civilian. I'd trip over me own—"

"Stop," she cuts in. "The gosh-shucks routine works with others, you great bloody git, but I know you. You're the one sussed out Harker and Thiago. Not I. You deserve to be there."

Dez reaches up and grabs both of her shoulders, squeezing. "I would pay to see the look on that arsehole's face when you find him, love, but—"

"Don't call me love."

"But love, you earned this one. You did. I interfered in your world once. Won't do it again. Ring me up when you have his dick in the blender, will ye?"

She steps into him, hugs him. Hard.

Arabella Satti whispers, "Will do, love."

EPILOGUE

Ray Harker drinks until the bottle calls it quits.

He drinks solo, in a thatched-roof beach bar until three in the morning, gets sick, sleeps in the cottage he's renting until noon, stumbles out to find some food, and some more booze.

He checks his watch. For nearly a month now, he's been on the run. He'd built a gold-plated reputation as the assassin known as Thiago, had been in demand, had contract jobs lined up through the next six months.

And then it all went to shit.

The death of the Tanzanian president had been meticulously set up by his assassination broker. The details had been exquisitely laid out. The three-million-euro payoff had been secured. Every detail had been accounted for.

And then a joint task force of British MI6 and the CIA, along with Tanzanian troops, had dropped on him like a hammer on the butt of a bullet casing. Helicopters, a gauntlet of military, spooks floating in on parachutes, frequency jammers. The ever-fucking works.

And they'd known his real name. They hadn't been chasing Thiago, they'd been chasing him. Raymond Wayne Harker. Former U.S. Marine. Former CIA officer.

Once considered the Golden Boy at Langley's ops division.

It wasn't that the Tanzanian assassination had gone tits up. Harker's whole existence had gone tits up.

He knows a friend of a friend of a friend who could fly him out of Tanzania, across the Indian Ocean. Most of his international accounts had been found and frozen, but he had a little money stored elsewhere. He had traveled by fishing trawler to Phú Quốc, the Vietnamese island off the coast of Cambodia, where he could hole up for a while.

His broker has gone offline.

The contracts stopped pouring in.

He made the Top 5 most-wanted list for every Western intelligence agency on Earth.

And how long till they found him on this pissant island in the Gulf of Thailand? Find him and lock his ass up in a dark site for the rest of his days?

Weeks?

Optimistically, yeah. Maybe weeks.

Harker has almost made it back to his favorite bar when his phone vibrates. His Thiago phone. He'd been charging it every day, but it hadn't vibrated in a month. The communications silence on that phone had been as much an island of isolation as Phú Quốc itself.

But now it vibrates.

He pulls it, checks the incoming message.

I know what happened to you in Tanzania.
I know who set you up. And I can deliver
them.—RJ Sharpe.

He's seen that name somewhere. He gets to the bar, lays down his money, grabs his bottle of rum, and

tucks into a corner. He tries going to the Clockjack
search engine but then remembers that the company
has been taken over by federal authorities. Harker still
doesn't know the details of what happened; doesn't
much care.

He googles the name instead.

In one of life's weird twists, RJ Sharpe is directly
tied to Clockjack. She'd been the CEO, and now is being hunted by federal authorities due to her connection
to . . .

Project 404.

The last hit of Thiago's career. The Tanzanian job.

I know what happened to you in Tanzania.
I know who set you up. And I can deliver
them.—RJ Sharpe.

He gulps rum and types back a message. Who did it?
He watches the three bubbles dance on his text
screen.

Arabella Satti. And one other.

Harker leaves the bar and race-walks, stiff-legged,
half a mile up the white-sand beach, then turns around
and marches back. He needs the time to get his hands
to stop shaking. The hatred has risen in him like a tsu-
nami. The white noise in his skull makes typing impossible.

He sits at his table, gulps three fingers of rum.

When/where?

Nicosia. 48 hours.

NICOSIA, CYPRUS. FORTY-EIGHT HOURS
LATER

RJ Sharpe has chopped off her signature mane. She's
dyed her hair dishwater brown, wearing it boyishly
short. She gave up her glam-rock accoutrements, going for mom jeans and sneakers and oversized sweat-
ers that hide her athleticism. She bought fake, plain-lens
glasses. That bastard Limerick had drained one of her
accounts—drained it dry—but RJ has others he hadn't
known about. He'd taken tens of thousands. She has
more than a million left.

Nicosia is one of the last split cities on Earth. Like
Berlin before it. Today, she keeps in line with the
other tourists, next to the sand-filled, white-and-baby-
blue barrels with the United Nations logo, hard up
against brick walls with barbed-wire topping. Cyprus
has been at war between its Greek self (the south) and
its Turkish self (the north) since the 1970s. The hot
war long ago cooled to a glum détente, but the sullen
enmity prevails.

She gets to the first checkpoint and hands her passport over to a Greek soldier under a Greek flag. Brenda
Marie Linden of Ottawa, Canada. That ID had cost her
plenty, but she has plenty to spend.

Everyone in the queue steps past the Greek soldiers,
walks twenty paces, and goes through it all again. Now
with Turkish soldiers, under a Turkish flag.

This soldier waves RJ on, too.

She checks the address she'd written down. She wanders around the Turkish, north side of the city until she
spots the restaurant. Ajda's. The sign on the door reads
CLOSED, but she knocks anyway.

The woman on the other side is beautiful. Petite,
maybe five-two, with lustrous, wavy mahogany hair to

the middle of her back, very large eyes, an easy smile. She is barefoot, in yoga pants and a tank.

"Hallo! You are, ah, Brenda Marie Linden, yes?" The woman makes air-quotes around the name, then laughs. It's an infectious laugh. "RJ, please come in. I am Liv. And you are exactly on time."

RJ crosses the threshold. The restaurant itself is small and clean, with tile floors and a curved ceiling like the interior of an overturned barrel, with a total of six two-tops and a bar that can seat four more. It's intimate and very old, RJ guesses. Mid-eighteenth century, perhaps.

The woman, in her mid-thirties, pads around behind the bar. "I am told you are a red wine drinker, yes? I am not a big fan of Cypriot wines. I had a Barolo shipped in. I hope that works."

RJ can't place the accent. Middle Eastern, on some consonants, and Western European on some vowels. "I honestly have not had a good glass of wine in a month. Yes, please."

The woman pours for them both.

"Ray Harker . . . ?"

"Will be with us shortly. He is not as punctual as you, alas."

"And you are, again?"

Liv hands her the glass, then turns to press the cork back into the bottle, using both hands to push down. As she does, RJ catches a glimpse of a tattoo on her left shoulder blade, mostly obscured by the thin strap of her tank. It appears to be a tattoo of a couple of bearded guys.

"I am Olivia Gelman. Liv to my friends."

"And your role in all this?"

Liv beams. "Pourer of Tuscan reds. Plus, this and that."

Liv carries her drink and crosses toward the door. For the first time, RJ notices a larger than usual, ruggedized tablet computer sitting at the hostess's station. It's open, running some sort of a program.

"What's that?"

Liv taps the screen, studies the scroll. "It is known as a skimmer."

"What does it do?"

Liv sips her drink. They hear a knock on the door. "Ah! One moment."

She opens the door. Ray Harker fills the doorway.

"So pleased to see you! Come in."

Ray enters. He's done an internet search of RJ Sharpe, and recognizes her despite the haircut and fake glasses. He ignores the smaller woman, storms past her.

"You can get me to Satti?"

RJ blinks. "What?"

"You said you could deliver Satti. And the other. Do it! Now!"

RJ stands for a moment, feeling her world tip.

"I . . . wait. You're Ray Harker."

"Yeah."

"You contacted me. You said you could deliver Desmond Limerick."

Harker pauses. "Who?"

Liv Gelman giggles. Her large and luminous eyes fairly disappear when she laughs. The laugh wrinkles her nose, her shoulders bobbing.

"Oh my god, that's funny. You don't remember his name!"

Ray Harker growls, "Hang on, what the hell. Who's Desmond? What's?" as RJ Sharpe says, "I don't understand. Why did you reach out to me? Arabella?"

Liv's laughter rings out. Both of them turn to her.

"I'm so terrible! My god, that was good." She sighs. She sips. "Oh! Ray, there is rum. Behind the bar. And Zed Zed Eight Oh Niner."

Ray Harker blinks at the petite woman smiling up

at him. "Alpha Alpha Seven Twelve. Jesus, you're my broker! Where the fuck have you been?"

RJ is so upset she doesn't think to set her glass down. "I don't know who you are! Either of you! I'm from Canada. I don't know what this is about."

She grabs her shoulder bag and storms to the door of Ajda's.

Which is locked.

Liv addresses Ray first. "I am not your broker, but I work for him. The same as you. Rum." She points. "Just there. Help yourself."

She turns to RJ, all smiles.

"Open this damn door!"

"I can but I won't."

RJ sets down her glass, reaches into her shoulder bag and roots around. "You had better let me go, or—"

Liv lifts her hand, showed RJ an empty palm, then makes a dramatic, theatrical gesture. RJ's light, compact Ruger Max .380 pistol appears as if by magic. The gun had been in RJ's bag.

"Ta da!"

Liv makes the gesture again, and the small handgun disappears.

"Who are you?"

"First things first. You asked about the app on my computer, and I told you it was a skimmer, and you asked what that is, and the answer is that, when you walked through the door, I scanned your false passport and also your Brenda Marie Linden bank accounts, and I've been draining them as we spoke."

Behind the bar, Ray Harker gulped rum, watching it all, his thoughts pinging about, trying to catch up.

RJ turns and slams her shoulder into the restaurant door. It doesn't even shudder. She reaches for her glass of wine and smashes the bowl on the hostess's station, the Italian red spraying everywhere. She holds the broken end of the long stem in front of her like a bayonet.

"Get this fucking door open! Do you know who I am?"

"I do, actually. I know everything. Ray and I have work that needs to be done. And you're the bank."

"Fuck you!" RJ shoulders the door again. Nothing.

Liv laughs. "Oh, please. That's a door, my darling. And there is not a door on Earth I can't open, keep open, and control who gets through it. And who doesn't."

RJ glares at her.

Liv twists at the hips, revealing most of her back to the much taller woman with the longer arms. RJ's broken glass stem twitches, less than ten inches from Liv's back.

"I'll let you in on a secret." She pulls back the strap of her tank to show the tattoo. It's not two guys, as RJ thought. It's a two-faced man. "Janus. Roman god of beginnings and gates, transitions and time, duality and doors, passages and endings. He is a friend."

Behind Liv, Ray narrows his eyes, a memory breaching.

Liv twists back, smiling wide, hands elbow-height and to her side, revealing open palms.

RJ's broken glass stem wobbles in mid-air.

Liv makes the abracadabra gesture again, steps forward, brushes RJ's hand aside, and slides a spring-loaded, six-inch tactical stiletto blade into the heart of RJ Sharpe.

She pulls it free. The long, tapered blade is so narrow, so sharp, that RJ bleeds, but only internally.

RJ blinks, several times. She opens her mouth to speak.

Her legs give out as her heart stops.

Liv kneels and wipes the blade clean on RJ's sweater. She rises, the blade snicking back into its scabbard with the touch of a button. She slides it into a sheath clipped to the small of her back.

Ray gulps rum. "I heard someone say that shit. About gates and beginnings and whatever. I've heard that before."

Liv laughs. "Yes, you've heard it before. From a gatekeeper. Now drink up. We've tasks, and toils, and retribution aplenty. And old, old friends to find."

Turn the page for an exciting excerpt from the next Dez Limerick thriller, *Chain Reaction*, coming in early 2025!

Prologue

The innocuous-looking car approaches the research campus at five minutes before eleven at night. The driver's name is Dez. He's wearing civilian clothes today, which is unusual for him. Seated next to him is a fellow Englishman whose name is most decidedly not Jamison, even though his newly forged passport identifies him thusly.

The research campus is dark. There should be no one here except security and janitorial crew. And one fairly prickly biologist. Dez is idling the car just outside the gate, studying the sprawling, three-acre campus.

Jamison is smoking, his window cracked open, blowing the smoke out. He eyes his driver. Dez is wearing an olive sweater and khakis and lace-up boots. He isn't tall but he's beefy, with wide shoulders, a fifty-inch chest, powerfully cut forearms.

"Damn good of you to do this. And on short notice," Jamison says.

Dez grins in the dark. "I'm a soldier, me. Go where I'm ordered."

"How did you draw the short straw for babysitting duty?"

"I've a skill set. My commander thought I might be useful."

Jamison nods. "Let's do this."

Dez puts the Land Rover into gear. They slow roll up to the armored fence and gate, and a guard steps out of his shack. Dez lowers his window. "I've a Mister Jamison here t'see Professor Eduardo Castillo," Dez says in fluent Spanish.

The guard consults a clipboard. He shines a penlight into the car, focusing on Jamison, then on Dez. The guard is not armed.

"Very good. Building 17."

Dez puts it in first as the heavy gate rolls open.

"See what you mean about skill sets," Jamison says. "Glad you speak the lingo."

"No worries."

They roll into the quiet campus.

"Is Dez short for anything?"

"Desmond Aloysius Limerick."

Jamison smiles. "Vengeful parents?"

"It's quite a nice name." Dez sounds a little hurt. "Distinguished, if you was to ask me."

"Yes. Very."

They find building number 17 and Dez parks. Dez clips a holster to the belt of his khakis. The holster holds a PAMAS G1 9mm with a fifteen-round mag and a bullet preloaded in the pipe. Jamison eyes it, and Dez notices.

"You spy types learn t'carry your own weapons, you wouldn't need a soldier like me watchin' your back, squire."

Jamison throws away the stub of his cigarette. "Who said anything about spies?"

"Right, right."

Another guard is waiting for them, wearing the same sand-colored uniform as the man at the gate. Dez speaks to him briefly in Spanish. This guard looks nervous. He uses a magnetic ID card on a lanyard to open building number 17. He escorts them in, then into an elevator. The same magnetic ID gets the elevator car moving to the top floor.

The corridor is sterile, bland; the walls and ceiling white; the floor polished. Both newcomers wince at the glare.

"Lights are set on 'migraine,'" Dez observes.

The guard takes them to room 804 and uses his ID card on a monitor set into the wall. The door clacks open.

Room 804 is a biology lab. Spectacularly well out-fitted, from the looks of it. No expense spared.

They are met by a smallish man in an old tweed jacket and an enormous mustache. He wears round, wire-rim spectacles. He's perhaps in his midseventies. With him is a young woman wearing a plain skirt, orthopedic shoes, a simple blouse, and a white lab coat. Dez thinks she's quite lovely and strives to hide it; hair back in a severe bun, unattractive eye-glasses, no makeup that he can spot.

She steps forward and offers a hand. "Mr. Jamison?"

The guard stays out in the corridor. Dez stands back by the door, out of the way.

Jamison takes her hand. "Hallo. You must be Miss Gomez, Dr. Castillo's assistant."

She adjusts her glasses. "Yes. The doctor speaks no English, I'm afraid. You don't mind my translating?"

"Please."

Professor Castillo rolls out a standing vertical-flat-screen monitor on twin stands, upon which the image of a complex biological formula has been sketched. Lots of hexagons and letters. Dez reads the monitor: $C_8H_{10}N_4O_2$.

Professor Castillo nods to it. "Do you know what this is, Mr. Jamison?"

Miss Gomez translates into English.

"I'm hoping it's the formula you've been working

on, sir. The formula that would make synthetic opioids nonaddictive."

She translates.

The old man nods. "Yes, yes. This is the work that has driven the last seven years of my life for king and country, sir."

Dez has noted a security monitor on a table. He strolls that way. It shows a high-res black-and-white image of the guard who led them up, and the exterior of the door he'd just been leaning on. The guard checks his watch and, a beat later, checks it again.

"This bit of formula?" The professor finds a remote control. The hexagons shrink and are revealed to be part of a much, much larger chemical structure. "It works. It can eliminate the addictive qualities of synthetic opioids."

"This would . . . change many things," Jamison says, and the assistant translates. He gestures around to include the whole lab. "This is a government-owned facility. The formula is owned by you, and not the Spanish government, sir?"

Miss Gomez translates.

"It is mine. Wholly mine."

"Then Great Britain is prepared to meet your price, professor. But know that it is our intention to share this with every other nation on—"

Everyone starts at the distant sound of automatic gunfire.

Jamison turns to Dez, eyebrows raised.

Dez sits at the security monitor and begins typing on the keyboard.

Ms. Gomez spots him. "I . . . I believe they said the security monitors can only be accessed by campus personnel, Mister . . . ?"

"Dez," he says, keys clacking away. "Dez Limerick. And aye, likely. I've some small training with computers. Might be able to. . . ."

The screen changes, first to six separate images of the campus. Then twelve, then twenty-four. All from closed circuit security cameras.

Jamison hurries over, hovering over Dez in his chair. Dez targets the camera monitoring the main gate.

The gate is open. The guard who let them in lies on the ground, bleeding from a bullet wound.

Dez shifts to another camera: Two large SUVs are moving through the campus, lights off.

"Heading our way," Jamison says. He draws his phone and checks. "I've no signal."

"Aye. Professor? Who else did you tell about your fantastic discovery?"

The woman says, "*Profesor, con quien—*"

"That's not necessary, love. Your mate here's no more Spanish than I am. He speaks Spanish with the accent of one who learned it in the Southwest United States. I've an ear for dialects. An' the question stands: Who else knows about the formula."

Jamison turns to the professor and his assistant. "Well?"

She says, "There were other bidders, but . . ."

Dez changes to the camera that is right outside the lab.

Their guard is gone. So he'd been in on . . . whatever this is. Paid off, probably, Dez thinks.

On the security monitor, they see the two SUVs have arrived at building 17. Side doors slam open, and a dozen heavily armed men with balaclava masks and Kevlar begin jumping out. They carry HK-47s. They also have a magnetic card to bypass security.

"It strikes me," Dez drawls, "that there might be some what don't want nobody messin' with the addictive qualities of opioids. Yeah?"

Jamison sighs. "Quite."

Dez spots a tool kit under one of the tables, kneels,

draws a screwdriver, and moves to the door. He begins tearing apart the wall-mounted security monitor by the door.

Jamison says, "What are you doing?"

"Buying us time, squire. Here."

Dez draws his 9mm pistol and hands it butt first to the British agent, then goes back to fiddling with the innards of the security system.

"The professor speaks English?" Jamison asks.

"He does." Dez addresses the wiring he's now exposing. "An' his magical formula for opioids? The good professor was showing you a compound consistin' of, ah, eight carbon atoms, ten hydrogen, four nitrogen, an' two oxygen atoms, if I've done me sums right. Yeah? Less I miss my guess, they was showin' you the atomic structure of caffeine."

Miss Gomez says, "How did . . ." Then catches herself.

Jamison says, "Jesus."

A puff of smoke roils up from the security device. "Should do. Get me that acetylene torch over there, will ye?"

Jamison sees it, moves swiftly toward it.

Dez grins at Ms. Gomez as he takes the torch from Jamison. He quickly whisks up his left sleeve and shows her a tattoo of a two-faced Roman god.

"Janus. God of beginnings an' gates, transitions an' time, duality an' doors, passages an' endings. I'm what's called a gatekeeper, yeah? Can open any door. Can keep it open as long as is necessary. Can control who does—and who don't—get through. Means I've studied me chemistry, miss."

Jamison brings him a sparker, too. Dez fires up the acetylene torch.

He winks at Jamison. "Them's the skill sets my commander was thinkin' of when I drew the short straw."

Ten of the assault squad crowd into the elevator; two stay in the lobby. The elevator quickly rises to their floor.

He turns to Ms. Gomez. "This lot's not with you, I assume?"

"Oh, hell no!"

"Then we all need t'get out of here, pronto."

Dez holds the torch to the door knob on the inner side of the door. He speaks over the hiss of the flame. "Dr. Castillo and Miss Gomez, I'm guessin', are thieves. Was hopin' to take the British government for several million pounds sterling. An' if they're any good at what they do, they've an exit strategy. In case this caper went pear-shaped on 'em."

The assault squad is on their floor now. One man draws a magnetic key card and attempts to open the door. It's not working because Dez bollixed it from the inside.

Dez continues to hold the torch to the door knob.

"We . . . we do have a way out," Miss Gomez says.

The alleged Professor Castillo spins on her. "Cat! Shut the fuck up!" He speaks English. They both sound like Americans.

She ignores him, checks her watch. "If you can keep them out for eight minutes, we can get gone."

Dez says, "Well, love, your way out just became everyone's way out. Ta."

The woman—Cat—whisks off her glasses and throws them in a trash bin. "The building AC is set to go off in just over seven minutes. When it does, small packets of explosives will blow the air-filter mesh in a maintenance tunnel, back this way." She points deeper into the lab. "The AC will mask the vibration of the explosion. We can crawl out to the roof. There's a ladder down to the parking lot on the north side. The explosives are on a timer, so we can't blow it early."

"Cat, for fuck sake—" her accomplice growls.

Outside, the assault unit has given up hoping their stolen magnetic card will get them through the door and into the lab. One of them does what people always do in these situations: He grabs the doorknob and rattles it to see if, miraculously, it's unlocked.

The man screams in pain, smoke roiling from his charred hand.

"Door's got a steel core," Dez tells the room, turning off the torch. "Same with the wall around it. Spotted it as we entered. Watch what happens when they try t'shoot their way in. Which they will."

On the monitor, one of the men unslings his AK and fires a burst at the door.

His own ricochet nearly cuts him in two.

The oppo is down to nine on this floor, and one of those nine has third-degree burns on one palm, so he won't be using his AK. There are still two more in the lobby.

"Them lot's not getting in that way. Unless they brought explosives," Dez says. "Hang on a bit."

He moves around the lab, opening cabinet doors, searching behind desks.

"Aw! This is nice." He produces a canister of liquid nitrogen. "Ah, Cat, was it? Call out the time, love."

Two of the assault squad are kneeling and opening their backpacks. Jamison watches the monitor. "C4, Limerick. You called it."

"Aye. Tried the magnetic lock. Tried rattlin' the door to force it open. Tried shootin' through. Now they'll try blasting through." Dez shakes his head sadly. "It's how every tosser an' their cousin tries to get through a door. Feckin' amateurs. Cat?"

The American woman says, "Four minutes."

Dez holds the canister under one arm, a hose in his

other hand, and begins spraying the door hinges with liquid nitrogen.

"Right lovely ball-peen hammer in that cabinet yonder, squire. Fetch it smart-like, will ye?"

The inside of the door is turning white around first the upper hinge, then the lower one. Dez switches back and forth. Ice from the liquid nitrogen coats the metal, whisps of smoke curling off it.

Dez keeps pouring the nitrogen on the door. The icy buildup continues.

Jamison returns with the hammer. He and Cat are watching the monitor. He says, "They're attaching explosive packets near the hinges. Just as you said."

Cat glances at her watch. "Three minutes."

"Right then." Dez sets the empty canister down. He picks up the hammer. "You lot head back toward the maintenance tunnel. Right behind ye."

Jamison says, "I'll stay, all the same."

"No. Go. Right behind ye."

Jamison hesitates, then sprints after the two American thieves.

Dez is a gifted cricket player. A very good batsman, yes, but also a top-line bowler. He takes fifteen steps back, then winds up and hurls the ball-peen hammer, overhand, at the supercooled metal door.

He doesn't wait to see if he hit it. Instead, he turns and sprints after Jamison and the others.

In the corridor, two of the assault squad are kneeling, applying C4 explosives, gingerly attaching wires to blasting caps. The others are getting ready to back off.

Just as the supercooled hinges of the door shatter.

Triggering their explosives early.

Of the nine men they brought, two are disintegrated by the explosion. Four more die as shrapnel and the high-pressure energy wave radiates down the corridor.

Three survive, back by the elevator, but all three are on their asses, stunned by the explosion.

Three still alive on this floor. Two in the lobby. The odds are better but still bad.

Two minutes later, Dez, Jamison, and the con artists watch as a heavy, wire mesh grill over a maintenance tunnel sizzles and falls away from the tunnel entrance. The ersatz professor has doffed his mustache, glasses, and wig. Dez guesses his true age at midfifties.

The con artists lead, then Jamison, then Dez.

It's a winding, circuitous route, and they do it on their hands and knees. Thirty feet in, they find a metal ladder, leading upward. Cat takes the lead. She's quick and sure-footed. The non-professor goes next.

Jamison pauses to slide Dez's gun into his belt, freeing his hand, then he climbs as well. Dez on his six. Jamison's jacket catches on a rung at one point, costing them about five seconds.

By the time Jamison and Dez get to the roof, the two thieves are long gone.

Jamison checks his phone. "I've a signal." He starts dialing. "We're assuming the welcoming committee represents an organization making its piles pushing opioids in Europe?"

"Seems likely, aye." Dez says. He walks to the edge of the building near the metal ladder and peers over. No sign of the thieves. "Appears organized crime bought the cock-an'-bull story about the professor's ingenious discovery."

Jamison presses a series of buttons on his phone. "SOS. We'll have backup here within minutes." He looks up, smiling ruefully. "His Majesty's Government bought the cock-and-bull story, too, Dez. We're as gullible as the bad guys."

Dez glances down behind an air-conditioning unit

and spots Cat. She's seated, legs drawn up against her chest, arms wrapped around her knees. She looks up into his eyes.

Jamison sighs. "Our thieves will be far away before the cavalry arrives, I assume."

"Oh, aye," Dez says, and winks at Cat. She blinks in surprise. Dez puts a vertical finger to his lips, turns, and saunters back toward Jamison. "They got away with naught, though. Not much point in pursuin' them."

"Agreed. Besides which, there are still two gentlemen in the lobby with AKs."

"I'm betting a few survived in the corridor, too. Best to stay up here. Wait for the cavalry."

Jamison finds a cigarette pack and a lighter. "You saved my life, Mr. Limerick."

"Which means you're buyin' the first round, squire."

"Quite. You were very calm back there. Methodical. Do you do this a lot? Tangle with armed gangs?"

"Me?" Dez laughs. "Course not! I'm the peaceable type. I never go lookin' for trouble."